SUSANNA MUSGROVE HASWELL ROWSON, destined to be one of the founding mothers of American literature, was born in Portsmouth, England, in 1762; she was taken to America in 1767 but returned to England in 1778. In 1793, with her husband, William Rowson, she moved to America for good and began a long and successful career—first in Philadelphia, then in the Boston area—as an actress, author, and feminist educator. She died in 1828. Among her most popular works were the novels *Rebecca; or, The Fille de Chambre* (1792), *Charlotte Temple* (1791 [England]; 1794 [America]), *Charlotte's Daughter; or, The Three Orphans* (1828), the play *Slaves in Algiers* (1794), and the song "America, Commerce, and Freedom."

ANN DOUGLAS is Professor of English and an associate of the Center for American Cultural Studies at Columbia University. She is the author of *The Feminization of American Culture,* as well as many articles and reviews on nineteenth- and twentieth-century American culture.

PENGUIN CLASSICS

TEMPLE and LUCY

Charlotte Temple

and

Lucy Temple

Susanna Rowson

EDITED AND
WITH AN INTRODUCTION BY
ANN DOUGLAS

PENGUIN BOOKS

PENGUIN BOOKS
Published by the Penguin Group
Viking Penguin, a division of Penguin Books USA Inc.,
375 Hudson Street, New York, New York 10014, U.S.A.
Penguin Books Ltd, 27 Wrights Lane,
London W8 5TZ, England
Penguin Books Australia Ltd, Ringwood,
Victoria, Australia
Penguin Books Canada Ltd, 2801 John Street,
Markham, Ontario, Canada L3R 1B4
Penguin Books (N.Z.) Ltd, 182–190 Wairau Road,
Auckland 10, New Zealand

Penguin Books Ltd, Registered Offices:
Harmondsworth, Middlesex, England

Charlotte Temple was first published in the United States of America in 1794.
Lucy Temple as Charlotte's Daughter: The Three Orphans
was first published in 1828. This edition with an introduction by
Ann Douglas published in Penguin Books 1991.

1 3 5 7 9 10 8 6 4 2

Introduction and notes copyright © Viking Penguin,
a division of Penguin Books USA Inc., 1991
All rights reserved

LIBRARY OF CONGRESS CATALOGING IN PUBLICATION DATA
Rowson, Mrs., 1762–1824.
[Charlotte Temple]
Charlotte Temple; and, Lucy Temple/ by Susanna Rowson; edited
and with an introduction by Ann Douglas.
p.   cm.—(Penguin classics)
Includes bibliographic references.
ISBN 0 14 03.9080 4
I. Douglas, Ann, 1942–   . II. Rowson, Mrs., 1762–1824. Lucy
Temple. 1990. III. Title. IV. Title: Charlotte Temple. V. Title:
Lucy Temple. VI. Series.
PS2736.R3C5   1990
813'.2—dc20   90–7776

Printed in the United States of America

Set in Fairfield Medium
Designed by Ann Gold

Except in the United States of America, this
book is sold subject to the condition that it
shall not, by way of trade or otherwise, be lent,
re-sold, hired out, or otherwise circulated
without the publisher's prior consent in any form
of binding or cover other than that in which it
is published and without a similar condition
including this condition being imposed on the
subsequent purchaser.

Contents

◇   ◇

Introduction

◇   ◇

Susanna Rowson, like many American authors, was of mixed nationality. Born in England in 1762 and raised in America, she returned to England in 1778 and shortly thereafter began her career as actress, dramatist, and novelist. In 1793 she re-emigrated to America with her husband, William Rowson. In America—"My dear adopted country," as she called it—she met with vastly more success as an actress and author (and, later, a teacher) than she had in England; she died in the United States in 1824. In the course of a long and enterprising life, Rowson wrote ten novels, six theatrical works, two volumes of poetry, innumerable songs, and six textbooks for her progressive "Young Ladies Academy" in Boston and other schools like it. Independent-minded and feminist in her sympathies, she set her mark on early American drama, fiction, and education. In Constance Rourke's admiring words, Rowson "tethered a buoyant temperament to a prolonged series of tasks" and "gave momentum to broad tendencies.'

Yet Rowson is best remembered for a single book, *Charlotte Temple: A Tale of Truth,* the story of a young English girl seduced to America and abandoned there to die. *Charlotte Temple* was published in England in 1791, where it attracted little attention; Rowson herself arranged for its separate publication in America in 1794 shortly after she re-emigrated there, and it became the biggest bestseller in American history until Harriet Beecher Stowe published

Uncle Tom's Cabin in 1852; Rowson's novel continued to sell into the twentieth century, going through at least two hundred editions. *Charlotte Temple*'s sequel, *Charlotte's Daughter; or, The Three Orphans*, published in 1828 (four years after Rowson's death), was reissued forty times in the course of the nineteenth century usually under the title *Lucy Temple*. *Charlotte Temple* is one of the earliest American novels (the first is William Hill Brown's *The Power of Sympathy*, of 1789); more important, it is, in Leslie Fiedler's words in *Love and Death in the American Novel* (1960), "the first book by an American to move American readers." Yet critics past and present, aware of Rowson's undeniable artistic deficiencies, have been able to give few explanations for the book's powerful influence on American soil.

In 1917, Carl van Doren speculated in *The Cambridge History of American Fiction* that Rowson had "imposed" on a "naive wonderworld of fiction readers." In 1960, Leslie Fiedler remarked that *Charlotte Temple* is "hardly written at all." The novel, Fiedler concluded, is a "subliterate myth." Many of the better educated among Rowson's contemporaries would apparently have concurred in Fiedler's estimate of Rowson's literary skills. An English critic reviewing Rowson's novel *Mary; or the Test of Honor* in 1789 ventured the opinion that it seemed to have been written by one "evidently unaccustomed to the use of a pen." Another reviewer praised Rowson's "feeling heart" but noted the absence of "style and the various graces of composition." Such mentions were rare: Rowson attracted only a scant handful of reviews in England; in America, her adopted country and the one in which her books found the readers they failed to attract in England, she was not reviewed at all.

If the working supposition is that literature gets reviewed, "subliterate myths," in Leslie Fiedler's phrase, apparently do not. One understands the lack of critical attention given to Rowson's work. Any candid look at the novels of the feminine contemporaries Rowson most admired—say *Belinda* (1801), by Maria Edgeworth, or

Evalina (1778), by Fanny Burney, or *A Simple Story* (1791), by Elizabeth Inchbald, or even the American best-seller *The Coquette* (1797), by Hannah Foster, whose heroine Eliza Wharton ran a close second to Charlotte Temple in the affections of American readers—reveals Rowson's limitations as a stylist and delineator of character. She herself confessed candidly in *Mary; or the Test of Honor* that "my talent is small." But a book's popularity is itself a kind of criticism, complex evidence that the best-seller in question expressed the hopes and fears of people who found them nowhere else so forcibly put. If *Charlotte Temple* did not meet the taste of the few, it answered the needs of the many; and in their need lay Rowson's art.

In an earlier work, a collection of tales called *The Inquisitor; or the Invisible Rambler* (1788), Rowson's narrator (a stock eighteenth-century sentimental "man of feeling") is magically granted "the power of visiting unseen the receptacles of the miserable and the habitations of vice and poverty." What has been bestowed on the narrator here—and Rowson by proxy—is the novelist's gift, and privilege, the pass key of vicarious and significant experience, and the power to describe that experience for others eager for it, for readers, that new segment of the population in the 1780s, a kind of embryo class unto itself. Rowson always knows how eager her readers are for what she fetchingly calls "a little private history." In a Rowson intrusion that will become a kind of signature for her over the next forty years, she gives voice in *The Inquisitor* to those readers whose impatience she loves to tease, educate, and reward: "But the tale!" she imagines them exclaiming. "You shall have it directly," the narrator promises. If *The Inquisitor* did not fully deliver the goods, *Charlotte Temple,* of course, did. It is as "a tale," that obsessive chiming of what happened with why, that sheerest appeal to the appetitive curiosity by which we live, that *Charlotte Temple* moves its readers. Rowson's book is eloquent, not with the power of skillful language, portraiture, or form, but with the momentum of a story that must be told, a story whose readers

Rowson provokes at every turn into active participation in its meaning. *Charlotte Temple*, like all true tales, is for, about, and by its
readers.

Who were they? Rowson's asides in her fiction suggest that she
expected an audience mainly of middle-class young women and
those concerned with their fate, but her actual audience was far
larger. Literary historian Cathy N. Davidson has recently turned
up invaluable information on *Charlotte*'s readers over the century
of the novel's greatest popularity: middle-class girls like one Uri
Decker, who inscribed her copy of *Charlotte Temple* in the 1820s
"Uri Decker's Book and Heart Shall Never Part"; working-class
girls, men of all ranks who lent or gave the book to daughters,
wives, and fiancées; even a group of black women in Ohio after
the Civil War. This is an audience marked by class diversification
and gender inclusion; the only common denominator among them,
Davidson notes, seems to be that they were all Americans, and
that a good number of them were Americans whose rights in the
new republic were questioned or curtailed by reason of gender,
race, and class. Charlotte Temple herself, as an immigrant and a
female, has no political or economic rights in the country to which
she has been abducted by deception and force; she will die in a
"poor little hovel," one of those "receptacles of the miserable" to
which the narrator of *The Inquisitor* gained magical access, "habitations" of "poverty," if not "vice," that Rowson herself had known
at first hand on American soil. If *Charlotte Temple* is a "subliterate
myth," and I think it is, it is a peculiarly American one.

Rowson's special gift—to use Constance Rourke's phrase—was
to take "broad tendencies" in early American culture and to give
them "momentum" in the just evolving theatrical and literary genres of the day; more specifically, in the stage melodrama and the
novel. Genres, those fluid constellations of psychological and cultural motifs that express and tap the collective psyche, are instant
pop history, by definition closer to popular taste than a highly
individuated and authored autonomous text. One might speculate

that the American writer, impelled by the democratic imperative
of American society that culture gain part of its power from broad
and deep accessibility, was lured, like the writer of no other nation,
towards the creation of high-voltage genres; that the finest American authors, whether "highbrow" or "low" (to revert to critic Van
Wyck Brooks's terms), aspired to encapsulate the force of an entire
genre—indeed, of several genres—within the strained confines of
a single text. This was Melville's achievement in *Moby Dick* (1851),
Harriet Beecher Stowe's in *Uncle Tom's Cabin* (1852), and, indisputably, Susanna Rowson's in *Charlotte Temple*. *Charlotte Temple*,
in its way, like *Moby Dick* and *Uncle Tom's Cabin* in theirs, infused
the hospitable form of the novel with the energies of the stage
melodrama. Rowson's choice of forms was appropriate, even inevitable. Melodrama and the novel, both genres destined to be so
powerful that they would spill into other genres and almost lose
their distinct identity, share an extreme devotion to the "tale" and
a commitment to audience involvement unmatched in any other
literary or theatrical form.

   Charlotte Temple, of course, is part of the literature of seduction
(and abandonment) that commanded the talents of many of the
best novelists of the eighteenth and nineteenth centuries in England and Europe. Whatever her deficiencies, Charlotte is the
American version of the "Crazy Jane" and "Mad Ophelia" figures,
victims of love gone wrong, who regularly appeared on the pages
of sentimentalists Lawrence Sterne and Oliver Goldsmith and in
the Gothic tales of "Monk" Lewis; she is sister to Samuel Richardson's Clarissa of 1748, Choderlos de Laclos's Madame de Tour-
vel in *Les Liaisons Dangereuses* of 1782, Charles Dickens's Little
Emily in *David Copperfield* of 1850, and Flaubert's Emma Bovary
of 1857. From the start, the seduction motif was a genre-hopper,
running the gamut from literate to illiterate or nonliterate forms;
its longest, most extensive life would be in the novel, and on the
stage (and later on the screen) as melodrama.

   When Rowson wrote *Charlotte Temple*, both genres were new.

The novel dated from the early to mid-eighteenth century; the stage melodrama was just coming into existence in the 1780s and 1790s in France, England, and America. In their evolution, the novel and the melodrama can be seen as siblings, successive and overlapping agents of a vast democratization of cultural authority. The novel developed in tandem with liberal political and educational movements that promised a broad expansion of literacy, once the monopoly of the upper classes, among the middle and working classes. Melodrama's appearance coincided with the French (and American) revolutions of the later eighteenth century; the earliest Boulevard theaters in Paris devoted to melodrama were located in lower-class districts. Its appeal lay in its ability to elicit and activate powerfully shared energies and values in those just beginning to seize a recognized role in history's making.

The early novel tapped and extended a public that had but recently learned to read and made these new readers unprecedentedly active and equal collaborators with the author in the task of creating the meaning and interest of the text. As Ben Franklin said of Defoe: "The reader is admitted into the company and present at the conversation." Melodrama reached beyond the novel, to those who did not yet possess the skills of literacy. The official father of melodrama, French playwright Guilbert de Pixérécourt, author-translator of *Coelina; ou L'Enfant du Mystère* (1800), claimed he wrote plays for those who could not read.

The novel, in Peter Brooks's words, was "the first medium to realize the importance of persecuted woman struggling to preserve the impulse of moral vision"; the stage melodrama, with its focus on "The Maid, the Mother, the Maniac"—to borrow the title of an early English melodrama—furthered the theme. Pixérécourt's *Coelina* and *Nellie*, L. C. Caignie's *Annette* of *La Pie Voleus*, Frederick Maddox's *Louise* of *Infanticide*, brought the trials and pains of Pamela, Clarissa, and a host of early fictional heroines to the stage. But if early novels told the story of their young protagonists' education by the world, early melodrama depicted their battles against it, and within it. Where the novel taught, melodrama excited. Melodrama dealt not in the written word but in "subliterate myths" marketed to that "feeling heart." An early critic found Rowson's single strength by freighting and straining individual utterances and gestures with a charge of collectivized and totalized inchoate meaning. If the novel made the reader the author's equal, melodrama gave its audience precedence, top billing, so to speak, over the author—indeed, over all established authority.

Late eighteenth- and nineteenth-century novels, sometimes issued anonymously or pseudo-anonymously and unprotected by copyright laws, were exuberantly pirated; but the author (or the author's other works) were always cited. Indeed, the author's name or credits ("By the Author of . . .") helped to sell the book. The author of an early melodrama mattered far less to begin with; the actor-manager who put the play on, the actors who took the leading roles, and, above all, the spectators who watched it created the play. Histories of the early stage always give the names of the manager, actors, and the theater involved in a particular production but often omit the playwright. Not surprisingly, in this atmosphere of collective authorship, dramatists, managers, and actors translated and adapted the work of others with little thought and less acknowledgment. Melodramas, like novels, were unprotected by copyright; but unlike novels, they often were not printed at all. The life of melodrama, in other words, was synonymous with live-audience participation. Melodrama emerged at home and abroad as the product of a few recognizable artists, many anonymous craftsmen, and a host of transient audience members collaborating seamlessly over a period of time; melodrama's emergence is genre formation in strikingly pure form, a collective work of popular need and taste.

The interaction between the just-forming melodrama and the early novel was a close, lively, and long-lived one, and it worked both ways. If the novels of Ann Radcliffe, "Monk" Lewis, Sir Walter Scott, Charles Dickens, Harriet Beecher Stowe, Mrs. E. D. E. N. Southworth, Mrs. Henry Wood, and Mary E. Braddon became smash-hit melodramas between the 1790s and the 1860s (melodrama's heyday), a number of the later authors, most notably Dickens, were influenced by the theater as they wrote their novels. Melville's *Moby Dick* was not dramatized; but if Ahab never returned to the stage, he in good part originated there. Ahab could only have sprung from a culture that melodramatized Shakespeare and produced the magnificent rantings of all-American actor Edwin Forrest in specially chosen vehicles like John Augustus Stone's *Metamora, the Last of the Wampanoags* (1829), Robert Montgomery Bird's *The Gladiator* (1831), and Robert T. Conrad's *Jack Cade* (1835). Rowson as a cultural broker between the stage and the page was at the start of a long line of literary middlemen and -women of immense importance to American culture. The early publishers who issued *Charlotte Temple* with and without Rowson's permission listed the author as "Mrs. Rowson of the New Theatre, Philadelphia"; although she left the stage forever in 1797, publishers continued this description for the next century. They did so surely as a reminder to readers that Rowson had been an American, or at least had held an American job; but they did so also as a pledge to readers that this author would bring the illiterate pleasures of the theater to the literate tastes of the novel, and even as a hint that to do so is an American activity.

The first melodramas were French, the literary sources were English and German, but the trademark excitement of the genre was American, and America was arguably more hospitable to melodrama for a longer time than any other country. In the twentieth century, America would export Americanized melodramatic fare back to Europe and a world beyond it through the mass arts of cinema and television. If a nation, or its collective assertions and explanations of its own nature, can be said to have a cultural analogy in a genre, America, home of the rags-to-riches scenario, *is* melodrama. Where the novel particularizes, the melodrama totalizes and mythologizes. In *Charlotte Temple,* melodrama gives the ring of grandiosity to the "little private history" (to return to Rowson's phrase) of the novel; it transforms the story of one girl's fate into the most compelling of tales, a passionate dramatization of the meaning of America, the "subliterate myth" of the hopes and fears of those who came to its shores to find a new life.

Susanna Rowson, herself a wide-ranging if mediocre actress and a popular author of comic and melodramatic scenarios, was among melodrama's early founders. With an avidity that would characterize later American authors, she sensed the possibilities of the form. From nascent melodrama—and its sources in pantomime, musical shows, domestic or "serious" drama, sentimental and gothic tales of seduction and violence—Rowson drew the emphasis on compelling tableaus, gestures, and hyperbole, the impatience and at times ineptness with written language, the commitment to a democratic ethos of audience participation, and the heart-breaking tale of "The Maid, the Mother and the Maniac" that would make *Charlotte Temple* an underworld classic.

It is no coincidence that *Charlotte Temple* was dramatized by at least three different authors between 1826 and 1896: first by a scene painter who has survived only as "Ferry," next by Rollin Howard, then by Glascott, both also unknown; Charlotte Pixley Plumb published yet another dramatization in 1899. Until later in the nineteenth century, *Charlotte Temple* the play ran often, a tried and true favorite, in the company of such like-minded domestic melodramas as W. H. Smith's *The Drunkard, or the Fallen Saved* (1844), George L. Aiken's *Uncle Tom's Cabin* (1852), and Dumas's variously adapted *Camille* (1852). *Charlotte* the play was put on most frequently in two of the biggest of the popular theaters of New York: P. T. Barnum's Museum (whose productions the young Henry James viewed with enthralled if skeptical attention) and the Bowery Theatre. There may have been other dramatizations of *Charlotte Temple* running in New York and in "the provinces"; theater records from the period are far from complete. No text of any *Charlotte Temple* scenario survives as far as I can tell, but, as I have suggested, few texts of any of the popular domestic melodramas of which Charlotte was one survive. Just as we have lost pioneering cinematic treasures to early indifference or incredulity regarding their possible artistic value, so have we lost most of our domestic melodramas. But although no one knew melodramas were art, many were convinced they were life.

Charlotte Temple's readers trusted Rowson when she promised them that hers was "a tale of truth." Thousands of nineteenth-century Americans made the pilgrimage to Trinity Churchyard in New York; they ignored the nearby (authentic) graves of statesman Alexander Hamilton and inventor Samuel Fulton to leave tears, flowers, locks of hair, and crude verses on the tombstone marking the supposed gravesite of "poor Charlotte"; plates of the tombstone adorned new editions of *Charlotte* in the 1840s and after. They believed (with Rowson's tacit encouragement) Charlotte to be a real historic personage—one Charlotte Stanley, an English nobleman's descendant who eloped to the new world; they found the originator of Montraville in Rowson's own cousin, British Army engineer John Montresor, who worked in America just prior to the Revolution. If they were mistaken—and they probably were, in any strict factual sense—they were nonetheless obeying the injunction every melodramatist delivers to his or her audience: *take this story literally*. Swear to a reality that includes yet supersedes mere reality of fact for the truth of desire, the "feeling heart"; consent whole-heartedly to a process that promises your own liberation into larger-than-life realization as moral and feeling beings. Thrill and weep for Charlotte as if her life and death are all that matter; she will live, and so will you.

Rowson is usually given the title of the first professional American author, although no American author until the somewhat later days of Washington Irving and James Fenimore Cooper was able to make a living solely by the pen. Rowson reminds us of how many of our writers, from the English-born William Bradford and the

Frenchman Jean de Crèvecoeur to the Polish Henry Roth and the French-speaking Jack Kerouac, have been immigrants or children of immigrants. Born Susanna Musgrove Haswell on February 5, 1762, in Portsmouth, England, into a solid middle-class naval family, Rowson would cheerfully and vigorously live out what later, more sentimental American writers would term "the melodrama of beset womanhood"; the genteel woman thrown early on the mercies of the world and forced to earn her economic and moral livelihood there without significant male support. Rowson lost her mother only ten days after her birth, presumably as a victim to puerperal fever, a daily killer in those days of frequent births and ignorance of germs. Her widowed father, William, left for New England at the behest of the navy in 1763 and brought the five-year-old Susanna over to Boston in 1767.

The crossing, lasting some three months, was a difficult one for the lively child; she would describe the stormy weather and near starvation that beset the passengers in the partly autobiographical novel *Rebecca: or the Fille de Chambre* in 1792, a book unnoticed in England but a steady best-seller in America. If *Rebecca* is to be trusted, on Susanna's arrival in Boston, harbor and boat alike were sheeted in winter "sleet" and "ice" and cut with a bitter wind. The child was tied up in a bundle and lowered over the ship's side by a kind sailor. Her waiting father received her amid imminent fear of the ship's foundering; "a false step or slip might destroy them both." Another boat brought her to Nantasket (where she would live for most of the next decade) and a very different prospect:

a beautiful little peninsula [consisting of] . . . two gradually rising hills beautifully diversified with orchards, cornfields, and pasture lands. In the valley is built a little village. . . . The peninsula . . . forms [on one side] a charmingly picturesque harbor in which are a variety of small but delightfully fertile islands, and, on the other, it is washed by the ocean, to which it lays open.

The hospitable New Englanders "revived in the mind . . . the golden age so celebrated by poets." The start of Rowson's American adventure, like that of the immigrants who preceded and succeeded her, was marked by a double vision: on the one hand, a perilous wilderness dominated by the elements, in which one must depend on the good nature of common men; on the other, a civilized rural utopia easily yielding to agrarian and domestic needs, ideals, and pleasures.

During these American years, William Haswell married again (he picked an American, Rachel Woodward, whom Rowson found uncongenial) and had two sons. Susanna wandered the beautiful country, read avidly (Homer, Shakespeare, Dryden, and Spenser) from her father's small library, and enjoyed conversations with James Otis, an early and eloquent formulator of American rights in the colonies' approaching struggle for independence. Hard times befell the Haswell family as conflict with the mother country sharpened; Haswell, his sympathies divided between his adopted and native land, was nonetheless an employee of the crown and imprisoned as such with his family in 1775. Moved from one spot of captivity under armed guard to another and yet another over the next three years, suffering isolation and actual privation, the Haswells found their support in the teenaged Susanna, who oversaw the moves, gathered firewood, tended what home they had, and sought provisions and aid from friends old and new whose generosity she never forgot. Finally, in May 1778, in an exchange of prisoners, the Haswells were allowed to return to London. Again Rowson had had a double experience in America: on the one hand, severe hardship amid unforgettable revolutionary violence (the Revolution would provide background for half of her novels); on the other, an opportunity to test her capacity to survive amid difficult circumstances with the help of the good-hearted friends and common citizens of a fledgling New World.

Back in London (where the record gets dim), the young Rowson continued to support her family (both William and Rachel were ill), working at various jobs, probably including that of governess and companion. Some time in the early 1780s, she went on the stage, still a questionable but by no means a prohibited activity for a middle-class girl who meant to keep her reputation; her first book, *A Trip to Parnassus* (1784), a book of shrewd drama criticism, shows a wide knowledge of the London theater world. In 1786, she married William Rowson, a hardware merchant and inept handyman of the stage; he would do mediocre and transient work as an actor and prompter and enjoy some small fame as a trumpet-player. He would also ask his wife to tend his bastard son, William Rowson Jr., by another woman. (She did; the couple had no children of their own.) Eventually he settled down to a small-time customs job in the 1800s, outlived his wife, remarried, and died in 1843.

There is concrete evidence that William was a drinker, a shift-less worker, a running embarrassment to Rowson. She seems to have married him not out of love but out of a belief that she could accomplish more of what she wanted to do as a wife. even as William Rowson's wife, than—in her words in *Sarah; or the Exemplary Wife* (1813)—as a single and "poor" woman "thrown on the world . . . open to the pursuits and insults of the profligate." "Do not marry a fool," she once cautioned, apparently from experience, but she lived under the same roof with William the rest of her life and wrote a poem to him on their twenty-fifth wedding anniversary, declaring herself "ready to renew [her marriage vows] now." If William did not enhance her status, he did not obstruct it, and her eventual large success was visibly her own.

Unlike later Victorian heroines of "the melodrama of beset wom-anhood"—Sarah Joseph Hale, "Fanny Fern" (Sara Willis Parton), E. D. E. N. Southworth, and Harriet Beecher Stowe, all best-selling authors compelled to write, they liked to announce, by economic necessity in the form of an incompetent or runaway or deceased spouse—Rowson never complained in public and seldom in private about her lot; daughter of the Revolution that she was, a modest but sturdy feminist independence was her native style.

In matriarchal fashion she would eventually support a sister-in-law, three nieces, and an adopted daughter, as well as William and his illegitimate son. Even though, in keeping with the legal system of the day, it was William who signed her publishing and theatrical contracts in England and America, and William who became an American citizen in 1802 (women were not accredited citizens or voters in the Republic), it was undoubtedly she who was the presiding spirit in all their enterprises.

After nearly a decade of unsuccessful struggle in the London theater, the Rowsons responded to the solicitations of the distinguished American actor-playwright Thomas Wignell to return with his newly assembled company to the New Theatre (still under construction) in Philadelphia. After the American theater companies had been banned by the colonies at the start of the Revolution, many of their actors had gone into other pursuits or emigrated to England and Europe's busy theaters. When the ban against theaters was lifted in America in the late 1780s, an American manager like Wignell found few actors still on hand. Just as the Virginia Company had done in the 1620s and 1630s, Wignell prospected abroad for talent; he went direct to the London theater. The English corps he collected in the early 1790s under his management and that of his collaborator, the popular composer Alexander Reinagle, was destined to be the best in early post-Revolutionary America. Rowson could not play many leads in a company that boasted Mrs. Eliza Kemble Whitlock, Mrs. Oldmixon, and Mrs. Anne Brunton Merry, except in her own patriotic and comic-melodramatic plays (of which only *Slaves of Algiers* [1794] survives), but she essayed secondary matron roles like the Nurse and Mrs. Capulet in *Romeo and Juliet,* Mrs. Quickley in *The Merry Wives of Windsor,* and the Player Queen in *Hamlet* to temperate praise. Rowson prospered under Wignell and more especially Reinagle, for whose lively tunes she wrote a number of spirited and witty lyrics; one sees in this team a faint but real predecessor to Ira and George Gershwin.

In 1796 the Rowsons left the Wignell company for the Federal Street Theatre of Boston. Susanna Rowson's last appearance as an actress was in May 1797; later in that year she would open her "Young Ladies Academy" in Boston. Fittingly, Rowson, the author of a runaway best-seller whose audience included those who seldom and barely read, was in good part self-educated, but she was widely so; she disdained the prejudicially scanty decorative skills to which girls' education was largely confined. In all her work, whether on stage, at a desk, or in a classroom, Rowson dramatized and tried to narrow the gap between the literate and illiterate, the privileged and the disenfranchised, the female and the male, the enslaved and the free. Her Academy, moved to various sites in the Boston area over the next quarter century and flanked by half a dozen innovative and wide-selling textbooks written by Rowson for female students, was a modest pioneer in the movement for serious education for women that would culminate in the founding of Mt. Holyoke, Bryn Mawr, Smith, and Vassar over the next century.

Rowson emigrated, then, to America not once but twice, sketching a kind of paradigm of the motives behind all such emigrations: the first time as a child, a dependent caught in a father's career move; the second time voluntarily, as a professional, an author-actress-playwright, looking self-consciously to better and further her prospects. For Rowson the American dream, even a feminist version of it, came true. She parlayed her industry as actress and author into a respectable career as an educator to Boston's best families; her books sold in America as they never had in England. In 1809 she bought a house on Hollis Street in Boston worth $4600, a considerable sum for that day. But Rowson had also known a passage to America that had something in common with the experience of the slaves carried as live cargo to the New World; moreover, her father had suffered a dizzying reverse in status there, and she had seen gaol, hard labor, and want. She was well aware that the American dream was not even-handedly available to all its applicants or believers and that it could turn bad even on those it favored. When she wrote in her hit play *Slaves of Algiers* (1794) that America was a land where "There are no bolts and bars" and "women do just as they please," she may have expected to get a laugh as well as a patriotic round of applause.

Charlotte Temple bears witness to Rowson's darker knowledge of her "dear adopted country." Charlotte comes to America apparently during the Revolution* at the age of fifteen, just the age Rowson was when she and her family suffered imprisonment in the strife-filled colonies. Charlotte leaves a safe home and makes the trip, like any other immigrant, seduced by the hope of a new and more exciting life: Montraville (very much a "catch" for Charlotte) has promised to marry her in America. Charlotte's crossing is a calamitous one; it is there midway between the Old World and the New that she presumably loses her virtue. "We trusted our happiness [she writes her evil angel, La Rue, shortly before her death] on a tempestuous ocean where mine has been wrecked."

Charlotte is still on shipboard when she is brought with casual brutality to her first awareness of the deception that has been practiced on her. When the designing La Rue switches her attentions from the knavish Belcour to the easily duped and wealthy Crayton, "the inexperienced Charlotte was astonished." She has assumed that La Rue ran away with Belcour just as she did with Montraville, out of love and the belief that he would marry her on their arrival in New York. "I am sure Belcour promised to marry [La Rue]," she tells Montraville uneasily. "Well, and suppose he did?" Montraville returns. "[If] he has changed his mind, . . .

---

*The historical date is not precise in *Charlotte Temple*; adding the facts supplied by *Charlotte's Daughter*—that Lucy is twenty in 1794 and that Charlotte died at nineteen—Charlotte would have come to New York in 1770–1 and died there in 1774. This does not coincide with the picture of New York in *Charlotte Temple* as a town filled with Loyalist troops, nor with Montraville and Belcour's suggestion that Montraville may well meet "a musket ball" there. The overwhelming and time-honored impression that Charlotte is lost in a city under military rule and in a country at war must win the day.

then, you know, the case is altered." Male caprice is a statute independent of any country's law or creed. By the end Charlotte longs for nothing but a return to England, "that dear happy land which now contains all that is dear to wretched Charlotte." If America is a land of promise, it is also an academy in promises deferred, broken and betrayed. All those capable of enterprise, like Rowson herself, have a fighting chance to better their lot in the New World; but those who are dependent, like Charlotte, scarcely individuated from a familial and educative network of supportive care, will perish.

And who is most likely to be dependent? Not a young man— not, for instance, Montraville, a classic case of the "youngest son" in English society, given a gentleman's rank and little of a gentleman's income; he will marry up and prosper financially in the New World. Montraville's father gives us the tip-off to the inequitable property and education divisions by gender that will preoccupy Rowson through every phase of her long career. His sons can train themselves, the elder Montraville knows, "to genteel professions" and then "exert their talents, make themselves friends and raise their fortunes on the basis of merit." His daughters cannot so train themselves and remain ladies; their only hope is in a marriage that will save them from "the snares and temptations" attendant on an "accomplished female when oppressed by the frowns of poverty and the sting of dependence." We may recall that Rowson herself married to escape just this fate.

If professional exertion is forbidden a "lady," how can she survive in a culture that prides itself on awarding "fortune on the basis of merit"? Montraville is upwardly mobile, but Charlotte is in a downward spiral. One of the most powerful scenes in *Charlotte Temple* is the abandoned and penniless Charlotte's interview with her irate and brutal landlady. This self-righteous matron urges Charlotte to go to work if only as a laundress or a cook or (she barely veils her meaning here) as a prostitute ("go to the barracks and work for a morsel of bread") and evicts her. Charlotte, wandering pregnant in the snowstorm through New York's streets, destitute, ill-clad, and barely sane, aided too late only by chance kindness of two working-class men (the soldier and the butler), is one of the homeless, a member of the underclass.

Few of Charlotte's best-known fictive successors like Harriet Beecher Stowe's Little Eva and Mara, "the Pearl of Orr's Island," and Henry James's Daisy Miller and Milly Theale, would fall into sexual degradation, abject poverty, and insanity, although they would all, like Charlotte, die in protracted deathbed sequences. But they owe much to her. Alexis Comte de Tocqueville, the most celebrated of all travelers to the American scene, would remark in the 1830s on the striking contrast between the "freedom" of the American girl and the "extreme dependence" of the American wife. Although he does not say so, Tocqueville is noting not just the difference between the American woman's single and married status, but also that between the masculine and feminine versions of the rags-to-riches-and-back-again American social dynamic. The American woman is free or dependent according to the value the male market sets on her or stores in her; she does not make that value and she cannot control it. Charlotte is a powerful predecessor of the "American Girl," the major protagonist of Henry James and William Dean Howells, who would be ineffably updated and commercialized by Marilyn Monroe in *The Prince and the Showgirl* (1957), *Some Like It Hot* (1959), and *The Misfits* (1961). The American girl is always the symbol of the American dream, never its continuous active agent.

I do not forget Julia Franklin, who wins Montraville's love from Charlotte. She plays the "lively girl" (to borrow a term melodrama favored) to Charlotte's helplessly victimized ingenue, and she would have her heirs in Stowe's Topsy and James's Kate Croy, in the Mitzi Gaynors and Debbie Reynolds of fifties' screen musicals. As a middle-aged woman at the dénouement of *Charlotte's Daughter*, Julia leaves England, "the country where she had known nothing but misfortune and trial," for America, where she had known all her "happiness." But Julia at any age is always, in Rowson's words, "the very reverse of Charlotte Temple." In *Charlotte Temple*, Julia is independently wealthy, as Charlotte is not; she is older and clearly better educated than Charlotte. She is not quite the "American Girl"; Rowson always describes Charlotte as a "girl" but Julia as a "woman." Julia's character strengths are those of "energy and decision," not the "passive virtues" that are clearly Charlotte's. She can take care of herself without her author's help. Because she does not depend on male aid or need it, it will not fail her as it brutally fails Charlotte.

What of the two men more or less in love with Charlotte? Belcour has no traffic with female passivity except to destroy it; he will eventually take off, drawn by "the blooming health of a farmer's daughter," who seems a stray from the robust and lusty world of *Tom Jones*. Montraville is more ambivalent. He entertains the possibility of marrying Charlotte before learning her financial standing; he would never have abandoned her, Rowson tells us, if he had not believed Belcour's lies. But while the cloistered female may attract Montraville, she does not interest him. Montraville will fall truly in love with Julia Franklin, who calls men out into their own world—"Do you bury yourself in the house this fine evening, gents?" is her jaunty summons to Montraville and Belcour—not into a feminine, private realm. Neither Montraville nor Belcour is governed by the insistent query of the classic seducer, like Richardson's Lovelace in *Clarissa* or La Clos's Valmont in *Les Liaisons Dangereuses*: is there a woman capable of resisting seduction? Can the Diogenes-seducer find on this earth one honest maid? This obsessive quest, which magnifies even as it attacks the worth of the valiantly chaste female, is not Montraville's nor Belcour's. No, poor Charlotte is not much more than a side interest; an off-fancy, to them; where she gives her tiny all, they give only a momentary if large caprice.

It is essential to her story that Charlotte is of consuming interest only to women: to her adoring mother, Lucy; to her feminized father and grandfather, denizens of their beloved Lucy's gardenscape; to Madame du Pont, head of the academy from which Charlotte is seduced, who "loved Charlotte truly"; to the cunning French teacher La Rue, who, driven—much like Melville's Claggart in his attempt to bring down Billy Budd—by the sinner's hatred of the innocent, is, all the characters agree, Charlotte's real seducer; to Mrs. Beauchamp, who will try to help Charlotte rejoin her parents and cradle Charlotte's head on her own maternal "bosom" in the girl's final moments; above all to the "dear young ladies" for whom Rowson writes; and to Rowson herself.

Rowson's often-noted authorial intrusions in *Charlotte Temple* (there are nine full-scale ones) at first glance read like moralizings directed against the tenor of the story. Her constant command to her readers is not to do what Charlotte did: "Oh my dear girls, for such only am I writing, listen not to the voice of love unless sanctioned by paternal approbation!" But in fact each authorial remark is designed to clear away, not reinforce, the obstacles that lie between Rowson's readers and full identification with the story. She meets the objections of "sober matrons," men "of philosophic temperament," frowning "madams," any "Sir" who "cavils" at the accuracy of her account, even her dear "young, volatile readers" who may be growing restless. In Chapter XXVIII, just before *Charlotte*'s thrilling dénouement—the mad pilgrimage in the snowstorm—Rowson calls her readers sharply to attention. Perhaps they are getting bored with Charlotte's long-drawn-out victimization; they would not if they realized that, as it is for Charlotte, "thus it might have been with me." Rowson means to make them "acutely feel the woes of Charlotte," to empathize, agonize, identify with her: "I am writing a tale of truth: I mean to write it to the heart."

Each authorial intrusion screws up reader involvement another notch, and Rowson herself suffers with her story: "Gracious heavens! When I think of . . . [the miseries of the parent of a seduced girl], I want . . . to extirpate those monsters of seduction from the earth"; "my heart aches while I write"; "from my soul I pity [the merciless]"; "the burning blush of indignation and shame tinges my cheek while I write." Charlotte too will "burn" with "shame"; she too will exclaim "Gracious Heaven!" Rowson knows how thin a line separates her readers and herself from Charlotte's fate, and at one point she takes a moment off from her story to speak straight out to those kind friends and strangers who once saved her in her darkest hour on American soil from Charlotte's fate; she "mourns" that like assistance "cannot extend to all the sons and daughters of affliction."

This reaching off the page is Rowson's signature. Again and again, she reminds us that words are her only medium, but that they are nonetheless inadequate pointers to the meaning she seeks. She refers to "an agony of grief which it is impossible to describe"; she queries "Who can form an adequate idea of Charlotte's misery?"; she concludes that "it would be impossible to do justice [to the meeting of Charlotte's mother and her daughter]." Charlotte herself is almost mute, until desperation and madness electrify her to passionately abject if fruitless appeals. As Charlotte's agony deepens, this "subliterate myth" moves us away from the interference of language into gesture, the only expression of hyperbolic feeling so intense as to constitute (in Peter Brooks's words) "primal" language, the "sign language" of the body.

It is crucial to melodrama, which began in wordless pantomime set to music, that body and heart take up the work of articulation at the point that language fails. Increasingly, as the noose of Charlotte's fate and Rowson's story tightens, the book turns into tableaux, in Peter Brooks's words, "visual summaries of emotional situations," set pieces in which body placement, posture, and expression cast off the secrecy of language: Charlotte's abduction in the carriage; Charlotte pleading with Montraville not to desert her, with her landlady not to evict her, with La Rue to give her refuge, with Mrs. Beauchamp to comfort her, with her mother (by letter) and her father in person not to "curse" her. Charlotte repeatedly uses stock melodramatic gestures, which Rowson inserts almost as if they were stage directions. She "clasps her hands" in supplication, "lifts her eyes" in prayer, kneels "in shame," and "faints" away in agony. If *Charlotte Temple* is "subliterate myth," one must remember that such subliterature includes the very sources of language in body and heart, in blushes, tears and gesture, sources that language masks as well as indicates; one must remember that myths are, to paraphrase Freud's famous words, the history of our instincts, amalgams of physical and psychological needs and drives. We see in *Charlotte Temple*—and this is a large part of the book's power—the refusal of desire, ever balked of its end, of its wished-for consummation, to use any language but its own.

Desire as female sexuality is not altogether absent in the novel. Sexual desire, if of a shy and affectionate nature, is Charlotte's motive for her elopement. We see her lying down timidly but unmistakably by the sleeping Montraville; she waits with utter expectancy for his rare visits, "counting the minutes and straining her eyes to catch the first glimpse of his person." Even as he begins to grow cruel, she is "tortured with the pangs of disappointed love." But, at bottom, Charlotte is looking for a parent, not a lover; she is a child in years and even more so in mind. Her enormous pathos in the later portions of her story comes from our sense of her as a helpless child, a trapped and defenseless animal, looking frantically to see where it can reattach and be safe. She wants what a child wants: food, shelter, care. But her world has become a "barren waste," her needs in their displaced extremity a "Medusa's head" that turns the hearts in which she would find mercy to "stone." Without love—without, to be more precise, symbiosis—the child must die.

Charlotte is helpless to decide her fate—that is the province of adults; she can only enact adult decrees. If she has sinned, it is not an adult's sin but a child's. Like any child, she is forced to trust and to trust most those with the most power to hurt her—namely adults. Her sin is to trust the wrong adults: first La Rue, then Montraville. The sin of the adults in *Charlotte Temple* is not one of trust but of judgment. They imagine they are literate in society's and reality's workings; they read the evidence and then act on it. La Rue sees that this is an unjust world, particularly for women, and behaves accordingly. Montraville believes Belcour's accusations about Charlotte not because he trusts Belcour but because he believes his eyes when he sees them on her bed together. Even Charlotte's parents, even Mrs. Beauchamp, commit the unpardonable sin as a child understands it—the crime of desertion. We know why Charlotte's parents don't seek her out: they need information they haven't got. We know why Mrs. Beauchamp takes a trip with her husband, leaving Charlotte on her own: a married woman has her priorities. But these deeds still function like an act of brutality as deliberate as La Rue's simply because Charlotte doesn't understand them.

The child never understands its own abandonment. Charlotte's most heartrending words are spoken as she is taking the full meaning of her lover's behavior: "Gracious heaven! Is Montraville then unjust to none but me?" The adult's crimes are finally necessary in the melodramatic world of *Charlotte Temple* because they highlight and empower the victimized child; she becomes a figure whose awful plight exposes a broader adult guilt. Charlotte has been seduced and abandoned in the New World, not only of America, but of that world that is always new to children, the landscape of adult passion and betrayal. In her postpartum dementia, Charlotte knows that a child "partakes not of its mother's guilt," and at the deepest level she is that innocent infant, not its guilty parent.

A monopathic being, Charlotte cannot bear more than one feeling at a time; she is dominated by what critic Franco Moretti calls "the excessive desire for one-sidedness." She can only transfer her dependence from one person to another, intact; she cannot discriminate. She replaces her love of her mother ("I will not break her heart!" she tells Montraville as she tries in vain to resist him) with love of Montraville; then, punished (to her mind) for her betrayal of parents and home, she converts her love of Montraville back to love of her mother. There is scant evidence that she still loves Montraville once he cuts her off and she begins her trek into the barren wasteland. The only piece of jewelry she has left is a locket containing a lock of her mother's hair, "which the greatest extremity of want could not have forced her to part with." Charlotte's only virtue is, in several senses, her mother's; her life *is* her mother's. She cannot sustain independent life; her own child is, to her confused mind, not simply herself but herself "parted" from the mother whose "bosom bleeds at every vein." Dying, she has become once again only her parents' daughter, not Montraville's mistress; she calls her child the "offspring of disobedience," not the fruit of guilty passion. Seduction in classic melodrama is never merely a love affair; it is also a family romance. It is a matter, if not of incest, of what Peter Brooks calls the "temptation of over-sameness." Heterosexual passion is at bottom a decoy from home; desire sets its own ambush. By the end, Charlotte ceases to be "an object of desire" even for the sadistic Belcour.

But, while Charlotte's status as an object of desire and her own objects of desire shift, her *longing* permeates the text, and her longing is not denied its culmination. Charlotte's fatal melancholia (to use an eighteenth-century term for her suicidal depression) is what Freud called "a pure culture of the death instinct." The power of her story comes from a kind of death wish; for what is the death wish but the drive to escape separation, individuation, and maturation? Her flight to New York is not so much a quest for life as a desperate intent to die in her own way, on her own terms; she wants both to embrace her punishment and to thrust its injustice into the faces of those who have betrayed her. Her eloquence is elicited and consumed by acts of conspicuous self-nomination; she begins to refer to herself in the third person as "the lost abandoned Charlotte," "the heart-broken Charlotte," "the wretched Charlotte," "a poor forsaken wanderer." "What will become of me?" she exclaims. Emotionally anorexic, she demands a mere crust, but that she demands implacably.

Charlotte's aim in the novel's last quarter is to be seen, to be heard. "Kill me, but for pity's sake . . . do not doubt my innocence," she implores Montraville as he is leaving her. She craves, as virtue in melodrama always does, absolute visibility: to be in her corporeal self coterminal with any interpretation of herself, to be believed, to be taken as testimony in the full legal and religious sense of the word. When Mrs. Beauchamp first sees Charlotte, she learns she is "the mistress of Montraville." But Mrs. Beauchamp discards the words, the interpretation, in favor of the physical evidence: "the goodness of her heart is depicted in her ingenuous countenance," Mrs. Beauchamp tells her husband; she longs to befriend the English girl. No wonder she is Charlotte's good "Angel"; she alone can read Charlotte's language.

Charlotte, who becomes increasingly weak, languid, "pale" with "sunk and heavy" eyes, "deathlike" and "emaciated," a kind of seduced saint of what was once called "holy anorexia," records physically that which is within her, that which defies words but not show. Remember: This is "a subliterate myth." Charlotte's eloquence, belated but powerful, is the spillover of physical agony, not an effort at the separate articulation that is the goal of language. It is her "tortured nerves" that write the last portion of the book. Her body becomes her text, and her last agonized journey is a sustained feverish attack of what the prima donna of melodrama, Sarah Bernhardt, called "le trac," the stage fright that attacks "le cage," the diaphragm and nerves of the body gearing into ultimate performative expression.

Like the raped Philomel of classical myth, the archetype of all ravished maidens, Charlotte is seduced, abandoned, mutilated, and silenced; as Philomel's tongue was cut out lest she betray her seducer to her sister, Charlotte's letters home are stolen or lost. Like Philomel, Charlotte must make out of muteness a language. Because it is Charlotte's body that speaks, when she tries to describe her hell of shame and pain, she projects it as physical ordeal, an ordeal that works by a hysterical engrossment and identification with the feelings that she has caused others. When she left her mother, she later writes her, her "heart bled at the thought of what you would suffer." The "agony of that moment" can never be "erased." She describes the parting as the sundering of a single organism; it was "the separation of soul and body," "like tearing the chords of life asunder." She would go back to her mother if it meant walking "barefoot over a burning desert."

Literalism is the key to Charlotte's story; everything real must be transformed into something true. Before the story started, we learn, the intriguing La Rue had eloped from a convent with a man who presumably deserted her; she had then "lived with several different men in open defiance" of morality. She was subsequently accepted as a teacher at Charlotte's school because she fooled a friend and the headmistress with a false tale of seduction and "penitence"; they believed she was "sincere." La Rue will tell the same story of seduction, betrayal, and remorse (with variations) to the gullible Colonel Crayton on shipboard to America. But the penalty for lying in the melodramatic world of *Charlotte Temple* is that the lie will come true; lies magnetize substantiation. First, La Rue's story is displaced and projected; for it is of course Charlotte, not La Rue, who is seduced, abandoned, and heart-rendingly repentant. The name "La Rue" reminds us that its possessor is a creature of the streets—as Charlotte will be. But as Charlotte's fate makes La Rue's script fact, La Rue will be compelled to re-enact Charlotte's doom, to literalize her own perjury, and end poor, friendless, miserable, and dying on the doorstep of Charlotte's family. If Charlotte, like some late Victorian female hysteric, must manifest in her heart and body the feelings she has caused or believes she has caused in others, others must in turn manifest her feelings.

In *Charlotte Temple*, there are no uninvolved passersby; everyone is drafted into the needs of the story for self-emblazonment. As Charlotte's anguish externalizes itself into action, into the terrible trek through New York City, its power increases until it becomes a law that the actions of others must obey. Right after Charlotte's death, Montraville echoes step by step Charlotte's path through the city. It is his turn now to live through his "tortured nerves"; he, like Charlotte, will fall ill and go insane, and although he will not die, he will not fully recover. As he searches for Charlotte, *the* world has become *her* world. The story he elicits from a soldier about a 'poor girl" abandoned when "big with child" by a "cruel man" is Charlotte's version of their story not his, but it has become the popular and the true version and he must subscribe to it. In melodramatic fashion, the fiction of Charlotte Temple has indeed become "a tale of truth."

Pacing here is everything. Charlotte's crime is finally dependence; the tale works to expose her incompleteness, her mutilation, by knocking her supports out from under her one by one. Like all melodramas, *Charlotte Temple* entoils its readers in an experience of the unbearable. The story does not get fully charged and empowered until Charlotte's suffering becomes her identity—the pain *is* the story—but from the very start, the trivial, even the uninteresting details and scenes compel us because we know, we sniff out, that they foreshadow the end, that they will be ironized by later developments, that this story is enacted from the viewpoint of its finish. Montraville's casual query to Belcour, "Are you for a walk," opens the book. The friends go to "take a survey of the Chichester ladies as they returned from their devotions." The sauntering male is pitted against the sheltered, devout female; adventure is stalking domesticity; the chase has begun.

The two young men quickly sight their quarry, the "tall, elegant" Charlotte, but we do not get on at once with the hunt. The tale works by melodramatic conventions of action and content as Peter Brooks has formulated them, conventions that would become the staple of stage melodrama in the 1790s, 1800s, and 1810s. Before taking off, so to speak, Rowson must invoke the domestic background against which we can take the measure of Charlotte's coming degradation. We are given the "garden" utopia of Charlotte's home that will be penetrated and nearly destroyed by the serpent-seducer La Rue; then the family history (Mr. Temple's model courtship of Charlotte's mother) that went into its making. There is the "violated banquet"—Charlotte's birthday party lovingly planned by her parents that Charlotte does not attend. There is the "thwarted escape"—Charlotte's misgivings, her twists in the trap as she tries to love Montraville without succumbing to him. Then we have the "journey"—the trip to America, the false paradise of Charlotte and Montraville's cottage outside New York.

And then, like a tapestry shuddering in a powerful current of air, the story begins to quiver, to shift, to reveal new and extreme designs. Efforts to find help fail, letters are lost, language is useless, Charlotte is betrayed, Montraville leaves, Belcour decamps, she is evicted, logic is gone, and Charlotte is mad. The urtext written by pain swamps the overt text; like the "Crazy Mary" or "Jane" figure who comes into literature about the same time *Charlotte* was written, this victim of male sexual violence begins to speak the only language at her disposal; the body usurps the word. Charlotte goes to New York, her father comes to America, she dies. Montraville learns the truth, then searches out and kills the drunken Belcour in a duel; he goes mad, he partly recovers and fully regrets. The nightmare is over, the storm of significance is past, and we return to a muted version of the opening pastoral: Eden after the fall, little Lucy united with her grandparents in England. It is all a bit like the dynamic of the midnineteenth-century opera—*Rigoletto, La Traviata, Lucia di Lamamoor*—that sprang direct from early melodrama: chance collaborations of voices turn into driven enmeshed trios and quartets, the solitary voice of the soprano-heroine soars in agony and ecstasy above its accompaniment, the orchestra's music quickens to crash in the turmoil of complete expression and then subsides, diminishes into one sharp clap, and silence.

Charlotte Temple is no *bildungsroman*: Charlotte learns nothing; the reader, despite Rowson's injunctions, learns nothing. In the "barren waste" of urban America, Charlotte can only be a "wanderer"—not a voyager, not a discoverer, not even a pilgrim. There is no tragic catharsis—for Charlotte, for Montraville, for the reader. Such a catharsis is an instantaneous fusion of just-acquired intellectual perception with powerfully tapped primal reserves of feeling, and it does not attend *Charlotte Temple*. As the child is to the adult, as the illiterate is to the literate, as gesture is to language, so the dénouement of melodrama, *Charlotte Temple*'s affect, is to catharsis. We do not think; we only experience, we only feel more and more. We tap the reserves of emotion until they are empty; exhaustion, not understanding, is the result. When Charlotte's body usurps the text, the text, like her body, becomes a metaphor of desire as *symptom*, as a sign of illness. As such, text and body are caught in their own involutions amid the self-referential workings of the somatic psyche, involutions out of which development *can* rise but need not, of which maturation is one possible expression but not the goal, not the inevitable form. Charlotte does not undergo the conflict that indicates the unwilling acknowledgment of what Freud called "the reality principle"; her "heart," in her own words, is "torn" apart, not conflicted, by identifications that involve all of her.

Since there is no conflict in Charlotte to be resolved, only a split that cannot be healed, she must work herself out of her story. "Let me die unlamented and my name sink into oblivion," she begs. Her body becomes a symptom of the illness maturation entails, but it cannot transmit back to her heart and mind the knowledge that finally achieves maturation; it must die and be placed on view as a corpse. Charlotte becomes that quintessential creature of memory, the child we once were, the child that died so we might become the judging, divided adult creatures we are. Her "plaintive . . . voice," singing its deathless theme, "let me be at peace," must be silenced, but it will sound in that country in which we are always children, the country of dreams. When Montraville, aflame with his crime, raves for "Charlotte!", he is mourning not

Charlotte but his lost self, the adventurous boy who went for a "walk" and ended up in America at Charlotte's tomb. Mr. Temple refuses to let Montraville act out his grief, refuses to strike him dead and spare him "the misery of reflection"; he condemns him to "look at that little heap of earth" where Charlotte is buried, to "look at it often." He could be issuing a summons to all the Americans who would make the pilgrimage to Charlotte Temple's grave in Trinity Church over the next century. Charlotte's name cannot "sink into oblivion," for her readers, like Charlotte, come to America again and again, children who will die in the shock of reality.

Rowson did not want to leave the theme of feminine maturation on the regressive note of *Charlotte Temple*; to promote and facilitate such maturation was her pragmatic goal, as a resourceful, innovative, and dedicated teacher of girls and as a robust if crude chronicler of the young woman setting heart and mind to the task of living in a mixed world of deprivation and opportunity. And so we have *Charlotte's Daughter*—or *Lucy Temple,* the title under which almost all publishers after the first edition marketed the tale. Lucy Blackeney does not, despite the insistent and telling retitling by publishers and readers, even bear her mother's name. "A splendid heiress" living with a loving adoptive family in England and ignorant of her mother's story, she is by circumstance, training, and temperament shockproof; Lucy is a girl who laughs "when I hear of love at first sight." Where her mother found a depopulated world of disaster, she finds a populous but ordered social scene, a live sermon on the possibilities and necessities of her development. Lucy's body undergoes no ordeal; her lesson—and she learns it— is one of the mind and conscience.

Early on in *Lucy Temple,* we meet a humble, elderly serving-class couple on Sir Robert Ainslie's estate who subsist largely on tea, the Bible, and the kindness of their pastor. They accept their meager fate in part because class distinctions are strangely vital to Rowson here but also, it seems, as penance. In earlier days, they brought up their daughter, Alice, to think herself a "lady"; Alice made an ill-starred marriage that culminated in abandoment and early death. "I did not teach her to know herself," Gammer Lounsdale confesses. Perhaps the ill-fated Alice Lounsdale was not taught to know herself, but Lucy is. She watches her mother's fate overtake one of her two adopted sisters, Lady Mary Lumly—snobbish, sentimental, ready to leave behind property rights and self-respect in the interest of being, "in the language of romantic misses, sworn friends" with the weak-principled Miss Brenton (a faint echo of La Rue) and romantic lover (and, she hopes, wife) to the dissipated Stephen Haynes (another portrait of Belcour).

Mary, of course, has done too much reading under the eyes first of an "indulgent" mother and then of a "flattering" governess. This is the fault by which so many early novelists, Rowson among them, anxious over the many girls for the first time in history "living"— as Henry James would later put it with some asperity—"by the aid of the novel," mark out the female character destined to fall. Read this novel, such authors seem to tell their readers in a profusion of mixed motives ranging from business instinct to moral conviction; it can't hurt you because it tells you that novels—I mean other novels—can. In *Lucy Temple*'s predecessor, we might note, if Charlotte overindulged in fiction, and even if La Rue did, Rowson did not tell us of it. Charlotte was to be read: she was the text. Lucy is nowhere more significantly different from her mother than in the fact that she is herself a reflective reader, much like the young female reader Rowson theoretically hoped to educate by the tale of *Charlotte*. *Lucy Temple* is about Lucy reading *Charlotte*'s text, displaced, trivialized, and half comical, in Mary Lumley's re-enactment of Charlotte's melodramatic scenario "The Maid, the Mother, the Maniac."

But there are texts Lucy cannot read and they have, notably, to do with her mother. Her grandfather's letter detailing her mother's shame is broken off in just the crucial place. Is the letter that begins the name of Charlotte's seducer an "N" or an "M"? No one knows. The miniature of Charlotte given to Lucy at her coming-of-age birthday party is the most striking presence in *Lucy Temple*, far more powerful than any of the so-called living characters. But Lucy cannot guess its meaning; the miniature can be read aright only by the unhappy survivor of the terrors of the earlier text. Montraville knows at once who the portrait represents and what it means, and his language shuttles us back to the melodramatic realm of *Charlotte Temple*: "it is—it is come again to blast my vision in my last hour!—The woman you would marry [he tells his son] is my own daughter!—Just Heaven!—Oh that I could have been spared this!" He takes all the blame, exonerates poor Charlotte, and expresses the grim wish that he had changed "not his name only but himself!" The tactic of changing one's name may have saved Lucy from her mother's fate, but it cannot protect the man who kicked that drama off from living his part to the bitter end. This is the transformative power of Charlotte Temple the character and *Charlotte Temple* the text: they issue their largest edicts to those empowered to feel them but powerless to enact them.

In *Lucy Temple*, Gammer Lounsdale expresses a curious contentment with the early death of her little granddaughter, the offspring of the unhappy Alice who did not "know herself" and fell. The child faced the same "temptation," Gammer explains, the conjunction of "poverty" and "beauty" her mother knew; she "might have been lost [like her mother] both body and soul." Gammer seems a stand-in here for her author, unwilling to create another fictive Charlotte and participate again in her heart-wrenching fall. In *Lucy Temple*, Rowson has banished the strong emotional affects that vivified *Charlotte*. After Montraville's death scene, the mimetic world Rowson has established in *Lucy* with its humdrum daily-life talk of cakes and ale, its birthday feast of hams and pies and plum puddings, quickly returns. This version of Charlotte, Lady Mary, will survive her seduction to find shelter and tempered happiness with her adoptive family. Lucy's other adoptive sister, Aura, without "one showy accomplishment," Rowson insists, much less a romantic adventure, will make a rational and happy love match, with economic prosperity thrown in. The father figure here, the Reverend Matthews, in contrast to Charlotte's father, always knows best. When he loses one of his adopted daughters, his realization is quick: Mary is no sooner missing than he jumps to the epithet "[the] poor stray lamb!" His grief is, to say the least, tempered, and his forgiveness will be equally easy. Montraville's death scene is the only melodramatic tableau or, indeed, scene of any kind Rowson gives us in *Lucy Temple*. She skips the big love sequences, the encounters of shock and rapture, as "dull in detail" or best left to be "imagined by the readers."

Old Blandford begins a tale to Lucy about her mother that gives her a stab of "terror," but it is broken off like her grandfather's letter, never to be continued. When her fiancé, Montraville's son, Lieutenant Franklin, learns the terrible truth—that they are half-brother and -sister and must not marry—he does not carry the news in person to Lucy. He sends a friend with the message *"God Bless Her!"* His eventual heroic and suicidal death is safely far off stage. Lucy will never be caught up in a living dénouement of passion; Rowson always provides her the time and distance needed to take thought, to learn, to develop and mature. The third-hand news of the full meaning of her mother's story is swiftly converted into the motive for a prosperous, happy. and selfless life as the teacher of young girls.

In the late nineteenth century a theater critic would defend the "old melodrama" in the face of its new adversary—the realistic drama of Ibsen, Shaw, and Chekhov—by talking of the extraordinary parts it had offered the actress in the grip of an ordeal. "Melodrama gives an actress such a chance to display [the extremes of emotions] . . . melodrama shows all the women in the theater . . . woman in the supreme moments of life." Lucy has gained the sanity and prosperity that Charlotte lacked, but she has paid for them in significance and force. The feminine victim deformed and exalted by the exhaustion of her ordeal is an emblem of indelible if obscure authority. As Alexander Dumas would say of the lost "Dame aux Cameliás": "she had changed . . . she had suffered, she was still suffering." The frail reed tossed in a cruel wind *becomes* the wind. The price of feminism in *Lucy Temple*, unfairly and surely not consciously on Rowson's part, seems to be dramatic interest.

But Rowson does not waver. Writing Lucy Temple, she has disentangled herself from the web of emotions and ambiguities that came from her younger experience of the two-sided nature of the profoundly ambivalent American dream: on the one hand, the ice-imprisoned ship in the snow and sleet of Boston Harbor, from which she was handed to shore at five years of age in 1767; on the other, the unpretentious yet prosperous "Golden Age" of the small towns of New England in which she lived from 1767 till 1775. On the one hand, the cruel imprisonment, penury, and deportment she knew in the Revolutionary years in the colonies; on the other, her shrewdly managed felicitous return to the republic as actress-author-teacher in 1793. The contrast is that between *Charlotte Temple* and *Lucy Temple*. When she embarks on her version of Rowson's prosperous pedagogy, Lucy, looking for a site for her school, chooses "a pleasant spot . . . a quiet little nook bosomed among the wooded hills and commanding a view of the village and a wide expanse of soft meadow scenery." It sounds rather like Nantasket as Rowson remembered spotting it as an emigré child, a "beautiful little peninsula" with a charming "village" and gentle pasture land. Rowson has firmly sided with Lucy Temple and rendered Charlotte, if not a ghost, a genie in a bottle that the novel *Lucy Temple* can and does cap.

But only at the price of protecting Lucy from the melodramatic materials of *Charlotte* and, in a parallel act of diminution, removing her from America. *Lucy Temple* is a fascinating book, a correction to *Charlotte Temple*'s image of the American dream as nightmare, an act of self-criticism that later American authors would also undertake, often with equally little success. If the American dream can only be mended, made to turn out, by transplanting it back to England, it has not so much criticized itself as cancelled itself out. Unlike Charlotte, *Lucy Temple* is a *bildungsroman*, a portrayal of traditional processes of development and self-assessment; Lucy grows up as Charlotte never did and never could. Like many another American author, Rowson's best talents did not lie with the *bildungsroman*, though her sustained efforts—perhaps even her affections—did. If America is the stage for melodrama's most striking tableaux of electrified stasis from *Metamora* (1829) to Ignatius Donnelly's *Caesar's Column* (1891), England is the home of the *bildungsroman* at its finest: *Tom Jones* (1749), *Great Expectations* (1861), and *Middlemarch* (1872). But for Americans, for Rowson, England may be safe, England may be loved; but England is also, they inadvertently confess, dull and derivative. There, *Lucy Temple*'s stilted, well-meant story tells us, one lives out the consequences, bad and good, of crimes committed in America; England keeps the records of American aggression. The colony has become the main text, the mother nation the footnote.

Charlotte Temple's efforts, such as they were, at separation and individuation failed, but America's of course did not. In her lifetime, Rowson saw a new nation born and launched. She contributed her best dramatic writing and songs to the jubilant patriotism of independence, the national confidence that America would indeed, as the Statue of Liberty would proclaim a century later, take in the poor, hungry, friendless multitudes "yearning to be free" of whom Charlotte Temple was so frail yet so persistent a representative. "America, Commerce, and Freedom," Rowson's most popular song, enjoined its listeners:

Then drink round, my boys [and 'my lasses'], 'tis the first of our joys,
   To relieve the distressed, clothe and feed 'em;
'Tis a duty we share with the brave and the fair,
   In this land of commerce and freedom.

Yet Rowson's most powerful work, *Charlotte Temple*, is indisputably one of the variants of that half-buried regressive streak evident in America's romances and melodramas in its first half-century or so of independent life. The feminine domestic novelists who succeeded Susanna Rowson—Catherine Maria Sedgwick, Susan Warner, Maria Cummins, Ann Stephens, Maria McIntosh, Marion Harland, even Louisa May Alcott—would, like Rowson herself, try to balance their attraction to an inchoate melodrama that starred and segregated the female as victim, patient, saint, and avenger with their loyalties to a pragmatic functional feminist ideal; they too tried to balance *Charlotte Temple* with *Lucy Temple*. But the greatest works of American fiction, whether verbally complex or crude, would swerve, as *Charlotte Temple* swerved, into the realm of "subliterate myth." One thinks of Charles Brockden Brown's *Wieland* (1798), Edgar Allan Poe's "The Fall of the House of Usher" (1839), Mrs. E. D. E. N. Southworth's *Retribution* (1849), Herman Melville's *Pierre* (1852), Harriet Beecher Stowe's *Uncle Tom's Cabin* (1852)—texts that, like *Charlotte*, strain and swell and crack with their inability to escape from incestuous symbiosis into adult individuation, an inability to break a family paradigm that strangles and seduces maturation from its goal.

All of Stowe's most important characters in *Uncle Tom's Cabin*, like Rowson's in *Charlotte Temple* and its sequel, either meet their death in America or escape it by repatriating elsewhere. In a famous sequence in *Uncle Tom's Cabin*, the runaway mulatto slave Eliza, clutching her baby to her breast, leaps across the frozen river on the cracking and perilous ice; Eliza relives Charlotte's desperate flight to New York on that "cold stormy day in the latter end of December." The scene would live yet again in D. W. Griffith's hugely popular masterpiece, the silent film *Way Down East* of 1920; the film was based on a melodrama of 1897 by Lottie Blair Parker that owes much to *Charlotte Temple*. In *Way Down East*, Lillian Gish, branded as an unwed mother and turned out of doors, battles the snow and ice in her instinctive, near-fatal drive toward the frozen and treacherous river. "The image of flight," Leslie Fiedler has said in his evocation of the deepest hieroglyph of American culture, "is the image of life": a flight forwards and back, toward individuation and away, etched then blurred, life-as-death and death-as-life. Reading Susanna Rowson's *Charlotte Temple* and its sequel *Lucy Temple,* we read through the words to sight the kingdom Flaubert summoned in *Emma Bovary:* "the alluring phantasmagoric realm of genuine feeling."

Suggestions for
Further Reading

◇　　◇

Bakhtin, M. M. *The Dialogic Imagination,* ed. Michael Holquist. Austin: University of Texas Press, 1981.

Baym, Nina. "The Melodrama of Beset Manhood," in *Feminist Criticism,* ed. Elaine Showalter. New York: Pantheon Books, 1985.

Brooks, Peter. *The Melodramatic Imagination.* New York: Columbia University Press, 1988.

————. *Reading for the Plot.* New York: Random House, 1985.

Brumberg, Joan Jacobs. *Fasting Girls: The History of Anorexia Nervosa.* New York: Penguin Books, 1988.

Davidson, Cathy N., ed. *Reading in America: Literary and Social History.* Baltimore and London: Johns Hopkins University Press, 1989.

————. *Revolution and the Word: The Rise of the Novel in America.* New York and London: Oxford University Press, 1986.

Fiedler, Leslie. *Love and Death in the American Novel.* New York: Dell Publishing Company, 1967.

————. *What Was Literature?* New York: Simon and Schuster, 1982.

McNall, Sally Allen. *Who Is in the House: A Psychological Study of Two Centuries of Women's Fiction in America, 1795 to the Present.* New York: Elsevier, 1981.

Meserve, Walter J. *An Emerging Entertainment: The Drama of the*

American People to 1828. Bloomington and London: Indiana University Press, 1977.

Moretti, Franco. "Kindergarten," in *Signs Taken for Wonders,* trans. Susan Fischer, David Lorgacs, and David Miller. New York and London: Verso, 1988.

Munch-Pedersen, Ole. "Crazy Jane: A Cycle of Popular Literature." *Eire-Ireland* XIV (Spring 1979), 56–73.

Odell, George C. D. *Annals of the New York Stage* (15 vols). New York: Columbia University Press, 1927–49.

Parker, Patricia L. *Susanna Rowson.* Boston: Twayne Publishers, 1986.

Rourke, Constance. *The Roots of American Culture,* ed. Van Wyck Brooks. Port Washington, New York: Kennicat Press, Inc., 1942.

Rowson, Susanna. [*Rebecca; or*] *The Fille de Chambre.* London: William Lane, 1792.

————. *The Inquisitor; or Invisible Rambler.* London: G. G. J. & J. Robinson, 1788.

————. *Reuben and Rachel; or, the Tales of Old Times.* Boston: Manning & Loring, 1798.

————. *Sarah, or the Exemplary Wife.* Boston: Charles Williams, 1813.

————. *Slaves in Algiers; or a Struggle for Freedom.* Philadelphia: Wrigley & Berriman, 1794.

Vail, R. W. G. *Susanna Haswell Rowson, The Author of Charlotte Temple: A Bibliographical Study.* Worcester, Mass.: The American Antiquarian Society, 1932.

Weil, Dorothy. *In Defense of Women: Susanna Rowson* (1762–1824). University Park and London: The Pennsylvania State University Press, 1976.

A NOTE ON THE TEXTS

The text of *Charlotte Temple* is taken from the first American edition, *Charlotte: A Tale of Truth* (Philadelphia: M. Carey, 1794). *Lucy Temple* is taken from the first American edition, *Charlotte's Daughter; or, The Three Orphans: A Sequel to Charlotte Temple* (Boston: Richardson & Lord, 1828).

Author's Preface

◊   ◊

For the perusal of the young and thoughtless of the fair sex, this Tale of Truth is designed; and I could wish my fair readers to consider it as not merely the effusion of Fancy, but as a reality. The circumstances on which I have founded this novel were related to me some little time since by an old lady who had personally known Charlotte, though she concealed the real names of the characters, and likewise the place where the unfortunate scenes were acted: yet as it was impossible to offer a relation to the public in such an imperfect state, I have thrown over the whole a slight veil of fiction, and substituted names and places according to my own fancy. The principal characters in this little tale are now consigned to the silent tomb: it can therefore hurt the feelings of no one; and may, I flatter myself, be of service to some who are so unfortunate as to have neither friends to advise, or understanding to direct them, through the various and unexpected evils that attend a young and unprotected woman in her first entrance into life.

While the tear of compassion still trembled in my eye for the fate of the unhappy Charlotte, I may have children of my own, said I, to whom this recital may be of use, and if to your own children, said Benevolence, why not to the many daughters of Misfortune who, deprived of natural friends, or spoilt by a mistaken education, are thrown on an unfeeling world without the least power to defend themselves from the snares not only of the other sex, but from the more dangerous arts of the profligate of their own.

Sensible as I am that a novel writer, at a time when such a variety of works are ushered into the world under that name, stands but a poor chance for fame in the annals of literature, but conscious that I wrote with a mind anxious for the happiness of that sex whose morals and conduct have so powerful an influence on mankind in general; and convinced that I have not wrote a line that conveys a wrong idea to the head or a corrupt wish to the heart, I shall rest satisfied in the purity of my own intentions, and if I merit not applause, I feel that I dread not censure.

If the following tale should save one hapless fair one from the error which ruined poor Charlotte, or rescue from impending misery the heart of one anxious parent, I shall feel a much higher gratification in reflecting on this trifling performance, than could possibly result from the applause which might attend the most elegant finished piece of literature whose tendency might deprave the heart or mislead the understanding.

Charlotte Temple

◇　◇

A Tale of Truth

CHAPTER I

A Boarding School

◇   ◇

"Are you for a walk," said Montraville to his companion, as they arose from table; "are you for a walk? or shall we order the chaise and proceed to Portsmouth?" Belcour preferred the former; and they sauntered out to view the town, and to make remarks on the inhabitants, as they returned from church.

Montraville was a Lieutenant in the army: Belcour was his brother officer: they had been to take leave of their friends previous to their departure for America, and were now returning to Portsmouth, where the troops waited orders for embarkation. They had stopped at Chichester to dine; and knowing they had sufficient time to reach the place of destination before dark, and yet allow them a walk, had resolved, it being Sunday afternoon, to take a survey of the Chichester ladies as they returned from their devotions.

They had gratified their curiosity, and were preparing to return to the inn without honouring any of the belles with particular notice, when Madame Du Pont, at the head of her school, descended from the church. Such an assemblage of youth and innocence naturally attracted the young soldiers: they stopped; and, as the little cavalcade passed, almost involuntarily pulled off their hats. A tall, elegant girl looked at Montraville and blushed: he instantly recollected the features of Charlotte Temple, whom he had once seen and danced with at a ball in Portsmouth. At that time he thought on her only as a very lovely child, she being then only thirteen; but the improvement two years had made in her person, and the blush of recollection which suffused her cheeks as she passed, awakened in his bosom new and pleasing ideas. Vanity led him to think that pleasure at again beholding him might have occasioned the emotion he had witnessed, and the same vanity led him to wish to see her again.

"She is the sweetest girl in the world," said he, as he enterd the inn. Belcour stared. "Did you not notice her?" continued Montraville: "she had on a blue bonnet, and with a pair of lovely eyes of the same colour, has contrived to make me feel devilish odd about the heart."

"Pho," said Belcour, "a musket ball from our friends, the Americans, may in less than two months make you feel worse."

"I never think of the future," replied Montraville; "but am determined to make the most of the present, and would willingly compound with any kind Familiar who would inform me who the girl is, and how I might be likely to obtain an interview."

But no kind Familiar at that time appearing, and the chaise which they had ordered, driving up to the door, Montraville and his companion were obliged to take leave of Chichester and its fair inhabitant, and proceed on their journey.

But Charlotte had made too great an impression on his mind to be easily eradicated: having therefore spent three whole days in thinking on her and in endeavouring to form some plan for seeing her, he determined to set off for Chichester, and trust to chance either to favour or frustrate his designs. Arriving at the verge of the town, he dismounted, and sending the servant forward with the horses, proceeded toward the place, where, in the midst of an extensive pleasure ground, stood the mansion which contained the lovely Charlotte Temple. Montraville leaned on a broken gate, and looked earnestly at the house. The wall which surrounded it was high, and perhaps the Argus's who guarded the Hesperian fruit within, were more watchful than those famed of old.

" 'Tis a romantic attempt;" said he; "and should I even succeed in seeing and conversing with her, it can be productive of no good: I must of necessity leave England in a few days, and probably may never return; why then should I endeavour to engage the affections of this lovely girl, only to leave her a prey to a thousand inquietudes, of which at present she has no idea? I will return to Portsmouth and think no more about her."

The evening now was closed; a serene stillness reigned; and the chaste Queen of Night with her silver crescent faintly illuminated the hemisphere. The mind of Montraville was hushed into composure by the serenity of the surrounding objects. "I will think on her no more," said he, and turned with an intention to leave the place; but as he turned, he saw the gate which led to the pleasure grounds open, and two women come out, who walked arm-in-arm across the field.

"I will at least see who these are," said he. He overtook them, and giving them the compliments of the evening, begged leave to see them into the more frequented parts of the town: but how was he delighted, when, waiting for an answer, he discovered, under the concealment of a large bonnet, the face of Charlotte Temple.

He soon found means to ingratiate himself with her companion, who was a French teacher at the school, and, at parting, slipped a letter he had purposely written, into Charlotte's hand, and five guineas into that of Mademoiselle, who promised she would endeavour to bring her young charge into the field again the next evening.

CHAPTER II

Domestic Concerns

◊   ◊

M r. Temple was the youngest son of a nobleman whose fortune was by no means adequate to the antiquity, grandeur, and I may add, pride of the family. He saw his elder brother made completely wretched by marrying a disagreeable woman, whose fortune helped to prop the sinking dignity of the house; and he beheld his sisters legally prostituted to old, decrepit men, whose titles gave them consequence in the eyes of the world, and whose affluence rendered them splendidly miserable. "I will not sacrifice internal happiness for outward shew," said he: "I will seek Content; and, if I find her in a cottage, will embrace her with as much cordiality as I should if seated on a throne."

Mr. Temple possessed a small estate of about five hundred pounds a year; and with that he resolved to preserve independence, to marry where the feelings of his heart should direct him, and to confine his expenses within the limits of his income. He had a heart open to every generous feeling of humanity, and a hand ready to dispense to those who wanted part of the blessings he enjoyed himself.

As he was universally known to be the friend of the unfortunate, his advice and bounty was frequently solicited; nor was it seldom that he sought out indigent merit, and raised it from obscurity, confining his own expenses within a very narrow compass.

"You are a benevolent fellow," said a young officer to him one day; "and I have a great mind to give you a fine subject to exercise the goodness of your heart upon."

"You cannot oblige me more," said Temple, "than to point out any way by which I can be serviceable to my fellow creatures."

"Come along then," said the young man, "we will go and visit a man who is not in so good a lodging as he deserves; and, were it not that he has an angel with him, who comforts and supports him, he must long since have sunk under his misfortunes." The young man's heart was too full to proceed; and Temple, unwilling to irritate his feelings by making further enquiries, followed him in silence, til they arrived at the Fleet prison.

The officer enquired for Captain Eldridge: a person led them up several pair of dirty stairs, and pointing to a door which led to a miserable, small apartment, said that was the Captain's room, and retired.

The officer, whose name was Blakeney, tapped at the door, and was bid to enter by a voice melodiously soft. He opened the door, and discovered to Temple a scene which rivetted him to the spot with astonishment.

The apartment, though small, and bearing strong marks of poverty, was neat in the extreme. In an arm-chair, his head reclined upon his hand, his eyes fixed on a book which lay open before him, sat an aged man in a Lieutenant's uniform, which though threadbare, would sooner call a blush of shame into the face of those who could neglect real merit, than cause the hectic of confusion to glow on the cheeks of him who wore it.

Beside him sat a lovely creature busied in painting a fan mount. She was fair as the lily, but sorrow had nipped the rose in her cheek before it was half blown. Her eyes were blue; and her hair, which was light brown, was slightly confined under a plain muslin cap, tied round with a black ribbon; a white linen gown and plain lawn handkerchief composed the remainder of her dress; and in this simple attire, she was more irresistibly charming to such a heart as Temple's, than she would have been, if adorned with all the splendor of a courtly belle.

When they entered, the old man arose from his seat, and shaking Blakeney by the hand with great cordiality, offered Temple his chair; and there being but three in the room, seated himself on the side of his little bed with evident composure.

"This is a strange place," said he to Temple, "to receive visitors of distinction in; but we must fit our feelings to our station. While I am not ashamed to own the cause which brought me here, why should I blush at my situation? Our misfortunes are not our faults; and were it not for that poor girl—"

Here the philosopher was lost in the father. He rose hastily from his seat, and walking toward the window, wiped off a tear which he was afraid would tarnish the cheek of a sailor.

Temple cast his eye on Miss Eldridge: a pellucid drop had stolen from her eyes, and fallen upon a rose she was painting. It blotted and discoloured the flower. " 'Tis emblematic," said he mentally: "the rose of youth and health soon fades when watered by the tear of affliction."

"My friend Blakeney," said he, addressing the old man, "told me I could be of service to you: be so kind then, dear Sir, as to point out some way in which I can relieve the anxiety of your heart and increase the pleasures of my own."

"My good young man," said Eldridge, "you know not what you offer. While deprived of my liberty I cannot be free from anxiety on my own account; but that is a trifling concern; my anxious thoughts extend to one more dear a thousand times than life: I am a poor weak old man, and must expect in a few years to sink into silence and oblivion; but when I am gone, who will protect that fair bud of innocence from the blasts of adversity, or from the cruel hand of insult and dishonour."

"Oh, my father!" cried Miss Eldridge, tenderly taking his hand, "be not anxious on that account; for daily are my prayers offered to heaven that our lives may terminate at the same instant, and one grave receive us both; for why should I live when deprived of my only friend."

Temple was moved even to tears. "You will both live many years," said he, "and I hope see much happiness. Cheerly, my friend, cheerly; these passing clouds of adversity will serve only to make the sunshine of prosperity more pleasing. But we are losing time: you might ere this have told me who were your creditors, what were their demands, and other particulars necessary to your liberation."

"My story is short," said Mr. Eldridge, "but there are some particulars which will wring my heart barely to remember; yet to one whose offers of friendship appear so open and disinterested, I will relate every circumstance that led to my present, painful situation. But my child," continued he, addressing his daughter, "let me prevail on you to take opportunity, while my friends are with me, to enjoy the benefit of air and exercise. Go, my love; leave me now; to-morrow at your usual hour I will expect you."

Miss Eldridge impressed on his cheek the kiss of filial affection, and obeyed.

CHAPTER III

Unexpected Misfortunes

◇ ◇

"My life," said Mr. Eldridge, "till within these few years was marked by no particular circumstance deserving notice. I early embraced the life of a sailor, and have served my King with unremitted ardour for many years. At the age of twenty-five I married an amiable woman; one son, and the girl who just now left us, were the fruits of our union. My boy had genius and spirit. I straitened my little income to give him a liberal education, but the rapid progress he made in his studies amply compensated for the inconvenience. At the academy where he received his education he commenced an acquaintance with a Mr. Lewis, a young man of affluent fortune: as they grew up their intimacy ripened into friendship, and they became almost inseparable companions.

"George chose the profession of a soldier. I had neither friends or money to procure him a commission, and had wished him to embrace a nautical life: but this was repugnant to his wishes, and I ceased to urge him on the subject.

"The friendship subsisting between Lewis and my son was of such a nature as gave him free access to our family; and so specious was his manner that we hesitated not to state to him all our little difficulties in regard to George's future views. He listened to us with attention, and offered to advance any sum necessary for his first setting out.

"I embraced the offer, and gave him my note for the payment

of it, but he would not suffer me to mention any stipulated time, as he said I might do it whenever most convenient to myself. About this time my dear Lucy returned to school, and I soon began to imagine Lewis looked at her with eyes of affection. I gave my child a caution to beware of him, and to look on her mother as her friend. She was unaffectedly artless; and when, as I suspected, Lewis made professions of love, she confided in her parents, and assured us her heart was perfectly unbiassed in his favour, and she would cheerfully submit to our direction.

"I took an early opportunity of questioning him concerning his intentions towards my child: he gave an equivocal answer, and I forbade him the house.

"The next day he sent and demanded payment of his money. It was not in my power to comply with the demand. I requested three days to endeavour to raise it, determining in that time to mortgage my half pay, and live on a small annuity which my wife possessed, rather than be under an obligation to so worthless man: but this short time was not allowed me; for that evening, as I was sitting down to supper, unsuspicious of danger, an officer entered, and tore me from the embraces of my family.

"My wife had been for some time in a declining state of health: ruin at once so unexpected and inevitable was a stroke she was not prepared to bear, and I saw her faint into the arms of our servant, as I left my own habitation for the comfortless walls of a prison. My poor Lucy, distracted with her fears for us both, sunk on the floor and endeavoured to detain me by her feeble efforts; but in vain; they forced open her arms; she shrieked, and fell prostrate. But pardon me. The horrors of that night unman me. I cannot proceed."

He rose from his seat, and walked several times across the room: at length, attaining more composure, he cried—"What a mere infant I am! Why, Sir, I never felt thus in the day of battle."

"No," said Temple; "but the truly brave soul is tremblingly alive to the feelings of humanity."

"True," replied the old man, (something like satisfaction darting across his features) "and painful as these feelings are, I would not exchange them for that torpor which the stoic mistakes for philosophy. How many exquisite delights should I have passed by unnoticed, but for these keen sensations, this quick sense of happiness or misery? Then let us, my friend, take the cup of life as it is presented to us, tempered by the hand of a wise Providence; be thankful for the good, be patient under the evil, and presume not to enquire why the latter predominates."

"This is true philosophy," said Temple.

" 'Tis the only way to reconcile ourselves to the cross events of life," replied he. "But I forget myself. I will not longer intrude on your patience, but proceed in my melancholy tale.

"The very evening that I was taken to prison, my son arrived from Ireland, where he had been some time with his regiment. From the distracted expressions of his mother and sister, he learnt by whom I had been arrested; and, late as it was, flew on the wings of wounded affection, to the house of his false friend, and earnestly enquired the cause of this cruel conduct. With all the calmness of a cool deliberate villain, he avowed his passion for Lucy; declared her situation in life would not permit him to marry her; but offered to release me immediately, and make any settlement on her, if George would persuade her to live, as he impiously termed it, a life of honour.

"Fired at the insult offered to a man and a soldier, my boy struck the villain, and a challenge ensued. He then went to a coffee-house in the neighbourhood and wrote a long affectionate letter to me, blaming himself severely for having introduced Lewis into the family, or permitted him to confer an obligation, which had brought inevitable ruin on us all. He begged me, whatever might be the event of the ensuing morning, not to suffer regret or unavailing sorrow for his fate, to encrease the anguish of my heart, which he greatly feared was already insupportable.

"This letter was delivered to me early in the morning. It would be vain to attempt describing my feelings on the perusal of it; suffice it to say, that a merciful Providence interposed, and I was for three weeks insensible to miseries almost beyond the strength of human nature to support.

"A fever and strong delirium seized me, and my life was despaired of. At length, nature, overpowered with fatigue, gave way to the salutary power of rest, and a quiet slumber of some hours restored me to reason, though the extreme weakness of my frame prevented my feeling my distress so acutely as I otherways should.

"The first object that struck me on awaking, was Lucy sitting by my bedside; her pale countenance and sable dress prevented my enquiries for poor George: for the letter I had received from him, was the first thing that occurred to my memory. By degrees the rest returned: I recollected being arrested, but could no ways account for being in this apartment, whither they had conveyed me during my illness.

"I was so weak as to be almost unable to speak. I pressed Lucy's hand, and looked earnestly round the apartment in search of another dear object.

" 'Where is your mother?' said I, faintly.

"The poor girl could not answer: she shook her head in expressive silence; and throwing herself on the bed, folded her arms about me, and burst into tears.

" 'What! both gone?' said I.

" 'Both,' she replied, endeavouring to restrain her emotions: 'but they are happy, no doubt.' "

Here Mr. Eldridge paused: the recollection of the scene was too painful to permit him to proceed.

CHAPTER IV

Change of Fortune

◇　◇

"It was some days," continued Mr. Eldridge, recovering himself, "before I could venture to enquire the particulars of what had happened during my illness: at length I assumed courage to ask my dear girl how long her mother and brother had been dead: she told me, that the morning after my arrest, George came home early to enquire after his mother's health, staid with them but a few minutes, seemed greatly agitated at parting, but gave them strict charge to keep up their spirits, and hope every thing would turn out for the best. In about two hours after, as they were sitting at breakfast, and endeavouring to strike out some plan to attain my liberty, they heard a loud rap at the door, which Lucy running to open, she met the bleeding body of her brother, borne in by two men who had lifted him from a litter, on which they had brought him from the place where he fought. Her poor mother, weakened by illness and the struggles of the preceding night, was not able to support this shock; gasping for breath, her looks wild and haggard, she reached the apartment where they had carried her dying son. She knelt by the bed side; and taking his cold hand, 'my poor boy,' said she, 'I will not be parted from thee: husband! son! both at once lost. Father of mercies, spare me!' She fell into a strong convulsion, and expired in about two hours. In the mean time, a surgeon had dressed George's wounds; but they were in such a situation as to bar the smallest hopes of recovery. He never was sensible from the time he was brought home, and died that evening in the arms of his sister.

"Late as it was when this event took place, my affectionate Lucy insisted on coming to me. 'What must he feel,' said she, 'at our apparent neglect, and how shall I inform him of the afflictions with which it has pleased heaven to visit us?'

"She left the care of the dear departed ones to some neighbours who had kindly come in to comfort and assist her; and on entering the house where I was confined, found me in the situation I have mentioned.

"How she supported herself in these trying moments, I know not: heaven, no doubt, was with her; and her anxiety to preserve the life of one parent in some measure abated her affliction for the loss of the other.

"My circumstances were greatly embarrassed, my acquaintance few, and those few utterly unable to assist me. When my wife and son were committed to their kindred earth, my creditors seized my house and furniture, which not being sufficient to discharge all their demands, detainers were lodged against me. No friend stepped forward to my relief; from the grave of her mother, my beloved Lucy followed an almost dying father to this melancholy place.

"Here we have been nearly a year and a half. My half-pay I have given up to satisfy my creditors, and my child supports me by her industry: sometimes by fine needlework, sometimes by painting. She leaves me every night, and goes to a lodging near the bridge; but returns in the morning, to cheer me with her smiles, and bless me by her duteous affection. A lady once offered her an asylum in her family; but she would not leave me. 'We are all the world to each other,' said she. 'I thank God, I have health and spirits to improve the talents with which nature has endowed me; and I trust if I employ them in the support of a beloved parent, I shall not be thought an unprofitable servant. While he lives, I pray for strength to pursue my employment; and when it pleases heaven to take one of us, may it give the survivor resignation to bear the separation as we ought: till then I will never leave him.' "

"But where is this inhuman persecutor?" said Temple.

"He has been abroad ever since," replied the old man; "but he has left orders with his lawyers never to give up the note till the utmost farthing is paid."

"And how much is the amount of your debts in all?" said Temple.

"Five hundred pounds," he replied.

Temple started: it was more than he expected. "But something must be done," said he: "that sweet maid must not wear out her life in a prison. I will see you again to-morrow, my friend," said he, shaking Eldridge's hand: "keep up your spirits: light and shade are not more happily blended than are the pleasures and pains of life; and the horrors of the one serve only to increase the splendor of the other."

"You never lost a wife and son," said Eldridge.

"No," replied he, "but I can feel for those that have." Eldridge pressed his hand as they went toward the door, and they parted in silence.

When they got without the walls of the prison, Temple thanked his friend Blakeney for introducing him to so worthy a character; and telling him he had a particular engagement in the city, wished him a good evening.

"And what is to be done for this distressed man," said Temple, as he walked up Ludgate Hill. "Would to heaven I had a fortune that would enable me instantly to discharge his debt: what exquisite transport, to see the expressive eyes of Lucy beaming at once with pleasure for her father's deliverance, and gratitude for her deliverer: but is not my fortune affluence," continued he, "nay superfluous wealth, when compared to the extreme indigence of Eldridge; and what have I done to deserve ease and plenty, while a brave worthy officer starves in a prison? Three hundred a year is surely sufficient for all my wants and wishes: at any rate Eldridge must be relieved."

When the heart has will, the hands can soon find means to execute a good action.

Temple was a young man, his feelings warm and impetuous; unacquainted with the world, his heart had not been rendered callous by being convinced of its fraud and hypocrisy. He pitied their sufferings, overlooked their faults, thought every bosom as generous as his own, and would cheerfully have divided his last guinea with an unfortunate fellow creature.

No wonder, then, that such a man (without waiting a moment for the interference of Madam Prudence) should resolve to raise money sufficient for the relief of Eldridge, by mortgaging part of his fortune.

We will not enquire too minutely into the cause which might actuate him in this instance: suffice it to say, he immediately put the plan in execution; and in three days from the time he first saw the unfortunate Lieutenant, he had the superlative felicity of seeing him at liberty, and receiving an ample reward in the tearful eye and half articulated thanks of the grateful Lucy.

"And pray, young man," said his father to him one morning, "what are your designs in visiting thus constantly that old man and his daughter?"

Temple was at a loss for a reply: he had never asked himself the question: he hesitated; and his father continued—

"It was not till within these few days that I heard in what manner your acquaintance first commenced, and cannot suppose any thing but attachment to the daughter could carry you such imprudent lengths for the father: it certainly must be her art that drew you in to mortgage part of your fortune."

"Art, Sir!" cried Temple eagerly. "Lucy Eldridge is as free from art as she is from every other error: she is—"

"Everything that is amiable and lovely," said his father, interrupting him ironically: "no doubt in your opinion she is a pattern of excellence for all her sex to follow; but come, Sir, pray tell me what are your designs towards this paragon. I hope you do not intend to complete your folly by marrying her."

"Were my fortune such as would support her according to her merit, I don't know a woman more formed to insure happiness in the married state."

"Then prithee, my dear lad," said his father, "since your rank and fortune are so much beneath what your *Princess* might expect, be so kind as to turn your eyes on Miss Weatherby; who, having only an estate of three thousand a year, is more upon a level with you, and whose father yesterday solicited the mighty honour of your alliance. I shall leave you to consider on this offer; and pray remember, that your union with Miss Weatherby will put it in your power to be more liberally the friend of Lucy Eldridge."

The old gentleman walked in a stately manner out of the room; and Temple stood almost petrified with astonishment, contempt, and rage.

CHAPTER V

Such Things Are

◇ ◇

M iss Weatherby was the only child of a wealthy man, almost idolized by her parents, flattered by her dependants, and never contradicted even by those who called themselves her friends: I cannot give a better description than by the following lines.

> *The lovely maid whose form and face*
> *Nature has deck'd with ev'ry grace,*
> *But in whose breast no virtues glow,*
> *Whose heart ne'er felt another's woe,*
> *Whose hand ne'er smooth'd the bed of pain,*
> *Or eas'd the captive's galling chain;*
> *But like the tulip caught the eye,*
> *Born just to be admir'd and die;*
> *When gone, no one regrets its loss,*
> *Or scarce remembers that it was.*

Such was Miss Weatherby: her form lovely as nature could make it, but her mind uncultivated, her heart unfeeling, her passions impetuous, and her brain almost turned with flattery, dissipation, and pleasure; and such was the girl, whom a partial grandfather left independent mistress of the fortune before mentioned.

She had seen Temple frequently; and fancying she could never be happy without him, nor once imagining he could refuse a girl of her beauty and fortune, she prevailed on her fond father to offer the alliance to the old Earl of D——, Mr. Temple's father.

The Earl had received the offer courteously: he thought it a great match for Henry; and was too fashionable a man to suppose a wife could be any impediment to the friendship he professed for Eldridge and his daughter.

Unfortunately for Temple, he thought quite otherwise: the conversation he had just had with his father, discovered to him the situation of his heart; and he found that the most affluent fortune would bring no increase of happiness unless Lucy Eldridge shared it with him; and the knowledge of the purity of her sentiments, and the integrity of his own heart, made him shudder at the idea his father had started, of marrying a woman for no other reason than because the affluence of her fortune would enable him to injure her by maintaining in splendor the woman to whom his heart was devoted: he therefore resolved to refuse Miss Weatherby, and be the event what it might, offer his heart and hand to Lucy Eldridge.

Full of this determination, he fought his father, declared his resolution, and was commanded never more to appear in his presence. Temple bowed; his heart was too full to permit him to speak; he left the house precipitately, and hastened to relate the cause of his sorrows to his good old friend and his amiable daughter.

In the mean time, the Earl, vexed to the soul that such a fortune should be lost, determined to offer himself a candidate for Miss Weatherby's favour.

What wonderful changes are wrought by that reigning power, ambition! The love-sick girl, when first she heard of Temple's refusal, wept, raved, tore her hair, and vowed to found a protestant nunnery with her fortune; and by commencing abbess, shut herself up from the sight of cruel ungrateful man for ever.

Her father was a man of the world: he suffered this first transport

to subside, and then very deliberately unfolded to her the offers of
the old Earl, expatiated on the many benefits arising from an elevated title, painted in glowing colours the surprise and vexation
of Temple when he should see her figuring as a Countess and his
mother-in-law, and begged her to consider well before she made
any rash vows.

The *distressed* fair one dried her tears, listened patiently, and at
length declared she believed the surest method to revenge the slight
put on her by the son, would be to accept the father: so said so
done, and in a few days she became the Countess D——.

Temple heard the news with emotion: he had lost his father's
favour by avowing his passion for Lucy, and he saw now there
was no hope of regaining it: "But he shall not make me miserable," said he. "Lucy and I have no ambitious notions: we can live
on three hundred a year for some little time, till the mortgage is
paid off, and then we shall have sufficient not only for the comforts but many of the little elegancies of life. We will purchase a
little cottage, my Lucy," said he, "and thither with your reverend
father we will retire; we will forget there are such things as splendor, profusion, and dissipation: we will have some cows, and you
shall be queen of the dairy; in a morning, while I look after my
garden, you shall take a basket on your arm, and sally forth to feed
your poultry; and as they flutter round you in token of humble
gratitude, your father shall smoke his pipe in a woodbine alcove,
and viewing the serenity of your countenance, feel such real pleasure dilate his own heart, as shall make him forget he had ever
been unhappy."

Lucy smiled; and Temple saw it was a smile of approbation. He
sought and found a cottage suited to his taste; thither, attended by
Love and Hymen, the happy trio retired; where, during many years
of uninterrupted felicity, they cast not a wish beyond the little
boundaries of their own tenement. Plenty, and her handmaid,
Prudence, presided at their board, Hospitality stood at their gate,

Peace smiled on each face, Content reigned in each heart, and Love and Health strewed roses on their pillows.

Such were the parents of Charlotte Temple, who was the only pledge of their mutual love, and who, at the earnest entreaty of a particular friend, was permitted to finish the education her mother had begun, at Madame Du Pont's school, where we first introduced her to the acquaintance of the reader.

CHAPTER VI

An Intriguing Teacher

◇ ◇

Madame Du Pont was a woman every way calculated to take the care of young ladies, had that care entirely devolved on herself; but it was impossible to attend the education of a numerous school without proper assistants; and those assistants were not always the kind of people whose conversation and morals were exactly such as parents of delicacy and refinement would wish a daughter to copy. Among the teachers at Madame Du Pont's school, was Mademoiselle La Rue, who added to a pleasing person and insinuating address, a liberal education and the manners of a gentlewoman. She was recommended to the school by a lady whose humanity overstepped the bounds of discretion: for though she knew Miss La Rue had eloped from a convent with a young officer, and, on coming to England, had lived with several different men in open defiance of all moral and religious duties, yet, finding her reduced to the most abject want, and believing the penitence which she professed to be sincere, she took her into her own family, and from thence recommended her to Madame Du Pont, as thinking the situation more suitable for a woman of her abilities. But Mademoiselle possessed too much of the spirit of intrigue to remain long without adventures. At church, where she constantly appeared, her person attracted the attention of a young man who was upon a visit at a gentleman's seat in the neighbourhood she had met him several times clandestinely; and being invited to come out that evening, and eat some fruit and pastry in a summer-house belonging to the gentleman he was visiting, and requested to bring some of the ladies with her, Charlotte being her favourite, was fixed on to accompany her.

The mind of youth eagerly catches at promised pleasure: pure and innocent by nature, it thinks not of the dangers lurking beneath those pleasures, till too late to avoid them: when Mademoiselle asked Charlotte to go with her, she mentioned the gentleman as a relation, and spoke in such high terms of the elegance of his gardens, the sprightliness of his conversation, and the liberality with which he ever entertained his guests, that Charlotte thought only of the pleasure she should enjoy in the visit,—not on the imprudence of going without her governess's knowledge, or of the danger to which she exposed herself in visiting the house of a gay young man of fashion.

Madame Du Pont was gone out for the evening, and the rest of the ladies retired to rest, when Charlotte and the teacher stole out at the back gate, and in crossing the field, were accosted by Montraville, as mentioned in the first chapter.

Charlotte was disappointed in the pleasure she had promised herself from this visit. The levity of the gentlemen and the freedom of their conversation disgusted her. She was astonished at the liberties Mademoiselle permitted them to take; grew thoughtful and uneasy, and heartily wished herself at home again in her own chamber.

Perhaps one cause of that wish might be, an earnest desire to see the contents of the letter which had been put into her hand by Montraville.

Any reader who has the least knowledge of the world, will easily imagine the letter was made up of encomiums on her beauty, and vows of everlasting love and constancy; nor will he be surprised that a heart open to every gentle, generous sentiment, should feel itself warmed by gratitude for a man who professed to feel so much for her; nor is it improbable but her mind might revert to the agreeable person and martial appearance of Montraville.

In affairs of love, a young heart is never in more danger than when attempted by a handsome young soldier. A man of an indifferent appearance, will, when arrayed in a military habit, shew to advantage; but when beauty of person, elegance of manner, and an easy method of paying compliments, are united to the scarlet coat, smart cockade, and military sash, ah! well-a-day for the poor girl who gazes on him: she is in imminent danger; but if she listens to him with pleasure, 'tis all over with her, and from that moment she has neither eyes nor ears for any other object.

Now, my dear sober matron, (if a sober matron should deign to turn over these pages, before she trusts them to the eye of a darling daughter,) let me intreat you not to put on a grave face, and throw down the book in a passion and declare 'tis enough to turn the heads of half the girls in England; I do solemnly protest, my dear madam, I mean no more by what I have here advanced, than to ridicule those romantic girls, who foolishly imagine a red coat and silver epaulet constitute the fine gentleman; and should that fine gentleman make half a dozen fine speeches to them, they will imagine themselves so much in love as to fancy it a meritorious action to jump out of a two pair of stairs window, abandon their friends, and trust entirely to the honour of a man, who perhaps hardly knows the meaning of the word, and if he does, will be too much the modern man of refinement, to practice it in their favour.

Gracious heaven! when I think on the miseries that must rend the heart of a doating parent, when he sees the darling of his age at first seduced from his protection, and afterwards abandoned, by the very wretch whose promises of love decoyed her from the paternal roof—when he sees her poor and wretched, her bosom torn between remorse for her crime and love for her vile betrayer—when fancy paints to me the good old man stooping to raise the weeping penitent, while every tear from her eye is numbered by drops from his bleeding heart, my bosom glows with honest indignation, and I wish for power to extirpate those monsters of seduction from the earth.

Oh my dear girls—for to such only am I writing—listen not to the voice of love, unless sanctioned by paternal approbation: be assured, it is now past the days of romance: no woman can be run away with contrary to her own inclination: then kneel down each morning, and request kind heaven to keep you free from temptation, or, should it please to suffer you to be tried, pray for fortitude to resist the impulse of inclination when it runs counter to the precepts of religion and virtue.

CHAPTER VII

Natural Sense of Propriety Inherent in the Female Bosom

◊   ◊

"I cannot think we have done exactly right in going out this evening, Mademoiselle," said Charlotte, seating herself when she entered her apartment: "nay, I am sure it was not right; for I expected to be very happy, but was sadly disappointed."

"It was your own fault, then," replied Mademoiselle: "for I am sure my cousin omitted nothing that could serve to render the evening agreeable."

"True," said Charlotte: "but I thought the gentlemen were very free in their manner: I wonder you would suffer them to behave as they did."

"Prithee, don't be such a foolish little prude," said the artful woman, affecting anger: "I invited you to go in hopes it would divert you, and be an agreeable change of scene; however, if your delicacy was hurt by the behaviour of the gentlemen, you need not go again; so there let it rest."

"I do not intend to go again," said Charlotte, gravely taking off her bonnet, and beginning to prepare for bed: "I am sure, if Madame Du Pont knew we had been out to-night, she would be very angry; and it is ten to one but she hears of it by some means or other."

"Nay, Miss," said La Rue, "perhaps your mighty sense of propriety may lead you to tell her yourself: and in order to avoid the censure you would incur, should she hear of it by accident, throw the blame on me: but I confess I deserve it: it will be a very kind return for that partiality which led me to prefer you before any of the rest of the ladies; but perhaps it will give you pleasure," continued she, letting fall some hypocritical tears, "to see me deprived of bread, and for an action which by the most rigid could only be esteemed an inadvertency, lose my place and character, and be driven again into the world, where I have already suffered all the evils attendant on poverty."

This was touching Charlotte in the most vulnerable part: she rose from her seat, and taking Mademoiselle's hand—"You know, my dear La Rue," said she, "I love you too well, to do anything that would injure you in my governess's opinion: I am only sorry we went out this evening."

"I don't believe it, Charlotte," said she, assuming a little vivacity; "for if you had not gone out, you would not have seen the gentleman who met us crossing the field; and I rather think you were pleased with his conversation."

"I had seen him once before," replied Charlotte, "and thought him an agreeable man; and you know one is always pleased to see a person with whom one has passed several chearful hours. But," said she pausing, and drawing the letter from her pocket, while a gentle suffusion of vermillion tinged her neck and face, "he gave me this letter; what shall I do with it?"

"Read it, to be sure," returned Mademoiselle.

"I am afraid I ought not," said Charlotte: "my mother has often told me, I should never read a letter given me by a young man, without first giving it to her."

"Lord bless you, my dear girl," cried the teacher smiling, "have you a mind to be in leading strings all your life time. Prithee open the letter, read it, and judge for yourself; if you show it your mother, the consequence will be, you will be taken from school, and a strict guard kept over you; so you will stand no chance of ever seeing the smart young officer again."

"I should not like to leave school yet," replied Charlotte, "till I have attained a greater proficiency in my Italian and music. But you can, if you please, Mademoiselle, take the letter back to Montraville, and tell him I wish him well, but cannot, with any propriety, enter into a clandestine correspondence with him." She laid the letter on the table, and began to undress herself.

"Well," said La Rue, "I vow you are an unaccountable girl: have you no curiosity to see the inside now? for my part I could no more let a letter addressed to me lie unopened so long, that I could work miracles: he writes a good hand," continued she, turning the letter, to look at the superscription.

" 'Tis well enough," said Charlotte, drawing it towards her.

"He is a genteel young fellow," said La Rue carelessly, folding up her apron at the same time; "but I think he is marked with the small pox."

"Oh you are greatly mistaken," said Charlotte eagerly; "he has a remarkable clear skin and fine complexion."

"His eyes, if I could judge by what I saw," said La Rue, "are grey and want expression."

"By no means," replied Charlotte; "they are the most expressive eyes I ever saw."

"Well, child, whether they are grey or black is of no consequence: you have determined not to read his letter; so it is likely you will never either see or hear from him again."

Charlotte took up the letter, and Mademoiselle continued—

"He is most probably going to America; and if ever you should hear any account of him, it may possibly be that he is killed; and though he loved you ever so fervently, though his last breath should be spent in a prayer for your happiness, it can be nothing to you: you can feel nothing for the fate of the man, whose letters you will not open, and whose sufferings you will not alleviate, by permitting him to think you would remember him when absent, and pray for his safety."

Charlotte still held the letter in her hand: her heart swelled at the conclusion of Mademoiselle's speech, and a tear dropped upon the wafer that closed it.

"The wafer is not dry yet," said she, "and sure there can be no great harm—" She hesitated. La Rue was silent. "I may read it, Mademoiselle, and return it afterwards."

"Certainly," replied Mademoiselle.

"At any rate I am determined not to answer it," continued Charlotte, as she opened the letter.

Here let me stop to make one remark, and trust me my very heart aches while I write it; but certain I am, that when once a woman has stifled the sense of shame in her own bosom, when once she has lost sight of the basis on which reputation, honour, every thing that should be dear to the female heart, rests, she grows hardened in guilt, and will spare no pains to bring down innocence and beauty to the shocking level with herself: and this proceeds from that diabolical spirit of envy, which repines at seeing another in the full possession of that respect and esteem which she can no longer hope to enjoy.

Mademoiselle eyed the unsuspecting Charlotte, as she perused the letter, with a malignant pleasure. She saw, that the contents had awakened new emotions in her youthful bosom: she encouraged her hopes, calmed her fears, and before they parted for the night, it was determined that she should meet Montraville the ensuing evening.

CHAPTER VIII

Domestic Pleasures
Planned

◇　　◇

"I think, my dear," said Mrs. Temple, laying her hand on her husband's arm as they were walking together in the garden, "I think next Wednesday is Charlotte's birth day: now I have formed a little scheme in my own mind, to give her an agreeable surprise; and if you have no objection, we will send for her home on that day." Temple pressed his wife's hand in token of approbation, and she proceeded.—"You know the little alcove at the bottom of the garden, of which Charlotte is so fond? I have an inclination to deck this out in a fanciful manner, and invite all her little friends to partake of a collation of fruit, sweetmeats, and other things suitable to the general taste of young guests; and to make it more pleasing to Charlotte, she shall be mistress of the feast, and entertain her visitors in this alcove. I know she will be delighted; and to complete all, they shall have some music, and finish with a dance."

"A very fine plan, indeed," said Temple, smiling; "and you really suppose I will wink at your indulging the girl in this manner? You will quite spoil her, Lucy; indeed you will."

"She is the only child we have," said Mrs. Temple, the whole tenderness of a mother adding animation to her fine countenance; but it was withal tempered so sweetly with the meek affection and submissive duty of the wife, that as she paused expecting her husband's answer, he gazed at her tenderly, and found he was unable to refuse her request.

"She is a good girl," said Temple.

"She is, indeed," replied the fond mother exultingly, "a grateful, affectionate girl; and I am sure will never lose sight of the duty she owes her parents."

"If she does," said he, "she must forget the example set her by the best of mothers."

Mrs. Temple could not reply; but the delightful sensation that dilated her heart sparkled in her intelligent eyes and heightened the vermillion on her cheeks.

Of all the pleasures of which the human mind is sensible, there is none equal to that which warms and expands the bosom, when listening to commendations bestowed on us by a beloved object, and are conscious of having deserved them.

Ye giddy flutterers in the fantastic round of dissipation, who eagerly seek pleasure in the lofty dome, rich treat, and midnight revel—tell me, ye thoughtless daughters of folly, have ye ever found the phantom you have so long sought with such unremitted assiduity? Has she not always eluded your grasp, and when you have reached your hand to take the cup she extends to her deluded votaries, have you not found the long-expected draught strongly tinctured with the bitter dregs of disappointment? I know you have: I see it in the wan cheek, sunk eye, and air of chagrin, which ever mark the children of dissipation. Pleasure is a vain illusion; she draws you on to a thousand follies, errors, and I may say vices, and then leaves you to deplore your thoughtless credulity.

Look, my dear friends, at yonder lovely Virgin, arrayed in a white robe devoid of ornament; behold the meekness of her countenance, the modesty of her gait; her handmaids are *Humility, Filial Piety, Conjugal Affection, Industry,* and *Benevolence;* her name is *Content;* she holds in her hand the cup of true felicity, and when once you have formed an intimate acquaintance with these her attendants, nay you must admit them as your bosom friends and chief counsellors, then, whatever may be your situation in life, the meek eyed Virgin will immediately take up her abode with you.

Is poverty your portion?—she will lighten your labours, preside at your frugal board, and watch your quiet slumbers.

Is your state mediocrity?—she will heighten every blessing you enjoy, by informing you how grateful you should be to that bountiful Providence who might have placed you in the most abject situation; and, by teaching you to weigh your blessings against your deserts, show you how much more you receive than you have a right to expect.

Are you possessed of affluence?—what an inexhaustible fund of happiness will she lay before you! To relieve the distressed, redress the injured, in short, to perform all the good works of peace and mercy.

Content, my dear friends, will blunt even the arrows of adversity, so that they cannot materially harm you. She will dwell in the humblest cottage; she will attend you even to a prison. Her parent is Religion; her sisters, Patience and Hope. She will pass with you through life, smoothing the rough paths and tread to earth those thorns which every one must meet with as they journey onward to the appointed goal. She will soften the pains of sickness, continue with you even in the cold gloomy hour of death, and, chearing you with the smiles of her heaven-born sister, Hope, lead you triumphant to a blissful eternity.

I confess I have rambled strangely from my story: but what of that? if I have been so lucky as to find the road to happiness, why should I be such a niggard as to omit so good an opportunity of pointing out the way to others. The very basis of true peace of mind is a benevolent wish to see all the world as happy as one's self; and from my soul do I pity the selfish churl, who, remembering the little bickerings of anger, envy, and fifty other disagreeables to which frail mortality is subject, would wish to revenge the affront which pride whispers him he has received. For my own part, I can safely declare, there is not a human being in the universe, whose prosperity I should not rejoice in, and to whose happiness I would not contribute to the utmost limit of my power: and may my offences be no more remembered in the day of general retribution, than as from my soul I forgive every offence or injury received from a fellow creature.

Merciful heaven! who would exchange the rapture of such a reflexion for all the gaudy tinsel which the world calls pleasure!

But to return.—Content dwelt in Mrs. Temple's bosom, and spread a charming animation over her countenance, as her husband led her in, to lay the plan she had formed (for the celebration of Charlotte's birth day,) before Mr. Eldridge.

CHAPTER IX

We Know Not What a Day May Bring Forth

◊   ◊

Various were the sensations which agitated the mind of Charlotte, during the day preceding the evening in which she was to meet Montraville. Several times did she almost resolve to go to her governess, show her the letter, and be guided by her advice: but Charlotte had taken one step in the ways of imprudence; and when that is once done, there are always innumerable obstacles to prevent the erring person returning to the path of rectitude: yet these obstacles, however forcible they may appear in general, exist chiefly in imagination.

Charlotte feared the anger of her governess: she loved her mother, and the very idea of incurring her displeasure, gave her the greatest uneasiness: but there was a more forcible reason still remaining: should she show the letter to Madame Du Pont, she must confess the means by which it came into her possession; and what would be the consequence? Mademoiselle would be turned out of doors.

"I must not be ungrateful," said she. "La Rue is very kind to me; besides I can, when I see Montraville, inform him of the impropriety of our continuing to see or correspond with each other, and request him to come no more to Chichester."

However prudent Charlotte might be in these resolutions, she certainly did not take a proper method to confirm herself in them.

Several times in the course of the day, she indulged herself in reading over the letter, and each time she read it, the contents sunk deeper in her heart. As evening drew near, she caught herself frequently consulting her watch. "I wish this foolish meeting was over," said she, by way of apology to her own heart, "I wish it was over; for when I have seen him, and convinced him my resolution is not to be shaken, I shall feel my mind much easier."

The appointed hour arrived. Charlotte and Mademoiselle eluded the eye of vigilance; and Montraville, who had waited their coming with impatience, received them with rapturous and unbounded acknowledgments for their condescension: he had wisely brought Belcour with him to entertain Mademoiselle, while he enjoyed an uninterrupted conversation with Charlotte.

Belcour was a man whose character might be comprised in a few words; and as he will make some figure in the ensuing pages, I shall here describe him. He possessed a genteel fortune, and had a liberal education; dissipated, thoughtless, and capricious, he paid little regard to the moral duties, and less to religious ones: eager in the pursuit of pleasure, he minded not the miseries he inflicted on others, provided his own wishes, however extravagant, were gratified. Self, darling self, was the idol he worshipped, and to that he would have sacrificed the interest and happiness of all mankind. Such was the friend of Montraville: will not the reader be ready to imagine, that the man who could regard such a character, must be actuated by the same feelings, follow the same pursuits, and be equally unworthy with the person to whom he thus gave his confidence?

But Montraville was a different character: generous in his disposition, liberal in his opinions, and good-natured almost to a fault; yet eager and impetuous in the pursuit of a favorite object, he staid not to reflect on the consequence which might follow the attainment of his wishes; with a mind ever open to conviction, had he been so fortunate as to possess a friend who would have pointed out the cruelty of endeavouring to gain the heart of an innocent artless girl, when he knew it was utterly impossible for him to marry her, and when the gratification of his passion would be unavoidable infamy and misery to her, and a cause of never-ceasing remorse to himself: had these dreadful consequences been placed before him in a proper light, the humanity of his nature would have urged him to give up the pursuit: but Belcour was not this friend; he rather encouraged the growing passion of Montraville; and being pleased with the vivacity of Mademoiselle, resolved to leave no argument untried, which he thought might prevail on her to be the companion of their intended voyage; and he made no doubt but her example, added to the rhetoric of Montraville, would persuade Charlotte to go with them.

Charlotte had, when she went out to meet Montraville, flattered herself that her resolution was not to be shaken, and that, conscious of the impropriety of her conduct in having a clandestine intercourse with a stranger, she would never repeat the indiscretion.

But alas! poor Charlotte, she knew not the deceitfulness of her own heart, or she would have avoided the trial of her stability.

Montraville was tender, eloquent, ardent, and yet respectful. "Shall I not see you once more," said he, "before I leave England? will you not bless me by an assurance, that when we are divided by a vast expanse of sea I shall not be forgotten?"

Charlotte sighed.

"Why that sigh, my dear Charlotte? could I flatter myself that a fear for my safety, or a wish for my welfare occasioned it, how happy would it make me."

"I shall ever wish you well, Montraville," said she; "but we must meet no more."

"Oh say not so, my lovely girl: reflect, that when I leave my native land, perhaps a few short weeks may terminate my existence; the perils of the ocean—the dangers of war—"

"I can hear no more," said Charlotte in a tremulous voice. "I must leave you."

"Say you will see me once again."

"I dare not," said she.

"Only for one half hour to-morrow evening: 'tis my last request. I shall never trouble you again, Charlotte."

"I know not what to say," cried Charlotte, struggling to draw her hands from him: "let me leave you now."

"And you will come to-morrow," said Montraville.

"Perhaps I may," said she.

"Adieu then. I will live upon that hope till we meet again."

He kissed her hand. She sighed an adieu, and catching hold of Mademoiselle's arm, hastily entered the garden gate.

CHAPTER X

When We Have Excited Curiosity, It Is but an Act of Good Nature to Gratify It

◇   ◇

Montraville was the youngest son of a gentleman of fortune, whose family being numerous, he was obliged to bring up his sons to genteel professions, by the exercise of which they might hope to raise themselves into notice.

"My daughters," said he, "have been educated like gentlewomen; and should I die before they are settled, they must have some provision made, to place them above the snares and temptations which vice ever holds out to the elegant, accomplished female, when oppressed by the frowns of poverty and the sting of dependance: my boys, with only moderate incomes, when placed in the church, at the bar, or in the field, may exert their talents, make themselves friends, and raise their fortunes on the basis of merit."

When Montraville chose the profession of arms, his father presented him with a commission, and made him a handsome provision for his private purse. "Now, my boy," said he, "go! seek glory in the field of battle. You have received from me all I shall ever have it in my power to bestow: it is certain I have interest to gain you promotion; but be assured that interest shall never be exerted, unless by your future conduct you deserve it. Remember, therefore, your success in life depends entirely on yourself. There is one thing

I think it my duty to caution you against; the precipitancy with which young men frequently rush into matrimonial engagements, and by their thoughtlessness draw many a deserving woman into scenes of poverty and distress. A soldier has no business to think of a wife till his rank is such as to place him above the fear of bringing into the world a train of helpless innocents, heirs only to penury and affliction. If, indeed, a woman, whose fortune is sufficient to preserve you in that state of independence I would teach you to prize, should generously bestow herself on a young soldier, whose chief hope of future prosperity depended on his success in the field—if such a woman should offer—every barrier is removed, and I should rejoice in an union which would promise so much felicity. But mark me, boy, if, on the contrary, you rush into a precipitate union with a girl of little or no fortune, take the poor creature from a comfortable home and kind friends, and plunge her into all the evils a narrow income and increasing family can inflict, I will leave you to enjoy the blessed fruits of your rashness; for by all that is sacred, neither my interest or fortune shall ever be exerted in your favour. I am serious," continued he, "therefore imprint this conversation on your memory, and let it influence your future conduct. Your happiness will always be dear to me; and I wish to warn you of a rock on which the peace of many an honest fellow has been wrecked; for believe me, the difficulties and dangers of the longest winter campaign are much easier to be borne, than the pangs that would seize your heart, when you beheld the woman of your choice, the children of your affection, involved in penury and distress, and reflected that it was your own folly and precipitancy had been the prime cause of their sufferings."

As this conversation passed but a few hours before Montraville took leave of his father, it was deeply impressed on his mind: when, therefore, Belcour came with him to the place of assignation with Charlotte, he directed him to enquire of the French woman what were Miss Temple's expectations in regard to fortune.

Mademoiselle informed him, that though Charlotte's father possessed a genteel independence, it was by no means probable that he could give his daughter more than a thousand pounds; and in case she did not marry to his liking, it was possible he might not give her a single *sou;* nor did it appear the least likely, that Mr. Temple would agree to her union with a young man on the point of embarking for the feat of war.

Montaville therefore concluded it was impossible he should ever marry Charlotte Temple; and what end he proposed to himself by continuing the acquaintance he had commenced with her, he did not at that moment give himself time to enquire.

CHAPTER XI

Conflict of Love
and Duty

◇　◇

Almost a week was now gone, and Charlotte continued every
evening to meet Montraville, and in her heart every meeting
was resolved to be the last; but alas! when Montraville at parting
would earnestly intreat one more interview, that treacherous heart
betrayed her; and, forgetful of its resolution, pleaded the cause of
the enemy so powerfully, that Charlotte was unable to resist. Another and another meeting succeeded; and so well did Montraville
improve each opportunity, that the heedless girl at length confessed
no idea could be so painful to her as that of never seeing him again.

"Then we will never be parted," said he.

"Ah, Montraville," replied Charlotte, forcing a smile, "how can
it be avoided? My parents would never consent to our union; and
even could they be brought to approve it, how should I bear to be
separated from my kind, my beloved mother?"

"Then you love your parents more than you do me, Charlotte?"

"I hope I do," said she, blushing and looking down, "I hope my
affection for them will ever keep me from infringing the laws of
filial duty."

"Well, Charlotte," said Montraville gravely, and letting go her
hand, "since that is the case, I find I have deceived myself with
fallacious hopes. I had flattered my fond heart, that I was dearer
to Charlotte than any thing in the world beside. I thought that

you would for my sake have braved the dangers of the ocean, that you would, by your affection and smiles, have softened the hardships of war, and, had it been my fate to fall, that your tenderness would chear the hour of death, and smooth my passage to another world. But farewel, Charlotte! I see you never loved me. I shall now welcome the friendly ball that deprives me of the sense of my misery."

"Oh stay, unkind Montraville," cried she, catching hold of his arm, as he pretended to leave her, "stay, and to calm your fears, I will here protest that was it not for the fear of giving pain to the best of parents, and returning their kindness with ingratitude, I would follow you through every danger, and, in studying to promote your happiness, insure my own. But I cannot break my mother's heart, Montraville; I must not bring the grey hairs of my doating grand-father with sorrow to the grave, or make my beloved father perhaps curse the hour that gave me birth.' She covered her face with her hands, and burst into tears.

"All these distressing scenes, my dear Charlotte," cried Montraville, "are merely the chimeras of a disturbed fancy. Your parents might perhaps grieve at first; but when they heard from your own hand that you was with a man of honour, and that it was to insure your felicity by an union with him, to which you feared they would never have given their assent, that you left their protection, they will, be assured, forgive an error which love alone occasioned, and when we return from America, receive you with open arms and tears of joy."

Belcour and Mademoiselle heard this last speech, and conceiving it a proper time to throw in their advice and persuasions, approached Charlotte, and so well seconded the entreaties of Montraville, that finding Mademoiselle intended going with Belcour, and feeling her own treacherous heart too much inclined to accompany them, the hapless Charlotte, in an evil hour, consented that the next evening they should bring a chaise to the end of the town, and that she would leave her friends, and throw herself entirely on the protection of Montraville. "But should you," said she, looking earnestly at him, her eyes full of tears, "should you, forgetful of your promises, and repenting the engagement you here voluntarily enter into, forsake and leave me on a foreign shore—"

"Judge not so meanly of me," said he. "The moment we reach our place of destination, Hymen shall sanctify our love; and when I shall forget your goodness, may heaven forget me."

"Ah," said Charlotte, leaning on Mademoiselle's arm as they walked up the garden together, "I have forgot all that I ought to have remembered, in consenting to this intended elopement."

"You are a strange girl," said Mademoiselle: "you never know your own mind two minutes at a time. Just now you declared Montraville's happiness was what you prized most in the world; and now I suppose you repent having insured that happiness by agreeing to accompany him abroad."

"Indeed I do repent," replied Charlotte, "from my soul: but while discretion points out the impropriety of my conduct, inclination urges me on to ruin."

"Ruin! fiddlestick!" said Mademoiselle; "am I not going with you? and do I feel any of these qualms?"

"You do not renounce a tender father and mother," said Charlotte.

"But I hazard my dear reputation," replied Mademoiselle, bridling.

"True," replied Charlotte, "but you do not feel what I do." She then bade her good night: but sleep was a stranger to her eyes, and the tear of anguish watered her pillow.

CHAPTER XII

◇   ◇

Nature's last, best gift:
Creature in whom excell'd, whatever could
To sight or thought be nam'd!
Holy, divine! good, amiable, and sweet!
How thou art fall'n!—

When Charlotte left her restless bed, her languid eye and pale cheek discovered to Madame Du Pont the little repose she had tasted.

"My dear child," said the affectionate governess, "what is the cause of the languor so apparent in your frame? Are you not well?"

"Yes, my dear Madam, very well," replied Charlotte, attempting to smile, "but I know not how it was; I could not sleep last night, and my spirits are depressed this morning."

"Come chear up, my love," said the governess; "I believe I have brought a cordial to revive them. I have just received a letter from your good mama, and here is one for yourself."

Charlotte hastily took the letter: it contained these words—

"As to-morrow is the anniversary of the happy day that gave my beloved girl to the anxious wishes of a maternal heart, I have requested your governess to let you come home and spend it with us; and as I know you to be a good affectionate child, and make it your study to improve in those branches of education which you know will give most pleasure to your delighted parents, as a reward for your diligence and attention I have prepared an agreeable surprise for your reception. Your grand-father, eager to embrace the darling of his aged heart, will come in the chaise for you; so hold yourself in readiness to attend him by nine o'clock. Your dear father joins in every tender wish for your health and future felicity, which warms the heart of my dear Charlotte's affectionate mother,

L. Temple."

"Gracious heaven!" cried Charlotte, forgetting where she was, and raising her streaming eyes as in earnest supplication.

Madame Du Pont was surprised. "Why these tears, my love?" said she. "Why this seeming agitation? I thought the letter would have rejoiced, instead of distressing you."

"It does rejoice me," replied Charlotte, endeavouring at composure, "but I was praying for merit to deserve the unremitted attentions of the best of parents."

"You do right," said Madame Du Pont, "to ask the assistance of heaven that you may continue to deserve their love. Continue, my dear Charlotte, in the course you have ever pursued, and you will insure at once their happiness and your own."

"Oh!" cried Charlotte, as her governess left her, "I have forfeited both for ever! Yet let me reflect:—the irrevocable step is not yet taken: it is not too late to recede from the brink of a precipice, from which I can only behold the dark abyss of ruin, shame, and remorse!"

She arose from her seat, and flew to the apartment of La Rue. "Oh Mademoiselle!" said she, "I am snatched by a miracle from destruction! This letter has saved me: it has opened my eyes to the folly I was so near committing. I will not go, Mademoiselle; I will not wound the hearts of those dear parents who make my happiness the whole study of their lives."

"Well," said Mademoiselle, "do as you please, Miss; but pray understand that my resolution is taken, and it is not in your power to alter it. I shall meet the gentlemen at the appointed hour, and shall not be surprised at any outrage which Montraville may commit, when he finds himself disappointed. Indeed I should not be astonished, was he to come immediately here, and reproach you for your instability in the hearing of the whole school: and what will be the consequence? you will bear the odium of having formed the resolution of eloping, and every girl of spirit will laugh at your want of fortitude to put it in execution, while prudes and fools will load you with reproach and contempt. You will have lost the confidence of your parents, incurred their anger, and the scoffs of the world; and what fruit do you expect to reap from this piece of heroism, (for such no doubt you think it is?) you will have the pleasure to reflect, that you have deceived the man who adores you, and whom in your heart you prefer to all other men, and that you are separated from him for ever."

This eloquent harangue was given with such volubility, that Charlotte could not find an opportunity to interrupt her, or to offer a single word till the whole was finished, and then found her ideas so confused, that she knew not what to say.

At length she determined that she would go with Mademoiselle to the place of assignation, convince Montraville of the necessity of adhering to the resolution of remaining behind; assure him of her affection, and bid him adieu.

Charlotte formed this plan in her mind, and exulted in the certainty of its success. "How shall I rejoice," said she, "in this triumph of reason over inclination, and, when in the arms of my affectionate parents, lift up my soul in gratitude to heaven as I look back on the dangers I have escaped!"

The hour of assignation arrived: Mademoiselle put what money and valuables she possessed in her pocket, and advised Charlotte to do the same; but she refused; "my resolution is fixed," said she; "I will sacrifice love to duty."

Mademoiselle smiled internally; and they proceeded softly down the back stairs and out of the garden gate. Montraville and Belcour were ready to receive them.

"Now," said Montraville, taking Charlotte in his arms, "you are mine for ever."

"No," said she, withdrawing from his embrace, "I am come to take an everlasting farewel."

It would be useless to repeat the conversation that here ensued; suffice it to say, that Montraville used every argument that had formerly been successful, Charlotte's resolution began to waver, and he drew her almost imperceptibly towards the chaise.

"I cannot go," said she: "cease, dear Montraville, to persuade. I must not: religion, duty, forbid."

"Cruel Charlotte," said he, "if you disappoint my ardent hopes, by all that is sacred, this hand shall put a period to my existence. I cannot—will not live without you."

"Alas! my torn heart!" said Charlotte, "how shall I act?"

"Let me direct you," said Montraville, lifting her into the chaise.

"Oh! my dear forsaken parents!" cried Charlotte.

The chaise drove off. She shrieked, and fainted into the arms of her betrayer.

CHAPTER XIII

Cruel Disappointment

◇   ◇

"What pleasure," cried Mr. Eldridge, as he stepped into the chaise to go for his grand-daughter, "what pleasure expands the heart of an old man when he beholds the progeny of a beloved child growing up in every virtue that adorned the minds of her parents. I foolishly thought, some few years since that every sense of joy was buried in the graves of my dear partner and my son; but my Lucy, by her filial affection, soothed my soul to peace, and this dear Charlotte has twined herself round my heart, and opened such new scenes of delight to my view, that I almost forget I have ever been unhappy."

When the chaise stopped, he alighted with the alacrity of youth; so much do the emotions of the soul influence the body.

It was half past eight o'clock; the ladies were assembled in the school room, and Madame Du Pont was preparing to offer the morning sacrifice of prayer and praise, when it was discovered, that Mademoiselle and Charlotte were missing.

"She is busy, no doubt," said the governess, "in preparing Charlotte for her little excursion; but pleasure should never make us forget our duty to our Creator. Go, one of you, and bid them both attend prayers."

The lady who went to summon them, soon returned, and informed the governess, that the room was locked, and that she had knocked repeatedly, but obtained no answer.

"Good heaven!" cried Madame Du Pont, "this is very strange:" and turning pale with terror, she went hastily to the door, and ordered it to be forced open. The apartment instantly discovered, that no person had been in it the preceding night, the beds appearing as though just made. The house was instantly a scene of confusion: the garden, the pleasure grounds were searched to no purpose, every apartment rang with the names of Miss Temple and Mademoiselle; but they were too distant to hear; and every face wore the marks of disappointment.

Mr. Eldridge was sitting in the parlour, eagerly expecting his grand-daughter to descend, ready equipped for her journey: he heard the confusion that reigned in the house; he heard the name of Charlotte frequently repeated. "What can be the matter?" said he, rising and opening the door: "I fear some accident has befallen my dear girl."

The governess entered. The visible agitation of her countenance discovered that something extraordinary had happened.

"Where is Charlotte?" said he, "Why does not my child come to welcome her doating parent?"

"Be composed, my dear Sir," said Madame Du Pont, "do not frighten yourself unnecessarily. She is not in the house at present; but as Mademoiselle is undoubtedly with her, she will speedily return in safety; and I hope they will both be able to account for this unseasonable absence in such a manner as shall remove our present uneasiness."

"Madam," cried the old man, with an angry look, "has my child been accustomed to go out without leave, with no other company or protector than that French woman. Pardon me, Madam, I mean no reflections on your country, but I never did like Mademoiselle La Rue; I think she was a very improper person to be entrusted with the care of such a girl as Charlotte Temple, or to be suffered to take her from under your immediate protection."

"You wrong me, Mr. Eldridge," replied she, "if you suppose I have ever permitted your grand-daughter to go out unless with the other ladies. I would to heaven I could form any probable conjecture concerning her absence this morning, but it is a mystery which her return can alone unravel."

Servants were now dispatched to every place where there was the least hope of hearing any tidings of the fugitives, but in vain. Dreadful were the hours of horrid suspense which Mr. Eldridge passed till twelve o'clock, when that suspense was reduced to a shocking certainty, and every spark of hope which till then they had indulged, was in a moment extinguished.

Mr. Eldridge was preparing, with a heavy heart, to return to his anxiously-expecting children, when Madame Du Pont received the following note without either name or date.

"Miss Temple is well, and wishes to relieve the anxiety of her parents, by letting them know she has voluntarily put herself under the protection of a man whose future study shall be to make her happy. Pursuit is needless; the measures taken to avoid discovery are too effectual to be eluded. When she thinks her friends are reconciled to this precipitate step, they may perhaps be informed of her place of residence. Mademoiselle is with her."

As Madame Du Pont read these cruel lines, she turned pale as ashes, her limbs trembled, and she was forced to call for a glass of water. She loved Charlotte truly; and when she reflected on the innocence and gentleness of her disposition, she concluded that it must have been the advice and machinations of La Rue, which led her to this imprudent action; she recollected her agitation at the receipt of her mother's letter, and saw in it the conflict of her mind.

"Does that letter relate to Charlotte?" said Mr. Eldridge, having waited some time in expectation of Madame Du Pont's speaking.

"It does," said she. "Charlotte is well, but cannot return today."

"Not return, Madam? where is she? who will detain her from her fond, expecting parents?"

"You distract me with these questions, Mr. Eldridge. Indeed I know not where she is, or who has seduced her from her duty."

The whole truth now rushed at once upon Mr. Eldridge's mind. "She has eloped then," said he. "My child is betrayed; the darling, the comfort of my aged heart, is lost. Oh would to heaven I had died but yesterday."

A violent gush of grief in some measure relieved him, and, after several vain attempts, he at length assumed sufficient composure to read the note.

"And how shall I return to my children?" said he: "how approach that mansion, so late the habitation of peace? Alas! my dear Lucy, how will you support these heart-rending tidings? or how shall I be enabled to console you, who need so much consolation myself?"

The old man returned to the chaise, but the light step and chearful countenance were no more; sorrow filled his heart, and guided his motions; he seated himself in the chaise, his venerable head reclined upon his bosom, his hands were folded, his eye fixed on vacancy, and the large drops of sorrow rolled silently down his cheeks. There was a mixture of anguish and resignation depicted in his countenance, as if he would say, henceforth who shall dare to boast his happiness, or even in idea contemplate his treasure, lest, in the very moment his heart is exulting in its own felicity, the object which constitutes that felicity should be torn from him.

CHAPTER XIV

Maternal Sorrow

◇　◇

S low and heavy passed the time while the carriage was conveying Mr. Eldridge home; and yet when he came in sight of the house, he wished a longer reprieve from the dreadful task of informing Mr. and Mrs. Temple of their daughter's elopement.

It is easy to judge the anxiety of these affectionate parents, when they found the return of their father delayed so much beyond the expected time. They were now met in the dining parlour, and several of the young people who had been invited were already arrived. Each different part of the company was employed in the same manner, looking out at the windows which faced the road. At length the long-expected chaise appeared. Mrs. Temple ran out to receive and welcome her darling: her young companions flocked round the door, each one eager to give her joy on the return of her birthday. The door of the chaise was opened: Charlotte was not there. "Where is my child?" cried Mrs. Temple, in breathless agitation.

Mr. Eldridge could not answer: he took hold of his daughter's hand and led her into the house; and sinking on the first chair he came to, burst into tears, and sobbed aloud.

"She is dead," cried Mrs. Temple. "Oh my dear Charlotte!" and clasping her hands in an agony of distress, fell into strong hysterics.

Mr. Temple, who stood speechless with surprize and fear, now ventured to enquire if indeed his Charlotte was no more. Mr.

Eldridge led him into another apartment; and putting the fatal note into his hand, cried—"Bear it like a Christian," and turned from him, endeavouring to suppress his own too visible emotions.

It would be vain to attempt describing what Mr. Temple felt whilst he hastily ran over the dreadful lines: when he had finished, the paper dropt from his unnerved hand. "Gracious heaven!" said he, "could Charlotte act thus?" Neither tear nor sigh escaped him; and he sat the image of mute sorrow, till roused from his stupor by the repeated shrieks of Mrs. Temple. He rose hastily, and rushing into the apartment where she was, folded his arms about her, and saying—"Let us be patient, my dear Lucy," nature relieved his almost bursting heart by a friendly gush of tears.

Should any one, presuming on his own philosophic temper, look with an eye of contempt on the man who could indulge a woman's weakness, let him remember that man was a father, and he will then pity the misery which wrung those drops from a noble, generous heart.

Mrs. Temple beginning to be a little more composed, but still imagining her child was dead, her husband, gently taking her hand, cried—"You are mistaken, my love. Charlotte is not dead."

"Then she is very ill, else why did she not come? But I will go to her: the chaise is still at the door: let me go instantly to the dear girl. If I was ill, she would fly to attend me, to alleviate my sufferings, and chear me with her love."

"Be calm, my dearest Lucy, and I will tell you all," said Mr. Temple. "You must not go, indeed you must not; it will be of no use."

"Temple," said she, assuming a look of firmness and composure, "tell me the truth I beseech you. I cannot bear this dreadful suspense. What misfortune has befallen my child? Let me know the worst, and I will endeavour to bear it as I ought."

"Lucy," replied Mr. Temple, "imagine your daughter alive, and in no danger of death: what misfortune would you then dread?"

"There is one misfortune which is worse than death. But I know my child too well to suspect—"

"Be not too confident, Lucy."

"Oh heavens!" said she, "what horrid images do you start: is it possible she should forget—"

"She has forgot us all, my love; she has preferred the love of a stranger to the affectionate protection of her friends."

"Not eloped?" cried she eagerly.

Mr. Temple was silent.

"You cannot contradict it," said she. "I see my fate in those tearful eyes. Oh Charlotte! Charlotte! how ill have you requited our tenderness! But, Father of Mercies," continued she, sinking on her knees, and raising her streaming eyes and clasped hands to heaven, "this once vouchsafe to hear a fond, a distracted mother's prayer. Oh let thy bounteous Providence watch over and protect the dear thoughtless girl, save her from the miseries which I fear will be her portion, and oh! of thine infinite mercy, make her not a mother, lest she should one day feel what I now suffer."

The last words faultered on her tongue, and she fell fainting into the arms of her husband, who had involuntarily dropped on his knees beside her.

A mother's anguish, when disappointed in her tenderest hopes, none but a mother can conceive. Yet, my dear young readers, I would have you read this scene with attention, and reflect that you may yourselves one day be mothers. Oh my friends, as you value your eternal happiness, wound not, by thoughtless ingratitude, the peace of the mother who bore you: remember the tenderness, the care, the unremitting anxiety with which she has attended to all your wants and wishes from earliest infancy to the present day; behold the mild ray of affectionate applause that beams from her eye on the performance of your duty: listen to her reproofs with silent attention; they proceed from a heart anxious for your future felicity: you must love her; nature, all-powerful nature, has planted the seeds of filial affection in your bosoms.

Then once more read over the sorrows of poor Mrs. Temple, and remember, the mother whom you so dearly love and venerate will feel the same, when you, forgetful of the respect due to your maker and yourself, forsake the paths of virtue for those of vice and folly.

CHAPTER XV

Embarkation

◇   ◇

It was with the utmost difficulty that the united efforts of Mademoiselle and Montraville could support Charlotte's spirits during their short ride from Chichester to Portsmouth, where a boat waited to take them immediately on board the ship in which they were to embark for America.

As soon as she became tolerably composed, she entreated pen and ink to write to her parents. This she did in the most affecting, artless manner, entreating their pardon and blessing, and describing the dreadful situation of her mind, the conflict she suffered in endeavouring to conquer this unfortunate attachment, and concluded with saying, her only hope of future comfort consisted in the (perhaps delusive) idea she indulged, of being once more folded in their protecting arms, and hearing the words of peace and pardon from their lips.

The tears streamed incessantly while she was writing, and she was frequently obliged to lay down her pen: but when the task was completed, and she had committed the letter to the care of Montraville to be sent to the post office, she became more calm, and indulging the delightful hope of soon receiving an answer that would seal her pardon, she in some measure assumed her usual chearfulness.

But Montraville knew too well the consequences that must unavoidably ensue, should this letter reach Mr. Temple: he therefore wisely resolved to walk on the deck, tear it in pieces, and commit the fragments to the care of Neptune, who might or might not, as it suited his convenience, convey them on shore.

All Charlotte's hopes and wishes were now concentrated in one, namely that the fleet might be detained at Spithead till she could receive a letter from her friends: but in this she was disappointed, for the second morning after she went on board, the signal was made, the fleet weighed anchor, and in a few hours (the wind being favourable) they bid adieu to the white cliffs of Albion.

In the mean time every enquiry that could be thought of was made by Mr. and Mrs. Temple; for many days did they indulge the fond hope that she was merely gone off to be married, and that when the indissoluble knot was once tied, she would return with the partner she had chosen, and entreat their blessing and forgiveness.

"And shall we not forgive her?" said Mr. Temple.

"Forgive her!" exclaimed the mother. "Oh yes, whatever be our errors, is she not our child? and though bowed to the earth even with shame and remorse, is it not our duty to raise the poor penitent, and whisper peace and comfort to her desponding soul? would she but return, with rapture would I fold her to my heart, and bury every remembrance of her faults in the dear embrace."

But still day after day passed on, and Charlotte did not appear, nor were any tidings to be heard of her: yet each rising morning was welcomed by some new hope—the evening brought with it disappointment. At length hope was no more; despair usurped her place; and the mansion which was once the mansion of peace, became the habitation of pale, dejected melancholy.

The chearful smile that was wont to adorn the face of Mrs. Temple was fled, and had it not been for the support of unaffected piety, and a consciousness of having ever set before her child the fairest example, she must have sunk under this heavy affliction.

"Since," said she, "the severest scrutiny cannot charge me with any breach of duty to have deserved this severe chastisement, I will bow before the power who inflicts it with humble resignation to his will; nor shall the duty of a wife be totally absorbed in the feelings of the mother; I will endeavour to appear more chearful, and by appearing in some measure to have conquered my own sorrow, alleviate the sufferings of my husband, and rouse him from that torpor into which this misfortune has plunged him. My father too demands my care and attention: I must not, by a selfish indulgence of my own grief, forget the interest those two dear objects take in my happiness or misery: I will wear a smile on my face, though the thorn rankles in my heart; and if by so doing, I in the smallest degree contribute to restore their peace of mind, I shall be amply rewarded for the pain the concealment of my own feelings may occasion."

Thus argued this excellent woman: and in the execution of so laudable a resolution we shall leave her, to follow the fortunes of the hapless victim of imprudence and evil counsellors.

CHAPTER XVI

Necessary Digression

◊　　◊

On board of the ship in which Charlotte and Mademoiselle were embarked, was an officer of large unincumbered fortune and elevated rank, and whom I shall call Crayton.

He was one of those men, who, having travelled in their youth, pretend to have contracted a peculiar fondness for every thing foreign, and to hold in contempt the productions of their own country; and this affected partiality extended even to the women.

With him therefore the blushing modesty and unaffected simplicity of Charlotte passed unnoticed; but the forward pertness of La Rue, the freedom of her conversation, the elegance of her person, mixed with a certain engaging *je ne sais quoi*, perfectly enchanted him.

The reader no doubt has already developed the character of La Rue: designing, artful, and selfish, she had accepted the devoirs of Belcour because she was heartily weary of the retired life she led at the school, wished to be released from what she deemed a slavery, and to return to that vortex of folly and dissipation which had once plunged her into the deepest misery; but her plan she flattered herself was now better formed: she resolved to put herself under the protection of no man till she had first secured a settlement; but the clandestine manner in which she left Madame Du Pont's prevented her putting this plan in execution, though Belcour solemnly protested he would make her a handsome settlement the moment they arrived at Portsmouth. This he afterwards contrived to evade by a pretended hurry of business. La Rue readily conceiving he never meant to fulfill his promise, determined to change her battery, and attack the heart of Colonel Crayton. She soon discovered the partiality he entertained for her nation; and having imposed on him a feigned tale of distress representing Belcour as a villain who had seduced her from her friends under promise of marriage, and afterwards betrayed her, pretending great remorse for the errors she had committed, and declaring whatever her affection for Belcour might have been, it was now entirely extinguished, and she wished for nothing more than an opportunity to leave a course of life which her soul abhorred; but she had no friends to apply to, they had all renounced her, and guilt and misery would undoubtedly be her future portion through life.

Crayton was possessed of many amiable qualities, though the peculiar trait in his character, which we have already mentioned, in a great measure threw a shade over them. He was beloved for his humanity and benevolence by all who knew him, but he was easy and unsuspicious himself, and became a dupe to the artifice of others.

He was, when very young, united to an amiable Parisian lady, and perhaps it was his affection for her that laid the foundation for the partiality he ever retained for the whole nation. He had by her one daughter, who entered into the world but a few hours before her mother left it. This lady was universally beloved and admired, being endowed with all the virtues of her mother, without the weakness of the father: she was married to Major Beauchamp, and was at this time in the same fleet with her father, attending her husband to New York.

Crayton was melted by the affected contrition and distress of La Rue: he could converse with her for hours, read to her, play cards with her, listen to all her complaints, and promise to protect her to the utmost of his power. La Rue easily saw his character; her sole aim was to awaken a passion in his bosom that might turn out to her advantage, and in this aim she was but too successful, for before the voyage was finished, the infatuated Colonel gave her from under his hand a promise of marriage on their arrival at New-York, under forfeiture of five thousand pounds.

And how did our poor Charlotte pass her time during a tedious and tempestuous passage? naturally delicate, the fatigue and sickness which she endured rendered her so weak as to be almost entirely confined to her bed: yet the kindness and attention of Montraville in some measure contributed to alleviate her sufferings, and the hope of hearing from her friends soon after her arrival, kept up her spirits, and cheered many a gloomy hour.

But during the voyage a great revolution took place not only in the fortune of La Rue but in the bosom of Belcour: whilst in pursuit of his amour with Mademoiselle, he had attended little to the interesting, inobtrusive charms of Charlotte, but when, cloyed by possession, and disgusted with the art and dissimulation of one, he beheld the simplicity and gentleness of the other, the contrast became too striking not to fill him at once with surprise and admiration. He frequently conversed with Charlotte; he found her sensible, well informed, but diffident and unassuming. The languor which the fatigue of her body and perturbation of her mind spread over her delicate features, served only in his opinion to render her more lovely: he knew that Montraville did not design to marry her, and he formed a resolution to endeavour to gain her himself whenever Montraville should leave her.

Let not the reader imagine Belcour's designs were honourable. Alas! when once a woman has forgot the respect due to herself, by yielding to the solicitations of illicit love, they lose all their consequence, even in the eyes of the man whose art has betrayed them, and for whose sake they have sacrificed every valuable consideration.

The heedless Fair, who stoops to guilty joys,
A man may pity—but he must despise.

Nay, every libertine will think he has a right to insult her with his licentious passion; and should the unhappy creature shrink from the insolent overture, he will sneeringly taunt her with pretence of modesty.

CHAPTER XVII

A Wedding

◇   ◇

On the day before their arrival at New-York, after dinner, Crayton arose from his seat, and placing himself by Mademoiselle, thus addressed the company—

"As we are now nearly arrived at our destined port, I think it but my duty to inform you, my friends, that this lady," (taking her hand,) "has placed herself under my protection. I have seen and severely felt the anguish of her heart, and through every shade which cruelty or malice may throw over her, can discover the most amiable qualities. I thought it but necessary to mention my esteem for her before our disembarkation, as it is my fixed resolution, the morning after we land, to give her an undoubted title to my favour and protection by honourably uniting my fate to hers. I would wish every gentleman here therefore to remember that her honour henceforth is mine, and," continued he, looking at Belcour, "should any man presume to speak in the least disrespectfully of her, I shall not hesitate to pronounce him a scoundrel."

Belcour cast at him a smile of contempt, and bowing profoundly low, wished Mademoiselle much joy in the proposed union; and assuring the Colonel that he need not be in the least apprehensive of any one throwing the least odium on the character of his lady, shook him by the hand with ridiculous gravity, and left the cabin.

The truth was, he was glad to be rid of La Rue, and so he was but freed from her, he cared not who fell victim to her infamous arts.

The inexperienced Charlotte was astonished at what she heard. She thought La Rue had, like herself, only been urged by the force of her attachment to Belcour, to quit her friends, and follow him to the feat of war: how wonderful then, that she should resolve to marry another man. It was certainly extremely wrong. It was indelicate. She mentioned her thoughts to Montraville. He laughed at her simplicity, called her a little ideot, and patting her on the cheek, said she knew nothing of the world. "If the world sanctifies such things, 'tis a very bad world I think," said Charlotte. "Why I always understood they were to have been married when they arrived at New-York. I am sure Mademoiselle told me Belcour promised to marry her."

"Well, and suppose he did?"

"Why, he should be obliged to keep his word I think."

"Well, but I suppose he has changed his mind," said Montraville, "and then you know the case is altered."

Charlotte looked at him attentively for a moment. A full sense of her own situation rushed upon her mind. She burst into tears, and remained silent. Montraville too well understood the cause of her tears. He kissed her cheek, and bidding her not make herself uneasy, unable to bear the silent but keen remonstrance, hastily left her.

The next morning by sun-rise they found themselves at anchor before the city of New-York. A boat was ordered to convey the ladies on shore. Crayton accompanied them; and they were shewn to a house of public entertainment. Scarcely were they seated when the door opened, and the Colonel found himself in the arms of his daughter, who had landed a few minutes before him. The first transport of meeting subsided, Crayton introduced his daughter to Mademoiselle La Rue, as an old friend of her mother's, (for the artful French woman had really made it appear to the credulous

Colonel that she was in the same convent with his first wife, and, though much younger, had received many tokens of her esteem and regard.)

"If, Mademoiselle," said Mrs. Beauchamp, "you were the friend of my mother, you must be worthy the esteem of all good hearts."

"Mademoiselle will soon honour our family," said Crayton, "by supplying the place that valuable woman filled: and as you are married, my dear, I think you will not blame—"

"Hush, my dear Sir," replied Mrs. Beauchamp: "I know my duty too well to scrutinize your conduct. Be assured, my dear father, your happiness is mine. I shall rejoice in it, and sincerely love the person who contributes to it. But tell me," continued she, turning to Charlotte, "who is this lovely girl? Is she your sister, Mademoiselle?"

A blush, deep as the glow of the carnation, suffused the cheeks of Charlotte.

"It is a young lady," replied the Colonel, "who came in the same vessel with us from England." He then drew his daughter aside, and told her in a whisper, Charlotte was the mistress of Montraville.

"What a pity!" said Mrs. Beauchamp softly, (casting a most compassionate glance at her.) "But surely her mind is not depraved. The goodness of her heart is depicted in her ingenuous countenance."

Charlotte caught the word pity. "And am I already fallen so low?" said she. A sigh escaped her, and a tear was ready to start, but Montraville appeared, and she checked the rising emotion. Mademoiselle went with the Colonel and his daughter to another apartment. Charlotte remained with Montraville and Belcour. The next morning the Colonel performed his promise, and La Rue became in due form Mrs. Crayton, exulted in her own good fortune, and dared to look with an eye of contempt on the unfortunate but far less guilty Charlotte.

CHAPTER XVIII

Reflections

◊　◊

"And am I indeed fallen so low," said Charlotte, "as to be only pitied? Will the voice of approbation no more meet my ear? and shall I never again possess a friend, whose face will wear a smile of joy whenever I approach? Alas! how thoughtless, how dreadfully imprudent have I been! I know not which is most painful to endure, the sneer of contempt, or the glance of compassion, which is depicted in the various countenances of my own sex: they are both equally humiliating. Ah! my dear parents, could you now see the child of your affections, the daughter whom you so dearly loved, a poor solitary being, without society, here wearing out her heavy hours in deep regret and anguish of heart, no kind friend of her own sex to whom she can unbosom her griefs, no beloved mother, no woman of character will appear in my company, and low as your Charlotte has fallen, she cannot associate with infamy."

These were the painful reflections which occupied the mind of Charlotte. Montraville had placed her in a small house a few miles from New-York: he gave her one female attendant, and supplied her with what money she wanted; but business and pleasure so entirely occupied his time, that he had little to devote to the woman, whom he had brought from all her connections, and robbed of innocence. Sometimes, indeed, he would steal out at the close of evening, and pass a few hours with her; and then so much was she attached to him, that all her sorrows were forgotten while blest with his society: she would enjoy a walk by moonlight, or sit by him in a little arbour at the bottom of the garden, and play on the harp, accompanying it with her plaintive, harmonious voice. But often, very often, did he promise to renew his visits, and, forgetful of his promise, leave her to mourn her disappointment. What painful hours of expectation would she pass! She would sit at a window which looked toward a field he used to cross, counting the minutes, and straining her eyes to catch the first glimpse of his person, till blinded with tears of disappointment, she would lean her head on her hands, and give free vent to her sorrows: then catching at some new hope, she would again renew her watchful position, till the shades of evening enveloped every object in a dusky cloud: she would then renew her complaints, and, with a heart bursting with disappointed love and wounded sensibility, retire to a bed which remorse had strewed with thorns, and court in vain that comforter of weary nature (who seldom visits the unhappy) to come and steep her senses in oblivion.

Who can form an adequate idea of the sorrow that preyed upon the mind of Charlotte? The wife, whose breast glows with affection to her husband, and who in return meets only indifference, can but faintly conceive her anguish. Dreadfully painful is the situation of such a woman, but she has many comforts of which our poor Charlotte was deprived. The duteous, faithful wife, though treated with indifference, has one solid pleasure within her own bosom, she can reflect that she has not deserved neglect—that she has ever fulfilled the duties of her station with the strictest exactness; she may hope, by constant assiduity and unremitted attention, to recall her wanderer, and be doubly happy in his returning affection; she knows he cannot leave her to unite himself to another: he cannot cast her out to poverty and contempt; she looks around her, and sees the smile of friendly welcome, or the tear of affectionate consolation, on the face of every person whom she favours with her esteem; and from all these circumstances she gathers comfort: but the poor girl by thoughtless passion led astray, who, in parting with her honour, has forfeited the esteem of the very man to whom she has sacrificed every thing dear and valuable in life, feels his indifference in the fruit of her own folly, and laments her want of power to recall his lost affection; she knows there is no tie but honour, and that, in a man who has been guilty of seduction, is but very feeble: he may leave her in a moment to shame and want; he may marry and forsake her for ever; and should he, she has no redress, no friendly, soothing companion to pour into her wounded mind the balm of consolation, no benevolent hand to lead her back to the path of rectitude; she has disgraced her friends, forfeited the good opinion of the world, and undone herself; she feels herself a poor solitary being in the midst of surrounding multitudes; shame bows her to the earth, remorse tears her distracted mind, and guilt, poverty, and disease close the dreadful scene: she sinks unnoticed to oblivion. The finger of contempt may point out to some passing daughter of youthful mirth, the humble bed where lies this frail sister of mortality; and will she, in the unbounded gaiety of her heart, exult in her own unblemished fame, and triumph over the silent ashes of the dead? Oh no! has she a heart of sensibility, she will stop, and thus address the unhappy victim of folly—

"Thou had'st thy faults, but sure thy sufferings have expiated them: thy errors brought thee to an early grave; but thou wert a fellow-creature—thou hast been unhappy—then be those errors forgotten."

Then, as she stoops to pluck the noxious weed from off the sod, a tear will fall, and consecrate the spot to Charity.

For ever honoured be the sacred drop of humanity; the angel of mercy shall record its source, and the soul from whence it sprang shall be immortal.

My dear Madam, contract not your brow into a frown of disapprobation. I mean not to extenuate the faults of those unhappy women who fall victims to guilt and folly; but surely, when we reflect how many errors we are ourselves subject to, how many secret faults lie hid in the recesses of our hearts, which we should blush to have brought into open day (and yet those faults require the lenity and pity of a benevolent judge, or awful would be our prospect of futurity) I say, my dear Madam, when we consider this, we surely may pity the faults of others.

Believe me, many an unfortunate female, who has once strayed into the thorny paths of vice, would gladly return to virtue, was any generous friend to endeavour to raise and re-assure her; but alas! it cannot be, you say; the world would deride and scoff. Then let me tell you, Madam, 'tis a very unfeeling world, and does not deserve half the blessings which a bountiful Providence showers upon it.

Oh, thou benevolent giver of all good! how shall we erring mortals dare to look up to thy mercy in the great day of retribution, if we now uncharitably refuse to overlook the errors, or alleviate the miseries, of our fellow-creatures.

CHAPTER XIX

A Mistake Discovered

◇　　◇

Julia Franklin was the only child of a man of large property, who, at the age of eighteen, left her independent mistress of an unincumbered income of seven hundred a year; she was a girl of a lively disposition, and humane, susceptible heart: she resided in New-York with an uncle, who loved her too well, and had too high an opinion of her prudence, to scrutinize her actions so much as would have been necessary with many young ladies, who were not blest with her discretion: she was, at the time Montraville arrived at New-York, the life of society, and the universal toast. Montraville was introduced to her by the following accident.

One night when he was upon guard, a dreadful fire broke out near Mr. Franklin's house, which, in a few hours, reduced that and several others to ashes; fortunately no lives were lost, and, by the assiduity of the soldiers, much valuable property was saved from the flames. In the midst of the confusion an old gentleman came up to Montraville, and, putting a small box into his hands, cried—"Keep it, my good Sir, till I come to you again;" and then rushing again into the thickest of the croud, Montraville saw him no more. He waited till the fire was quite extinguished and the mob dispersed; but in vain: the old gentleman did not appear to claim his property; and Montraville, fearing to make any enquiry, lest he should meet with impostors who might lay claim, without any legal right, to the box, carried it to his lodgings, and locked it up: he naturally imagined, that the person who committed it to his care knew him, and would, in a day or two, reclaim it; but several weeks passed on, and no enquiry being made, he began to be uneasy, and resolved to examine the contents of the box, and if they were, as he supposed, valuable, to spare no pains to discover, and restore them to the owner. Upon opening it, he found it contained jewels to a large amount, about two hundred pounds in money, and a miniature picture set for a bracelet. On examining the picture, he thought he had somewhere seen features very like it, but could not recollect where. A few days after, being at a public assembly, he saw Miss Franklin, and the likeness was too evident to be mistaken: he enquired among his brother officers if any of them knew her, and found one who was upon terms of intimacy in the family: "then introduce me to her immediately," said he, "for I am certain I can inform her of something which will give her peculiar pleasure."

He was immediately introduced, found she was the owner of the jewels, and was invited to breakfast the next morning in order to their restoration. This whole evening Montraville was honoured with Julia's hand; the lively sallies of her wit, the elegance of her manner, powerfully charmed him: he forgot Charlotte, and indulged himself in saying every thing that was polite and tender to Julia. But on retiring, recollection returned. "What am I about?" said he: "though I cannot marry Charlotte, I cannot be villain enough to forsake her, nor must I dare to trifle with the heart of Julia Franklin. I will return this box," said he, "which has been the source of so much uneasiness already, and in the evening pay a visit to my poor melancholy Charlotte, and endeavour to forget this fascinating Julia."

He arose, dressed himself, and taking the picture out, "I will reserve this from the rest," said he, "and by presenting it to her when she thinks it is lost, enhance the value of the obligation." He repaired to Mr. Franklin's, and found Julia in the breakfast parlour alone.

"How happy am I, Madam," said he, "that being the fortunate instrument of saving these jewels has been the means of procuring me the acquaintance of so amiable a lady. There are the jewels and money all safe."

"But where is the picture, Sir?" said Julia.

"Here, Madam. I would not willingly part with it."

"It is the portrait of my mother," said she, taking it from him: " 'tis all that remains." She pressed it to her lips, and a tear trembled in her eyes. Montraville glanced his eye on her grey night gown and black ribbon, and his own feelings prevented a reply.

Julia Franklin was the very reverse of Charlotte Temple: she was tall, elegantly shaped, and possessed much of the air and manner of a woman of fashion; her complexion was a clear brown, enlivened with the glow of health, her eyes, full, black, and sparkling, darted their intelligent glances through long silken lashes; her hair was shining brown, and her features regular and striking; there was an air of innocent gaiety that played about her countenance, where good humour sat triumphant.

"I have been mistaken," said Montraville. "I imagined I loved Charlotte: but alas! I am now too late convinced my attachment to her was merely the impulse of the moment. I fear I have not only entailed lasting misery on that poor girl, but also thrown a barrier in the way of my own happiness, which it will be impossible to surmount. I feel I love Julia Franklin with ardour and sincerity; yet, when in her presence, I am sensible of my own inability to offer a heart worthy her acceptance, and remain silent."

Full of these painful thoughts, Montraville walked out to see Charlotte: she saw him approach, and ran out to meet him: she banished from her countenance the air of discontent which ever appeared when he was absent, and met him with a smile of joy.

"I thought you had forgot me, Montraville," said she, "and was very unhappy."

"I shall never forget you, Charlotte," he replied, pressing her hand.

The uncommon gravity of his countenance, and the brevity of his reply, alarmed her.

"You are not well," said she; "your hand is hot; your eyes are heavy; you are very ill."

"I am a villain," said he mentally, as he turned from her to hide his emotions.

"But come," continued she tenderly, "you shall go to bed, and I will sit by, and watch you; you will be better when you have slept."

Montraville was glad to retire, and by pretending sleep, hide the agitation of his mind from her penetrating eye. Charlotte watched by him till a late hour, and then, lying softly down by his side, sunk into a profound sleep, from whence she awoke not till late the next morning.

CHAPTER XX

◇　　◇

Virtue never appears so amiable as when reaching forth her hand
to raise a fallen sister.   *Chapter of Accidents.*

When Charlotte awoke, she missed Montraville; but thinking
he might have arisen early to enjoy the beauties of the
morning, she was preparing to follow him, when casting her eye
on the table, she saw a note, and opening it hastily, found these
words—

"My dear Charlotte must not be surprised, if she does not see
me again for some time: unavoidable business will prevent me that
pleasure: be assured I am quite well this morning; and what your
fond imagination magnified into illness, was nothing more than
fatigue, which a few hours rest has entirely removed. Make yourself
happy, and be certain of the unalterable friendship of

"Montraville."

"Friendship!" said Charlotte emphatically, as she finished the
note, "is it come to this at last? Alas! poor, forsaken Charlotte, thy
doom is now but too apparent. Montraville is no longer interested
in thy happiness; and shame, remorse, and disappointed love will
henceforth be thy only attendants."

Though these were the ideas that involuntarily rushed upon the
mind of Charlotte as she perused the fatal note, yet after a few
hours had elasped, the syren Hope again took possession of her
bosom, and she flattered herself she could, on a second perusal,
discover an air of tenderness in the few lines he had left, which
at first had escaped her notice.

"He certainly cannot be so base as to leave me," said she, "and in stiling himself my friend does he not promise to protect me. I will not torment myself with these causeless fears; I will place a confidence in his honour; and sure he will not be so unjust as to abuse it."

Just as she had by this manner of reasoning brought her mind to some tolerable degree of composure, she was surprised by a visit from Belcour. The dejection visible in Charlotte's countenance, her swoln eyes and neglected attire, at once told him she was unhappy: he made no doubt but Montraville had, by his coldness, alarmed her suspicions, and was resolved, if possible, to rouse her to jealousy, urge her to reproach him, and by that means occasion a breach between them. "If I can once convince her that she has a rival," said he, "she will listen to my passion if it is only to revenge his slights." Belcour knew but little of the female heart; and what he did know was only of those of loose and dissolute lives. He had no idea that a woman might fall a victim to imprudence, and yet retain so strong a sense of honour, as to reject with horror and contempt every solicitation to a second fault. He never imagined that a gentle, generous female heart, once tenderly attached, when treated with unkindness might break, but would never harbour a thought of revenge.

His visit was not long, but before he went he fixed a scorpion in the heart of Charlotte, whose venom embittered every future hour of her life.

We will now return for a moment to Colonel Crayton. He had been three months married, and in that little time had discovered that the conduct of his lady was not so prudent as it ought to have been: but remonstrance was vain; her temper was violent; and to the Colonel's great misfortune he had conceived a sincere affection for her: she saw her own power, and, with the art of a Circe, made every action appear to him in what light she pleased: his acquaintance laughed at his blindness, his friends pitied his infatuation, his amiable daughter, Mrs. Beauchamp, in secret deplored the loss of her father's affection, and grieved that he should be so entirely swayed by an artful, and, she much feared, infamous woman.

Mrs. Beauchamp was mild and engaging; she loved not the hurry and bustle of a city, and had prevailed on her husband to take a house a few miles from New-York. Chance led her into the same neighbourhood with Charlotte; their houses stood within a short space of each other, and their gardens joined: she had not been long in her new habitation before the figure of Charlotte struck her; she recollected her interesting features; she saw the melancholy so conspicuous in her countenance, and her heart bled at the reflection, that perhaps deprived of honour, friends, all that was valuable in life, she was doomed to linger out a wretched existence in a strange land, and sink broken-hearted into an untimely grave. "Would to heaven I could snatch her from so hard a fate," said she; "but the merciless world has barred the doors of compassion against a poor weak girl, who, perhaps, had she one kind friend to raise and reassure her, would gladly return to peace and virtue; nay, even the woman who dares to pity, and endeavour to recall a wandering sister, incurs the sneer of contempt and ridicule, for an action in which even angels are said to rejoice."

The longer Mrs. Beauchamp was a witness to the solitary life Charlotte led, the more she wished to speak to her, and often as she saw her cheeks wet with the tears of anguish, she would say— "Dear sufferer, how gladly would I pour into your heart the balm of consolation, were it not for the fear of derision."

But an accident soon happened which made her resolve to brave even the scoffs of the world, rather than not enjoy the heavenly satisfaction of comforting a desponding fellow-creature.

Mrs. Beauchamp was an early riser. She was one morning walking in the garden, leaning on her husband's arm, when the sound of a harp attracted their notice: they listened attentively, and heard a soft melodious voice distinctly sing the following stanzas:

Thou glorious orb, supremely bright,
Just rising from the sea,
To chear all nature with thy light,
What are thy beams to me?
In vain thy glories bid me rise,
To hail the new-born day,
Alas! my morning sacrifice
Is still to weep and pray.
For what are nature's charms combin'd,
To one, whose weary breast
Can neither peace nor comfort find,
Nor friend whereon to rest?
Oh! never! never! whilst I live
Can my heart's anguish cease:
Come, friendly death, thy mandate give,
And let me be at peace.

" 'Tis poor Charlotte!" said Mrs. Beauchamp, the pellucid drop of humanity stealing down her cheek.

Captain Beauchamp was alarmed at her emotion. "What Charlotte?" said he; "do you know her?"

In the accent of a pitying angel did she disclose to her husband Charlotte's unhappy situation, and the frequent wish she had formed of being serviceable to her. "I fear," continued she, "the poor girl has been basely betrayed; and if I thought you would not blame me, I would pay her a visit, offer her my friendship, and endeavour to restore to her heart that peace she seems to have lost, and so pathetically laments. Who knows, my dear," laying her hand affectionately on his arm, "who knows but she has left some kind, affectionate parents to lament her errors, and would she return, they might with rapture receive the poor penitent, and wash away her faults in tears of joy. Oh! what a glorious reflexion would it be for me could I be the happy instrument of restoring her. Her heart may not be depraved, Beauchamp."

"Exalted woman!" cried Beauchamp, embracing her, "how dost thou rise every moment in my esteem. Follow the impulse of thy generous heart, my Emily. Let prudes and fools censure if they dare, and blame a sensibility they never felt; I will exultingly tell them that the heart that is truly virtuous is ever inclined to pity and forgive the errors of its fellow-creatures."

A beam of exulting joy played round the animated countenance of Mrs. Beauchamp, at these encomiums bestowed on her by a beloved husband, the most delightful sensations pervaded her heart, and, having breakfasted, she prepared to visit Charlotte.

CHAPTER XXI

◇　　◇

Teach me to feel another's woe,
　　To hid the fault I see,
That mercy I to others show,
　　That mercy show to me.　　*Pope.*

When Mrs. Beauchamp was dressed, she began to feel embarrassed at the thought of beginning an acquaintance with Charlotte, and was distressed how to make the first visit. "I cannot go without some introduction," said she, "it will look so like impertinent curiosity." At length recollecting herself, she stepped into the garden, and gathering a few fine cucumbers, took them in her hand by way of apology for her visit.

A glow of conscious shame vermillioned Charlotte's face as Mrs. Beauchamp entered.

"You will pardon me, Madam," said she, "for not having before paid my respects to so amiable a neighbour; but we English people always keep up that reserve which is the characteristic of our nation wherever we go. I have taken the liberty to bring you a few cucumbers, for I observed you had none in your garden."

Charlotte, though naturally polite and well-bred, was so confused she could hardly speak. Her kind visitor endeavoured to relieve her by not noticing her embarrassment. "I am come, Madam," continued she, "to request you will spend the day with me. I shall be alone; and, as we are both strangers in this country, we may hereafter be extremely happy in each other's friendship."

"Your friendship, Madam," said Charlotte blushing, "is an hon-

our to all who are favoured with it. Little as I have seen of this
part of the world, I am no stranger to Mrs. Beauchamp's goodness
of heart and known humanity: but my friendship—" She paused,
glanced her eye upon her own visible situation, and, spite of her
endeavours to suppress them, burst into tears.

Mrs. Beauchamp guessed the source from whence those tears
flowed. "You seem unhappy, Madam," said she: ' shall I be thought
worthy your confidence? will you entrust me with the cause of your
sorrow, and rest on my assurances to exert my utmost power to
serve you." Charlotte returned a look of gratitude, but could not
speak, and Mrs. Beauchamp continued—" My heart was interested
in your behalf the first moment I saw you, and I only lament I had
not made earlier overtures towards an acquaintance; but I flatter
myself you will henceforth consider me as your friend."

"Oh Madam!" cried Charlotte, "I have forfeited the good opinion
of all my friends; I have forsaken them, and undone myself."

"Come, come, my dear," said Mrs. Beauchamp, "you must not
indulge these gloomy thoughts: you are not I hope so miserable as
you imagine yourself: endeavour to be composed, and let me be
favoured with your company at dinner, when, if you can bring
yourself to think me your friend, and repose a confidence in me,
I am ready to convince you it shall not be abused." She then arose,
and bade her good morning.

At the dining hour Charlotte repaired to Mrs. Beauchamp's,
and during dinner assumed as composed an aspect as possible; but
when the cloth was removed, she summoned all her resolution and
determined to make Mrs. Beauchamp acquainted with every circumstance preceding her unfortunate elopement, and the earnest
desire she had to quit a way of life so repugnant to her feelings.

With the benignant aspect of an angel of mercy did Mrs. Beauchamp listen to the artless tale: she was shocked to the soul to find
how large a share La Rue had in the seduction of this amiable girl,
and a tear fell, when she reflected so vile a woman was now the
wife of her father. When Charlotte had finished, she gave her a

little time to collect her scattered spirits, and then asked her if she had never written to her friends.

"Oh yes, Madam," said she, "frequently: but I have broke their hearts: they are either dead or have cast me off for ever, for I have never received a single line from them."

"I rather suspect," said Mrs. Beauchamp, "they have never had your letters: but suppose you were to hear from them, and they were willing to receive you, would you then leave this cruel Montraville, and return to them?"

"Would I!" said Charlotte, clasping her hands; "would not the poor sailor, tost on a tempestuous ocean, threatened every moment with death, gladly return to the shore he had left to trust to its deceitful calmness? Oh, my dear Madam, I would return, though to do it I were obliged to walk barefoot over a burning desart, and beg a scanty pittance of each traveller to support my existence. I would endure it all chearfully, could I but once more see my dear, blessed mother, hear her pronounce my pardon, and bless me before I died; but alas! I shall never see her more; she has blotted the ungrateful Charlotte from her remembrance, and I shall sink to the grave loaded with her's and my father's curse."

Mrs. Beauchamp endeavoured to sooth her. "You shall write to them again," said she, "and I will see that the letter is sent by the first packet that sails for England; in the mean time keep up your spirits, and hope every thing, by daring to deserve it."

She then turned the conversation, and Charlotte having taken a cup of tea, wished her benevolent friend a good evening.

Sorrows of the Heart

◇   ◇

W hen Charlotte got home she endeavoured to collect her
thoughts, and took up a pen in order to address those dear
parents, whom, spite her errors, she still loved with the utmost
tenderness, but vain was every effort to write with the least co-
herence; her tears fell so fast they almost blinded her; and as she
proceeded to describe her unhappy situation she became so agitated
that she was obliged to give over the attempt and retire to bed,
where, overcome with the fatigue her mind had undergone, she
fell into a slumber which greatly refreshed her, and she arose in
the morning with spirits more adequate to the painful task she had
to perform, and, after several attempts, at length concluded the
following letter to her mother—

TO MRS. TEMPLE

New-York

"Will my once kind, my ever beloved mother, deign to receive a
letter from her guilty, but repentant child? or has she, justly in-
censed at my ingratitude, driven the unhappy Charlotte from her
remembrance? Alas! thou much injured mother! shouldst thou even
disown me, I dare not complain, because I know I have deserved
it: but yet, believe me, guilty as I am, and cruelly as I have disappointed the hopes of the fondest parents, that ever girl had, even
in the moment when, forgetful of my duty, I fled from you and

83

happiness, even then I loved you most, and my heart bled at the thought of what you would suffer. Oh! never, never! whilst I have existence, will the agony of that moment be erased from my memory. It seemed like the separation of soul and body. What can I plead in excuse for my conduct? alas! nothing! That I loved my seducer is but too true! yet powerful as that passion is when operating in a young heart glowing with sensibility, it never would have conquered my affection to you, my beloved parents, had I not been encouraged, nay, urged to take the fatally imprudent step, by one of my own sex, who, under the mask of friendship, drew me on to ruin. Yet think not your Charlotte was so lost as to voluntarily rush into a life of infamy; no, my dear mother, deceived by the specious appearance of my betrayer, and every suspicion lulled asleep by the most solemn promises of marriage, I thought not those promises would so easily be forgotten. I never once reflected that the man who could stoop to seduction, would not hesitate to forsake the wretched object of his passion, whenever his capricious heart grew weary of her tenderness. When we arrived at this place, I vainly expected him to fulfil his engagements, but was at last fatally convinced he had never intended to make me his wife, or if he had once thought of it, his mind was now altered. I scorned to claim from him his humanity what I could not obtain from his love: I was conscious of having forfeited the only gem that could render me respectable in the eye of the world. I locked my sorrows in my own bosom, and bore my injuries in silence. But how shall I proceed? This man, this cruel Montraville, for whom I sacrificed honour, happiness, and the love of my friends, no longer looks on me with affection, but scorns the credulous girl whom his art has made miserable. Could you see me, my dear parents, without society, without friends, stung with remorse, and (I feel the burning blush of shame die my cheeks while I write it) tortured with the pangs of disappointed love; cut to the soul by the indifference of him, who, having deprived me of every other comfort, no longer thinks it worth his while to sooth the heart where he has planted the thorn of never-ceasing regret. My daily employment is to think of you and weep, to pray for your happiness and deplore my own folly: my nights are scarce more happy, for if by chance I close my weary eyes, and hope some small forgetfulness of sorrow, some little time to pass in sweet oblivion, fancy, still waking, wafts me home to you: I see your beloved forms, I kneel and hear the blessed words of peace and pardon. Extatic joy pervades my soul; I reach my arms to catch your dear embraces; the motion chases the illusive dream; I wake to real misery. At other times I see my father angry and frowning, point to horrid caves, where, on the cold damp ground, in the agonies of death, I see my dear mother and my revered grand-father. I strive to raise you; you push me from you, and shrieking cry—"Charlotte, thou hast murdered me!" Horror and despair tear every tortured nerve; I start, and leave my restless bed, weary and unrefreshed.

"Shocking as these reflexions are, I have yet one more dreadful than the rest. Mother, my dear mother! do not let me quite break your heart when I tell you, in a few months I shall bring into the world an innocent witness of my guilt. Oh my bleeding heart, I shall bring a poor little helpless creature, heir to infamy and shame.

"This alone has urged me once more to address you, to interest you in behalf of this poor unborn, and beg you to extend your protection to the child of your lost Charlotte; for my own part I have wrote so often, so frequently have pleaded for forgiveness, and entreated to be received once more beneath the paternal roof, that having received no answer, not even one line, I much fear you have cast me from you for ever.

"But sure you cannot refuse to protect my innocent infant: it partakes not of its mother's guilt. Oh my father, oh beloved mother, now do I feel the anguish I inflicted on your hearts recoiling with double force upon my own.

"If my child should be a girl (which heaven forbid) tell her the unhappy fate of her mother, and teach her to avoid my errors; if a boy, teach him to lament my miseries, but tell him not who inflicted them, lest in wishing to revenge his mother's injuries, he should wound the peace of his father.

"And now, dear friends of my soul, kind guardians of my infancy, farewell. I feel I never more must hope to see you; the anguish of my heart strikes at the strings of life, and in a short time I shall be at rest. Oh could I but receive your blessing and forgiveness before I died, it would smooth my passage to the peaceful grave, and be a blessed foretaste of a happy eternity. I beseech you, curse me not, my adored parents, but let a tear of pity and pardon fall to the memory of your lost

Charlotte."

CHAPTER XXIII

A Man May Smile, and Smile, and Be a Villain

◊   ◊

While Charlotte was enjoying some small degree of comfort in the consoling friendship of Mrs. Beauchamp, Montraville was advancing rapidly in his affection towards Miss Franklin. Julia was an amiable girl; she saw only the fair side of his character; she possessed an independent fortune, and resolved to be happy with the man of her heart, though his rank and fortune were by no means so exalted as she had a right to expect; she saw the passion which Montraville struggled to conceal; she wondered at his timidity, but imagined the distance fortune had placed between them occasioned his backwardness, and made every advance which strict prudence and a becoming modesty would permit. Montraville saw with pleasure he was not indifferent to her, but a spark of honour which animated his bosom would not suffer him to take advantage of her partiality. He was well acquainted with Charlotte's situation, and he thought there would be a double cruelty in forsaking her at such a time; and to marry Miss Franklin, while honour, humanity, every sacred law, obliged him still to protect and support Charlotte, was a baseness which his soul shuddered at.

He communicated his uneasiness to Belcour: it was the very thing this pretended friend had wished. "And do you really," said he, laughing, "hesitate at marrying the lovely Julia, and becoming master of her fortune, because a little foolish, fond girl chose to leave her friends, and run away with you to America. Dear Montraville, act more like a man of sense; this whining, pining Charlotte, who occasions you so much uneasiness, would have eloped with somebody else if she had not with you."

"Would to heaven," said Montraville, "I had never seen her; my regard for her was but the momentary passion of desire, but I feel I shall love and revere Julia Franklin as long as I live; yet to leave poor Charlotte in her present situation would be cruel beyond description."

"Oh my good sentimental friend," said Belcour, "do you imagine no body has a right to provide for the brat but yourself."

Montraville started. "Sure," said he, "you cannot mean to insinuate that Charlotte is false."

"I don't insinuate it," said Belcour, "I know it."

Montraville turned pale as ashes. "Then there is no faith in woman," said he.

"While I thought you attached to her," said Belcour with an air of indifference, "I never wished to make you uneasy by mentioning her perfidy, but as I know you love and are beloved by Miss Franklin, I was determined not to let these foolish scruples of honour step between you and happiness, or your tenderness for the peace of a perfidious girl prevent your uniting yourself to a woman of honour."

"Good heavens!" said Montraville, "what poignant reflections does a man endure who sees a lovely woman plunged in infamy, and is conscious he was her first seducer; but are you certain of what you say, Belcour?"

"So far," replied he, "that I myself have received advances from her which I would not take advantage of out of regard to you: but hang it, think no more about her. I dined at Franklin's to-day, and Julia bid me seek and bring you to tea: so come along, my lad, make good use of opportunity, and seize the gifts of fortune while they are within your reach."

Montraville was too much agitated to pass a happy evening even in the company of Julia Franklin: he determined to visit Charlotte early the next morning, tax her with her falsehood, and take an everlasting leave of her; but when the morning came, he was commanded on duty, and for six weeks was prevented from putting his design in execution. At length he found an hour to spare, and walked out to spend it with Charlotte: it was near four o'clock in the afternoon when he arrived at her cottage; she was not in the parlour, and without calling the servant he walked up stairs, thinking to find her in her bed room. He opened the door, and the first object that met his eyes was Charlotte asleep on the bed, and Belcour by her side.

"Death and distraction," said he, stamping, "this is too much. Rise, villain, and defend yourself." Belcour sprang from the bed. The noise awoke Charlotte; terrified at the furious appearance of Montraville, and seeing Belcour with him in the chamber, she caught hold of his arm as he stood by the bed-side, and eagerly asked what was the matter.

"Treacherous, infamous girl," said he, "can you ask? How came he here?" pointing at Belcour.

"As heaven is my witness," replied she weeping, "I do not know. I have not seen him for these three weeks."

"Then you confess he sometimes visits you?"

"He came sometimes by your desire."

" 'Tis false; I never desired him to come, and you know I did not: but mark me, Charlotte, from this instant our connexion is at an end. Let Belcour, or any other of your favoured lovers, take you and provide for you; I have done with you for ever."

He was then going to leave her; but starting wildly from the bed, she threw herself on her knees before him, protesting her innocence and entreating him not to leave her. "Oh Montraville," said she, "kill me, for pity's sake kill me, but do not doubt my fidelity. Do not leave me in this horrid situation; for the sake of your unborn child, oh! spurn not the wretched mother from you."

"Charlotte," said he, with a firm voice, "I shall take care that neither you nor your child want any thing in the approaching painful hour; but we meet no more." He then endeavoured to raise her from the ground; but in vain; she clung about his knees, entreating him to believe her innocent, and conjuring Belcour to clear up the dreadful mystery.

Belcour cast on Montraville a smile of contempt: it irritated him almost to madness; he broke from the feeble arms of the distressed girl; she shrieked and fell prostrate on the floor.

Montraville instantly left the house and returned hastily to the city.

CHAPTER XXIV

Mystery Developed

◇   ◇

Unfortunately for Charlotte, about three weeks before this unhappy rencontre, Captain Beauchamp, being ordered to Rhode-Island, his lady had accompanied him, so that Charlotte was deprived of her friendly advice and consoling society. The afternoon on which Montraville had visited her she had found herself languid and fatigued, and after making a very slight dinner had lain down to endeavour to recruit her exhausted spirits, and, contrary to her expectations, had fallen asleep. She had not long been lain down, when Belcour arrived, for he took every opportunity of visiting her, and striving to awaken her resentment against Montraville. He enquired of the servant where her mistress was, and being told she was asleep, took up a book to amuse himself: having sat a few minutes, he by chance cast his eyes towards the road, and saw Montraville approaching; he instantly conceived the diabolical scheme of ruining the unhappy Charlotte in his opinion for ever; he therefore stole softly up stairs, and laying himself by her side with the greatest precaution, for fear she should awake, was in that situation discovered by his credulous friend.

When Montraville spurned the weeping Charlotte from him, and left her almost distracted with terror and despair, Belcour raised her from the floor, and leading her down stairs, assumed the part of a tender, consoling friend; she listened to the arguments he advanced with apparent composure; but this was only the calm of a moment: the remembrance of Montraville's recent cruelty again rushed upon her mind: she pushed him from her with some violence, and crying—"Leave me, Sir, I beseech you leave me, for much I fear you have been the cause of my fidelity being suspected; go, leave me to the accumulated miseries my own imprudence has brought upon me."

She then left him with precipitation, and retiring to her own apartment, threw herself on the bed, and gave vent to an agony of grief which it is impossible to describe.

It now occurred to Belcour that she might possibly write to Montraville, and endeavour to convince him of her innocence: he was well aware of her pathetic remonstrances, and, sensible of the tenderness of Montraville's heart, resolved to prevent any letters ever reaching him: he therefore called the servant, and, by the powerful persuasion of a bribe, prevailed with her to promise whatever letters her mistress might write should be sent to him. He then left a polite, tender note for Charlotte, and returned to New-York. His first business was to seek Montraville, and endeavour to convince him that what had happened would ultimately tend to his happiness: he found him in his apartment, solitary, pensive, and wrapped in disagreeable reflexions.

"Why how now, whining, pining lover?" said he, clapping him on the shoulder. Montraville started; a momentary flush of resentment crossed his cheek, but instantly gave place to a death-like paleness, occasioned by painful remembrance—remembrance awakened by that monitor, whom, though we may in vain endeavour, we can never entirely silence.

"Belcour," said he, "you have injured me in a tender point."

"Prithee, Jack," replied Belcour, "do not make a serious matter of it: how could I refuse the girl's advances? and thank heaven she is not your wife."

"True," said Montraville; "but she was innocent when I first knew her. It was I seduced her, Belcour. Had it not been for me, she had still been virtuous and happy in the affection and protection of her family."

"Pshaw," replied Belcour, laughing, "if you had not taken advantage of her easy nature, some other would, and where is the difference, pray?"

"I wish I had never seen her," cried he passionately, and starting from his seat. "Oh that cursed French woman," added he with vehemence, "had it not been for her, I might have been happy—" He paused.

"With Julia Franklin," said Belcour. The name, like a sudden spark of electric fire, seemed for a moment to suspend his faculties—for a moment he was transfixed; but recovering, he caught Belcour's hand, and cried—"Stop! stop! I beseech you, name not the lovely Julia and the wretched Montraville in the same breath. I am a seducer, a mean, ungenerous seducer of unsuspecting innocence. I dare not hope that purity like her's would stoop to unite itself with black, premeditated guilt: yet by heavens I swear, Belcour, I thought I loved the lost, abandoned Charlotte till I saw Julia—I thought I never could forsake her; but the heart is deceitful, and I now can plainly discriminate between the impulse of a youthful passion, and the pure flame of disinterested affection."

At that instant Julia Franklin passed the window, leaning on her uncle's arm. She curtseyed as she passed, and, with the bewitching smile of modest chearfulness, cried—"Do you bury yourselves in the house this fine evening, gents?" There was something in the voice! the manner! the look! that was altogether irresistible. "Perhaps she wishes my company," said Montraville mentally, as he snatched up his hat: "if I thought she loved me, I would confess my errors, and trust to her generosity to pity and pardon me." He soon overtook her, and offering her his arm, they sauntered to pleasant but unfrequented walks. Belcour drew Mr. Franklin on one side and entered into a political discourse: they walked faster than the young people, and Belcour by some means contrived entirely to lose sight of them. It was a fine evening in the beginning of autumn; the last remains of day-light faintly streaked the western sky, while the moon, with pale and virgin lustre in the room of gorgeous gold and purple, ornamented the canopy of heaven with silver, fleecy clouds, which now and then half hid her lovely face, and, by partly concealing, heightened every beauty; the zephyrs whispered softly through the trees, which now began to shed their leafy honours; a solemn silence reigned: and to a happy mind an evening such as this would give serenity, and calm, unruffled pleasure: but to Montraville, while it soothed the turbulence of his passions, it brought increase of melancholy reflexions. Julia was leaning on his arm: he took her hand in his, and pressing it tenderly, sighed deeply, but continued silent. Julia was embarrassed; she wished to break a silence so unaccountable, but was unable; she loved Montraville, she saw he was unhappy, and wished to know the cause of his uneasiness, but that innate modesty, which nature has implanted in the female breast, prevented her enquiring. "I am bad company, Miss Franklin," said he, at last recollecting himself; "but I have met with something to-day that has greatly distressed me, and I cannot shake off the disagreeable impression it has made on my mind."

"I am sorry," she replied, "that you have any cause of inquietude. I am sure if you were as happy as you deserve, and as all your friends wish you—" She hesitated. "And might I," replied he with some animation, "presume to rank the amiable Julia in that number?"

"Certainly," said she, "the service you have rendered me, the knowledge of your worth, all combine to make me esteem you."

"Esteem, my lovely Julia," said he passionately, "is but a poor cold word. I would if I dared, if I thought I merited your attention— but no, I must not—honour forbids. I am beneath your notice, Julia, I am miserable and cannot hope to be otherwise."

"Alas!" said Julia, "I pity you."

"Oh thou condescending charmer," said he, "how that sweet

word cheers my sad heart. Indeed if you knew all, you would pity; but at the same time I fear you would despise me."

Just then they were again joined by Mr. Franklin and Belcour. It had interrupted an interesting discourse. They found it impossible to converse on indifferent subjects, and proceeded home in silence. At Mr. Franklin's door Montraville again pressed Julia's hand, and faintly articulating "good night," retired to his lodgings dispirited and wretched, from a consciousness that he deserved not the affection, with which he plainly saw he was honoured.

CHAPTER XXV

Reception of a Letter

◇   ◇

"And where now is our poor Charlotte?" said Mr. Temple one evening, as the cold blasts of autumn whistled rudely over the heath, and the yellow appearance of the distant wood, spoke the near approach of winter. In vain the chearful fire blazed on the hearth, in vain was he surrounded by all the comforts of life; the parent was still alive in his heart, and when he thought that perhaps his once darling child was ere this exposed to all the miseries of want in a distant land, without a friend to sooth and comfort her, without the benignant look of compassion to chear, or the angelic voice of pity to pour the balm of consolation on her wounded heart; when he thought of this, his whole soul dissolved in tenderness; and while he wiped the tear of anguish from the eye of his patient, uncomplaining Lucy, he struggled to suppress the sympathizing drop that started in his own.

"Oh, my poor girl," said Mrs. Temple, "how must she be altered, else surely she would have relieved our agonizing minds by one line to say she lived—to say she had not quite forgot the parents who almost idolized her."

"Gracious heaven," said Mr. Temple, starting from his seat, "who would wish to be a father, to experience the agonizing pangs inflicted on a parent's heart by the ingratitude of a child?" Mrs.

Temple wept: her father took her hand; he would have said, "be comforted my child," but the words died on his tongue. The sad silence that ensued was interrupted by a loud rap at the door. In a moment a servant entered with a letter in his hand.

Mrs. Temple took it from him: she cast her eyes upon the superscription; she knew the writing. " 'Tis Charlotte," said she, eagerly breaking the seal, "she has not quite forgot us." But before she had half gone through the contents, a sudden sickness seized her; she grew cold and giddy, and putting it into her husband's hand, she cried—"Read it: I cannot." Mr. Temple attempted to read it aloud, but frequently paused to give vent to his tears. "My poor deluded child," said he, when he had finished.

"Oh, shall we not forgive the dear penitent?" said Mrs. Temple. "We must, we will, my love; she is willing to return, and 'tis our duty to receive her."

"Father of mercy," said Mr. Eldridge, raising his clasped hands, "let me but live once more to see the dear wanderer restored to her afflicted parents, and take me from this world of sorrow whenever it seemeth best to thy wisdom."

"Yes, we will receive her," said Mr. Temple; "we will endeavour to heal her wounded spirit, and speak peace and comfort to her agitated soul. I will write to her to return immediately."

"Oh!" said Mrs. Temple, "I would if possible fly to her, support and chear the dear sufferer in the approaching hour of distress, and tell her how nearly penitence is allied to virtue. Cannot we go and conduct her home, my love?" continued she, laying her hand on his arm. "My father will surely forgive our absence if we go to bring home his darling."

"You cannot go, my Lucy," said Mr. Temple: "the delicacy of your frame would but poorly sustain the fatigue of a long voyage; but I will go and bring the gentle penitent to your arms: we may still see many years of happiness."

The struggle in the bosom of Mrs. Temple between maternal

and conjugal tenderness was long and painful. At length the former triumphed, and she consented that her husband should set forward to New-York by the first opportunity: she wrote to her Charlotte in the tenderest, most consoling manner, and looked forward to the happy hour, when she should again embrace her, with the most animated hope.

CHAPTER XXVI

What Might Be Expected

◇   ◇

In the mean time the passion Montraville had conceived for Julia Franklin daily encreased, and he saw evidently how much he was beloved by that amiable girl: he was likewise strongly prepossessed with an idea of Charlotte's perfidy. What wonder then if he gave himself up to the delightful sensation which pervaded his bosom; and finding no obstacle arise to oppose his happiness, he solicited and obtained the hand of Julia. A few days before his marriage he thus addressed Belcour:

"Though Charlotte, by her abandoned conduct, has thrown herself from my protection, I still hold myself bound to support her till relieved from her present condition, and also to provide for the child. I do not intend to see her again, but I will place a sum of money in your hands, which will amply supply her with every convenience; but should she require more, let her have it, and I will see it repaid. I wish I could prevail on the poor deluded girl to return to her friends: she was an only child, and I make no doubt but that they would joyfully receive her; it would shock me greatly to see her henceforth leading a life of infamy, as I should always accuse myself of being the primary cause of all her errors. If she should chuse to remain under your protection, be kind to her, Belcour, I conjure you. Let not satiety prompt you to treat her in such a manner, as may drive her to actions which necessity might urge her to, while her better reason disapproved them: she shall never want a friend while I live, but I never more desire to behold her; her presence would be always painful to me, and a glance from her eye would call the blush of conscious guilt into my cheek.

"I will write a letter to her, which you may deliver when I am gone, as I shall go to St. Eustatia the day after my union with Julia, who will accompany me."

Belcour promised to fulfil the request of his friend, though nothing was farther from his intentions, than the least design of delivering the letter, or making Charlotte acquainted with the provision Montraville had made for her; he was bent on the complete ruin of the unhappy girl, and supposed, by reducing her to an entire dependance on him, to bring her by degrees to consent to gratify his ungenerous passion.

The evening before the day appointed for the nuptials of Montraville and Julia, the former retired early to his apartment; and ruminating on the past scenes of his life, suffered the keenest remorse in the remembrance of Charlotte's seduction. "Poor girl," said he, "I will at least write and bid her adieu; I will too endeavour to awaken that love of virtue in her bosom which her unfortunate attachment to me has extinguished." He took up the pen and began to write, but words were denied him. How could he address the woman whom he had seduced, and whom, though he thought unworthy his tenderness, he was about to bid adieu for ever? How should he tell her that he was going to abjure her, to enter into the most indissoluble ties with another, and that he could not even own the infant which she bore as his child? Several letters were begun and destroyed: at length he completed the following:

TO CHARLOTTE

"Though I have taken up my pen to address you, my poor injured girl, I feel I am inadequate to the task; yet, however painful the endeavour, I could not resolve upon leaving you for ever without one kind line to bid you adieu, to tell you how my heart bleeds at the remembrance of what you was, before you saw the hated Montraville. Even now imagination paints the scene, when, torn by contending passions, when, struggling between love and duty, you fainted in my arms, and I lifted you into the chaise: I see the agony of your mind, when, recovering, you found yourself on the road to Portsmouth: but how, my gentle girl, how could you, when so justly impressed with the value of virtue, how could you, when loving as I thought you loved me, yield to the solicitations of Belcour?

"Oh Charlotte, conscience tells me it was I, villain that I am, who first taught you the allurements of guilty pleasure; it was I who dragged you from the calm repose which innocence and virtue ever enjoy; and can I, dare I tell you, it was not love prompted to the horrid deed? No, thou dear, fallen angel, believe your repentant Montraville, when he tells you the man who truly loves will never betray the object of his affection. Adieu, Charlotte: could you still find charms in a life of unoffending innocence, return to your parents; you shall never want the means of support both for yourself and child. Oh! gracious heaven! may that child be entirely free from the vices of its father and the weakness of its mother.

"To-morrow—but no, I cannot tell you what to-morrow will produce; Belcour will inform you: he also has cash for you, which I beg you will ask for whenever you may want it. Once more adieu: believe me could I hear you was returned to your friends, and enjoying that tranquillity of which I have robbed you, I should be as completely happy as even you, in your fondest hours, could wish me, but till then a gloom will obscure the brightest prospect of

Montraville."

After he had sealed this letter he threw himself on the bed, and enjoyed a few hours repose. Early in the morning Belcour tapped at his door: he arose hastily, and prepared to meet his Julia at the altar.

"This is the letter to Charlotte," said he, giving it to Belcour: "take it to her when we are gone to Eustatia; and I conjure you, my dear friend, not to use any sophistical arguments to prevent her return to virtue; but should she incline that way, encourage her in the thought, and assist her to put her design in execution."

CHAPTER XXVII

◇　　◇

Pensive she mourn'd, and hung her languid head,
Like a fair lily overcharg'd with dew.

Charlotte had now been left almost three months a prey to her
own melancholy reflexions—sad companions indeed; nor did
any one break in upon her solitude but Belcour, who once or twice
called to enquire after her health, and tell her he had in vain
endeavoured to bring Montraville to hear reason; and once, but
only once, was her mind cheared by the receipt of an affectionate
letter from Mrs. Beauchamp. Often had she wrote to her perfidious
seducer, and with the most persuasive eloquence endeavoured to
convince him of her innocence; but these letters were never suffered to reach the hands of Montraville, or they must, though on
the very eve of marriage, have prevented his deserting the wretched
girl. Real anguish of heart had in a great measure faded her charms,
her cheeks were pale from want of rest, and her eyes, by frequent,
indeed almost continued weeping, were sunk and heavy. Sometimes
a gleam of hope would play about her heart when she thought of
her parents—"They cannot surely," she would say, "refuse to
forgive me; or should they deny their pardon to me, they will not
hate my innocent infant on account of its mother's errors." How
often did the poor mourner wish for the consoling presence of the
benevolent Mrs. Beauchamp.

"If she were here," she would cry, "she would certainly comfort
me, and sooth the distraction of my soul."

She was sitting one afternoon, wrapped in these melancholy

reflexions, when she was interrupted by the entrance of Belcour. Great as the alteration was which incessant sorrow had made on her person, she was still interesting, still charming; and the unhallowed flame, which had urged Belcour to plant dissension between her and Montraville, still raged in his bosom: he was determined, if possible, to make her his mistress; nay, he had even conceived the diabolical scheme of taking her to New-York, and making her appear in every public place where it was likely she should meet Montraville, that he might be a witness to his unmanly triumph.

When he entered the room where Charlotte was sitting, he assumed the look of tender, consolatory friendship. "And how does my lovely Charlotte?" said he, taking her hand: "I fear you are not so well as I could wish."

"I am not well, Mr. Belcour," said she, "very far from it; but the pains and infirmities of the body I could easily bear, nay, submit to them with patience, were they not aggravated by the most insupportable anguish of my mind."

"You are not happy, Charlotte," said he, with a look of well-dissembled sorrow.

"Alas!" replied she mournfully, shaking her head, "how can I be happy, deserted and forsaken as I am, without a friend of my own sex to whom I can unburthen my full heart, nay, my fidelity suspected by the very man for whom I have sacrificed every thing valuable in life, for whom I have made myself a poor despised creature, an outcast from society, an object only of contempt and pity."

"You think too meanly of yourself, Miss Temple: there is no one who would dare to treat you with contempt: all who have the pleasure of knowing you must admire and esteem. You are lonely here, my dear girl; give me leave to conduct you to New-York, where the agreeable society of some ladies, to whom I will introduce you, will dispel these sad thoughts, and I shall again see returning chearfulness animate those lovely features."

"Oh never! never!" cried Charlotte, emphatically: "the virtuous part of my sex will scorn me, and I will never associate with infamy. No, Belcour, here let me hide my shame and sorrow, here let me spend my few remaining days in obscurity unknown and unpitied, here let me die unlamented, and my name sink to oblivion." Here her tears stopped her utterance. Belcour was awed to silence: he dared not interrupt her; and after a moment's pause she proceeded—"I once had conceived the thought of going to New-York to seek out the still dear, though cruel, ungenerous Montraville, to throw myself at his feet, and entreat his compassion; heaven knows, not for myself; if I am no longer beloved, I will not be indebted to his pity to redress my injuries, but I would have knelt and entreated him not to forsake my poor unborn—" She could say no more; a crimson glow rushed over her cheeks, and covering her face with her hands, she sobbed aloud.

Something like humanity was awakened in Belcour's breast by this pathetic speech: he arose and walked towards the window; but the selfish passion which had taken possession of his heart, soon stifled these finer emotions; and he thought if Charlotte was once convinced she had no longer any dependence on Montraville, she would more readily throw herself on his protection. Determined, therefore, to inform her of all that had happened, he again resumed his seat; and finding she began to be more composed, enquired if she had ever heard from Montraville since the unfortunate rencontre in her bed chamber.

"Ah no," said she. "I fear I shall never hear from him again."

"I am greatly of your opinion," said Belcour, "for he has been for some time past greatly attached—"

At the word "attached" a death-like paleness overspread the countenance of Charlotte, but she applied to some hartshorn which stood beside her, and Belcour proceeded.

"He has been for some time past greatly attached to one Miss Franklin, a pleasing lively girl, with a large fortune."

"She may be richer, may be handsomer," cried Charlotte, "but cannot love him so well. Oh may she beware of his art, and not trust him too far as I have done."

"He addresses her publicly," said he, "and it was rumoured they were to be married before he sailed for Eustatia, whither his company is ordered."

"Belcour," said Charlotte, seizing his hand, and gazing at him earnestly, while her pale lips trembled with convulsive agony, "tell me, and tell me truly, I beseech you, do you think he can be such a villain as to marry another woman, and leave me to die with want and misery in a strange land: tell me what you think; I can bear it very well; I will not shrink from this heaviest stroke of fate; I have deserved my afflictions, and I will endeavour to bear them as I ought."

"I fear," said Belcour, "he can be that villain."

"Perhaps," cried she, eagerly interrupting him, "perhaps he is married already: come, let me know the worst," continued she with an affected look of composure: "you need not be afraid, I shall not send the fortunate lady a bowl of poison."

"Well then, my dear girl," said he, deceived by her appearance, "they were married on Thursday, and yesterday morning they sailed for Eustatia."

"Married—gone—say you?" cried she in a distracted accent, "what without a last farewell, without one thought on my unhappy situation! Oh Montraville, may God forgive your perfidy." She shrieked, and Belcour sprang forward just in time to prevent her falling to the floor.

Alarming faintings now succeeded each other, and she was conveyed to her bed, from whence she earnestly prayed she might never more arise. Belcour staid with her that night, and in the morning found her in high fever. The fits she had been seized with had greatly terrified him; and confined as she now was to a bed of sickness, she was no longer an object of desire: it is true for several days he went constantly to see her, but her pale, emaciated appearance disgusted him: his visits became less frequent; he forgot the solemn charge given him by Montraville; he even forgot the money entrusted to his care; and, the burning blush of indignation and shame tinges my cheek while I write it, this disgrace to humanity and manhood at length forgot ever the injured Charlotte; and, attracted by the blooming health of a farmer's daughter, whom he had seen in his frequent excursions to the country, he left the unhappy girl to sink unnoticed to the grave, a prey to sickness, grief, and penury; while he, having triumphed over the virtue of the artless cottager, rioted in all the intemperance of luxury and lawless pleasure.

CHAPTER XXVIII

A Trifling Retrospect

◇   ◇

"**B**less my heart," cries my young, volatile reader, "I shall never have patience to get through these volumes, there are so many ahs! and ohs! so much fainting, tears, and distress, I am sick to death of the subject." My dear, chearful, innocent girl, for innocent I will suppose you to be, or you would acutely feel the woes of Charlotte, did conscience say, thus might it have been with me, had not Providence interposed to snatch me from destruction: therefore, my lively, innocent girl, I must request your patience; I am writing a tale of truth: I mean to write it to the heart: but if perchance the heart is rendered impenetrable by unbounded prosperity, or a continuance in vice, I expect not my tale to please, nay, I even expect it will be thrown by with disgust. But softly, gentle fair one; I pray you throw it not aside till you have perused the whole; mayhap you may find something therein to repay you for the trouble. Methinks I see a sarcastic smile sit on your countenance.—"And what," cry you, "does the conceited author suppose we can glean from these pages, if Charlotte is held up as an object of terror, to prevent us from falling into guilty errors? does not La Rue triumph in her shame, and by adding art to guilt, obtain the affection of a worthy man, and rise to a station where she is beheld with respect, and chearfully received into all companies. What then is the moral you would inculcate? Would you wish us to think that a deviation from virtue, if covered by art and hypocrisy, is not an object of detestation, but on the contrary shall raise us to fame and honour? while the hapless girl who falls a victim to her too great sensibility, shall be loaded with ignominy and shame?" No, my fair querist, I mean no such thing. Remember the endeavours of the wicked are often suffered to prosper, that in the end their fall may be attended with more bitterness of heart; while the cup of affliction is poured out for wise and salutary ends, and they who are compelled to drain it even to the bitter dregs, often find comfort at the bottom; the tear of penitence blots their offences from the book of fate, and they rise from the heavy, painful trial, purified and fit for a mansion in the kingdom of eternity.

Yes, my young friends, the tear of compassion shall fall for the fate of Charlotte, while the name of La Rue shall be detested and despised. For Charlotte, the soul melts with sympathy; for La Rue, it feels nothing but horror and contempt. But perhaps your gay hearts would rather follow the fortunate Mrs. Crayton through the scenes of pleasure and dissipation in which she was engaged, than listen to the complaints and miseries of Charlotte. I will for once oblige you; I will for once follow her to midnight revels, balls, and scenes of gaiety, for in such was she contanly engaged.

I have said her person was lovely; let us add that she was surrounded by splendor and affluence, and he must know but little of the world who can wonder, (however faulty such a woman's conduct,) at her being followed by the men, and her company courted by the women: in short Mrs. Crayton was the universal favourite: she set the fashions, she was toasted by all the gentlemen, and copied by all the ladies.

Colonel Crayton was a domestic man. Could he be happy with such a woman? impossible! Remonstrance was vain: he might as well have preached to the winds, as endeavour to persuade her from any action, however ridiculous, on which she had set her mind: in short, after a little ineffectual struggle, he gave up the attempt, and left her to follow the bent of her own inclinations: what those were, I think the reader must have seen enough of her character to form a just idea. Among the number who paid their devotions at her shrine, she singled one, a young Ensign of mean birth, indifferent education, and weak intellects. How such a man came into the army, we hardly know to account for, and how he afterwards rose to posts of honour is likewise strange and wonderful. But fortune is blind, and so are those too frequently who have the power of dispensing her favours: else why do we see fools and knaves at the very top of the wheel, while patient merit sinks to the extreme of the opposite abyss. But we may form a thousand conjectures on this subject, and yet never hit on the right. Let us therefore endeavour to deserve her smiles, and whether we succeed or not, we shall feel more innate satisfaction, than thousands of those who bask in the sunshine of her favour unworthily. But to return to Mrs. Crayton: this young man, whom I shall distinguish by the name of Corydon, was the reigning favourite of her heart. He escorted her to the play, danced with her at every ball, and when indisposition prevented her going out, it was he alone who was permitted to chear the gloomy solitude to which she was obliged to confine herself. Did she ever think of poor Charlotte?—if she did, my dear Miss, it was only to laugh at the poor girl's want of spirit in consenting to be moped up in the country, while Montraville was enjoying all the pleasures of a gay, dissipated city. When she heard of his marriage, she smiling said, so there's an end of Madam Charlotte's hopes. I wonder who will take her now, or what will become of the little affected prude?

But as you have lead to the subject, I think we may as well return to the distressed Charlotte, and not, like the unfeeling Mrs. Crayton, shut our hearts to the call of humanity.

CHAPTER XXIX

We Go Forward Again

◊ ◊

The strength of Charlotte's constitution combatted against her disorder, and she began slowly to recover, though she still laboured under a violent depression of spirits: how must that depression be encreased, when, upon examining her little store, she found herself reduced to one solitary guinea, and that during her illness the attendance of an apothecary and nurse, together with many other unavoidable expences, had involved her in debt, from which she saw no method of extricating herself. As to the faint hope which she had entertained of hearing from and being relieved by her parents; it now entirely forsook her. for it was above four months since her letter was dispatched, and she had received no answer: she therefore imagined that her conduct had either entirely alienated their affection from her, or broken their hearts, and she must never more hope to receive their blessing.

Never did any human being wish for death with greater fervency or with juster cause; yet she had too just a sense of the duties of the Christian religion to attempt to put a period to her own existence. "I have but to be patient a little longer," she would cry, "and nature, fatigued and fainting, will throw off this heavy load of mortality, and I shall be released from all my sufferings."

It was one cold stormy day in the latter end of December, as Charlotte sat by a handful of fire, the low state of her finances not allowing her to replenish her stock of fuel, and prudence teaching her to be careful of what she had, when she was surprised by the entrance of a farmer's wife, who, without much ceremony, seated herself, and began this curious harangue.

"I'm come to see if as how you can pay your rent, because as how we hear Captain Montable is gone away, and it's fifty to one if he b'ant killed afore he comes back again; an then, Miss, or Ma'am, or whatever you may be, as I was saying to my husband, where are we to look for our money."

This was a stroke altogether unexpected by Charlotte: she knew so little of the ways of the world that she had never bestowed a thought on the payment for the rent of the house; she knew indeed that she owed a good deal, but this was never reckoned among the others: she was thunder-struck; she hardly knew what answer to make, yet it was absolutely necessary that she should say something; and judging of the gentleness of every female disposition by her own, she thought the best way to interest the woman in her favour would be to tell her candidly to what a situation she was reduced, and how little probability there was of her ever paying any body.

Alas poor Charlotte, how confined was her knowledge of human nature, or she would have been convinced that the only way to insure the friendship and assistance of your surrounding acquaintance is to convince them you do not require it, for when once the petrifying aspect of distress and penury appear, whose qualities, like Medusa's head, can change to stone all that look upon it; when once this Gorgon claims acquaintance with us, the phantom of friendship, that before courted our notice, will vanish into unsubstantial air, and the whole world before us appear a barren waste. Pardon me, ye dear spirits of benevolence, whose benign smiles and chearful-giving hand have strewed sweet flowers on many a thorny path through which my wayward fate forced me to pass; think not, that, in condemning the unfeeling texture of the human heart, I forget the spring from whence flow all the comforts I enjoy: oh no! I look up to you as to bright constellations, gathering new splendours from the surrounding darkness; but ah! whilst I adore the benignant rays that cheared and illumined my heart, I mourn that their influence cannot extend to all the sons and daughters of affliction.

"Indeed, Madam," said poor Charlotte in a tremulous accent, "I am at a loss what to do. Montraville placed me here, and promised to defray all my expenses: but he has forgot his promise, he has forsaken me, and I have no friend who has either power or will to relieve me. Let me hope, as you see my unhappy situation, your charity—"

"Charity," cried the woman impatiently interrupting her, "charity indeed: why, Mistress, charity begins at home, and I have seven children at home, *honest, lawful* children, and it is my duty to keep them; and do you think I will give away my property to a nasty, impudent hussey, to maintain her and her bastard; an I was saying to my husband the other day what will this world come to; honest women are nothing now-a-days, while the harlotings are set up for fine ladies, and look upon us no more nor the dirt they walk upon: but let me tell you, my fine spoken Ma'am, I must have my money; so seeing as how you can't pay it, why you must troop, and leave all your fine gimcracks and fal der ralls behind you. I don't ask for no more nor my right, and nobody shall dare for to go for to hinder me of it."

"Oh heavens," cried Charlotte, clasping her hands, "what will become of me?"

"Come on ye!" retorted the unfeeling wretch: "why go to the barracks and work for a morsel of bread; wash and mend the soldiers cloaths, an cook their victuals and not expect to live in idleness on honest people's means. Oh I wish I could see the day when all such cattle were obliged to work hard and eat little; it's only what they deserve."

"Father of mercy," cried Charlotte, "I acknowledge thy correction just; but prepare me, I beseech thee, for the portion of misery thou may'st please to lay upon me."

"Well," said the woman, "I shall go an tell my husband as how you can't pay; and so d'ye see, Ma'am, get ready to be packing away this very night, for you should not stay another night in this house, though I was sure you would lay in the street."

Charlotte bowed her head in silence; but the anguish of her heart was too great to permit her to articulate a single word.

CHAPTER XXX

◇   ◇

And what is friendship but a name,
A charm that lulls to sleep,
A shade that follows wealth and fame,
But leaves the wretch to weep.

W hen Charlotte was left to herself, she began to think what
course she must take, or to whom she could apply, to prevent
her perishing for want, or perhaps that very night falling a victim
to the inclemency of the season. After many perplexed thoughts,
she at last determined to set out for New-York, and enquire out
Mrs. Crayton, from whom she had no doubt but she should obtain
immediate relief as soon as her distress was made known; she had
no sooner formed this resolution than she resolved immediately to
put it in execution: she therefore wrote the following little billet
to Mrs. Crayton, thinking if she should have company with her it
would be better to send it in than to request to see her.

To Mrs. Crayton.

"Madam,

"When we left our native land, that dear, happy land which
now contains all that is dear to the wretched Charlotte, our prospects were the same; we both, pardon me, Madam, if I say, we
both too easily followed the impulse of our treacherous hearts, and
trusted our happiness on a tempestuous ocean, where mine has
been wrecked and lost for ever; you have been more fortunate—
you are united to a man of honour and humanity, united by the
most sacred ties, respected, esteemed, and admired, and sur-

rounded by innumerable blessings of which I am bereaved, enjoying those pleasures which have fled my bosom never to return; alas! sorrow and deep regret have taken their place. Behold me, Madam, a poor forsaken wanderer, who has no where to lay her weary head, wherewith to supply the wants of nature, or to shield her from the inclemency of the weather. To you I sue, to you I look for pity and relief. I ask not to be received as an intimate or an equal; only for charity's sweet sake receive me into your hospitable mansion, allot me the meanest apartment in it, and let me breath out my soul in prayers for your happiness; I cannot, I feel I cannot long bear up under the accumulated woes that pour in upon me; but oh! my dear Madam, for the love of heaven suffer me not to expire in the street; and when I am at peace, as soon I shall be, extend your compassion to my helpless offspring, should it please heaven that it should survive its unhappy mother. A gleam of joy breaks in on my benighted soul while I reflect that you cannot, will not refuse your protection to the heart-broken.   Charlotte."

When Charlotte had finished this letter, late as it was in the afternoon, and though the snow began to fall very fast, she tied up a few necessaries which she had prepared against her expected confinement, and terrified lest she should be again exposed to the insults of her barbarous landlady, more dreadful to her wounded spirit than either storm or darkness, she set forward for New-York.

It may be asked by those, who, in a work of this kind, love to cavil at every trifling omission, whether Charlotte did not possess any valuable of which she could have disposed, and by that means have supported herself till Mrs. Beauchamp's return, when she would have been certain of receiving ever tender attention which compassion and friendship could dictate: but let me entreat these wise, penetrating gentlemen to reflect, that when Charlotte left England, it was in such haste that there was no time to purchase any thing more than what was wanted for immediate use on the voyage, and after her arrival at New-York, Montraville's affection soon began to decline, so that her whole wardrobe consisted of only necessaries, and as to baubles, with which fond lovers often load their mistresses, she possessed not one, except a plain gold locket of small value, which contained a lock of her mother's hair, and which the greatest extremity of want could not have forced her to part with.

I hope, Sir, your prejudices are now removed in regard to the probability of my story? Oh they are. Well then, with your leave, I will proceed.

The distance from the house which our suffering heroine occupied, to New-York, was not very great, yet the snow fell so fast, and the cold so intense, that, being unable from her situation to walk quick, she found herself almost sinking with cold and fatigue before she reached the town; her garments, which were merely suitable to the summer season, being an undress robe of plain white muslin, were wet through, and a thin black cloak and bonnet, very improper habiliments for such a climate, but poorly defended her from the cold. In this situation she reached the city, and enquired of a foot soldier whom she met, the way to Colonel Crayton's.

"Bless you, my sweet lady," said the soldier with a voice and look of compassion, "I will shew you the way with all my heart; but if you are going to make a petition to Madam Crayton it is all to no purpose I assure you: if you please I will conduct you to Mr. Franklin's, though Miss Julia is married and gone now, yet the old gentleman is very good."

"Julia Franklin," said Charlotte; "is she not married to Montraville?"

"Yes," replied the soldier, "and may God bless them, for a better officer never lived, he is so good to us all; and as to Miss Julia, all the poor folk almost worshipped her."

"Gracious heaven," cried Charlotte, "is Montraville unjust then to none but me."

The soldier now shewed her Colonel Crayton's door, and, with a beating heart, she knocked for admission.

CHAPTER XXXI

Subject Continued

◇   ◇

When the door was opened, Charlotte, in a voice rendered scarcely articulate, through cold and the extreme agitation of her mind, demanded whether Mrs. Crayton was at home. The servant hesitated: he knew that his lady was engaged at a game of picquet with her dear Corydon, nor could he think she would like to be disturbed by a person whose appearance spoke her of so little consequence as Charlotte; yet there was something in her countenance that rather interested him in her favour, and he said his lady was engaged, but if she had any particular message he would deliver it.

"Take up this letter," said Charlotte: "tell her the unhappy writer of it waits in her hall for an answer."

The tremulous accent, the tearful eye, must have moved any heart not composed of adamant. The man took the letter from the poor suppliant, and hastily ascended the stair case.

"A letter, Madam," said he, presenting it to his lady: "an immediate answer is required."

Mrs. Crayton glanced her eye carelessly over the contents. "What stuff is this," cried she haughtily; "have not I told you a thousand times that I will not be plagued with beggars, and petitions from people one knows nothing about? Go tell the woman I can't do any thing in it. I'm sorry, but one can't relieve every body."

The servant bowed, and heavily returned with this chilling message to Charlotte.

"Surely," said she, "Mrs Crayton has not read my letter. Go, my good friend, pray go back to her; tell her it is Charlotte Temple who requests beneath her hospitable roof to find shelter from the inclemency of the season."

"Prithee, don't plague me, man," cried Mrs. Clayton impatiently, as the servant advanced something in behalf of the unhappy girl. "I tell you I don't know her."

"Not know me," cried Charlotte, rushing into the room, (for she had followed the man up stairs) "not know me, not remember the ruined Charlotte Temple, who, but for you, perhaps might still have been innocent, still have been happy. Oh! La Rue, this is beyond every thing I could have believed possible."

"Upon my honour, Miss," replied the unfeeling woman with the utmost effrontery, "this is a most unaccountable address: it is beyond my comprehension. John," continued she, turning to the servant, "the young woman is certainly out of her senses: do pray take her away, she terrifies me to death."

"Oh God," cried Charlotte, clasping her hands in an agony, "this is too much; what will become of me? but I will not leave you; they shall not tear me from you; here on my knees I conjure you to save me from perishing in the streets; if you really have forgot me, oh for charity's sweet sake this night let me be sheltered from the winter's piercing cold."

The kneeling figure of Charlotte in her affecting situation might have moved the heart of a stoic to compassion; but Mrs. Crayton remained inflexible. In vain did Charlotte recount the time they had known each other at Chichester, in vain mention their being in the same ship, in vain were the names of Montraville and Belcour mentioned. Mrs. Crayton could only say she was sorry for her imprudence, but could not think of having her own reputation endangered by encouraging a woman of that kind in her own house, besides she did not know what trouble and expense she might bring upon her husband by giving shelter to a woman in her situation.

"I can at least die here," said Charlotte, "I feel I cannot long survive this dreadful conflict. Father of mercy, here let me finish my existence." Her agonizing sensations overpowered her, and she fell senseless on the floor.

"Take her away," said Mrs. Crayton, "she will really frighten me into hysterics; take her away I say this instant."

"And where must I take the poor creature?" said the servant with a voice and look of compassion.

"Any where," cried she hastily, "only don't let me ever see her again. I declare she has flurried me so I shan't be myself again this fortnight."

John, assisted by his fellow-servant, raised and carried her down stairs. "Poor soul," said he, "you shall not lay in the street this night. I have a bed and a poor little hovel, where my wife and her little ones rest them, but they shall watch to night, and you shall be sheltered from danger." They placed her in a chair; and the benevolent man, assisted by one of his comrades, carried her to the place where his wife and children lived. A surgeon was sent for: he bled her, she gave signs of returning life, and before the dawn gave birth to a female infant. After this event she lay for some hours in a kind of stupor; and if at any time she spoke, it was with a quickness and incoherence that plainly evinced the total deprivation of her reason.

CHAPTER XXXII

Reasons Why and Wherefore

◊   ◊

The reader of sensibility may perhaps be astonished to find Mrs. Crayton could so positively deny any knowledge of Charlotte; it is therefore but just that her conduct should in some measure be accounted for. She had ever been fully sensible of the superiority of Charlotte's sense and virtue; she was conscious that she had never swerved from rectitude, had it not been for her bad precepts and worse example. These were things as yet unknown to her husband, and she wished not to have that part of her conduct exposed to him, as she had great reason to fear she had already lost considerable part of that power she once maintained over him. She trembled whilst Charlotte was in the house, lest the Colonel should return; she perfectly well remembered how much he seemed interested in her favour whilst on their passage from England, and made no doubt, but, should he see her in her present distress, he would offer her an asylum, and protect her to the utmost of his power. In that case she feared the unguarded nature of Charlotte might discover to the Colonel the part she had taken in the unhappy girl's elopement, and she well knew the contrast between her own and Charlotte's conduct would make the former appear in no very respectable light. Had she reflected properly, she would have afforded the poor girl protection; and by enjoining her silence, ensured it by acts of repeated kindness; but vice in general blinds its votaries, and they discover their real characters to the world when they are most studious to preserve appearances.

Just so it happened with Mrs. Crayton: her servants made no scruple of mentioning the cruel conduct of their lady to a poor distressed lunatic who claimed her protection; every one joined in reprobating her inhumanity; nay even Corydon thought she might at least have ordered her to be taken care of, but he dare not even hint it to her, for he lived but in her smiles, and drew from her lavish fondness large sums to support an extravagance to which the state of his own finances was very inadequate; it cannot therefore be supposed that he wished Mrs. Crayton to be very liberal in her bounty to the afflicted suppliant; yet vice had not so entirely seared over his heart, but the sorrows of Charlotte could find a vulnerable part.

Charlotte had now been three days with her humane preservers, but she was totally insensible of everything: she raved incessantly for Montraville and her father: she was not conscious of being a mother, nor took the least notice of her child except to ask whose it was, and why it was not carried to its parents.

"Oh," said she one day, starting up on hearing the infant cry, "why, why will you keep that child here; I am sure you would not if you knew how hard it was for a mother to be parted from her infant: it is like tearing the cords of life asunder. Oh could you see the horrid sight which I now behold—there—there stands my dear mother, her poor bosom bleeding at every vein, her gentle, affectionate heart torn in a thousand pieces, and all for the loss of a ruined, ungrateful child. Save me—save me—from her frown. I dare not—indeed I dare not speak to her."

Such were the dreadful images that haunted her distracted mind, and nature was sinking fast under the dreadful malady which medicine had no power to remove. The surgeon who attended her was a humane man; he exerted his utmost abilities to save her, but he saw she was in want of many necessaries and comforts, which the poverty of her hospitable host rendered him unable to provide: he therefore determined to make her situation known to some of the officers' ladies, and endeavour to make a collection for her relief.

When he returned home, after making this resolution, he found a message from Mrs. Beauchamp, who had just arrived from Rhode-Island, requesting he would call and see one of her children, who was very unwell. "I do not know," said he, as he was hastening to obey the summons, "I do not know a woman to whom I could apply with more hope of success than Mrs. Beauchamp. I will endeavour to interest her in this poor girl's behalf; she wants the soothing balm of friendly consolation: we may perhaps save her; we will try at least."

"And where is she," cried Mrs. Beauchamp when he had prescribed something for the child, and told his little pathetic tale, "where is she, Sir? we will go to her immediately. Heaven forbid that I should be deaf to the calls of humanity. Come we will go this instant." Then seizing the doctor's arm, they sought the habitation that contained the dying Charlotte.

CHAPTER XXXIII

Which People Void of Feeling
Need Not Read

◊   ◊

When Mrs. Beauchamp entered the apartment of the poor
sufferer, she started back with horror. On a wretched bed,
without hangings and but poorly supplied with covering, lay the
emaciated figure of what still retained the semblance of a lovely
woman, though sickness had so altered her features that Mrs.
Beauchamp had not the least recollection of her person. In one
corner of the room stood a woman washing, and, shivering over a
small fire, two healthy but half naked children; the infant was
asleep beside its mother, and, on a chair by the bed side, stood a
porrenger and wooden spoon, containing a little gruel, and a tea-
cup with about two spoonfulls of wine in it. Mrs. Beauchamp had
never before beheld such a scene of poverty; she shuddered involuntarily, and exclaiming—"heaven preserve us!" leaned on the
back of a chair ready to sink to the earth. The doctor repented
having so precipitately brought her into this affecting scene; but
there was no time for apologies: Charlotte caught the sound of her
voice, and starting almost out of bed, exclaimed—"Angel of peace
and mercy, art thou come to deliver me? Oh, I know you are, for
whenever you was near me I felt eased of half my sorrows; but you
don't know me, nor can I, with all the recollection I am mistress
of, remember your name just now, but I know that benevolent

countenance, and the softness of that voice which has so often comforted the wretched Charlotte."

Mrs. Beauchamp had, during the time Charlotte was speaking, seated herself on the bed and taken one of her hands; she looked at her attentively, and at the name of Charlotte she perfectly conceived the whole shocking affair. A faint sickness came over her. "Gracious heaven," said she, "is this possible?" and bursting into tears, she reclined the burning head of Charlotte on her own bosom; and folding her arms about her, wept over her in silence. "Oh," said Charlotte, "you are very good to weep thus for me: it is a long time since I shed a tear for myself: my head and heart are both on fire, but these tears of your's seem to cool and refresh it. Oh now I remember you said you would send a letter to my poor father: do you think he ever received it? or perhaps you have brought me an answer: why don't you speak, Madam? Does he say I may go home? Well he is very good; I shall soon be ready."

She then made an effort to get out of bed; but being prevented, her frenzy again returned, and she raved with the greatest wildness and incoherence. Mrs. Beauchamp, finding it was impossible for her to be removed, contented herself with ordering the apartment to be made more comfortable, and procuring a proper nurse for both mother and child; and having learnt the particulars of Charlotte's fruitless application to Mrs. Crayton from honest John, she amply rewarded him for his benevolence, and returned home with a heart oppressed with many painful sensations, but yet rendered easy by the reflexion that she had performed her duty towards a distressed fellow-creature.

Early the next morning she again visited Charlotte, and found her tolerably composed; she called her by name, thanked her for her goodness, and when her child was brought to her, pressed it in her arms, wept over it, and called it the offspring of disobedience. Mrs. Beauchamp was delighted to see her so much amended, and began to hope she might recover, and, spite of her former errors, become an useful and respectable member of society; but the arrival of the doctor put an end to these delusive hopes: he said nature was making her last effort, and a few hours would most probably consign the unhappy girl to her kindred dust.

Being asked how she found herself, she replied—"Why better, much better, doctor. I hope now I have but little more to suffer. I had last night a few hours sleep, and when I awoke recovered the full power of recollection. I am quite sensible of my weakness; I feel I have but little longer to combat with the shafts of affliction. I have an humble confidence in the mercy of him who died to save the world, and trust that my sufferings in this state of mortality, joined to my unfeigned repentance, through his mercy, have blotted my offences from the sight of my offended maker. I have but one care—my poor infant! Father of mercy," continued she, raising her eyes, "of thy infinite goodness, grant that the sins of the parent be not visited on the unoffending child. May those who taught me to despise thy laws be forgiven; lay not my offences to their charge, I beseech thee; and oh! shower the choicest of thy blessings on those whose pity has soothed the afflicted heart, and made easy even the bed of pain and sickness."

She was exhausted by this fervent address to the throne of mercy, and though her lips still moved her voice became inarticulate: she lay for some time as it were in a doze, and then recovering, faintly pressed Mrs. Beauchamp's hand, and requested that a clergyman might be sent for.

On his arrival she joined fervently in the pious office, frequently mentioning her ingratitude to her parents as what lay most heavy at her heart. When she had performed the last solemn duty, and was preparing to lie down, a little bustle on the outside door occasioned Mrs. Beauchamp to open it, and enquire the cause. A man in appearance about forty, presented himself, and asked for Mrs. Beauchamp.

"That is my name, Sir," said she.

"Oh then, my dear Madam," cried he, "tell me where I may find my poor, ruined, but repentant child."

Mrs. Beauchamp was surprised and affected; she knew not what to say; she foresaw the agony this interview would occasion Mr. Temple, who had just arrived in search of his Charlotte, and yet was sensible that the pardon and blessing of her father would soften even the agonies of death to the daughter.

She hesitated. "Tell me, Madam," cried he wildly, "tell me, I beseech thee, does she live? shall I see my darling once again? Perhaps she is in this house. Lead, lead me to her, that I may bless her, and then lie down and die."

The ardent manner in which he uttered these words occasioned him to raise his voice. It caught the ear of Charlotte: she knew the beloved sound: and uttering a loud shriek, she sprang forward as Mr. Temple entered the room. "My adored father." "My long lost child." Nature could support no more, and they both sunk lifeless into the arms of the attendants.

Charlotte was again put into bed, and a few moments restored Mr. Temple: but to describe the agony of his sufferings is past the power of any one, who, though they may readily conceive, cannot delineate the dreadful scene. Every eye gave testimony of what each heart felt—but all were silent.

When Charlotte recovered, she found herself supported in her father's arms. She cast on him a most expressive look, but was unable to speak. A reviving cordial was administered. She then asked, in a low voice, for her child: it was brought to her: she put it in her father's arms. "Protect her," said she, 'and bless your dying—"

Unable to finish the sentence, she sunk back on her pillow: her countenance was serenely composed; she regarded her father as he pressed the infant to his breast with a steadfast look; a sudden beam of joy passed across her languid features, she raised her eyes to heaven—and then closed them for ever.

CHAPTER XXXIV

Retribution

◇   ◇

In the meantime Montraville having received orders to return to New-York, arrived, and having still some remains of compassionate tenderness for the woman whom he regarded as brought to shame by himself, he went out in search of Belcour, to enquire whether she was safe, and whether the child lived. He found him immersed in dissipation, and could gain no other intelligence than that Charlotte had left him, and that he knew not what was become of her.

"I cannot believe it possible," said Montraville, "that a mind once so pure as Charlotte Temple's, should so suddenly become the mansion of vice. Beware, Belcour," continued he, "beware if you have dared to behave either unjust or dishonourably to that poor girl, your life shall pay the forfeit:—I will revenge her cause."

He immediately went into the country, to the house where he had left Charlotte. It was desolate. After much enquiry he at length found the servant girl who had lived with her. From her he learnt the misery Charlotte had endured from the complicated evils of illness, poverty, and a broken heart, and that she had set out on foot for New-York, on a cold winter's evening; but she could inform him no further.

Tortured almost to madness by this shocking account, he returned to the city, but, before he reached it, the evening was drawing to a close. In entering the town he was obliged to pass several little huts, the residence of poor women who supported themselves by washing the cloaths of the officers and soldiers. It was nearly dark: he heard from a neighbouring steeple a solemn toll that seemed to say some poor mortal was going to their last mansion: the sound struck on the heart of Montraville, and he involuntarily stopped, when, from one of the houses, he saw the appearance of a funeral. Almost unknowing what he did, he followed at a small distance; and as they let the coffin into the grave, he enquired of a soldier who stood by, and had just brushed off a tear that did honour to his heart, who it was that was just buried. "An please your honour," said the man, " 'tis a poor girl that was brought from her friends by a cruel man, who left her when she was big with child, and married another.' Montraville stood motionless, and the man proceeded—"I met her myself not a fortnight since one night all wet and cold in the streets; she went to Madam Crayton's, but she would not take her in, and so the poor thing went raving mad." Montraville could bear no more; he struck his hands against his forehead with violence; and exclaiming "poor murdered Charlotte!" ran with precipitation towards the place where they were heaping the earth on her remains. "Hold, hold, one moment," said he. "Close not the grave of the injured Charlotte Temple till I have taken vengeance on her murderer."

"Rash young man," said Mr. Temple, "who are thou that thus disturbest the last mournful rites of the dead, and rudely breakest in upon the grief of an afflicted father."

"If thou art the father of Charlotte Temple," said he, gazing at him with mingled horror and amazement—"if thou art her father— I am Montraville." Then falling on his knees, he continued—"Here is my bosom. I bare it to receive the stroke I merit. Strike—strike now, and save me from the misery of reflexion."

"Alas!" said Mr. Temple, "if thou wert the seducer of my child, thy own reflexions be thy punishment. I wrest not the power from the hand of omnipotence. Look on that little heap of earth, there hast thou buried the only joy of a fond father. Look at it often; and may thy heart feel such true sorrow as shall merit the mercy of heaven." He turned from him; and Montraville starting up from the ground, where he had thrown himself, and at that instant remembering the perfidy of Belcour, flew like lightning to his lodgings. Belcour was intoxicated; Montraville impetuous: they fought, and the sword of the latter entered the heart of his adversary. He fell, and expired almost instantly. Montraville had received a slight wound; and overcome with the agitation of his mind and loss of blood, was carried in a state of insensibility to his distracted wife. A dangerous illness and obstinate delirium ensued, during which he raved incessantly for Charlotte: but a strong constitution, and the tender assiduities of Julia, in time overcame the disorder. He recovered; but to the end of his life was subject to severe fits of melancholy, and while he remained at New-York frequently retired to the church-yard, where he would weep over the grave, and regret the untimely fate of the lovely Charlotte Temple.

CHAPTER XXXV

Conclusion

◊　　◊

Shortly after the interment of his daughter, Mr. Temple, with his dear little charge and her nurse, set forward for England. It would be impossible to do justice to the meeting scene between him, his Lucy, and her aged father. Every heart of sensibility can easily conceive their feelings. After the first tumult of grief was subsided, Mrs. Temple gave up the chief of her time to her grand-child, and as she grew up and improved, began to almost fancy she again possessed her Charlotte.

It was about ten years after these painful events, that Mr. and Mrs. Temple, having buried their father, were obliged to come to London on particular business, and brought the little Lucy with them. They had been walking one evening, when on their return they found a poor wretch sitting on the steps of the door. She attempted to rise as they approached, but from extreme weakness was unable, and after several fruitless efforts fell back in a fit. Mr. Temple was not one of those men who stand to consider whether by assisting an object in distress they shall not inconvenience them-selves, but instigated by the impulse of a noble feeling heart, im-mediately ordered her to be carried into the house, and proper restoratives applied.

She soon recovered; and fixing her eyes on Mrs. Temple, cried— "You know not, Madam, what you do; you know not whom you are relieving, or you would curse me in the bitterness of your heart.

Come not near me, Madam, I shall contaminate you. I am the viper that stung your peace. I am the woman who turned the poor Charlotte out to perish in the street. Heaven have mercy! I see her now," continued she looking at Lucy; "such, such was the fair bud of innocence that my vile arts blasted ere it was half blown."

It was in vain that Mr. and Mrs. Temple intreated her to be composed and to take some refreshment. She only drank half a glass of wine; and then told them that she had been separated from her husband seven years, the chief of which she had passed in riot, dissipation, and vice, till, overtaken by poverty and sickness, she had been reduced to part with every valuable, and thought only of ending her life in a prison; when a benevolent friend paid her debts and released her; but that her illness encreasing, she had no possible means of supporting herself, and her friends were weary of relieving her. "I have fasted," said she, "two days, and last night lay my aching head on the cold pavement: indeed it was but just that I should experience those miseries myself which I had unfeelingly inflicted on others."

Greatly as Mr. Temple had reason to detest Mrs. Crayton, he could not behold her in this distress without some emotions of pity. He gave her shelter that night beneath his hospitable roof, and the next day got her admission into an hospital; where having lingered a few weeks, she died, a striking example that vice, however prosperous in the beginning, in the end leads only to misery and shame.

FINIS

Lucy Temple

CHAPTER I

False Pride and
Unsophisticated Innocence

◇   ◇

"What are you doing there Lucy?" said Mrs. Cavendish to a lovely girl, about fifteen years old. She was kneeling at the feet of an old man sitting just within the door of a small thatched cottage situated about five miles from Southampton on the coast of Hampshire. "What are you doing there child?" said she, in rather a sharp tone, repeating her question.

"Binding up sergeant Blandford's leg ma'am," said the kind hearted young creature, looking up in the face of the person who spoke to her. At the same time, rising on one knee she rested the lame limb on a stool on which was a soft cushion which this child of benevolence had provided for the old soldier.

"And was there no one but you Miss Blakeney who could perform such an office? You demean yourself strangely." "I did not think it was any degradation," replied Lucy, "to perform an act of kindness to a fellow creature, but I have done now," continued she rising, "and will walk home with you ma'am if you please." She then wished the sergeant a good night, and tying on her bonnet which had been thrown on the floor during her employment, she took Mrs. Cavendish's arm, and they proceeded to the house of the Rector of the village.

"There! Mr. Matthews," exclaimed the lady on entering the

parlour, "there! I have brought home Miss Blakeney, and where do you think I found her? and how employed?"

"Where you found her," replied Mr. Matthews, smiling, "I will not pretend to say, for she is a sad rambler; but I dare be bound that you did not find her either foolishly or improperly employed."

"I found her in old Blandford's cottage, swathing up his lame leg." "And how my good madam," inquired Mr. Matthews, "could innocence be better employed than in administering to the comforts of the defender of his country?"

"Well, well, you always think her right, but we shall hear what my sister says to it. Mrs. Matthews, do you approve of a young lady of rank and fortune making herself familiar with all the beggars and low people in the place?"

"By no means," said the stately Mrs. Matthews, "and I am astonished that Miss Blakeney has not a higher sense of propriety and her own consequence."

"Dear me, ma'm," interrupted Lucy, "it was to make myself of consequence that I did it; for Lady Mary, here at home, says I am nobody, an insignificant Miss Mushroom, but sergeant Blandford calls me his guardian angel, his comforter; and I am sure those are titles of consequence."

"Bless me," said Mrs. Cavendish, "what plebeian ideas the girl has imbibed! It is lucky for you child, that you were so early removed from those people."

"I hope madam," replied Lucy, "you do not mean to say that it was fortunate for me that I was so early deprived of the protection of my dear grandfather? Alas! it was a heavy day for me; he taught me that the only way to become of real consequence is to be useful to my fellow creatures." Lucy put her hand before her eyes to hide the tears she could not restrain, and courtesying respectfully to Mr. Matthews, his wife and sister, she left the room.

"Well, I protest sister," said Mrs. Cavendish, "that is the most extraordinary girl I ever knew; with a vast number of low ideas and habits, she can sometimes assume the *hauteur* and air of a dutchess. In what a respectful yet independent manner she went out of the room! I must repeat she is a most extraordinary girl."

Mrs. Matthews was too much irritated to reply with calmness; she therefore wisely continued silent. Mr. Matthews was silent from a different cause, and supper being soon after announced, the whole family went into the parlour; Lucy had dried her tears, and with a placid countenance seated herself by her reverend friend, Mr. Matthews. "*You*, I hope, are not angry with me, Sir?" said she with peculiar emphasis. "No my child," he replied, pressing the hand she had laid upon his arm, "No, I am not angry, but my little Lucy must remember that she is now advancing towards womanhood, and that it is not always safe, nor perfectly proper, to be rambling about in the dusk of the evening without a companion."

"Then if you say so sir, I will never do it again; but indeed you do not know how happy my visits make old Mr. Blandford; you know, sir, he is very poor; so Lady Mary would not go with me if I asked her; and he is very lame, so if Aura went with me, she is such a mad-cap, perhaps she might laugh at him; besides, when I sometimes ask Mrs. Matthews to let her walk with me, she has something for her to do, and cannot spare her."

"Well, my dear," said the kind hearted old gentleman, "when you want to visit him again ask me to go with you." "Oh! you are the best old man in the world," cried Lucy, as rising she put her arms round his neck and kissed him. "There now, there is a specimen of low breeding," said Mrs. Cavendish, "you ought to know, Miss Blakeney, that nothing can be more rude than to call a person old." "I did not mean to offend," said Lucy. "No! I am sure you did not," replied Mr. Matthews, "and so let us eat our supper; for when a man or woman, sister, is turned of sixty they may be termed old without much exaggeration, or the smallest breach of politeness."

But the reader will perhaps like to be introduced to the several individuals who compose this family.

CHAPTER II

The Little Heiress, and the Master of the Mansion

◇　　◇

Lucy Blakeney had from her earliest infancy been under the protection of her maternal grandfather; her mother had ushered her into life at the expense of her own, and captain Blakeney of the navy having been her godfather, she was baptized by the name of Blakeney in addition to her own family name. Captain Blakeney was the intimate friend of her grandfather; he had loved her mother as his own child, and dying a bachelor when Lucy was ten years old, he left her the whole of the property he had acquired during the war which had given to the United States of America, rank and consequence among the nations of the earth; and during which period he had been fortunate in taking prizes, so that at the time of his death, his property amounted to more than twenty thousand pounds sterling. This he bequeathed to his little favourite on condition that she took the name and bore the arms of Blakeney; indeed, she had never been called by any other name, but the will required that the assumption should be legally authorized, and a further condition was that whoever married her should change his own family name to that of Blakeney, but on a failure of this, the original sum was to go to increase the pensions of the widows of officers of the navy dying in actual service, Lucy only retaining the interest which might have accumulated during her minority.

About two years after this rich bequest, Lucy literally became an orphan by the death of both her grandparents within a few months of each other. She inherited from her grandfather a handsome patrimony, enough to support and educate her in a very superior style, without infringing on the bequest of captain Blakeney, the interest of which yearly accumulating would make her by the time she was twenty-one a splendid heiress.

The reverend Mr. Matthews had lived in habits of intimacy with both the grandfather of Lucy and captain Blakeney, though considerably younger than either; he was nominated her guardian in conjunction with Sir Robert Ainslie, a banker in London, a man of strict probity, to whom the management of her fortune was intrusted.

To Mr. Matthews the care of her person was consigned; he had promised her grandfather that she should reside constantly in his family, and under his eye receive instruction in the accomplishments becoming the rank she would most probably fill in society from the best masters; whilst the cultivation of her mental powers, the formation of her moral and religious character, and the correction of those erring propensities which are the sad inheritance of all the sons and daughters of Adam, he solemnly promised should be his own peculiar care.

Mr. Matthews was, what every minister of the Gospel should be, the profound scholar, the finished gentleman, and the sincere, devout christian. Plain and unaffected in his address to his parishioners, on the sabbath day, or any day set apart for devotional exercises, he at all other time exemplified in his own conduct the piety and pure morality he had from the pulpit forcibly recommended to others. Liberal as far as his circumstances would allow, without ostentation; strictly economical without meanness; conscientiously pious without bigotry or intolerance; mild in his temper, meek and gentle in his demeanour, he kept his eye steadily fixed on his divine master, and in perfect humility of spirit endeavoured as far as human nature permits, to tread in his steps.

Alfred Matthews was the youngest son of a younger branch of

an honourable but reduced family. He received his early education at Eton, on the foundation, from whence he removed to Cambridge, where he finished his studies, and received the honours of the university; his moral character, steady deportment, and literary abilities had raised him so high in the esteem of the heads of the college, that he was recommended as private tutor, and afterwards became the travelling companion to the young Earl of Hartford and his brother, Lord John Milcombe. Returning from this tour, he for a considerable time became stationary as domestic chaplain in the family of the Earl. This nobleman had two sisters, the children of his mother by a former marriage, both by several years his seniors. The elder, Philippa, was of a serious cast, accomplished, sensible, well informed, pleasing in her person, and engaging in her manners. Constantia, the younger of the two, had been celebrated for her beauty, she was stately, somewhat affected, and very dictatorial. They were both highly tinctured with family pride, thinking the name of Cavendish might rank almost with royalty itself; but withal so strongly attached to each other, that whatever one resolved to do or say, the other upheld as unquestionably right.

To both these ladies Mr. Matthews was an acceptable companion, and from the society of both he reaped the most unaffected pleasure. He admired their talents, and esteemed their virtues; but his heart felt no warmer sentiment till from several concurring circumstances he could not but perceive that the amiable Philippa envinced a tenderer attachment than her sister. On some subjects she could never converse with him without hesitation and blushes, while Constantia was easy and unembarrassed upon all topics. This discovery awakened his gratitude, but honour told him that the sister of his patron was in too elevated a station for him to hope to obtain her brother's consent to their union; he therefore requested permission to retire from the family.

"I am sorry to lose you from our family circle Mr. Matthews," said the Earl, when he mentioned his desire; "but it is natural that you should wish to have a fire side of your own, and it is probable that you may also wish for a companion to make that fire side cheerful. I must beg you to accept the Rectory of L— which has lately become vacant and is in my gift, till something better can be offered " Every thing being arranged for his leaving the family, it was mentioned the next evening at supper. Philippa felt her colour vary, but she neither looked up nor spoke; Constantia, turning towards him, with vivacity, inquired, "How long he had taken the whim of keeping bachelor's hall, though I beg your pardon for the suggestion," said she, "perhaps some fair lady"—here she stopped, for Philippa's agitation was evident, and Constantia perceived that her brother noticed it.

When the ladies had retired, the Earl suddenly addressed his friend. "If I am not very much mistaken, Mr. Matthews, one of my sisters would have no objection to break in upon your bachelor scheme. Come, be candid, is the inclination mutual?" "I hope, my lord," replied Mr. Matthews, "that you do not suspect me of the presumption."—"I see no presumption in it my friend," rejoined the Earl; "your family, your education, your talents, set you upon an equality with any woman, and though Philippa is not rich, yet her fortune and your income from the Rectory will supply the comforts, conveniences, and many of the elegances of life."

The conversation continued till the hour of repose, when after taking counsel of his pillow, Mr. Matthews resolved to solicit the favour of Miss Cavendish, and proved a successful wooer—a few months after, he became master of the Rectory—had a fire side of his own, and an amiable companion to render that fire side cheerful.

In the course of twenty years many changes had taken place: the Earl of Hartford had married a beautiful, but very dissipated woman, who, though she brought him but a very small fortune, knew extremely well how to make use of his, and diffuse its benefits in a most elegant and fashionable style. Her profusion knew no bounds, and, the Earl being taken off by a rapid fever, his affairs were found in so embarrassed a state that his sisters' fortunes, which had never been paid, though they had regularly received the interest, were reduced to less than half their original value, which was twenty thousand pounds. With this comparatively small portion, Mrs. Matthews and Mrs. Constantia Cavendish were obliged to be content.

Mr. Matthews continued Rector of L—, but no change of circumstances could lead him to accept a plurality of livings. It was a point of conscience with him to be paid for no more duty than he was able to perform himself; and as he was not able to allow a curate a liberal stipend, he employed none. When Mrs. Constantia argued with him on the subject, as she sometimes would, and wondered that he would perform all offices of the Rectorship himself, when he might have a curate who would think himself well paid by fifty pounds a year, and who would take the most troublesome part upon himself. "I should be sorry sister," he would reply "to consider any part of my duty a trouble, and what right have I to expect another to do for fifty pounds, what I am paid five hundred for doing? Every clergyman is, or should be a gentleman, and I think it highly disgraceful for one minister of the gospel to be lolling on velvet cushions, rolling in his carriage, and faring sumptuously every day, while many, very many of his poor brethren, labourers in the same vineyard, bowed with poverty, burthened with large families, would, like Lazarus, be glad to feed on the crumbs that fall from the rich man's table."

But Mr. Matthews was an old fashioned person, and perhaps will not be thought very entertaining, so I will bring forward the young ladies.

CHAPTER III

The Three Orphans

◊　◊

We have already announced Lucy Blakeney, and if what has been said, does not give a competent idea of her character, we must leave it to time to develop; as to her person, it was of the middle size, perfectly well proportioned, and her figure and limbs had that roundness, which, in the eye of an artist, constitutes beauty. Her complexion was rather fair than dark, her eyes open, large, full hazel, her hair light brown, and her face animated with the glow of health and the smile of good humour

Lady Mary Lumly had lost her mother a few years previous to the commencement of our story. She was an only child and had been indulged to a degree of criminality by this doatingly fond but weak mother, so that she had reached her sixteenth year without having had one idea impressed upon either head or heart that could in the least qualify her for rational society, or indeed for any society, but such as her fancy had created from an indiscriminate perusal of every work of fiction that issued from the press. Her father died when she was an infant; his estates which had never been adequate to his expenses, passed with the title to a male branch of the family, her mother retired to her jointure house in Lancashire. Ill health secluded her from company, and finding her dear Mary averse from study, she sought in a governess for her daughter, more an easy companion for herself, than a conscientious able instructress for her child. The common elements of education, reading, writing, and English grammar, a little dancing, a little music, and a trifling knowledge of the French language constituted the whole of her accomplishments when at the death of her mother, the guardian to whom the care of her little fortune had been intrusted, entreated Mrs. Matthews to receive her into her family. There was some relationship in the case, and Mrs. Cavendish thinking, that with her romantic ideas, and uninformed mind, a boarding school, such as her income could afford, would not be a proper asylum for her, prevailed on her sister to accede to the proposal.

When scarcely past the age of childhood or indeed infancy, she had been allowed to sit beside her mother, while the tale of misfortune, of love or folly, was read aloud by the governess, and being possessed of a quick apprehension, strong sensibility, and a fertile imagination, she peopled the world, to which she was in effect a stranger, with lords and ladies, distressed beauties, and adoring lovers, to the absolute exclusion of every natural character, every rational idea, and truly moral or christian like feeling. Wealth and titles, which were sure to be heaped on the hero or heroine of the tale at last, she considered as the *ultimatum* of all sublunary good. Her mother had been a woman of high rank, but small fortune; she had therefore amongst other weak prejudices imbibed a strong predilection in favour of ancient nobility, and not to have a particle of noble blood flowing through one's veins was, in her opinion, to be quite insignificant.

This orphan of quality was as handsome as flaxen hair, light eyebrows, fair skin, blooming cheeks, and large glossy blue eyes could make her. The features of her face were perfectly regular but there was no expression in them; her smile was the smile of innocence, but it was also the smile of vacancy. She was tall, her limbs were long and her figure flat and lean; yet she thought herself a perfect model for a statuary. Her temper was naturally good, but the overweening pride and morbid sensibility, which were the fruits of the imprudent system of her education, rendered her quick to take offence where no offence was meant, and not unfrequently bathed her in tears, without any real cause. At the period when we introduced her to our readers, she was nearly seventeen years old, and had been under the care of Mr. Matthews, for the last four years.

Aura Melville completed the trio of fair orphans. Aura was the only child of a poor clergyman to whom Mr. Matthews had been, during a long and painful illness, an undeviating friend; she was ten years old when death released her father from a state of suffering—her mother had been dead several years previous to this event.

It was an evening towards the end of July, the pale light of a moon just entered on its second quarter shone faintly into the chamber of the feeble invalid, a chamber to which he had been confined for more than eight months; the casement was open and the evening breeze passing through the blooming jessamine that climbed the thatch of the humble cottage, wafted its refreshing perfume to cool the hectic cheek of the almost expiring Melville. He was seated in an easy chair, Mr. Matthews by his side, and the little Aura on a cushion at his feet. "Look, my own papa," said she, "how beautifully the moon shines; does not this cool breeze make you feel better? I love to look at the moon when it is new," continued she, "I do not know why, but it makes me feel so pleasantly, and yet sometimes I feel as if I could cry; and I say to myself what a good God our God is, to give us such a beautiful light to make our nights pleasant and cheerful, that, without it, are so dark and gloomy. Oh! my own dear papa, if it would but please our good God to make you well!" Melville pressed her hand, Mr. Matthews felt the drop of sensibility rise to his eye; but neither of them spoke.

The child, finding both remained silent, continued. "I hope you will be better, a great deal better, before next new moon." "I shall be well, quite well, my darling, in a very little time," said her father, "for before this moon is at the full, I shall be at rest." "You will rest a good deal before that, I hope,' said she with tender simplicity, then pausing a moment, she sprang up, and throwing her arms round his neck, she exclaimed, "Ah! I understand you now: Oh, my own dear papa! what will become of Aura! Oh, my good God, if it please you to let me die with my papa! for when he is gone there will be no one to love or care for his poor Aura." Her sobs impeded farther utterance—Melville had clasped the interesting child in his arms, his head sunk on her shoulder, her cheek rested on his. Mr. Matthews, fearing this tender scene would be too much for his debilitated frame, went towards them and endeavoured to withdraw her from his embrace. At the slightest effort, his arms relaxed their hold, his head was raised from her shoulder, but instantly falling back against the chair, Mr. Matthews, shocked to the very soul, perceived that Aura was an orphan.

The poor child's anguish, when she discovered the truth, is not to be described. "She shall never want a protector," said he mentally, as he was leading her from the house of death to his own mansion.

"Philippa," said he, presenting Aura to his wife, "Providence has sent us a daughter; be a mother to her my dear companion, love her, correct her, teach her to be like yourself, she will then be most estimable."

Mrs. Matthews with all her family pride, possessed a kind and feeling heart; that heart loved most tenderly Alfred Matthews,—could she do otherwise than comply with his request? She took the poor girl to her bosom, and though she experienced not the most tender affection, yet Aura Melville found in her all the care and solicitude of a mother.

Her father had laid good foundation in her innocent mind, and Mr. Matthews carefully completed the education he had begun, and at the age of nineteen, the period when first she appears in our pages, she was a pleasing well informed young woman; highly polished in her manners, yet without one showy accomplishment. She knew enough of music to enjoy and understand its simple beauties, but she performed on no instrument. She moved gracefully, and could, if called upon, join a cotillion or contra dance, without distressing others; her understanding was of the highest order, and so well cultivated that she could converse with sense and propriety on almost any subject. Yet unobtrusive, modest and humble, she was silent and retired, unless called forth by the voice of kindness and encouragement. She was beloved in the family; industrious, discreet, cheerful, good humoured, grateful to her benefactors, and contented with her lot; she won the regard and without exacting it, gained the respect of all who knew her.

CHAPTER IV

Romance, Piety, Sensibility

◇　◇

L ucy, after the gentle reproof she received from Mr. Matthews, was careful not to go out in the evening without a companion; she frequently visited the cottages of the poor class of industrious peasants, and as her allowance for clothes and pocket money was liberal and her habits by no means expensive, she had many opportunities of relieving the distresses of some, and adding to the comforts of others. Sometimes she would tempt Lady Mary to ramble with her, but that young lady but little understood the common incidents, and necessities of life, and even had she comprehended them ever so well, she was so thoughtless in her expenditure on dress and trifles, that she seldom had any thing to bestow. Aura Melville was therefore her usual associate and adviser in these visits of charity. Her bosom sympathized in their sufferings, and her judgment suggested the relief likely to be of most benefit.

One evening Lady Mary had been walking with a young lady in the neighbourhood, whose tastes and feelings resembled her own, when, just as the family were preparing to take their tea, she rushed into the parlour and in a flood of tears exclaimed, "Oh, my dear sir, my kind Mr. Matthews, if you do not help me I shall lose my senses." "How, my dear?" said he, approaching the seat on which she had thrown herself in an attitude of the utmost distress. "Oh, sir," said she, sobbing, "I must have five guineas directly, for I wanted so many things when you paid me my last quarter's allowance, that I have not a guinea left." "I am sorry for that," replied Mr. Matthews, "for you know that it will be six weeks before another payment is due." "Oh yes, I know that: but I thought you would be so good as to lend it to me on this very, very urgent occasion!" "And pray what may the very, very urgent occasion be?" asked he smiling, and placing a chair near the tea table, he motioned with his hand for her to draw nigh and partake the social meal, for which the rest of the family were now waiting

"I cannot eat, indeed I cannot, sir," she replied with an hysterical sob, "I can do nothing till you comply with my request."

"That I certainly shall not do at present, child. I must understand for what this sum is required, and how you mean to dispose of it. Five guineas, Lady Mary, is a considerable sum; it should not be hastily or unadvisedly lavished away. It might rescue many suffering individuals from absolute want."

"Yes, sir, it is for that I want it, I know you will let me have it." "I am not quite so sure about that. But come, Mary Lumly," for so the good man was wont to call her when he was pleased with her, "come, draw nigh and take your tea, after which you shall tell your story and to-morrow morning we will see what can be done."

"To-morrow! sir, to-morrow!" exclaimed she wildly, "to-morrow, it may be too late, they are suffering the extremity of want, and are you so cold hearted as to talk of to-morrow?"

Miss Blakeney and Aura Melville exchanged looks with each other. Mr. Matthews sat down and began his tea. "You must permit me to tell you, Lady Mary Lumly," said Mrs. Cavendish, in her stately manner, "that this is very unbecoming behaviour; you call it no doubt sensibility, but you give it too dignified a name. It is an affectation of fine feeling, it arises more from a wish to display your own humanity, than from any genuine sympathy. The heart has little to do with it. You have spoken rudely to my brother

Matthews; he, worthy man, knows what true sensibility is, and is actuated by its dictates, though you, disrespectful girl, have called him cold hearted."

Resentment at being spoken to, in so plain a style, soon dried Lady Mary's tears. She seated herself at the tea table, took her cup, played with her spoon, poured the tea into the saucer, then back into the cup; in short, did every thing but drink it.

The tea service removed, Mr. Matthews said, "come hither, Mary Lumly, and now let us hear your tragical tale." Lady Mary's excessive enthusiasm had by this time considerably abated, but she felt somewhat vexed at the plain, well meant reproof of Mrs. Cavendish. However, she seated herself on the sofa beside Mr. Matthews, and in a conciliatory tone began. "I am afraid that I have not been so respectful as I ought to be, sir, but my feelings ran away with me." "Your impetuosity, you should say, child," interrupted Mrs. Cavendish.—Lady Mary coloured highly. "The evening is really very fine," said the good Rector, "come, Mary, you and I will go and inhale the sweets of the flowers;" then drawing her arm under his, he led her into the garden.

"So you have been taking a ramble with Miss Brenton this afternoon."

"Yes, sir, and we went farther than we intended, for we went through the little copse, and took a path which neither of us had any knowledge of, and having walked a considerable way without seeing any house, or meeting any one, we began to feel alarmed." "I think you were very imprudent, Mary; you might have encountered ill bred clowns or evil minded persons who would have insulted you."

"I know it, sir, but I am very glad I went, for all that."

"How so?"

"Why, just as we began to feel a little frightened, we heard a child cry, and following the sound, we came to a very wretched hovel, for it could not be called even a cottage. At the door sat a child about four years old, crying. 'What is the matter child?' said

Miss Brenton. 'Mammy is sick and Granny fell out of her chair, and Daddy a'n't come home yet.' We both of us were in the hut in a moment, Oh! dear sir, I never shall forget it, on the bed as they called it, but it was only some straw laid upon a kind of shelf made of boards and covered with a ragged blanket, so dirty that I was almost afraid to go near it, and—and—on this wretched bed lay a poor pale woman with a little, very little baby on her arm."

Lady Mary's lip quivered, Mr. Matthews presssed her hand and said, "But the poor old Granny? you have not told me about her."

"She had been up all the preceding night with her daughter, and not having any help all day, or much nourishment I believe, she had fainted and fell out of her chair; the little girl whose crying had brought us to the place, had run out in great alarm; but when we entered the house, the old woman had recovered, and was sitting, pale as a ghost and unable to articulate, by the handful of fire, over which hung an iron pot."

"Why this is a most deplorable tale, my dear Mary."

"But I have not told you the worst, sir."

"Why I suppose the worst was, you had no money to give them?"

"No, I had a crown in my purse, and I gave it to the old woman, who as she looked at it burst into tears and recovering her speech, said, 'God forever bless you.' "

"But had Miss Brenton nothing to give?"

"Oh no, sir, she said her sensibility was so great she could not stay in the hovel, and they were so dirty that she was afraid of contracting some infectious disorder."

"Then that was the worst, for I suppose she ran away and left you?"

"Yes, she did, and said she would wait for me by the road side, so while I was inquiring what they most wanted, and the poor sick woman with the baby, said 'every thing,' a rough looking man with two boys and a girl came in; he went to the sick woman, asked her how she did, and then turning to the old woman said, 'Mother, is there any thing for supper?' 'Yes, thank God,' said the mother, "I have got summut for ye, John, which a kind hearted christian man gave me this morn.' She then opened the pot, took out a small piece of meat, and two or three turnips, and said, 'there, John, is a nice piece of mutton, and Sally has supped a little of the broth, oh! 'twas a great comfort to her, and here, dears,' taking up some of the water in which the meat had been boiled in porringers, 'here's a nice supper for ye all.' She then gave the children each a piece of bread, so black, that I ran out of the place ashamed that my curiosity had kept me there so long, when I had so little to give.''

"It was not curiosity, Mary, it was a better feeling: but had you been mistress of five guineas, and had them in your purse at that moment would you have given them?''

"Oh yes, ten, if I could have commanded them, but now, sir, that you know the whole, you will, I am sure, lend me the money.''

"We will see about it to-morrow; your crown will for the present provide a few necessaries, so rest in quiet, my good girl, for believe me the bit of boiled mutton and turnips were heartily relished by the man; and the water as you call it, the children, who I suppose had been out at work all day, ate with a keener appetite than you would have partaken of the most delicate viands.''

The next morning Lady Mary, who was not an early riser, and did not generally make her appearance till the rest of the family were seated at the breakfast table, was surprised, upon entering the parlour, to find Miss Blakeney, and Miss Melville had just returned from a walk in which they had been accompanied by their guardian, their hair disordered by the morning breeze and their countenances glowing with health and pleasure.

"You are an idler, Mary Lumly,'' said Mr. Matthews, "but exercise is so necessary to preserve health that I am resolved that you shall accompany me in a round of visits to some of my parishioners this morning.'' This was an invitation he frequently gave to one or the other of the fair orphans under his protection. The morning was fine, and Lady Mary hoping he would take the path through the copse, readily assented, and being soon equipped for her walk, gaily tripped by his side till she found that he took a directly opposite path to what she had expected.

"I was in hopes you would have gone with me to visit the poor people I mentioned," said she in rather a supplicating voice. "All in good time, child," he replied, "I have several poor and some sick persons to visit." The first cottage they entered, they saw a pale looking woman at her spinning; near her, two children seated on a stool, held a spelling book between them, and in an old high backed arm chair sat a man, the very picture of misery; his feet and hands were wrapped in coarse flannel. Every thing around them indicated extreme poverty, yet every thing was perfectly clean: the children's clothes were coarse, but not ragged, the mother preferring a patch of a different colour, to a hole or rent.

"How are you, neighbour?" said Mr. Matthews, "and how are you, my good Dame, and how do you contrive to keep all so tight and orderly, when you have a sick husband to attend, and nothing but your own labour to support him, yourself and your children?" "Oh, sir," said the woman rising, "we have much to be thankful for. The good Sir Robert Ainslie has ordered his steward to let us live in this cottage, rent free, till my husband shall get better, and the house keeper lets little Bessey here have a pitcher of milk and a plate of cold meat every now and then, so, please your Reverence, we are not so bad off as we might be."

"What is the matter with your husband?" asked Lady Mary, with a look of wonder at the woman's expression of contentment, when there was so much apparent wretchedness around her.

"Why, your Ladyship, Thomas, though he be an industrious kind husband, was never over strong; he worked too hard, and last summer took a bad fever; and when he was getting better he would go to work again before he had got up his strength; the season was very wet and he was out late and early, so, you see, he got a bad cold, and his fever came on worse than ever, and the rheumatics set in, and ever since he has been a cripple like, not being able to use his hands or feet."

"Dear me, that is very terrible," said Lady Mary, "how can you possibly live? How do you get time to work?"

"I gets up early, my Lady, and sits up late; sometimes I can earn, one way or another, three and sixpence a week, and sometimes, but not very often, five shillings."

"Five shillings!" repeated the astonished Mary, "can four people live on five shillings a week?"

Mr. Matthews had been, during this time, talking with the invalid, but catching her last words he replied, "Aye, child, and many worthy honest christians with larger families are obliged to do with less."

"We, I am sure," said Thomas, "ought not to complain, thanks be to God and my good Dame, we are main comfortable, but I fear me, your Reverence, she will kill herself; she washes and mends our clothes when she ought to be resting, after spinning all day or going out to work, to help the gentlefolks' servants to wash and clean house. I sometimes hope and pray that I may soon recover the use of my hands and feet, or that it will please my Maker to lay me at rest."

"No! no! heaven forbid, Thomas, I can work very well, I can be contented with any thing, so you are spared, and you will get well by and by, and then we shall all be happy again."

The tears which had for some time trembled in Lady Mary's eyes, now rushed down her cheeks, she drew forth her empty purse and looked beseechingly at Mr. Matthews. He did not particularly notice her, but asked, "Does the doctor attend you regularly? Is he kind and considerate."

"Oh yes, sir, and we gets all the physic and such stuff from the Potticary without paying, thanks to you, reverend sir; then the housekeeper at the great house sent us some oatmeal and sago, a nutmeg and a whole bottle of wine, and that has made poor Thomas comfortable for above a month past. Oh we have so many blessings."

Mr. Matthews gave the woman an approving smile, and presenting her with half a crown, said, "This young lady desires me to give you this, it may enable you to add a little to your comforts. Good morning, continue this humble contented frame of mind and rely on your heavenly Father, he will in his own good time relieve you from your difficulties, or enable you to support them with patience."

"My dear sir," said Lady Mary when they had left the cottage, "what a trifle you gave to that distressed family."

"Mary," replied the Rector, "it is not the bestowing large sums that constitutes real benevolence, nor do such donations ultimately benefit the persons on whom they are bestowed, they rather serve to paralyze the hand of industry, while they lead the individual to depend on adventitious circumstances for relief, instead of exerting his own energies to soften or surmount the difficulties with which he may be surrounded."

Many other calls were made in the course of the morning, till at length they stopped at a very small cottage, and on entering, Mary was struck with the appearance of an elderly man and woman both seemingly past the period of being useful either to themselves or others. A few embers were in the grate, over which hung a teakettle, and on a deal table stood a pewter teapot, some yellow cups and saucers and a piece of the same kind of bread, the sight of which had filled her with such disgust the evening before. A little dark brown sugar and about a gill of skimmed milk completed the preparation for their humble meal.

"Why, you are early at your tea, or late at your breakfast, Gammer," said Mr. Matthews as he entered. The old dame laid down the patchwork with which she had been employing herself, and her husband closed the Bible in which he was reading.

"Bless you, good sir," said he, "tea is often all our sustenance and serves for breakfast, dinner and supper, but we are old, and can take but little exercise, so a little food suffices; if sometimes we can get a morsel of bacon or a crumb of cheese to relish our bread, it is quite a treat, and a herring laid on the coals is a feast indeed; but it is long since we have known better times, and we be got used to the change. I wish indeed sometimes that I had something to comfort my poor old dame, but since the death of our little darlings, what sustains our tottering frames is of little consequence; we are thankful for what we have."

"Thankful," said Lady Mary internally, "thankful for such a poor shed to keep them from the weather, such a miserable looking bed to rest their old limbs upon, and some black tea and dry bread for their only meal."

Mr. Matthews saw that she was struck, and willing to give her time for rumination sat down beside the old man on a stool. The only vacant wooden chair being dusted by the dame, Lady Mary seated herself and pursuing her train of thought, audibly said, "I should think, poor woman, you had cause for repining and discontent rather than thankfulness."

"Ah no, lady," she replied, "what right have I to expect more than others; how many thousands in this kingdom have not even a hovel to shelter them, scarcely a rag to cover them, and only the bare ground to sleep on, whilst their poor children beg their daily bread from door to door."

"Dreadful!" said Lady Mary, and her cheek assumed a marble hue.

"But that is not the worst," continued the woman, "many of these poor souls are as ignorant as the blackamoors of Africa; they cannot read their Bibles; they do not know that idleness is next to thieving; they do not know the God who made them, or the Saviour who redeemed them. How much happier are we! This is a poor place to be sure, but it is our own, and if our bed is hard, we can lie down with quiet consciences; if we have but little food we eat it with thankfulness; and when we are low spirited, our frames feeble and our hearts oppressed, we can read the word of consolation in God's own book. Oh lady, these are great blessings."

"But I understood from what your husband said, that you had seen better days. How can you bring your mind to bear the ills of age and poverty without complaint?"

"It is because I know that He who has allotted my portion knows what is best for me. It is because I am fully sensible that his bounties are far beyond my deserts."

"What? such poor fare! such a hut! and you a good well conducted woman, and these wretched accommodations more than you deserve?"

"Yes, Lady, had the best of us no more than we deserve, our portion would be hard indeed. You say I have seen better days, so I have. But I weary you, and I beg your pardon, too, Reverend Sir."

"You have it, dame, go on, tell your story to that young lady; I have much to say to your good man."

Thus encouraged, Gammer Lonsdale again addressed her attentive auditor. "When I married my good man there, I had three hundred pounds, which had been left me by my grandfather, and my husband had scraped together about as much more. So we stocked a farm, and for years went on quite well; we never had but one child, it was a girl, and, God forgive us! we were very proud of her, for Alice Lonsdale grew up a very pretty young woman. I taught her to be domestic, and to use her needle, but alack-a-day, I did not teach her to know herself. There was our first great fault, and when people praised her beauty or her singing, (for Alice sung sweetly, Lady) we used to join in the praise, and her father, poor man, would chuck her under the chin, and say aye! aye! in good time we shall see our girl either a 'squire's or a parson's lady. So Alice grew vain and conceited, and in an evil hour we consented that she should pay a visit to a neighbouring market town, and attend a dancing school, for as we had settled it in our weak heads that she was to be a lady, it was but right that she should learn to dance.

"Alice was now turned of fifteen, and during the time of her visit to Dorking, (for at that period we lived in Surry) she became acquainted with a young man, the son of a reputable tradesman in that town. After her return, he sometimes called to see her, and, to make short of my story, when she was eighteen, with the consent of both his parents and her own, Alice became his wife. We gave her five hundred pounds, his father gave him seven hundred, which furnished a small house neatly in Croyden, where he had some family connections, and stocked a shop in the grocery line.

"For some time things went on smoothly; and when her father and I visited them about a year after their marriage, we thought they were getting before-hand. He appeared to be industrious and attentive, and Alice was cheerful and happy. I staid with my poor girl during her first confinement, and was very proud of the little grandson with which she presented me. After this I saw her no more for two years, but I used to fancy that her letters were not so sprightly as formerly. However, I knew that when a woman becomes a wife and mother, the vivacity of girlhood is sobered. However some reports having reached us that her husband was become unsteady, and that it was thought he was much involved in debt, my good man took a journey to inquire about it. He found things worse than had been represented. Alice was pale, dejected and miserable; her husband had got acquainted with a set of worthless beings who called themselves honest fellows, frequented clubs, and acted private plays, which being done once in the hall of a public house and money taken for admission, they were all taken up and had to pay a heavy fine.

"My husband had not been many days in Croyden, before he had reason to think that Alice was injured in the tenderest point, and that with her own domestic; but she made no complaint, and while her father was considering what he should do that might best promote her happiness, Lewis, for that was her husband's name, was arrested for fifteen hundred pounds on his note which he had given for stock, and as we afterwards learnt, sold at under price to supply his extravagance. Alice pleaded with her father to assist him; her situation was delicate, and old Mr. Lewis being sent for, his affairs were compromised, the two fathers being bound for him.

"My good man then returned home, where he had not been more than a month, when one evening just at dusk, a chaise stopped at the gate, and in a few moments, Alice, leading her little boy, ran up the walk, and throwing herself into my arms with an hysterical sob fainted. It was long before she could articulate. At length she told us old Mr. Lewis was dead, his property was not sufficient to pay his debts, that her heartless husband had taken what valuables he could collect, and raised money upon every thing that was not already mortgaged, and absconded with the abandoned woman I told you about. He had told Alice that he was going to Dorking to look into his late father's affairs. Ah, lady, he had been there before, and gleaned all he could from the wreck, even to the leaving his old widowed mother destitute. The same night the woman who lived with Alice, having asked leave to go out, never returned, and upon examination, it was found that she had taken her clothes, to which she had added some of the most valuable belongings of her mistress.

"The next day the furniture of the house was taken by a man who said he had advanced money upon it, and my poor girl was literally turned into the street. In this distress the landlord of a large inn had compassion on her. He advanced her a few guineas and sent her in his own chaise to her father, her best and only friend.

"I found upon inquiry that my child had not been altogether faultless. She had been thoughtless in her expenses, and never having been controlled in her youth, she could not practice the necessary patience and forbearance which her situation required; so that instead of weaning her unhappy partner from his pursuits, she perhaps irritated his temper and made him more dissipated. A few days after her return, my husband was arrested upon the note, and being unable to pay so large a sum, his stock upon the farm was seized, and not being able to meet his rent, which from various circumstances had run for six months, we were obliged to quit the farm and take a cottage a little way from Croyden. Here Alice gave birth to a daughter and a few days after was laid at rest in the grave. But our misfortunes were not ended. Though by working hard and living poor, we kept free from debt, yet it was a struggle to maintain the two children.

"But we managed to keep them clean and tidy, so that they went to school, and lovely babies they were, and my vain proud heart made them my idols, but it was God's will that I should be humbled to the very dust. One night the thatch of our cottage caught fire and we awoke almost suffocated with smoke. We sprang up; I caught up the girl and ran out, but before my husband could escape with the boy, a rafter fell, and I thought I had lost them both; but with great struggling he got out, though greatly bruised and burnt. The child was so hurt that he was a cripple as long as he lived.

"We were now houseless, pennyless and naked; neither of us very young, my health not good, and my husband likely to be confined months before he could go to work, if indeed he should be ever able to work again. A cottager who lived about a mile from us, who had got up early to carry something to Croyden market, saw the fire, and calling his son, they ran to our assistance, but nothing was saved. He took my husband on his back; the lad took the boy; both father and son had pulled off their outer jackets to wrap them round me and my little girl; and we proceeded as well as we could to neighbour Woodstock's cottage.

"They did all they could for us, but they were poor themselves. However, on applying to the 'squire, of whom we had rented the hut we had lived in, he bade his housekeeper send us some old clothes. She not only obeyed him in that, but brought us some little comforts, and with her came a sweet boy about the age of little Alice. When this dear child went back, he told his father, who was then visiting the 'squire, how poor and how sick we were, and the next day brought him to see us.

"Sir Robert Ainslie, for it was he himself, spoke to us kindly, gave us money to purchase some clothing, and procured a doctor to visit my husband and grandson; he also spoke to the minister about us, and he came to console and pray with us. Oh, lady, that was the greatest charity of all; for we did not know where to look for consolation till he taught us. We had never considered that a good and all wise Father has a right to chastise his children when and how he pleases; we had been full of complaining and discontent before. But he read to us and prayed with us, and at length convinced us that it was possible to be happy though poor.

"When my husband got able to move about, the dear boy, Master Ainslie, came with his father, one day, and laying a folded paper on my lap said, 'Papa gives you that.' So I opened it and found it was a gift of this place we now live in, and a promise of five guineas a year as long as I lived.

"I could not speak to thank him. He told me that he had lately purchased an estate in Hampshire; that he had been to look at it and have it put in repair, just before he came into Surry; that he recollected this cottage, and had written to his steward to have it got ready for us, and that he would have us sent to it free of all expense.

"Well, in a short time we moved here and were happier than we had ever been in our lives before, for Sir Robert wrote about us to our good Rector here, who has comforted and strengthened our minds. Our dear Alice grew apace; she earned a little towards clothing herself, and then she was so dutiful to her grandfather and me, and so kind to her crippled brother! But seven years agone last Lammas, the small pox came into the neighbourhood. The boy took it first. Nothing could separate his sister from him, and in one short week I followed both my darlings to the grave."

The old woman stopped a moment, put her hand to her forehead, then looking up meekly, cried in an under tone, "Thy will be done! It will not be long before I go to them, but they can never return to me. It was the hand of mercy that took them, for what had they to make life desirable? The boy's inheritance was decrepitude and poverty, and poor Alice had all her mother's beauty, and who knows what snares might have been laid, what temptations might have assailed her. She might have been lost both soul and body. Now, thanks be to God! she is safe in the house of her heavenly Father."

"Come, child, it is time for us to be walking," exclaimed Mr. Matthews, so taking leave of the old people, he led Lady Mary out of the cottage. Perceiving her cheeks wet with tears which she was endeavouring to conceal, "These are good tears," said he, "indulge them freely, they flow from pity and admiration."

"From pity, indeed," she replied, "but I cannot admire what I do not rightly understand." Then pausing a moment, she continued, "Pray, sir, are not these people Methodists?"

"What do you mean by a Methodist?"

"I hardly know how to explain myself, but I know I have often heard my mamma and governess laugh about some folks that lived in our neighbourhood, who used to talk a great deal about religion, and pray and sing psalms, even when they were in trouble, and they called them Methodists!"

"Is it then," said Mr. Matthews gravely, "a ridiculous thing to say our prayers, or praise the name of Him from whom all our blessings proceed?"

"No, sir, but when he has taken from us those we love, it is difficult to feel perfectly resigned. I am sure I could not praise Him when my mamma died."

"But you could pray to Him, I hope?"

"No, indeed I could not, I thought Him very cruel."

"Poor child," said he tenderly, "what a barren waste thy mind was at that time."

"But you have made me better, Sir."

"I hope God will make you wiser, my love! And now, Mary, let me advise you, never to use the term Methodist in this way again. Dame Lonsdale and her husband are good pious members of the church of England; they are what every christian should be, humble, devout, and grateful, but let the mode in which they worship, be what it may, if they are sincere, they will be accepted. There are many roads to the foot of the cross, and whichever may be taken, if it is pursued with a pure and upright heart, is safe, and He who suffered on it, will remove every burthen from us whether it be earthly affliction, or sorrow for committed offences." While Mr. Matthews was speaking, a sudden turn in the road made Lady Mary start, for she beheld just before her the identical cottage to which she had been so desirous to come when they first began their ramble.

CHAPTER V

A Lesson—Change of Scene

◊　　◊

"As I live, sir," said she in delight, "there is the place I wanted to visit."

"Then we will go in and see how the poor people are," said Mr. Matthews.

They entered, but how changed was the scene! A clean though coarsely furnished bed stood in one corner of the room; the old wooden frame had been removed; the room was neatly swept and sanded, a new sauce pan was by the fire, in which gruel was boiling, the sick woman and her infant were in clean clothes befitting their station, and the old mother also appeared in better habiliments, whilst a healthy looking young woman was busied about some domestic concerns.

Every thing wore such a look of comfort, that Lady Mary thought she had mistaken the place. But the old woman recognized her, and rising, began to say how lucky her good ladyship's visit had been to them all, for that morning two beautiful young ladies came to see them.

"Mayhap," continued she, "they be your sisters, though they were so good-natured and condescending, they seemed more like angels than aught else; and it was not more than two hours after they went away before a man came to the door with a cart, and what should be in it, think ye, but that nice bedstead and bed, with blankets, and sheets, and coverlet, and some clothes for Sally and her baby; and he brought that good young body to tend her, till she be up again. Dear heart! how John will be surprised when he comes home! He won't know his place, not he, but will think the fairies have been here."

"Ah!" said Lady Mary, looking at Mr. Matthews, "I fancy I know who the fairies were."

The Rector put his finger on his lip, and telling the women that he was glad to find they were so well provided for, he led his ward from the cottage.

"Now, Mary," said he smiling, "how much do you think those fairies whom you so shrewdly guess at, expended for all the comforts and conveniences these poor people seem to have acquired, since last evening."

"Oh! a great deal," said she, "more than five guineas, I dare say. First there is a bed—"

"That is not a bed, but a second hand mattress, which, though a good one, cost little or nothing. The blankets and coverlet, came from my house, and are with the bed linen *lent* only. If we find the woman on her recovery, industrious, clean, and well behaved, they will be given to her. The rest was very trifling, a little tea, oatmeal, sugar, and materials for brown bread, half a cheese, half a side of bacon, some coals and candles, were all purchased for less than a guinea and a half. Had you given the sum you intended, they would have squandered it away, and not made themselves half so comfortable. I make a point of inquiring the characters of any poor, who are my parishioners, before I give them any relief, and this morning while Lucy and Aura were visiting your protégés, I investigated their character. The man is an honest hard working fellow; his wife, I find from good authority, is idle, and by no means cleanly in her habits. You, child, have no idea how much the prosperity and comfort of a poor man, and often of a rich man too, depends on the conduct of his wife. The old woman is his wife's mother; she is old and feeble, can do but little, and often, by a querulous temper, makes things worse than they would otherwise be. You say the children were ragged and dirty; I shall see that they are comfortable clothed, and, if I find that the clothes are kept whole and clean, I will befriend the family farther. But if they are let run to rags, without washing or mending, I shall do no more."

Thus, in walking, chatting, making various calls, and commenting on the scenes they witnessed, time passed unobserved by Lady Mary. At length Mr. Matthews, drawing out his watch, exclaimed, "I protest, it is almost four o'clock."

"Indeed!" said Mary, "I am afraid we shall have dinner waiting." The Rector's hour of dining was half past three.

"I do not think they will wait," he replied, "I have frequently requested they would not wait for me, for you know I am frequently detained by a sick bed, or an unhappy person whose mind is depressed."

They had now a mile to walk, and Lady Mary assured the Rector that she was "very, very hungry!" Arriving at home they discovered that the family had dined, and the ladies gone out on some particular purpose. A cloth had been therefore laid in the study for the ramblers.

"Come," said Mr. Matthews, "sit down, Mary, you say you are hungry, we will waive ceremony on this occasion, and you shall dine in your morning dress. What have we here?" he continued raising a cover, and discovering part of a boiled leg of mutton, which had been kept perfectly hot, and on a dish beside it stood a few turnips not mashed.

"Are there no capers, John?"

"No sir, the cook did not recollect that they were out till it was too late to get any, and my mistress said she was sure you would excuse it."

"Well, well, we must do as well as we can," said he, laying a slice of mutton and one of the turnips, on Lady Mary's plate.

She did not wait for other sauce than a keen appetite, but having dispatched two or three slices of the meat, with a good quantity of the vegetable and bread, declared she never had relished a dinner so well in her life.

"You will have a bit of tart?" said the Rector. "I warrant John can find one, or a bit of cheese and biscuit."

"Oh no! my dear sir, I have eaten so heartily."

"Poor dear young woman!" said Mr. Matthews, in an affected tone of sensibility, "how my heart aches for you, out all the morning, walking from cottage to cottage, coming home hungry and weary, and had nothing to eat but a bit of boiled mutton and turnips, and to wash it down, a glass of cold water." Here Mr. Matthews pretended to sob; when Lady Mary comprehending the ridicule, burst out a laughing.

"You see, my child," said he, assuming his own kind and gracious manner, "how misplaced sensibility is, when it fancies any thing more than wholesome fare, however plain or coarse it may be, is necessary to satisfy the appetite of those whom exercise or labour have rendered really hungry. Where indeed there is a scanty quantity, it should awaken our good feelings, and lead us to extend the hand of charity."

"Dear Sir," said Lady Mary, "you have this day taught me a lesson that I trust through life I shall never forget."

Month after month, and year after year, passed on while Mr. Matthews was endeavouring to cultivate the understandings, fortify the principles, and, by air and exercise, invigorate the frames of his fair wards. During the six pleasantest months, masters in music and drawing from Southampton attended Lady Mary and Miss Blakeney. The other six, they employed themselves in imparting what they had gained to Aura Melville, in her leisure hours.

Thus they were improved in a far greater degree by the attention necessary to bestow on every acquirement in which they were desirous to instruct themselves. There were many genteel families in the neighbourhood, but none visited on a more intimate footing, than that of Sir Robert Ainslie. His son Edward, had become a great favourite at the Rectory, ever since they had known the story of old Dame Lonsdale and the cottage; but as he was pursuing his studies at Oxford, they saw him but seldom.

It was in the summer of 1794, when Lucy had just entered her twentieth year, that Mrs. Cavendish proposed that, to change the scene, and give the young people a glimpse of the fashionable world, a few weeks should be spent in Brighton, and that, the ensuing winter, they should go to London. Mr. and Mrs. Matthews were fondly attached to the place where they had passed so many happy years, yet, sensible that Lucy in particular, should be introduced properly into a world where she would most likely be called upon to act a prominent part, they consented, and about the latter part of June, they commenced their journey.

Sir Robert Ainslie and his son were to meet them there, for Edward was to be their escort to public places when Mr. Matthews felt disinclined to mix in the gay scenes of fashionable life, their attendant in walks upon the Stiene, or excursions in the beautiful environs of Brighton.

This was very pleasant to the whole party. The elderly ladies were fond of the society of Sir Robert. Mr. Matthews regarded him as an old and esteemed friend, and the young ones as a kind of parent, and his son as their brother. Lady Mary, indeed, could have fancied herself in love with Edward, and often in the most pathetic terms lamented to her young companions that he was not *nobly born*, he was so handsome, so generous, so gallant.

"Yes," said Aura, with an arch glance from under her long eyelashes, "so generally gallant that no one can have the vanity to suppose herself a particular favourite."

"No, indeed that is true, and I should lament to find *myself* particularized by him, as you know my poor mother used to say, she should not rest in her grave if she thought I should ever match myself with any one below the rank of nobility."

"I think," said Aura, laughing, "you need be under no apprehension, unless indeed it should be from the fear that should he offer, you might not be able to keep your resolution."

They were soon settled in their new abode at Brighton, their names enrolled on the books at the rooms, libraries, &c. and the unaffected manners of the three fair orphans, their simple style of dress, unobtrusive beauty, and the general report that they were all three heiresses, drew numerous admirers and pretenders, around them. But the grave and gentlemanly manners of Mr. Matthews, the stately hauteur of Mrs. Cavendish, with the brotherly attention of Edward Ainslie, kept impertinence and intrusion at an awe-full distance.

Edward felt kindly to all, but his heart gave the preference to Lucy, though he feared to give way to its natural impulse, lest the world, nay, even the object of his tenderness, should think him interested.

Sir Robert Ainslie had two sons and a daughter by a former marriage; these were married and settled, and were too much the seniors of the present young party to ever have been in habits of intimacy with them. The mother of Edward had survived his birth but a few years; and he became the consoler, delight, and darling of his father. The youth was endowed with fine talents, a mind of the strictest rectitude, and perhaps a remark that his cool, calculating, eldest brother once made, that it would be a fine *spec* for Ned, if he could catch the handsome heiress, led him to put a curb on that sensibility and admiration, which might otherwise have led him to appear as her professed lover.

One fine morning, as they were strolling on the Stiene, an elegant youth, in military uniform, accosted him with "Ainslie, my dear lad, how are you, this is a lucky encounter for me, for I hope you spend some time here, my regiment is here on duty for six months." Edward received his proffered hand with great cordiality, and presenting him to the ladies as Lieutenant Franklin, of the——regiment, named to his friend, each of the fair trio, and he joining the party, they sauntered on the sands an hour longer, waited on the ladies to Mr. Matthews' door, and then both gentlemen bade them good morning.

"Why, you are in luck's way, Ned," said the officer, "to be on such easy terms with the Graces, for really I must say your three beauties are worthy that appellation. Are you in any way related to any of them?"

"By no means," he replied, "my father is guardian to one, who is a splendid heiress, and in habits of great intimacy with the reverend Mr. Matthews, who is guardian to the other two."

"Heiresses also, eh! Ned?"

"Not exactly so, one has a genteel independence, the other, poor girl, is an orphan, whose family is only known to her guardian, and whose fortune, if report says true, depends entirely on his kindness."

"But which is the heiress?"

"That I shall leave to your sagacity to discover; but I hope you do not mean to set out in life, with interested views in the choice of a partner?"

"Oh no, my good grandfather took care I should have no occasion to do that. He left me enough for comfort, and even elegance, with prudent management, and as I have no propensities for gaming, racing, or other fashionable follies, I shall look out for good nature, good sense, and discretion in a wife, in preference to wealth. To be sure, a little beauty, and a handsome address, would, though not indispensable, be very acceptable qualities."

Lieutenant Franklin was the eldest of four sons, his father was an officer of artillery, had seen some hard service, passed a number of years abroad, and during that period had accumulated a large fortune. He had married the only daughter of a wealthy man, resident in the part of the world where he was stationed; he was intrusted by government with providing military stores, &c. during a seven years' war for a large army in actual service, and when the war was ended, returned to his own country which he had left nine years before, a Captain of Artillery, with little besides his pay, an honourable descent, and fair character, to receive the thanks of royalty for his intrepidity, and to dash into the world of splendour and gaiety. His house was one of the most elegant in Portland place, his equipage and establishment such as might have become a nobleman of the first rank. Bellevue, a large estate near Feversham in Kent, consisting of a large handsome and commodious mansion, several well tenanted farms, pleasure grounds, fish ponds, green and hot houses, was purchased for his summer residence.

Promoted to the rank of Colonel of artillery, and having held the office of chief engineer during his service abroad, the father of Lieutenant Franklin stood in an elevated rank, and associated with the first personages in the kingdom. His eldest son, as has been mentioned, was amply provided for, and had chosen the army for his profession. The others, as yet little more than boys, were finishing their education at some of the best establishments near London. His two daughters, Julia and Harriet, were attended by masters at home under the superintendence of an excellent governess.

From the moment of his introduction to the family of Mr. Matthews, Sir Robert Ainslie having spoken of him in high terms, Mr. Franklin became a frequent and always a welcome guest. Though Miss Blakeney was known to have an independent fortune, its extent was not confided even to herself; for Mr. Matthews knew that wealth attracts flattery, and good as he believed Lucy's heart to be, he feared for the frailty of human nature if exposed to the breath of that worst of mental poisons, injudicious and indiscriminate adulation.

A cursory observer would never have taken Lucy for the independent heiress; the retired modesty of her manners, the respectful deference which she paid her guardian and his family, united to an intuitive politeness and real affection with which she ever distinguished Aura Melville, would have led any one to think she was the dependent.

Lady Mary was afraid of Aura, her wit, though in general harmlessly playful, was sometimes sarcastic, and the vain girl of quality often smarted under its lash. If she met the steady eye of Aura, at a time when she was displaying airs of self complacency, her own would sink under it. The seniors of the family encouraged this involuntary respect paid to their protégée, and by their own manner towards her gave their visitors reason to think that they were receiving, rather than conferring a favour, by her residence among them.

Thus every circumstance coincided to establish the general idea entertained that Aura was the independent heiress, Lady Mary, a young person of rank, with only a moderate fortune, and Lucy Blakeney, the orphan, depending on the kindness of Mr. Matthews. Another circumstance contributed to the mistake. Miss Blakeney, though her guardian allowed her a very handsome stipend for clothes and pocket money, was yet extremely simple in her attire. Her apparel was ever of the best quality, but it was unostentatious; no display of splendour, no glitter or finery disfigured her interesting person, and she scarcely ever purchased a handsome article of dress for public occasions without presenting something of the same kind, perhaps more elegant or of a finer texture than her own, to her friend Miss Melville. Yet she contrived to do this without its being observed; for in all their little shopping parties, Aura was uniformly pursebearer, as Lucy used laughingly to say, to save herself trouble, but in reality to hide her own liberality.

Franklin then easily fell into the common error; and charmed with the person and manners of Miss Blakeney, feeling how proud and happy he should feel to raise so lovely a young woman from dependence to a state of comparative affluence, he determined to scrutinize her conduct, mark her disposition, and should all agree with the captivating external, to offer her his hand, and devote his life to her happiness. Lucy Blakeney, had she been really a destitute orphan, would, when she perceived Franklin's attentions to be serious, and supposed that he imagined her to be an heiress, have insisted on Mr. Matthews' explaining her real situation; but when the reverse was the case, what woman but would have felt highly flattered by the attentions of one of the handsomest officers of the corps to which he belonged, a man of honour and perfect rectitude of conduct, high in the esteem of personages of the first rank, and known to be in possession of a handsome fortune, who thus avowedly loved her for herself alone?

Mr. Matthews had a little spice of romance in his composition, and although he did not withdraw the veil from Miss Blakeney's situation, he would have shrunk with horror from the idea of obtaining a splendid alliance for Aura upon the false supposition of her being an heiress.

But there was no immediate call on the integrity of the conscientious guardian on this account. Though numerous were the moths and summer flies who, in expectation of a rich remuneration flitted round Aura Melville, she kept them at such a distance, that they neither disturbed her peace or annoyed her in any way. They were all treated alike, sometimes listened to with perfect nonchalance, sometimes laughed at, and often mortified with an hauteur which bordered on contempt.

A Rencontre—A Ball—
Love at First Sight

◇   ◇

It was on one of those mornings when the visitants of Brighton sally forth to ransack libraries, torment shopkeepers, and lounge upon the Stiene, when Edward Ainslie taking Lucy under one arm and Lady Mary under the other, having taken a walk upon the downs, strolled into one of the public Libraries, where raffles, scandal and flirtation were going forward amongst an heterogeneous crowd assembled there.

At the upper end of the room sat an elderly gentleman in a military undress, apparently in very ill health; beside him stood an elegant fashionable woman, evidently past the meridian of life, but still bearing on her countenance traces of beauty and strong intellectual endowments. Ainslie and his party had been conducted by the master of the shop to seats near these persons.

"I wonder where Mr. Franklin is?" said Lady Mary, as she seated herself, "he has neglected us all last evening and this morning, and I shall scold him well when I see him again."

"I have no doubt," said Lucy, "but Mr. Franklin can give a very good account."

"Heavens!" exclaimed the lady who stood by the military invalid. "What is the matter, my dear? Oh! pray make way, let him have air, he is very weak."

Lucy looked round, the veteran had sunk upon the shoulder of his wife, pale and almost lifeless. Having some *eau de Luce* in her hand which she had just before purchased, Lucy stepped forward and presented it to the languid sufferer. The volatile revived him, he opened his eyes, and gazing wildly on Lucy, pushed her hand away exclaiming,

"Take her away, this vision haunts me forever, sleeping or waking, it is still before me."

At that moment Lieutenant Franklin broke through the crowd, that filled the room, and giving Ainslie and the ladies a slight bow of recognition, helped the poor invalid to rise, and assisted by the lady, led him to a carriage which waited at the door of the shop. The footman helped him in, and Franklin handing in the lady, sprang in after them, and it drove off.

"Who is he?" "What is the matter?" was the general inquiry. Ainslie's party merely heard that it was a brave veteran, who had served many years abroad, and received a wound from the effects of which he still continued to suffer, and that he sometimes laboured under slight fits of insanity. Lucy's eyes filled. She thought of old sergeant Blandford. "But what is his disabled limb," said she mentally, "compared to the sufferings of this brave officer? Blandford has but a poor cottage and the pay of an invalid, 'tis true, but he is cheerful and even happy. This poor gentleman appears to be surrounded with affluence, but is yet miserable."

Ainslie sighed as he led them from the library, but made no remark. While Lady Mary said:

"Dear! what a pity that a man who has so beautiful an equipage, should be so sick and unhappy! Only think how elegant his liveries were, and how richly the arms were emblazoned on the pannels of the carriage." Lady Mary had become skilful in the language of heraldry, under the tuition of her mother who doated on rank, pedigree, &c. and could have held forth for hours on the crests, supporters, mottoes, and heraldic bearings of most of the noble families in England.

"Who was that young lady who offered your father the *eau de*

Luce, and to whom you bowed this morning, Jack," asked the mother of Franklin, as he sat tête-á-tête with her after a melancholy dinner on the evening of the day in which the events just related took place.

"A Miss Blakeney, a very amiable girl under the protection of the Rev. Mr. Matthews, who with his wife, and her sister, the Honourable Mrs. Cavendish, and two young ladies to whom he is guardian, are passing a few weeks in Brighton. They are a charming family. I wish my father's health would permit my bringing you acquainted with them."

"It is impossible," said his mother, sighing, "for besides that the health of your dear father is in a very precarious state, I fear that he has something heavy at his heart. He is much altered, Jack, within the last few months; his rest is disturbed, and indeed it is only by powerful opiates that he obtains any, and by them alone the smallest exhiliration of spirits."

"His wound is no doubt very painful, my dear madam," replied the son, "but we will hope that change of scene, and strict attention to the advice of the medical gentlemen who attend him, will in time restore him."

At that moment the Colonel's bell summoned his servant, and the mother of Franklin flew to the apartment of her husband, to strive to alleviate his sufferings by her tenderness and cheer him by her conversation.

"Where was I, Julia," said the Colonel, "when that faintness seized me?"

"At the Library near the Stiene, my dear. Do you not recollect the interesting girl who presented her smelling bottle?"

The Colonel put his hand to his head, spoke a few words in an under voice, and leaning back on a sofa on which he was seated, closed his eyes, and his wife continuing silent he dropped into a perturbed slumber.

"We will return to London," said he on awakening; "we will set off to-morrow, and then make an excursion to Margate and Ramsgate; from thence to Bellevue, where we will finish the summer."

"Why not go to your sister's for a few weeks? she will be much disappointed if we do not make her a visit this season."

"What, to Hampshire? no! no! I cannot go to Hampshire."

The next morning, Mr. Franklin having breakfasted with and taken leave of his parents, they set off from Brighton, where they had been but three days, in the vain hope that another place would contribute to restore the health and spirits of the Colonel.

As the delicacy of every member of Mr. Matthews' family forbade the smallest recurrence to the recontre in the library with the invalid officer who, they had learnt, was the father of Lieutenant Franklin, when two days after he mentioned the departure of his parents from Brighton, no remark was made, but the kind wish offered that his health might soon be restored.

The officers upon duty at Brighton having received many civilities from numerous families of distinction, temporary residents there, determined, as it drew near the close of the season, to give a splendid ball. Mr. Matthews' family were among the invited guests. Lady Mary was wild with delight, even Lucy felt somewhat exhilirated at the idea of a ball where all the splendor and fashion of the place would assemble, and where it was expected some personages of exalted rank would make their appearance.

Aura Melville was the most stoical of the trio, though it must be confessed her heart did palpitate a little quicker than usual, when Edward Ainslie requested to be her partner the two first dances.— Perhaps those quickened pulsations will in some measure account for the perfect indifference with which she had listened to all her admirers.

Balls in anticipation, and indeed in reality are very pleasant to those engaged in them, but most insufferably dull in detail. It will therefore be sufficient to say that our three orphans enjoyed themselves extremely well.

The attentions of Franklin to Lucy were very pointed. So much so, that Mr. Matthews was resolved should they continue, and the

Lieutenant follow them into Hampshire, to call upon him for an explanation of his intentions, and candidly state to him Miss Blakeney's real situation; in order that should an union take place, such settlements might be made as should secure to her independence for life, whatever events might hereafter happen.

The morning after the ball Lady Mary held forth for a full hour upon the splendid appearance, gallant manners, and evident admiration of a young baronet, who had danced, flirted, and flattered, till he had stirred up a strange commotion in her little vain heart. Lucy heard her and smiled. Aura smiled too, but it was with a look of arch meaning, while she replied to the often repeated question of:

"Do you not own he is very handsome?"

"Why yes, as far as tolerable features, good eyes and teeth, with more than tolerable dress goes, I think he is passable; but my dear Lady Mary, he has no noble blood in his veins: his Grandfather was *only* Lord Mayor of London, and you know you told me your mother would not rest in her grave if you matched with aught below nobility. Now, Sir Stephen Haynes's father and his father before him, were only stationers and booksellers—and who knows, my pretty Mary—*Lady* Mary, I beg your pardon—who knows but this very Sir Stephen Haynes, may on the female side be a collateral descendant of the renowned Whittington, who made such a fortunate voyage to St. Helena with his *cat*."

"How do you know it was to St. Helena, Aura?" said Mr. Matthews looking up, for he had been reading in the parlour where the young folks were talking over the events of the preceding evening.

"Oh! I only surmised, sir, because I read in some geographical work that the island of St. Helena was infested with rats, so that the inhabitants could neither raise or preserve grain of any kind upon it, in which case, a cat must have been a very valuable animal."

Lady Mary would have left the parlour in a pet, but that she hoped the Baronet would call in the course of the morning. He did so, and exercised the art of flattery so successfully, that Mary Lumley totally forgot the expressions of her dying mother, about her degrading herself by a plebeian marriage, and began to think she could be well content to be Lady Mary Haynes, though her husband was not a sprig of nobility.

Mr. Matthews had the interest and happiness of each of the orphans under his guardianship much at heart. He thought that Mary Lumley had many good natural qualities; he saw that they had been injured by the injudicious conduct of her mother; he had endeavoured to rectify some of her romantic notions and in some measure he had succeeded, but he knew enough of human nature, to be quite aware that when love and romance unite in the mind of a volatile young woman, there is scarcely a possibility of re-straining her from taking her own way. Yet he felt it his duty to inquire into the circumstances of the Baronet.

In three months Lady Mary would be her own mistress, and though her fortune was but trifling, yet settled on herself it might secure to her those comforts and conveniencies of life to which she had ever been accustomed. He found upon inquiry, that Sir Stephen Haynes, though the only son of a wealthy city knight, had pretty well dissipated his patrimony, and of the many thousand pounds and hundred acres he had inherited from his father, all that re-mained was Walstead Hall, a handsome seat in Wiltshire, with gardens, pinery, and farms for pasturage and tillage annexed, but which was deeply mortgaged; so that his whole income at that period would not amount to seven hundred pounds a year.

"Mary Lumley has good sense," said he to himself, "I will speak to her upon this momentous subject. For what will her seven thousand pounds do? It will not clear him of incumbrances, and when it is gone, what is she to do? Mary," said he, addressing her one morning when she was alone with him in the breakfast parlour, "does this young man, who is such a favourite with you, aspire to your hand?"

"He loves me, sir," replied she, "he has a noble estate in Wilt-shire, is the only son of a good family, and is willing to make any honourable arrangements previous to our union."

"You have then agreed to accept him?"

Lady Mary looked foolish. "I—I—have not refused him, sir."

"Well Mary, allow me to tell you that he is a bankrupt in both fortune and character. He has lost large sums at the gaming table, has associated with abandoned women, and unprincipled men. Can you hope for happiness in an union with such a person?"

"He may, and I have no doubt will reform, sir."

"*May* is barely possible, *will* hardly probable. Men who in early life have associated with profligate women form their opinion of the sex in general from that early knowledge. They will not believe any woman capable of resisting temptation, or practising self denial on principle, because they have found dissolute wives, and easy conquests in young women who are void of religion and virtue. Such men, Mary, may from passion, or from interest, protest that they love you. But, the passion gratified, the interested motives either complied with or disappointed ('tis of no consequence which) the stimulus loses its force, and the ardent lover sinks into the domestic tyrant, or the unfeeling savage."

"I cannot think, sir," said Lady Mary, "that Sir Stephen will degenerate into either."

"I would hope, Mary Lumley," he replied, "that you will not take a step of such consequence to your future peace as a matri-monial union without exercising, not only your own understanding, but consulting me, the guardian under whom you were placed, and whose knowledge of the world will enable him to direct you to avoid those rocks and quicksands on which the voyagers of youth and inexperience are liable to be wrecked. I am very earnest in this cause. I know the delicacy with which you have been brought up. I am well acquainted with the dangerous, I had almost said weak sensibility to which you too frequently yield. It is my duty as your guardian to take care that a proper settlement be made before you are married."

"I shall not marry directly, sir," said she, "and I believe in a short period the law will consider me of an age to dispose of my own person, and take care of my own interest."

"That is very true," said Mr. Matthews, with a sigh, "but let me conjure you, Lady Mary, not to be precipitate. Consult your friends. Be advised by those who love you. Ill could you support the deprivations a dissipated, heartless husband may bring upon you: dreadful would be the pangs that would agonize your heart, when that husband should treat with contempt and coldness, the woman he now pretends to idolize."

"I cannot believe either possible, sir."

"May you never find the suggestions realized, my poor child. I will however see Sir Stephen, and speak to him," continued Mr. Matthews.

"I must beg you will not," said the young lady petulantly, "Sir Stephen's views must be disinterested. What is my paltry fortune to his estates and possessions? he says he does not want a shilling with me."

"Then, Mary, let him prove the truth of his assertion by settling the whole of your fortune on yourself."

"What, sir, when his mind is so liberal, shall I prove myself a narrow minded selfish wretch, who has no confidence in the man she is about to make her husband? No, sir, when I make him master of my person, I shall also give him possession of my property, and I trust he is of too generous a disposition ever to abuse my confidence." Lady Mary left the room almost in tears, and Mr. Matthews in order to compose his temper, which had been somewhat irritated by this unpleasant discussion, walked toward the Stiene.

"What is the matter, Lady Mary," said Miss Blakeney, as she encountered her young associate on the stairs.

"Oh nothing very particular; only my guardian has been lecturing me about Haynes: as if a young woman nearly twenty-one was not competent to conduct herself and judge of her own actions."

"Why, as to that," replied Lucy, smiling, as they entered the drawing room together, "some women are not adequate to the task at forty. But jesting aside, I sincerely hope you will not take any decided step in this business contrary to the advice of Mr. Matthews. You have scarcely known Sir Stephen Haynes a fortnight, and are almost a stranger to his temper, habits and principles."

"You are nearly as much a stranger to Lieutenant Franklin, and yet I do not think that you would refuse him if he offered himself."

"You are mistaken, Lady Mary, I have no idea of romantic attachments, and laugh when I hear of love at first sight. I should never accept of any man without the approbation of Mr. Matthews and my guardian, Sir Robert Ainslie; and I must have taken leave of my senses, before I should enter into engagements with a young man not quite twenty, for I understand Mr. Franklin is nearly a year younger than myself!"

Here the conversation was interrupted by the entrance of the elder ladies and Aura Melville; pleasurable engagements occupied the remainder of the day, and no incident of consequence took place while they continued at Brighton.

About the middle of September, they returned to their delightful residence near Southampton, and for two months, Ainslie, Haynes, and Franklin, appeared not in the family circle. The first attended his father to London; the second was on the turf, dashing away upon the credit of intending soon to mary Lady Mary Lumley, whom he represented as a rich heiress; and the third confined to Brighton by his remaining term of duty.

CHAPTER VII

Folly—Rectitude—A Visit to Sergeant Blandford

◇　　◇

"Where in the world can Mary Lumley be," said Mrs. Cavendish, as the evening drew in, and the chill air of October reminded the inmates of Mr. Matthews' mansion that no one could be walking for pleasure at that hour. Lady Mary had gone out in the morning expressing her intention of spending the day with Miss Brenton. Now as it was customary for Mrs. Brenton's servant to attend the young lady home if she staid to a late hour, the family did not feel much alarmed until ten o'clock approached. Mr. Matthews broke off a game of chess he was playing with Lucy, and looked at his watch, Aura paced the room, and the two elder ladies expressed much uneasiness.

At length a ring at the gate made them start. Mr. Matthews in his anxiety preceded the servant to the door, and was well convinced by the precipitate retreat of the person who accompanied Lady Mary that it was no menial; nay, he fancied that he saw him kiss her hand, as he opened the door for her admittance.

"You are imprudent, Mary," said the anxious guardian, "to be out so late on this chilly evening, and with such slight covering. Who was the person who parted from you at the door?"

"A gentleman who dined at Mrs. Brenton's."

"And does Lady Mary Lumley allow herself to be escorted the

distance of nearly a mile in an unfrequented road, at this hour, by a stranger?"

"He was no stranger to Mrs. Brenton, sir."

"Nor to you, Mary, or I am mistaken."—

"I have seen him before," said she, hesitating, "I have met him several times," and taking a light from the sideboard where several were placed, she left the room.

"Mary will throw herself away," said Mrs. Matthews.

"Then she must abide the consequences," replied Mrs. Cavendish.

"Ah, much I fear," rejoined her sister, "the punishment will exceed the offence. That may be committed in a moment of romantic-folly; but the bitter repentance that will succeed may last through a long and miserable life."

Soon after Christmas, which no circumstances whatever would have prevented Mr. Matthews from celebrating in his own mansion and at his own church, the family removed to London, where a handsome ready furnished house in Southampton street, Bloomsbury Square, had been taken for them by Sir Robert Ainslie. Here Sir Stephen Haynes renewed his visits, but generally took care to call when he was sure of meeting other company, and assiduously avoided giving Mr. Matthews an opportunity of speaking to him alone. His manners to Lady Mary were polite, but distant, and her guardian began to surmise that he had altered his plans, and had some wealthier prize in view; he was therefore thrown off his guard, and determined to take no further notice of the subject to his fair ward.

The seventeeth of February was Lady Mary's birth day, that ardently desired day which freed her from the trammels of restraint, and made her, as she joyously expressed it, when Lucy and Aura affectionately kissed her and gave their congratulations, a free and independent agent.

"Then," said Aura, seriously, "I hope you will remain so at least for some years: enjoy this liberty you seem to prize so much; for, be assured there are shackles much less endurable than the salutary restraints of the excellent Mr. Matthews and his revered wife and sister, and not so easily thrown off."

At one o'clock, the writings necessary being prepared, Lady Mary was put in possession of her little fortune. When all was finished, Mrs. Matthews expressed her hope that she would remain in their family at least during the ensuing summer. She answered, formally, that "she had not yet determined how she should dispose of herself; she should remain with them during the time she staid in London, and then in all probability make a visit to her friend Miss Brenton."

About three weeks after this event, Lieutenant Franklin made a short visit to London, paid his respects to Lucy and her guardian's family, lamented that his father's ill health obliging him to pass the winter in Bath, he could not have the pleasure of making her acquainted with persons she was prepared so highly to esteem. "And for myself, Miss Blakeney," continued he, "I shall not be so happy as to see you above once more, as I have only a fortnight's leave of absence, and must devote the larger part of that time to attentions to my suffering father, and in striving to soothe and cheer the depressed spirits of my mother. But in June, I hope, my dear sir," turning to Mr. Matthews, "to be permitted to pay my respects to you in Hampshire."

Mr. Matthews expressed the pleasure it would give him to see him there, reflecting at the same time that at the period of the intended visit, he should decide upon the conduct to be observed in developing his intentions towards Lucy.

It was now determined that before Easter, Mr. Matthews and his family should return to their pleasant residence near Southampton. Lucy and Aura were delighted to leave London and return to inhale the sweets of the opening Spring and invigorating breezes from the sea. Lady Mary appeared indifferent; but three days before their intended departure, she showed Miss Blakeney a letter which she had received from Miss Brenton, which stated that she was going to pass Easter with an aunt who lived near Windsor, and entreated Lady Mary to accompany her.

"I never was at Windsor, Miss Blakeney, and I should like to see that celebrated castle. I have heard my poor mother talk of it."

As Lady Mary pronounced the words, *poor mother*, a deep blush suffused her face and neck, and her voice faltered almost to a sob as she finished the sentence. Lucy Blakeney did not want discernment; she looked earnestly at Lady Mary, and catching her hand, said tenderly, yet emphatically,

"But do not go to see it now, dear Mary, go with us into Hampshire, and I promise you when I am of age, which you know will be soon, we will make a most delectable excursion, take dear Guardy and Ma-Matthews, majestic Mrs. Cavendish and our lively Aura, and setting out in search of adventures, storm Windsor Castle in the course of our route; and you shall repeat all your lamented mother told you, for you know she was better acquainted with history than we are, especially when it was any thing concerning Kings and Princes, Dukes and Lords."

Now all this was said in a playful good humoured manner. But at her heart Lucy feared this excursion with Miss Brenton would lead to no good.

"I cannot retract my promise, dear Lucy," said Mary, in a soft tremulous voice. "Miss Brenton will be in town to-night, and will call for me to-morrow as she proceeds to Windsor."

"Would it not have been as well to have consulted"—Lucy would have proceeded, but Lady Mary stopped her with, "I cannot consent to ask leave of the stiff Mr. Matthews, his precise Lady, and the dictatorial Mrs. Cavendish."

"Oh fie! Lady Mary," replied Lucy, with something of sternness in her voice. "Can you forget the parental kindness they have shown you for five years past? You will say, perhaps, the interest of your fortune paid for your board, &c. True, those pecuniary debts were amply discharged. But who can repay the debt of gratitude due to those who cultivate the best feelings of the heart, and direct the understanding to the highest sources of improvement, whose precept and example go hand in hand to lead inexperienced youth into the path of happiness?"

"I never shall forget what I owe them, Miss Blakeney," she replied, "but I cannot consent to solicit permission to do what I like, and go where I please, from persons who, however good in their way, have no right now to control me. I shall myself mention my intention to the family, at the breakfast table to-morrow morning. Miss Brenton will commence her journey about noon, and will call for me; in the mean time I must beg it as a favour, you will not disclose this conversation to any one."

When she had left the room, Lucy stood for a moment irresolute what course to pursue. "It will do no good," said she mentally, "to distress the family by mentioning this intended excursion which however they may disapprove, they cannot prevent; and perhaps I judge too hardly of Lady Mary, when I think there is some other point in view than merely visiting Windsor Castle." Thus resolving upon silence, she joined the family at dinner, and found, to her surprise, that Lady Mary had complained of a head ache and requested to have some trifling refreshment in her own apartment.

The next morning at breakfast, no Lady Mary appeared, and when the footman was desired to send one of the female servants to call her, he replied,

"Lady Mary is not in the house."

"Not in the house?" cried Mr. Matthews, starting from his chair, "poor stray lamb, I fear the shepherd too easily gave up his trust, and thou wilt return no more to the fold."

Mrs. Matthews was turned deathly pale, and leaned back in her chair.

"It is no more than I expected," said Mrs. Cavendish, drawing herself up and taking a cup of tea from the trembling hand of Aura.

"Be not too much alarmed," said Lucy Blakeney. "I believe Lady Mary was engaged in a pleasurable excursion to Windsor, with

Miss Brenton, who arrived in town last evening, and was proceeding thither to visit her aunt. She mentioned it to me yesterday, but said they should not leave town till noon, and that at breakfast she would take leave of the family. Perhaps her friend went earlier than she expected, and Mary Lumley did not like to have the family disturbed, but I have no doubt she has left some letter or message."

"Lady Mary left the house at four o'clock in the morning," said the footman, "she went out through the area, because she was afraid of making a noise to alarm any one; the chaise did not draw up to the house, but stood at the bottom of the street. Betty, the house maid, took her bandbox, and I carried her trunk, when on her jumping in I saw she was received by a gentleman, and a lady seemed to be in the farther corner. There were four horses to the chaise, and a groom in livery followed it on horseback. 'To Windsor,' said the gentleman, as the door was shut, and they went off like lightning."

"Call Betty, this instant," said Mr. Matthews. Betty appeared. "Where is Lady Mary Lumley gone?" said he.

"To Windsor, with her friend Miss Brenton," she replied, pertly.

"Did she leave no letter or message, girl?"

"Lawes me, yes, there is a letter up stairs for you, I believes."

"Go fetch it, instantly."

"Stop," said he, when the girl gave him a sealed billet. "Why did you assist her out of the house in so clandestine a manner? Why not boldly open the front door; have the carriage drawn up, and call one of my servants to have adjusted her baggage, and if necessary to have proceeded with her?"

" 'Cause the poor dear lady cried, and said you and my ladies there wanted to make a slave of her, when she was as free to act for herself as you was, and if you knew of her going you would try to stop her."

" 'Tis well, go!" said Mr. Matthews, waving his hand. Betty

withdrew with an impertinent toss of her head, and Mr. Matthews opened the letter. It ran thus:

"SIR,

I am sensible you will blame the step I am about to take, but I cannot be happy unless as the wife of Sir Stephen Haynes. Before you will receive this, I shall be considerably advanced on the road to Scotland, not that, being my own mistress, any one has a right to control me, but I dreaded expostulation, shuddered at the idea of published banns, or a formal wedding by license, with settlements, lawyers, and parchments. These things have, I believe, little to do with love.—"

"But they have a great deal to do with prudence, I conceive," said the agitated Rector, pausing a moment from the perusal of the letter.

"Sir Stephen," he at length proceeded. "has promised to settle half his fortune on me, as a voluntary act of gratitude after I am his wife, and in return for this liberality I have given my little fortune into his hands. He talks of purchasing a peerage, and I begin to have different ideas of nobility since he has convinced me that all by nature are equal, and that distinctions have been always purchased by some means or other; and what matter is it whether by fighting for the rights of the monarch. or by advancing money to supply his necessities?

"My dear friend Miss Brenton accompanies me to Scotland. I shall, after a short tour, visit her in Hampshire, then, having taken a view of Sir Stephen's place in Wiltshire, and given our orders for repairs, new furnishing, &c. we shall make an excursion of a few months to the continent. On our return we shall pay our respects to you in Hampshire, and solicit a visit from any of the inmates of your mansion who may feel disposed so to honour us.

I beg you to accept my thanks for your care of my interest and happiness, although we happened not to think alike upon the latter subject, and make my acknowledgments to Mrs. Matthews and the other ladies of the family for their kind attentions.

I am, Sir, with Respect
and Esteem,

MARY LUMLEY."

Mr. Matthews folded the letter. "The die is cast," said he, "poor Mary Lumley, thou art fallen into bad hands. Settle half his fortune! according to the course he has pursued, by this time he may not have an acre of land, or a single guinea he can call his own.— That Miss Brenton has been of great injury to the unfortunate girl, for nothing can be more prejudicial to a young woman of strong imagination and ill regulated feelings, than those kind of artificial friendships and tender confidences, where flattery is substituted for real affection, and mutual self-complacency for disinterested attachment; where self willed folly is dignified with the name of enthusiastic liberality of sentiment, and the excitement of gratified vanity is mistaken for unchangeable, exalted love; such, I am persuaded, was the only friendship that subsisted between Julia Brenton, and our thoughtless Mary Lumley, and by her she has been led on to adopt the idea of 'All for Love or the World well lost,' and to act upon that mischievous, I could almost say dissolute, principle."

"I always knew Lady Mary to be vain and thoughtless, and from the romantic bias given to her early ideas easily led and highly enthusiastic," said Aura Melville, "but I do believe her mind is pure."

"There is the misery of it!" said Mr. Matthews, sighing, "for when that pure mind shall discover that it has allied itself to sensuality and profligacy, that it has chosen for its associate a being who will divide his time between jockeys and gamesters, and that he is never so happy as when in company with men and women of low breeding and gross conversation, what must it feel?"

No answer was made. The breakfast was removed almost untasted; no steps however could be taken to prevent this ill starred union. Mr. Matthews walked to Sir Robert Ainslie's, and discovered that the whole of Lady Mary's fortune had been the day before withdrawn from his hands, where it had been placed by her guardian on delivering up his trust, by an order under her own signature.

"What, all? principal and the few hundreds of interest I had saved for her, that she might have a little store to supply her purse upon coming of age?"

"All,' replied Sir Robert, "I was not aware of the circumstance till this morning, and was preparing to call on you when you were announced. The order was in favour of Julia Brenton. There was no authority by which we could refuse to pay it."

"Certainly not," said Mr. Matthews, "but she has ruined herself."

The second morning after this very painful occurrence, Mr. Matthews' family set off towards home, where they arrived in safety, and with real pleasure took possession of their old apartments, and began to pursue their usual avocations in that beloved mansion, reading, working, walking, arranging their plants and flowers, in the garden, and greenhouse, and occasionally riding round the country, accompanied by their paternal friend the Rector.

Mr. Matthews took an early opportunity to call on Mrs. Brenton, but the old lady knew nothing of her daughter's plans, had received but one letter from her since her departure. That indeed was dated from Windsor, but she appeared totally ignorant of the marriage of Lady Mary, or the active part her daughter had taken in the affair.

Lucy and Aura recommenced their rambles to the cottages of their poor neighbours, nor was the old sergeant forgotten, and be it known, that though Miss Blakeney sometimes thought that June would increase their party, yet was she never heard to complain of the leaden wings of time, or to sigh profoundly, and look interestingly sentimental.

The latter end of June brought Sir Robert Ainslie's family to their seat in Hampshire, and a few days after, Lieutenant Franklin, to visit his friend Edward.

"Lucy, my love," said Mr. Matthews, a few days after the arrival of these young men in their neighbourhood, "will you candidly answer me one question, and seriously make me one promise?"

"I will answer any question you may please to make, very honestly, my dear sir," said she smiling, "and as to promises, I am convinced you would require none but what was meant to secure my happiness."

"Now, my good girl, to put you to the test, has Mr. Franklin ever made any professions to you, or sought more than by general attentions to engage your affections?"

"Never, sir, Mr. Franklin never uttered a syllable to me that could be construed into any thing more than that politeness and gallantry which gentlemen of his profession think incumbent upon them to pay to our sex." A slight blush tinged her face as she spoke.

"But, my dear Lucy, have you never thought those polite gallantries, as you term them, were sometimes a little particular?"

"The thought"—she replied with a little hesitation. "But pray do not think me a vain girl, I have thought his looks and manner said more than his words."

"Good, ingenuous girl," said the Rector, "and you would not be displeased if you found yourself the object of his affection.—Well, well," he continued, "I will not insist on an answer to this last question. But now to your promise."

"Name it, sir."

"It is that you will enter into no engagements of a matrimonial kind till you have seen your twenty-first birth day. I have a letter in my possession written by your grandfather in the last hour of his life. It was designed to be delivered to you when your minority ended; you surely remember how very suddenly that good man was called out of time into eternity."

"Can I ever forget it?" replied Lucy, with emotion. "He had retired to his study as all imagined for a few hours repose, which it was his custom to take of an afternoon, and was found dead in his easy chair, I think I was told, with a written paper before him, and the pen still between his fingers."

"It was so, my child. I was in the house at the time, where I arrived after he had retired, and that paper was an unfinished letter to you. Promise me, therefore, Lucy, that you will enter into no serious engagements till you have read that letter."

"I do promise most solemnly, and also voluntarily add, that every behest in the letter of that dear lamented parent, shall be adhered to by me."

"I know I can depend on you," replied Mr. Matthews, "and am satisfied."

A few days after this conversation, Franklin having taken his tea at the Rectory, proposed a walk, and Aura being engaged in some domestic concerns which Mrs. Matthews had requested her to see performed, Lucy accepted the invitation. "I will take this young soldier to the cottage of my old friend sergeant Blandford," said she to Mr. Matthews, "and he shall tell him some of his famous stories, and fight over his battles."

It was a very fine evening, but as the sun descended, a dark cloud received the glorious orb, which as it shrouded his beams, transfused their radiance to itself, making the edges of its deep purple tint flame with gold and crimson.

"That cloud foretells a shower, I think," said Lucy, as approaching the old man's dwelling, she turned her eyes for the first time towards the declining sun.

"It will not come on very rapidly," said Franklin.

"We will make a short visit to the old soldier," said she. Then looking steadfastly at the advancing cloud, she continued, "That cloud is an emblem of misfortune overwhelming for a while the virtuous person; which though for a time it may prevent their general usefulness, and obscure the splendor of their actions, cannot entirely hide their brilliancy, but catches as it were a glory from the radiance it partially obscures."

"Or rather," said Franklin, "it is like a veil thrown over the face of a beautiful woman, which shades but cannot diminish her loveliness."

Before they reached old Blandford's hut, the cloud had spread rapidly and large drops of rain had fallen, so that Lucy's muslin dress was but a poor defence, and was easily wet through. She had thrown a black lace mantle over her shoulders when she began her walk, but pulling it off as she rushed into the house, and at the same time divesting her head of a straw cottage bonnet, her redundant hair fell over her face and shoulders.

"Bless me, is it you, Miss Blakeney?" said the old man, rising and supporting himself with his crutch.

"Yes, it is, good Blandford, and finely wet I am, but I use myself so much to all changes of atmosphere that I do not fear taking cold. I walked very fast when it began to rain, and am incommoded by the heat. So let me sit down, and give me a draught of water."

"Drink sparingly," said Franklin.

At the sound of his voice old Blandford started, and looking first at one and then at the other, asked,

"Who is this, Miss Lucy?"

"My name is Franklin," said the lieutenant, "and I come to visit an old brother soldier." He then presented the veteran his hand, who gazing earnestly on him exclaimed, "I could almost have sworn that you were—but I'm an old fool, it is impossible—and this dear lady has often made me think I had seen her face before, though not till this moment could I bring to mind whom she was so like. But just as she is now, only paler and in great distress, I once saw"—he paused—

"Saw whom?" said Lucy.

"It is a melancholy story, Miss, and you will not like to hear it, mayhap."

"I have no objection to hear it, if it is not very long, for the rain is almost over, and the moment it ceases, we must set off toward home."

Blandford stretched out his disabled leg, rested his chin on the handle of his crutch, and thus began.—

"You know, Miss Blakeney, I served abroad several years, and got my wound fighting with the—."

"Well, never mind, you have told me all that before, now to your story."

"Why, Miss, it was one cold night about the end of October, 1774, I was but a private then, when as I had been to the Colonel's quarters for orders, as I went from the door, a poor shivering young creature, her face pale as death, and nothing over her but a thin white gown, and a black something, like that you threw off just now, though the snow was falling fast, and the wind was very bleak."

Just then Mr. Matthews' carriage drove up to the cottage, and a request was delivered to Miss Blakeney that she would return in it, as her friends feared she might take cold. The sergeant was therefore obliged to break off his story, when it was scarcely begun, Lucy saying,

"You shall tell it me some other time, my good Blandford, but now good night."

Lieutenant Franklin handed her into the coach, bowing as he laughingly said, "A soldier is not afraid of the damp arising from a trifling shower, so I shall walk back to Sir Robert Ainslie's."

This delicate conduct was not lost upon Miss Blakeney, and raised the young man in the estimation of Mr. Matthews.

A short time after this, Mr. Franklin openly made a declaration of his sentiments to Lucy, who referred him to her guardian for the reason why she could not give a decided answer till her twenty-first birth day was passed. When Franklin heard that Miss Blakeney was in reality a wealthy heiress, instead of the dependant orphan he had depicted in his own mind, and found that he must adopt her name or relinquish her fortune, he felt something like hesitation; he had already laid aside his own family name and assumed that of his grandfather.

"I will be candid, my dear sir," said he. "Happiness to me appears unattainable unless in a union with Miss Blakeney, but I must consult my father, and I fear he will never consent to my changing the venerated name I now bear for any other. You know fortune has not been an object with me, for I loved and would have married your ward, though she had nothing but her invaluable self to bestow. But I cannot reconcile it to my own sense of integrity to despoil her of so fair an independence, which entitles her to those appendages and elegancies which my moderate fortune could not afford."

"You are a worthy young man," said Mr. Matthews, "persevere in this course of integrity, and perhaps things may turn out so as to obviate these difficulties. At any rate you will avoid self reproach, and happiness is so hardly attainable in this world, that it would be a pity while too eagerly pursuing it, to run the risk of mingling gall with the honey."

When Franklin took leave of Lucy, she held out her hand, and he pressed it to his lips. Her eyes were evidently full, while with a tremulous voice she said,

"Remember I have entered into no engagements, and whatever the import of my grandfather's letter may be, I am firmly resolved to abide by his directions. You have requested leave to commence a correspondence; you must allow me to decline it. It could be of no service. When the time comes that I shall see this formidable letter, you shall hear either from Mr. Matthews or myself the result: and let that be what it may, I shall ever retain a most grateful sense of your disinterested attachment, and if no nearer tie can ever connect us, I shall ever regard you as a friend and brother."

She then hastily left the room and shut herself in her own apartment, to give vent to feelings she was unwilling to have witnessed, though she was unable to suppress. Franklin returned to Sir Robert Ainslie's, from whence, at an early hour next morning, he departed with his young friend for London.

CHAPTER VIII

Unpleasant Discovery—
Bitter Repentance

◇   ◇

Though Sir Stephen Haynes had proposed to the credulous Lady Mary the delightful excursions which she stated in her letter to Mr. Matthews, he never seriously intended any other excursion than the one that made him master of her fortune, and indeed could he have obtained possession of that without incumbering himself with her person, he would gladly have done it. When however the hymeneal knot was tied, and the romantic, thoughtless girl had paid him the seven thousand pounds, he carelessly asked her if she had reserved any for her own use. Miss Brenton, who was present, not giving her friend time to speak, answered for her, "Certainly, Sir Stephen, Lady Mary has retained a trifle for her pocket expenses, till you have the settlements properly adjusted, and can pay her first quarter."

Sir Stephen looked out of the window and began to whistle. Miss Brenton laid her finger on her lip, looking earnestly at Lady Mary to impose silence upon her, for the truth was she had persuaded her to retain five hundred pounds, which was the sum Mr. Matthews had mentioned as having laid by for her, during her minority.

"It will be time enough to talk of these things when we have been to Wiltshire," said the new made bride. "Sir Stephen will then make his own generous arrangements, and I shall not have occasion for much money till I get to London, when I must have an entire new wardrobe, have the few jewels my mother left me more fashionably set—You will have a new carriage, I presume, Sir Stephen," addressing her husband, "and new liveries?"

"I don't know that I shall have either, madam," said he. It was the first time he had ever addressed her by the formal title of madam. She looked at him and her colour varied, but thinking he might suppose that she wished to hurry to London, she said,

"I did not mean that we should go directly there, if we are only there time enough to have everything ready for the birth day, when I shall expect to be presented by some of my mother's relations."

"Then you will be disappointed," he replied, sharply, "for, I do not think I shall go to London at all. It is a devilish expensive place, and you cannot suppose that your fortune entitles you to form such expectations, however your ladyship's rank may be."

"I never deceived you in regard to my fortune, Sir Stephen," she answered, her lip beginning to quiver, and a choaking sensation to arise in her throat.

"But I suppose you knew that your accommodating friend there had done it; she represented your fortune more than quadruple the paltry sum you have given me."—

"I have given you all, Sir Stephen," said she, "and had it been a thousand times as much, would have given it as freely." She hid her face with her handkerchief, and burst into an hysterical sob.

"Oh, pray don't let us have a crying match so early in the honey moon," said he, "I hate whimpering, it spoils a pretty face and makes an ugly one detestable." He snatched up his hat, and sauntered out.

It may be easily imagined what a young woman of such uncontrollable feelings as Lady Mary must have endured at this discovery of the selfish disposition of a man to whom she had entrusted her all of fortune, her all of earthly felicity—she threw herself into the arms of Miss Brenton and exclaimed,

"Theresa, why have you done this? I thought him disinterested,

I thought he loved me for myself, why, why did you lead him to think"—"My dear Mary," said Miss Brenton soothingly, "how can you blame me? I did not know the extent of your fortune, you were reputed an heiress, your guardian never contradicted the report, and knowing how immensely rich Sir Stephen was left by his father, I rejoiced in the prospect of seeing my dear friend, so amiable, so lovely, united to a man able to add to her exalted rank the gifts of fortune. And when I knew your sensitive heart was engaged by him, I thought in promoting your union, I was promoting your happiness."

"Forgive my petulance, Theresa," said Lady Mary, drying her eyes, "but what must I do, how must I conduct myself?"

Let it be remembered that Lady Mary was but a wife of three days, for on their return from Scotland they had stopped at Alnwick in Northumberland, where so much of antiquity and ancient splendor were to be seen, connected with historic tales of chivalry and renown, that Mary Lumley, as she passed through it on her imprudent expedition, had expressed a 'vish to stop on her return, and view the castle, the gates of the town, and other objects, to which her enthusiastic spirit of romance had given the highest interest.

Accordingly, on the second night of their retrograde journey, they stopped at an old fashioned but well attended comfortable inn, in the ancient town of Alnwick not very far from the beautiful seat so long descended from father to son in the noble family of Percy of Northumberland. On the second morning after her arrival there, the scene took place, which led to the question of "what must I do? how must I conduct myself?"

"Struggle to suppress your feelings," said Miss Brenton, "when Sir Stephen returns receive him with composure, and on no account let him know of the small sum you have retained, for from all I see and hear, I suspect it will be some time before you gain any thing from him."

Theresa Brenton was an artful, selfish young woman; her mother was a widow with a small jointure, and Theresa with a very trifling fortune of her own, looked round for ways and means to lead a life of ease and affluence, without infringing on a small patrimony inherited from her father, except to supply the articles of clothing and pocket money. She had early began to try her talent at flattery upon Lucy Blakeney, but Lucy had too much sense to be led, or hoodwinked by soft speeches, and a yielding versatility of manners. She was always polite, and treated Miss Brenton with that suavity of demeanour which was her general characteristic; but she could not love her as an associate, nor confide in her as a friend.

Lady Mary Lumley had been accustomed to the voice of adulation from her earliest remembrance; she had observed how subservient her governess always was to the will of her mother; she never contradicted her, and if at any time she was unreasonably petulant, from ennui, or irritable nerves, she was always silent, or soothed her into good humour again. Lady Mary thought this a proof of the strongest affection; she loved her governess, who was equally indulgent to her foibles, and glossed them over with the name of amiable weaknesses.

It may be here observed, that a conduct which was kind and consoling, to a woman formerly followed and courted by an admiring world, moving in the most splendid circles, indulged in every wish of her heart, but who was now weak in health, depressed in fortune, and neglected by that world; it was the height of cruelty to practice toward a young creature just entering into life.

When after the death of her mother Lady Mary was removed to the regular well conducted family of Mr. Matthews, where a kind of sedate cheerfulness went hand in hand with rational amusement and mental improvement; the change was so great that she was glad to meet a more congenial associate in Theresa Brenton. The consequence was, that they became in the language of romantic misses, "*sworn friends.*" Lady Mary would complain of the formality of Mrs. Cavendish, the strictness of Mr. Matthews, and the undeviating preciseness of his wife. Miss Brenton would reply, "I feel for you, my dear Mary, it must be very painful to your sensitive mind, but be patient, it cannot last forever, and the time will arrive when, being your own mistress, you can indulge those amiable sensibilities which throw a fascinating charm around you, and whilst constituting your own happiness, render you the delight of all who know you."

In the mean time Theresa Brenton would, when Mary Lumley received her quarterly allowance, accompany her from *pure good nature*, on her shopping expeditions, and when her friend purchased any elegant or expensive article, would lament, that she had not the power to indulge herself in any thing beyond usefulness, when often the thoughtless, yet generous minded Mary, would suffer considerable depredations on her purse, rather than dear Theresa should feel the want of an article that would set off her pretty person so well, but which her confined finances would not allow her to purchase.

Miss Brenton was herself deceived in regard to Sir Stephen's fortune, when following Lady Mary from Brighton he contrived to get an introduction to the family, where he found he could make a staunch auxiliary by a profusion of protestations and a few showy presents. His equipage and dress were so elegant, his disregard of expense so evident, that both Mrs. and Miss Brenton conceived his revenues to be immense, and Theresa thought by assisting her *friend* in eluding her guardian's watchfulness and forming a matrimonial union with Sir Stephen, she should secure to herself an invitation to pass one winter at least in London, during which period she might secure an establishment for herself, and, another season, dash forth, at parties, balls and routs, at the opera, theatre, or masquerade, as the rival or superior of her *angelic friend* Lady Mary Haynes. She therefore pretended not to know the extent of Lady Mary's fortune, but led the scheming selfish Baronet to conclude that it was above twenty thousand pounds.

Mary Lumley herself would have spurned at such an imposition, but Mary Lumley never made that mental exertion which is necessary when persons mean to judge and decide for themselves. She had been blindly led by the flattery and opinions of Theresa Brenton, and was taught to believe that in asking for or submitting to the advice of Mr. Matthews, she was making herself a slave to the will of one who being old and fastidious, was incapable of deciding upon what would constitute the happiness of a young and beautiful woman.

But Theresa Brenton in abetting the elopement had overreached herself. She had no idea that when she received, by Lady Mary's order, the whole of her little fortune from Sir Robert Ainslie, that the innocent confiding girl meant to give it unconditionally to her husband, before he had made the promised settlements, which even at that time she had no doubt that he had the power to make. But when she found it impossible to persuade her from so doing, she strongly urged her to retain the five hundred pounds in her own hands.

When dinner was announced and the ladies met Sir Stephen, Lady Mary strove to smile, Miss Brenton was remarkably cheerful, and when the cloth was removed, he made a proposal to visit Alnwick castle that afternoon. The smiles naturally returned to the face of his bride, and the carriage being ordered, they proceeded to the stately mansion of the Percys.

Sir Stephen knew when he made the proposal that some of the family being at that time in Northumberland, it was not likely that they would be admitted to view the castle; and when he received for answer on applying for admittance at the porter's lodge, that there was company there at present, turning to Lady Mary, he said,

"Well, it can't be helped, but we will take a drive round to view a little romantic spot which I am sure you will be pleased with; when I went out this morning, I met a friend I had not seen for many years who now lives within a short distance of Alnwick, I walked with him to his house where he resides with his mother, and from thence, on one of his horses, accompanied him on a ride in this delightful country, where there is so much to gratify both the taste and the judgment."

As they rode along, Sir Stephen was uncommonly attentive and entertaining. At an opening from a wood, he pointed out a cottage, built in the antique style, with a garden gay with early spring flowers and surrounded by a small patch of ground in which were a variety of beautiful flowering shrubs, though they now only shewed their under green leaves. The ladies both exclaimed,

"Well, what a lovely place, it is just a situation to realize the idea of love in a cottage."

Sir Stephen bade the postillion drive up to the gate.

"Come," said he, "we will alight and get some tea here. There will be a fine moon this evening, and we shall have a pleasant drive afterwards." But Miss Brenton observed, "that she thought the road they had come was very lonely; they had seen but few passengers and those not very prepossessing in their looks."

"Besides," said Lady Mary, "this is certainly not a house of entertainment."

"We shall try that," said he, jumping out, and insisting on the ladies alighting, he led the way up to an old fashioned porch, over which climbed the woodbine, and sweet brier, just bursting into vegetation. An elderly woman opened the door and ushered them into a not inelegant, but small parlour.

"Where is Mr. Craftly?" asked Sir Stephen.

"I expect him in every moment, your honour!" said the woman, whom we will call Janet, "and he told me should your honour arrive before him, to shew the ladies their rooms, and obey their orders in every thing."

The ladies were struck almost dumb with astonishment. "Our rooms? why, are we to remain here all night?" faintly articulated Lady Mary.

"Your lady, Sir Stephen, has no night clothes here," said Miss Brenton, with rather more firmness of voice, "and how can we be accommodated in this little place?"

"Pho! Theresa," he replied, half jocularly, "don't raise obstacles where none really exist: I have ordered the trunks to be brought; I did not like our situation at the Inn, and my friend having offered me the use of this cottage for a short period, I concluded it would just suit Lady Mary's taste, and you know you both declared just now it was exactly the situation to realize the idea of *love in a cottage.*"

"True," said Lady Mary, with a slight degree of acrimony, "but I do not know how I shall like the cottage without the love."

At this moment Craftly entered, and Sir Stephen taking his arm walked into the little shrubbery.

"What can this mean, Theresa?" inquired the pale and agitated bride. Miss Brenton shrugged her shoulders, but remained silent; and they concluded to go and inspect the apartments.

The cottage consisted of two parlours, a kitchen and four bed chambers, neatly but not elegantly furnished.

"I won't stay here," said Lady Mary.

"But how shall we get away?" rejoined her companion, "for I believe the carriage is gone in which we came. But be patient, dear Mary, this may only be a little frolic of Sir Stephen's to try your temper. Take no notice, ask no questions, endeavour to be cheerful, and all may be well yet. He knew your mother's attachment to rank and splendor, he may fear that you inherit her family pride."

"I wish to Heaven I had!" she ardently replied, "I should never have fallen into this humiliating situation."

"Well, what is done cannot be undone," said Theresa with a nonchalance surprizing to her friend.

At tea, though Mary was calm, she could not be cheerful. Miss Brenton was rather silent and observant. Craftly stayed the evening, and after supper challenged Sir Stephen to a game at piquet. The ladies retired to their chambers, where they found their trunks, but on looking round Lady Mary missed her dressing case, in which were her jewels and all her money except about twenty-five guineas which were in Theresa's purse.

She had inquired into the establishment of the cottage, and found it consisted only of the elderly person she had first seen, who acted as cook and housekeeper, and a rude country girl, who was to attend the ladies and take care of the chambers; a half grown boy, to clean knives and attend at meal times, and a poor old crone who occasionally came to superintend the garden and grounds. The girl accustomed to early hours, was gone to bed; the woman thought her work was finished when the supper table was cleared, and the boy expressed his discontent when he found he must sit up to wait on the gentlemen.

When, therefore, Lady Mary, on retiring to her room, found no one to assist her in undressing, or to go to Sir Stephen to inquire for her dressing case, Miss Brenton, who felt more alarmed than she was willing to own, snatched up the candle, for there was but one in the apartment, and without apology, hastened back to the parlour.

"Sir Stephen," said she, throwing open the door, "your lady's dressing case is not come."

"Well," he replied, "what of that? I suppose she can do without it for one night, lend her some of your things, Theresa, for I believe *they* are come."

"They may be, but I was so disturbed upon missing this valuable case, (for it belonged to your lady's mother, and she prized it very highly) that I did not look for, or even think of my own things."

"Well, well, I dare say it is safe enough, I will see about it tomorrow, so good Theresa, do go now, and leave us to play our game in peace."

"What a fool I have been, and how I have misled poor Lady Mary," said Miss Brenton, mentally, as she ascended the stairs. But endeavouring to suppress her feelings, and look cheerful as she entered the room where her friend was undressing, she said,

"The box will be here to-morrow, you must condescend, dear Mary, to use my dressing apparatus tonight and in the morning, I hope we shall prevail on Sir Stephen to give up the wild scheme of staying any time in this cottage, and commence a journey if not to London, at least into Hampshire, where I am sure my mother will be happy to receive you till Sir Stephen can look round and settle in a proper habitation."

After a few remarks, not very pleasant to either party, the ladies separated, but though they retired to bed, sleep visited neither of them till nearly daylight. When it did overtake them, it was so profound that they did not wake till after nine in the morning.

Lady Mary on looking round soon perceived Sir Stephen had not been in bed all night. A vague sensation of desolateness struck upon her heart she started up, searched for a bell, no bell was to be found. She opened the chamber door and called aloud for Theresa, and in a few moments, wrapped only in a dressing gown, her friend entered the room.

"Sir Stephen has not been in his apartment all night, Theresa, what can be the meaning of all this?" she exclaimed wildly. Before Miss Brenton could reply, Janet who had been listening, hearing the ladies speak, came up to say that breakfast had been ready above an hour.

"Where is your Master? good woman," asked Miss Brenton, as calmly as she could.

"My Master? Mr. Craftly, does your Ladyship mean. He walked out with his honour Sir Stephen, before five o'clock, and said he should not return to breakfast; but Dora when she was cleaning the parlour where their honours played cards last night, saw this bit of paper, but what it's about we can't tell, for neither she nor I can read joining hand."

Before Janet had finished her harangue, Theresa had snatched the note from her hand, eagerly broke the seal, and read as follows,

"TO MISS THERESA BRENTON,

You cannot be surprised, Theresa, after the explanation which took place between Lady Mary and myself yesterday, that I should declare my utter inability to make those settlements which I talked of before our excursion to the north. I must beg you to make my acknowledgments to the dear generous girl for all marks of favour and kindness bestowed by her on her unworthy, humble servant, but my finances are in such a state, that it is totally impossible for me to take a journey to Wilts, as proposed, or to solicit her company to France, whither I must repair as speedily as possible, to rusticate, whilst my affairs in England are put in train to restore me to some comparative degree of affluence. My friend, Richard Craftly, Esq. has offered the cottage to you and your lovely friend as long as you may please to occupy it. He is, Miss Brenton, a man of good abilities, amiable disposition, and possessed of a small but genteel and unincumbered estate, which upon the death of his mother will be augmented. He will call on you this afternoon, I *recommend him to your notice*. My best wishes attend you and your fair associate Lady Mary.

I am, Dear Theresa,
> Your Obliged friend, &c. &c.
> > Stephen Haynes."

"Give it me, give me that letter, Theresa!" exclaimed Lady Mary, snatching it from Miss Brenton. Her frenzied eye glanced rapidly over its contents, and muttering,

"*Friend! associate!*—yes, it flashes on my mind, I have no certificate; he gives me no name. I am undone! undone!—Oh! my Guardian, my dear! kind Lucy."

The letter fell from her hand, she clasped her fingers tightly across her forhead, and before the terrified and humane Janet could step forward to catch her, she fell lifeless on the floor.

CHAPTER IX

The Letter—The Birth Day

◊　　◊

October had almost expired; Lucy Blakeney began to count the hours when she should be relieved from the state of suspense which, notwithstanding her well regulated mind and subdued feelings was very painful. She had occasionally heard through the Ainslie family of Franklin's health and that his father still remained in a weak and sometimes deranged state. Her mind was harassed, she even no longer took pleasure in visiting Blandford's cottage.

"I cannot account for it, Aura," said she one day to Miss Melville, "but though my curiosity was awakened by the manner in which the old sergeant commenced his story, yet I cannot summon resolution to ask him to tell it me, a certain terror spreads through my frame, and I wish to hear no more of it till I can hear it in company with Mr. Franklin."

"Alas, and a-well-a-day," replied Aura, laughing, "what a sad thing this tender something is, which we hardly dare own, and know not how to describe."

"Well, I will not deserve to be laughed at, Aura: for I will act upon priciple, and am resolved to partake and enjoy all the comforts and innocent pleasures of life that may fall in my path, though one little thorn should pierce my foot in my pilgrimage."

"Your foot or your heart, Lucy?"

"Why my good Aura, I shall strive to keep it as far from my heart as I can."

"Do you remember, Lucy, what day next Thursday is?" asked Mr. Matthews, one morning as he sat at breakfast with his family.

"It is my birth day, sir, is it not?"

"Even so, my good little girl," for with Mr. Matthews every thing that was held very dear by him, was denominated *little*.

"Well," continued he, "and what shall we do to celebrate the day? I have no doubt but all the beaus and misses in the environs of Southampton, have long been anticipating splendid doings on the day when Miss Blakeney obtains her majority."

"I mean to have very splendid doings, sir."

"Indeed."

"Yes"—

"I wonder then, Miss Blakeney, you did not give my brother and sister intimation of your intent," said Mrs. Cavendish, "that proper preparations might have been made without the hurry which must now ensue."

"Oh, my dear madam," said Aura, "Lucy and I have been busy these two months past in preparing for this interesting occasion, and indeed our invitations are already sent out, and every one, I do assure you, accepted."

"Very extraordinary conduct, I think," said the consequential old lady.

"I wish you had given a little more time," said Mrs. Matthews, mildly, "but however we will see what can be done. But what is it to be? a ball and supper? or a breakfast in fashionable style?"

"Oh neither, madam, though I hope to make some dance, and some sing who are not much in the habit of doing such things."—

Mrs. Cavendish had taken a large pinch of snuff, and having wiped the *poudre tabac* from her upper lip with one of the finest coloured silk handkerchiefs, which together with her elegant snuff box she deposited in a fillagree work basket which always stood beside her, and opened her delicate white cambric one, and laid it on her lap, was beginning to speak, when Mr. Matthews said, "These girls are only playing tricks with us, sister. Lucy no more intends to have a party, than I intend to take a voyage to the moon."

"Don't you be too sure, my dear sir," said Lucy, laying her hand playfully on his arm. "I have really invited a party of forty to dine here on Thursday next, and all I have to ask is that you will lend me the hall, and that Mrs. Matthews will have the goodness to order John to lay the cloth in a simple manner for my guests, and permit the cook and housekeeper for all day on Wednesday to obey my injunctions."

"Well, children," said Mrs. Matthews, "I believe you must have your way this once. It shall be, Lucy, as you wish."

"But come, Lucy," said Mr. Matthews, "let us somewhat into the secret; I suspect you will want a little cash to carry your fine plans into effect."

"Not a doit, dear sir, till Thursday morning, when I shall want one hundred pounds, in guineas, half guineas, crowns and half crowns."

"Extravagant baggage," he replied, his fine venerable countenance glowing with pleasure. "Now tell us the arrangements of the day."

"Oh! they are very simple. You know, my ever venerated Mr. Matthews, on that day I expect to read a letter, the contents of which will most probably determine the hue of my future fate." She spoke with solemnity, and a slight convulsive tremor passed over her intelligent features.

"If you please, let that letter remain uninvestigated till I retire for the night. I would enjoy the innocent festivities I have projected for the day,—and now," she continued with more hilarity of manner, "I will tell you my plan. About twelve o'clock I expect my guests to begin to assemble; they will consist of a few of the oldest and most respected poor of your parish, with children and grandchildren. Aura and myself will receive them in the large sitting parlour, when yourself, with whom I shall deposit my hundred pounds, shall portion it out amongst them according to your judgment. For you must be the most proper person to decide upon their necessities and merits. You have ever been so liberal in your allowance to me, that having laid by a little hoard, Aura and myself have provided garments for the oldest and most infirm, the youngest and most desolate, and suitable presents for the rest."

"Oh! ho," said Mr. Matthews, "so now the secret is out of the cause of the many jaunts to Southampton lately, and the long conferences held in the dressing room, of a morning early, to which none but a few industrious young women were admitted."

"Even so, sir, for while we were gratifying our own whims, it was but just that they should not be selfish ones; so when Aura and I had cut the garments, we employed those young persons to make them, so that they might be benefited by forwarding our scheme, without feeling the weight of obligation, which I should think was a feeling most repugnant to the young and active. They have none of them been let into the secret of the use for which these garments are designed but some of them if not all will partake of our festivities."—

Mrs. Cavendish had during this explanation, sat with her eyes fixed on Miss Blakeney's face; she had folded and unfolded her cambric handkerchief several times, her eyes twinkled, she hemmed, applied the before mentioned silk handkerchief to her nose; and at length reaching her hand across the table she said in no very firm voice, "You are certainly a most extraordinary young lady, and I begin to think I have never rightly understood you. Pardon me, child, I fear I have this morning been both illiberal and rude."

"So well acquainted as I am with Mrs. Cavendish's good understanding, and highly cultivated mind," said Lucy, gracefully taking the extended hand, "it would be next to impossible that I could suspect her of ever being intentionally either illiberal or rude." "Well, well," replied the old lady, with one of her most knowing nods, "I trust I shall know you better in future."

On the Wednesday following several good sirloins of beef were roasted, hams boiled, pies baked, and on the Thursday morning plum puddings boiled for the expected regale. It was scarcely twelve o'clock when the company began to assemble; the young brimful of joy, and the old anticipating they hardly knew what, but all were cheerful and blithe with the most delightful sensations. Amongst the first arrived old Alice Lonsdale and her good man, brought by one of their neighbour's, whom Lucy had engaged for the purpose, in a chaise; nor were Thomas, who had now recovered the use of his limbs, with his good Dame and children, forgotten. While the family who had excited so warmly Lady Mary Lumley's romantic enthusiasm, were the blithest among the blithe in the happy group that not only filled the Rector's eating parlour, but partially filled the benches in the great hall; for Lucy's forty, when children, grandchildren, and in some cases great-grandchildren were collected, amounted to about sixty. Dishes of common cake were handed round, with cheese and ale for the men, and wine-sangaree for the women. Mr. Matthews then with a discriminating hand, portioned out the bounty of the heiress, according to the necessities of all; and many were that day provided with the means of passing through the ensuing winter with comfort, who else must have been pinched, both for fuel and sustenance.

At half past two, the tables were plentifully spread, at which amongst the elder guests, Mr. and Mrs. Matthews presided, and at that with the younger, sat Lucy and Aura, while Mrs. Cavendish walked round, looked at their happy faces and took her pinch of snuff with more exhilarated feelings than she had experienced for years before.

After dinner Lucy and Aura invited the Matrons to their own apartments which adjoined each other, where each received a present of clothing adapted to her age, circumstances and family. The young ones sported cheerfully in the grounds, the old men talked in groups round the hall chimney, where blazed an old fashioned large and cheerful fire. At six, a regale of coffee, tea, and simple cakes, with bread and butter were set forth; and before eight, all had retired to seek their homes, under the light of a brilliant full moon.

And how did Lucy feel when all were departed? She felt as a christian ought to feel; she had cheered and lightened the hearts of many; she had herself enjoyed the purest felicity during the whole day, and she mentally ejaculated as taking the letter from her guardian she sought her own apartment,

"If I have now a bitter cup to drain, let me not repine. I have much, very much, to be grateful for, and what right have I to expect to walk over beds of roses without feeling the briars which surround the stalks on which those beautiful and fragrant flowers blossom."—

She entered her chamber, bidding Aura good night at the door, which closing, she sat down, the letter in her hand, which though unsealed, she had not courage to open; at length rallying her spirits she unfolded the paper and read,

"TO MISS LUCY T. BLAKENEY,
To be delivered on the day she attains the age of 21.

"From the hour when I closed the eyes of your beloved, ill fated mother, you, my dear Lucy, have been the delight and solace of your grandmother and myself. And your amiable disposition has led us to hope, that you may in future be the happy inheritress of the estate and property on which we have lived above thirty-five years: happy, my child, in bestowing comfort on others, and doubly happy in the enjoyment of reflected joy from grateful hearts.

"You are in possession of independence from the bequest of Captain Blakeney, but you will find by my will, that it is my wish that not a farthing of that bequest, either principal or interest, should be expended on you during your minority. The income arising from your hereditary estate, &c. being amply sufficient to clothe, board, and educate you, in the style of a gentlewoman. You are by law entitled to the name and arms of Blakeney, but there was a clause annexed to your godfather's will which gave your dear grandmother and myself some uneasiness. It is that which insists that your future husband should change his own name to that of Blakeney, or the whole of the original bequest will be forfeited, an the accumulated interest only be yours.

"My lamented wife, in her last hours, Lucy, said to me, 'I wish, love, you may live to see our lovely child of an age when you may advise her never to shackle her sensibility by feeling as if she were obliged to reject the man whom she may love, and who might make her very happy, because himself or his friends should object to a change of name. I myself have such a predilection for family names, that had it not been for particular circumstances, and that the name of a female must at some time or other in all probability be changed, I should never have consented to our Lucy assuming the name of Blakeney. Should you be called hence before she is of a proper age to understand and be entrusted with every necessary communication on the subject of her birth, and other interesting circumstances, I must intrest you will be very explicit with her guardians, and also leave a letter addressed to herself.'

"Soon after this conversation, the companion and friend of my life, the heightener of all my joys, the consoler of all my sorrows, the only woman I ever loved, left this transitory sphere for a more blissful region. From that moment the world, my Lucy, has appeared a blank. Not even your endearing cheerfulness, your affectionate sympathy, could call me back to any enjoyment in life. I have endeavoured several times to nerve my feelings to the performance of this task, and have blamed myself for thus procrastinating it. But from several symptoms of failure in my mental and bodily vigour, I feel it will not be long before I follow my regreted partner into the world of spirits.

"I expect to see Mr. Matthews in the course of a few weeks. I shall then make him the confidant of many sorrows, which have sunk deep into my heart, and drank its vital energies, earlier than, perhaps, time might have impaired them. I intreat, my Lucy, my last earthly treasure, that in no momentous concern of your life you will act without consulting him, and when you have consulted, abide entirely by his decision.

"As it regards a matrimonial connection, let not the clause of your godfather's will have any influence. Your own patrimony will yield four hundred pounds a year; this must half be settled on yourself. The accumulation of the interest on my friend Blakeney's bequest will be very considerable in eleven years. This is your own to be settled or disposed of as yourself may direct. I have, by insisting on half your patrimony being settled on yourself previous to the day of marriage, secured to you the comforts and conveniences of life, as long as life may be continued; for the rest, I leave you in the charge of a good and heavenly Protector, who will never leave those to perish, who rely on his providence.

"There is one thing, my ever dear child, I am very anxious about, and on which my charge to you will be very solemn. It is, that you will never marry any one of the name of N —."

Here the stroke of death arrested the hand which held the pen, and the good old gentleman was found as already mentioned, dead in his easy chair.—

"What can I think, how must I act?" said Lucy, as with stunned faculties she still gazed on the open letter on the table before her. "I will determine on nothing till I know the opinion of my guardian on the subject: in the mean time I will implore the guidance and protection of HIM who knoweth best what is good for his children, and leave the event to time." So concluding, she folded the letter, performed her nightly devotions, and retired to her bed.—

Lieutenant Franklin was now in London; his father, whose health was still very feeble, had with his family, taken up their residence in their house in Portland Place. He had counted the days with anxiety, till the arrival of Lucy's birth day, after that, time seemed to have added lead to his pinions, and every hour and day were as an hundred. At length he received the following letter from Mr. Matthews,

"TO LIEUTENANT JOHN FRANKLIN.

"I have sat down, my dear sir, to fulfil a most unpleasant task in communicating to you by the desire of our lovely and esteemed friend, Miss Blakeney, a copy of her grandfather's letter, which I inclose, thinking it best to keep the original in my possession.

"You perceive that the old gentleman was by no means averse to her marrying to please herself though it might be to the diminution of her fortune. That there were some unhappy circumstances attending the birth of Miss Blakeney, I have every reason to conclude; though, what those circumstances were, I never could ascertain. For though my respected old friend frequently promised to impart them to me, the communication was deferred from time to time, till with him, poor man, time was no more.

"You will perceive that there is some particular family into which he had strong objections to her marrying, but the unfinished capital, which I am at a loss to decide whether meant for an N, an M, or an A, leads to no direct conclusion. I know he had a peculiar dislike to a family of the name of Lewis, the descendants of which in one branch are Mertons, in another Northalertons. There was a person also of the name of Allister, who gave him much trouble by a law suit. But I hardly could think my old friend was so little of a christian as to let his prejudice descend from generation to generation. However, be that as it may, there is nothing in the unfinished capital, that looks like F. Miss Blakeney is well, has kept her birth day in a most novel and splendid manner; I wish you could have seen her presiding amongst her guests; but I presume it will not be long before we see you at the Rectory, when you will hear from every tongue—yes, even from sister Cavendish, her eulogium.

I am, Dear Sir,

Yours, with Esteem,

ALFRED MATTHEWS."

The evening after Mr. Matthews had despatched this letter he entered the sitting parlour, where his family were assembled, some at work, some reading, and Aura Melville, strumming, as she called it, on the guitar. He took a morocco case from his waistcost pocket, and seated himself by a work table where Lucy was elaborately plying the needle's art, without having any definite end for which the work was designed when completed. He opened the case, a miniature of a lady set in wrought gold, and suspended by a superb chain was taken from it, and throwing the chain over Lucy's neck, he said,

"This, my little girl, should have been a birth day present, but you were so happy on that day, I thought you should not have too much satisfaction at once; it is good and prudent to portion out pleasure by degrees. If we are too lavish of it, the sense of enjoyment becomes torpid."

Lucy had taken the picture, it was that of a lovely female not more than sixteen years old: on the reverse was a braided lock of brown hair surmounted by the initials C. T—, in fine seed pearl.

"Who is this lovely creature?" said Lucy.

"Come to the glass, my child, and tell me who it is like," said Mr. Matthews, leading her to the glass, and raising a candle near her face. Lucy looked, and hesitated.

"Only," at length she said, "only, that it is much handsomer, and the eyes are blue, I should think."—

"That it was like yourself," said Mr. Matthews, leading her to the sofa, where Aura having laid aside her instrument, was ready to receive her.

"It is the portrait of your mother, Lucy! It was taken, your grandfather informed me, about three years previous to your birth, and was constantly worn by your grandmother, till some deeply afflicting occurrences, to which I am a stranger, induced her to lay it aside."

Lucy pressed the fair semblance of youth and innocence to her lips, to her heart, tears rushed from her eyes, and depositing the portrait in her bosom, she rested her head on the shoulder of Aura, and perfect silence for several minutes pervaded the apartment.

"So here is our friend Franklin!" said the good Rector, a few mornings after, presenting the young Lieutenant to the busy groups, drawn round the fire-side in the breakfast parlour.

Franklin bowed, and with a face half doubting, half delighted took a chair beside Lucy. She smiled, blushed, broke off her thread, unthreaded her needle, threaded it again, and worked most assiduously without one single idea of why or wherefore. Asked when he left London? What was the state of his father's health? When he last saw Edward Ainslie? till without being perceived by them, separately and silently every person but themselves had left the room.

Of all scenes to be repeated in narrative, love scenes are the most sickening, silly, and uninstructive. Suffice it to say that in an hour after they found themselves alone, Lucy had resolved to relinquish the principal of Blakeney's legacy. Franklin, with entire satisfaction, according to the terms of settling half her paternal inheritance on herself, and receiving the accumulated interest of eleven years on twenty thousand pounds, as a fortune to be disposed of according as his judgment should direct.

Friendship, love, and harmony, now took up their residence in the Rectory; the unostentatious though silently progressing preparations making for the wedding of Miss Blakeney, furnished occupation for every female of the family. Even Mrs. Cavendish relaxed her stern, yet really handsome features into smiles as she gave her opinion upon some new purchase, or told to the young persons whom Lucy chose to employ on this occasion, how such and such a dress was made and trimmed, when she was some few years younger.

It was one of Miss Blakeney's eccentricities, that nothing that could be performed by the industrious young women in the immediate vicinity of the Rectory, should be sent for from London;

and one morning when Mrs. Matthews and Mrs. Cavendish argued that her outward garments might be more tasteful and fashionable if made in the metropolis, she replied,

"But I am so vain as to think I should not look any handsomer in them, and I am sure I should not feel so happy. I know these good young women; some of them have aged parents to support, some young brothers and sisters to educate and put in a way to get their own bread. I am very sensible that with the assistance of Miss Melville, and our female domestics, more than two thirds of the work that is to be done, might be performed without any additional expense. But it has been a principle with me, ever since I was capable of reflecting on the subject, that those who can afford to pay for their clothes, &c. being made, defraud the industrious of what is their due, by making those articles themselves. I have also another odd fancy; I will not always employ those in the highest class of their profession, because having some taste of my own, and not being very fond of finery, or going to the extreme of fashion, I can generally give such directions as shall cause my clothes to be made in a neat becoming manner, and when I go to town it will be time enough to purchase whatever splendid dresses I may require for making my entrance into the gay world, so as not to disgrace the family, or impeach the judgment of Mr. Franklin."

A month had flitted by on rapid wings, when just at the close of a cold, dismal November day, as Franklin, having dined with the family at the Rectory, was proposing a game of chess with Mr. Matthews, a letter was delivered him by a servant, who said it was brought by one of Sir Robert Ainslie's grooms, who had ridden post from London, not stopping for any thing but slight refreshment, and to change horses.

Lucy watched his countenance as having apologized to the company, he eagerly broke the seal and read it. The colour fled from his cheeks, his lips quivered, and putting his hand to his forehead, he faintly articulated,

"My poor father! my mother!"

"Are they ill? Has any thing happened to either of them?" asked Lucy, as pale and agitated as himself.

"Something very dreadful has befallen them," he replied, "but of what nature, I cannot tell. These are a few, almost incoherent lines from Edward Ainslie, requesting I will not lose a moment in setting off for London; he will meet me a few miles from town, and explain what he did not choose to commit to paper. I shall set off for Southampton immediately on horseback, and from thence to my father's house as fast as a chaise and four horses can carry me."

"You will let us hear from you?" said Mr. Matthews.

"As early as the state of affairs will permit," was the reply.

"You know you have friends here who will not desert you in the day of adversity," said Mrs. Matthews, with one of her most benevolent looks.

The pale lips of Miss Blakeney moved, but no sound passed them; she held out her cold hand to Franklin, which having tenderly pressed, and respectfully kissed, he hastily said, "God bless you all!" and hurried out of the room.

In a moment his horse was heard going at a quick pace down the avenue, and anxiety and suspense became the inmates of the bosoms of Lucy and her sympathizing friends.

CHAPTER X

Manœuvring—Establishment
Formed—Change of
Circumstances Alters Cases

◊   ◊

It cannot be supposed but that in the length of time elapsed since Lady Mary Lumley left the protection of her friends to trust to the honour of a profligate, many conjectures had been formed concerning her situation, and the treatment she met with from her husband. All the family at the Rectory were anxious to hear from her, but how to direct their inquirers they were entirely at a loss.

Mr. Matthews once or twice called on Mrs. Brenton, but the old lady could give them no intelligence. The last letter she received from Theresa, was dated from Alnwick, and that was above seven months since; in that she said Sir Stephen and his Lady talked of making a short trip to the continent, and if they invited her to accompany them she should certainly go. The old lady did not express any uneasiness, concluding they were in France, and as Theresa never was a very attentive correspondent to her mother, supposed her time was too much absorbed in pleasure to think much about her old mother.

Mrs. Cavendish then wrote to some of Lady Mary's relations on the mother's side, to inquire if they had heard from her; but they, offended at her imprudent conduct, and the marriage connection she had formed, answered, that "They neither knew, nor wished to know any thing about her." The uneasiness of the family was much increased, when a day or two after Mr. Franklin's departure, a gentleman lately returned from France, called to deliver letters to Mr. Matthews, and staying dinner, mentioned having seen Sir Stephen Haynes in Paris some little time since.

"Was his lady with him?" asked Mrs. Cavendish.

"There certainly was a lady with him " replied the gentleman, "but I did not understand she was his wife. I saw her several times, but never in his company. She was a bold looking woman, of exceedingly free manners, and was said to lead a very gay life."

"That was not our poor Mary," whispered Aura to Miss Blakeney. Lucy shook her head, and the subject was dropped.

We left this victim of self will, and ill directed sensibility at a cottage not many miles distant from Alnwick castle, under the care of Mr. Craftly; but so ignorant were both Lady Mary and her friend of the country in which the cottage was situated, that they would have been unable to direct a servant, had any been allowed them, to find a post town or village by which means to transmit a letter to their friends. But for weeks after the departure of Sir Stephen, Lady Mary was in no state to write or hardly to think, being ill with a slow nervous fever, and at times delirious. Her highly excited state of feeling, her keen disappointment, added to a degree of self accusation which her ingenuous mind could not suppress, was more than she could support, and she had nearly sunk under it—perhaps would have done so, but that Craftly, who though he considered her as an imprudent young woman, pitied her sufferings and interested his mother and sister in her behalf.

These truly virtuous, respectable women did not think that the commission of one fault was sufficient to banish a human being from society, or excuse in others the want of humanity or kindness. They went to the cottage, they hovered over her like guardian angels, and when in her wanderings she would call for Lucy, Aura or Mrs. Matthews, they would one or the other present themselves at her bedside, soothe her, administer her medicines, talk of Sir

Stephen's return, of her reunion with her friends, and by degrees brought her back to health and a comparative degree of comfort.

Miss Brenton, taking her tone from these kind hearted women, was tender and attentive. Lady Mary revived, as to external appearance, but her warm enthusiastic heart had been chilled, the bright prospects of youth, to her were shrouded, and the sweet blossoms of hope were crushed forever.

Who and what was Craftly? A man of no mean capacity, nor bad feelings, who had been brought up to the profession of the law. He had lost his father early in life, but that father had secured to his wife and daughter, who was ten years the senior of her brother, a decent competency, and a genteel house in the vicinity of Alnwick. The residue of his estate and property he left to his son. There was considerable ready money. Craftly wished to taste the pleasures of a London winter; during that winter, being young and inexperienced, he became the prey of sharpers and gamesters; and among the rest became a debtor to Sir Stephen Haynes. His money was run out, and few and trifling rents he had to receive had not become due, and the only security he had to offer was the mortgage of a small cottage and grounds he held in Northumberland.

When therefore Haynes met Craftly upon his return from the north with his newly made lovely bride, it occurred to his unprincipled mind that he might make him subservient to his views in getting free from Lady Mary, and enjoying his intended tour to the continent in company with a dissolute woman, who had persuaded him, that though married and the mother of two lovely children, her invincible attachment to him had induced her to sacrifice all at the shrine of her illicit love.

This woman Sir Stephen Haynes had set up in his heart as a paragon of perfection; he did not feel that it was her blandishments that drew him first from the paths of rectitude; he did not know that a profligate unprincipled woman, is the bane of man's peace, both here and hereafter.

Mary Lumley was agreeable in her person, sportive in her manners, and easily assailed by flattery. Her fortune had been represented as more than treble its value. He sought to obtain that fortune, but shrunk from proclaiming her as his wife. Possessed of her little patrimony, his thoughts reverted to the woman who had enslaved his youthful mind, and leaving his confiding victim to what chance or time might produce, he took his adulterous paramour with him on his journey to France.

Lady Mary, recovered by the care of her unknown friends, began to think of living, and when she discovered that she was likely to become a mother, life itself became more endeared to her. Lady Mary Lumley, however headstrong in her resolves, however misled by the spirit of romance, and the flattery of pretended friends, had naturally a good heart, and an understanding above mediocrity. The time she had passed in the family of Mr. Matthews had been of infinite service to her. The principles and habits of the individuals who formed that family, were such as had taught her, that the neglect of duty in others, was no excuse for the same neglect in ourselves.

"I am forsaken," she mentally argued, "deceived, plundered of fortune and good name, but if my misconduct is the cause of a human being coming into the world, a being dependant on me for every thing, it is my duty to submit to the evils I have brought upon myself, and be to the little innocent, father! mother! all. How we are to be supported, God alone can tell; but my revered guardian used to tell me, that our Heavenly Father would maintain the cause of the orphan, and be the Judge of the widow. Alas! for me, I am more desolate than a widow; my infant, if it ever sees the light, unless his father be led to do us justice, more wretched than an orphan."

It may be asked why did she not write to those friends she now knew how to appreciate. She did write, but Craftly had received orders to forward no letters whatever; he had therefore requested his mother and sister, before he agreed to their attending the sick

bed of Lady Mary, to give all letters, whether written by her or
Miss Brenton, to him; alleging as a reason, that he could conve-
niently send them to the post office, without trouble to them.

It may be remembered that Haynes had represented Theresa
Brenton to Craftly as an object, in regard to fortune, worthy of
pursuit, and had intimated to that lady that Craftly was an independent man. A genteel establishment was the aim of the lady; a
little ready money would be very acceptable to the gentleman; therefore mutual civilities, condescension, and uniform politeness, was
scrupulously practised between them. He asserted, that Sir Stephen Haynes said he was not the husband of Lady Mary; that she
was a thoughtless romantic girl of fashion, who was so madly in
love with him that she had thrown herself upon his protection,
without waiting for those forms which her friends would have
insisted on, and which he had no inclination to submit to.

Theresa knew this in part to be true; but she also knew that
the marriage ceremony had passed at Gretna Green, and that Mary
Lumley was in her own opinion, though perhaps not in the eye of
the law, the wife of Sir Stephen Haynes. But Lady Mary was now
poor; where was the use of her (Theresa's) irritating Sir Stephen?
It would do her poor misguided friend no good, and might be of
injury to the plans she had formed for herself. Miss Brenton then
became in externals an entire new character; she had entirely
developed the pure, unassuming characters of Mrs. Craftly and
her daughter. Brought up in the country, mixing with but little
society, though that little was select, of plain good understandings,
they were urbane in their manners without being highly polished,
and very pleasant companions without being thought wits or aiming
to appear deeply learned. Of strict principles both as it regarded
religious duty and moral rectitude; cheerful without levity, and
grave without affected sanctity; their own minds, actuated by unsuspicious simplicity, thought no evil of others, until positive facts
obliged them to believe it.

With the son and brother, they had ever lived in harmony; for he was the idol of both, and they either did not, or could not perceive a fault in him. He, on his part, had so much regard for their peace, as to guard against any of his misconduct reaching them, or giving them any disturbance.

Theresa Brenton then to this family appeared every thing that was amiable. She was conciliating to the Craftlys; would talk most sagely upon economy, domestic concerns, quiet seclusion, love of mental improvement; and when the gentleman was present, would descant on the beauties of her mother's seat near Southampton, without betraying that it was only a hired place, and that its chief beauties consisted in the neat snug appearance of a small house and the garden surrounding it, and a view of the Bay from the upper windows. Then she would pathetically lament poor Lady Mary's misfortune, speak of her as a young woman of impetuous feelings, which had never been kept under any restraint, and conclude with a sigh,

"She fully believes herself Sir Stephen's wife, and it will be as well not to contradict her; in her present delicate state of health, it might produce fatal consequences. Though what is to become of her I cannot think, for by her not hearing from her friends I fear they have cast her off. I myself feel uneasy sometimes at not hearing from my mother, but elderly persons are not very fond of writing: so I do not think so much of it as I otherwise should."

Lady Mary endeavoured to obtain from Craftly her husband's address, but he always pretended that he believed him to be so unsettled that a letter would have but little chance of finding him.

All letters addressed to any member of Mr. Matthews' family were condemned to the flames, or thrown by in a drawer amongst waste paper; nor was he more careful of those written by Theresa to her mother, though to own the truth she did not trouble him with many. He well knew that to send intelligence to Mrs. Brenton was furnishing a direct clue to the discovery of Lady Mary, and this he had promised his friend Haynes should not be made in less than six months after his departure.

"Besides," thought Craftly, "Theresa might mention my attentions to her mother, and if I bring myself to marry the girl I might be plagued from that quarter about a settlement, and subject myself to have inquiries made which it may be neither easy nor convenient to answer."

"I have been thinking, my dear Theresa," said he one evening, as seated in the porch they were enjoying the full splendor of a harvest moon, "I have been thinking, and wishing—indeed it is the wish also of my mother and sister, they think it would be for the happiness of all concerned, to unite our hands, as I trust our hearts are already in unison with each other; and form our establishment before the winter commences."

He then proceeded to explain his actual fortune and his expectations, and made it appear that his annual income was above five hundred pounds a year, but in this he included the cottage, &c. without one word of the mortgage which Sir Stephen Haynes still held, though he had agreed to give up the interest which might arise from it for eighteen months to come, if Craftly would oblige him in the manner we have already seen he did. Finding the lady silent, the lover then went on to say,

"You will have no objection, my dear girl, to making this cottage our residence for the present. My mother will undoubtedly give us an invitation to pass part of the winter with her in Alnwick, which I do assure you is a very lively and genteel place, affording many rational and pleasant amusements; the society they mix in, is of the most respectable class."

"I can have no objection to pass a few weeks or months with Mrs. and Miss Craftly," said Theresa, interrupting him: "but as to agreeing to make this Gothic cottage a place of residence, except for a few months, in the heat of summer, I can never agree to it. I expect, at least the first winter after our marriage, that you will permit me to partake in your society, the pleasures of either York or London. I should prefer the latter. Indeed it will be almost impossible to give my little fortune into your hands without a journey to the metropolis, we can then also make a visit to my mother, who I am afraid must begin to think me very negligent."

"Well!" thought Craftly, "this is moderation with a vengeance! A winter in London! I have had enough of winters in London. I must persuade her out of this notion, or there is an end of the matter. She cannot be rich enough to justify such a piece of extravagance." Putting on therefore one of his most engaging smiles, he replied,

"But, my dear Theresa, have you duly considered the expense of a London winter, or even a winter in York? The whole of my yearly income would not pay our expenses, living in barely decent style. And though I do not know the amount of your fortune, yet I will take upon me to say, that the greater part of it might be run out in a single winter in London, without enabling either of us to be considered *somebody*. You are certainly too well versed in economy not to consider it better to spend only our income in cutting a good figure in the respectable town of Alnwick for many winters, than to spend half our fortunes in cutting *no figure at all* in the great city of London one winter. Think, better of that project, I entreat you, my Theresa."

There was reason in this. Determined however not to be too easily thwarted, she made some further attempts to carry her point; but finding the gentleman growing rather cool and distant during the several days that she held out, she prudently yielded, and the preparations for the marriage were commenced with great alacrity.

CHAPTER XI

Fruits of Error

◇　　◇

Lieutenant Franklin did not meet his friend Ainslie on the road to London as he had expected. On his arrival in town, he hastened to Portland Place. The blinds of his father's splendid mansion were closed, and every thing about it wore an aspect of gloom. The door was opened by a servant whose countenance indicated some terrible calamity.

Franklin hastened towards his mother's apartment, but was met on the stairs by one of his brothers, who had been summoned home from Eton. From him he learnt, that his father lay apparently at the point of death, having ruptured a blood vessel; that his mother had been by his bedside almost incessantly, since the accident had happened, and that the whole family were in a state of the greatest alarm and trepidation.

As he entered the sick chamber, the closed windows, the low whisperings of the attendants, the odours of medicinal preparations, and most of all, an occasional stifled sob from one of the children, who was permitted to be in the apartment for a few moments, brought home to his bosom the conviction that he was about to become fatherless. He approached the bed. His father lay perfectly motionless and silent, with closed eyes, watched by the partner of all his sorrows, who bent over him like some kind angel, with a ministry unremitted and untiring. An indifferent gazer might have read upon the marble forehead and classic features of the patient, noble and generous feelings, commanding talents—a promise of every thing that was excellent in character and desirable in fortune—all blighted by once yielding to the impulse of guilty passion.—The wife and the son saw nothing but the mysterious hand of Providence, visiting with severest affliction one whom they had ever regarded with reverence and love.

Franklin placed himself near the bed, and pressing the hand of his mother, waited in unutterable suspense the moment when his father should awake. At length he slowly opened his eyes, and fixing them on his son, with a faint smile he spoke, in a low voice, "My dear boy, I was this moment thinking of you. It gives me happiness to remember, how soon you are to be blest with the society of one you love, and who deserves your affection. I have not been so tranquil for years, as I am just now, in this thought. I wish that I could see her. I think I could read in her features the promise of your happiness, and then go to my account in peace."

Franklin pressed his father's hand. The big tears of mingled love, gratitude and sorrow, coursed down his cheeks. He could not speak in reply. He saw by his father's countenance that it was too late to comply literally with his request, but in the same moment, it occurred to him that he could almost accomplish his wish, by showing him the miniature of Lucy's mother, which he had playfully taken from her on the day of his departure, and in his haste and alarm, at the sudden summons, had forgotten to restore.

"I have a picture of her mother," said he, putting his hand in his bosom, "it is a good resemblance of herself."

He drew forth the miniature, and held it up before his father, who rose up, seized it with a convulsive grasp the moment the light fell on the features, and looking upon the initials on the back of it, shrieked out—

"It is—it is come again to blast my vision in my last hour!— The woman you would marry is my own daughter!—Just

Heaven!—Oh! that I could have been spared this!—Go, my son! Go to my private desk—you will there find the record of your father's shame, and your own fate!"

Nature was exhausted by the effort. He fell back on the bed, supported by his trembling wife, and in a few moments, the wretched Franklin, the once gay, gallant, happy Montraville, was no more.

CHAPTER XII

Disclosures

◇   ◇

The obsequies of Colonel Franklin, were attended with the circumstances of pomp and state which his rank required, and the journals of the day proclaimed his patriotism and public worth, while his family mourned in secret over the ruin caused by his unbridled passions.

Closeted with his bosom friend Edward Ainslie, young Franklin laid before him the manuscript which he had found by his father's direction. It had been written in a season of deep remorse, and its object was evidently to redeem from undeserved obloquy, the memory of the unfortunate Charlotte Temple, the mother of Lucy Temple Blakeney. Probably Colonel Franklin had intended to transmit it to her friends. Indeed a direction to that effect was found on a loose paper, in the desk. He took the whole blame of her ill-fated elopement upon himself. He disclosed circumstances which he had discovered after her decease, which proved her faithfulness to himself; and lamented in terms of the deepest sorrow, that it was in his power to make her no better reparation for all her love and all her injuries, than the poor one of thus bearing testimony to her truth and his own cruelty and injustice. He had never intended this paper to be seen until after his decease. He could not bear to make these full disclosures and afterwards look upon the countenances of his children; and he mentioned that the reason why he had so readily complied with the wish of a rich relation of his wife,

233

that he should change his family name of Montraville for that of Franklin, was, that under that name he had taken the fatal step which destroyed his peace—to use his own forcible expression, "he would willingly have lost all recollection of what he was, and changed not his name only but himself."

"Edward!" said the unfortunate youth, when the reading of this terrible record was finished, "I have disclosed to you the story of my ruined, blasted hopes. Receive this as the strongest mark of my friendship and confidence. Go to *her!*" he could not utter the name of Lucy. "Tell these dreadful truths in such a manner as your own feeling heart shall direct. She is a christian. This is her great trial, sent to purify and exalt her soul and fit her for a brighter sphere of existence. I cannot—I dare not see her again. I cannot even give you for her any other message than a simple, heartfelt *'God bless her!'* I have caused myself to be exchanged into a regiment which is ordered to India, and tomorrow I bid farewell to England!"

Edward promised implicitly to obey his friend's directions; and receiving from him the fatal miniature, he took leave of him for that day, and returned to his father's residence to dispatch a letter to Mr. Matthews, promising to be with him in a few days, and bring full intelligence of all that related to these unfortunate occurrences.

The next day he attended his friend for the last time, and witnessed the final preparations for his departure. There was a firmness, a sternness of purpose in Franklin's countenance, which indicated that his thoughts were fixed on some high and distant object; and though he spoke not of his future prospects, Edward who knew the force of his character, mentally predicted that his name would be found in the records of military renown. There was an impatience to be gone apparent in some of his movements, as if he feared to linger a moment on English ground. But this was inadvertently displayed, and he took leave of his mother, family and friend, with that deep emotion which must ever affect a feeling heart on such an occasion.

Edward was surprised at one circumstance, which was that Mrs. Franklin seemed to approve of her son's purpose to leave the kingdom. He had expected to find her very anxious to retain him, as a protector to herself. But he had not attributed to that lady all the judgment and firmness which belonged to her character. He had witnessed her enduring affection, and her noble example of all the passive virtues. Her energy and decision was yet to appear.

When the carriage, which bore his friend to the place of embarkation, had disappeared, he turned to the widow and made a most cordial tender of his services in whatever the most active friendship could perform for her in her new and trying situation. He mentioned his purpose of going to Hampshire, and offered to return and await her commands as soon as the purpose of his journey was accomplished. This friendly offer was very gratefully acknowledged, but the tender of his services in the city was declined. It was not her purpose, she said, to remain in London; but should any circumstances occur which would render it necessary to avail herself of his kind offer, she should not fail to do it, in virtue of the claim which his friendship for her son gave her. At any rate he should be apprized of the future movements of the family by some one of its members.

Satisfied with this arrangement, Ainslie retired.

CHAPTER XIII

An Arrival

◇　◇

It may well be supposed that the family at the Rectory were in a state of great anxiety after the departure of Franklin. The air of mystery which attended his hasty summons to town served to increase their distress. Lucy struggled, severely but vainly, to preserve an appearance of composure. Much of her time was spent in the retirement of her chamber, and when she was with the family and apparently deriving a temporary relief from her sorrows by joining in the usual occupations of the busy little circle, a sigh would escape from her in spite of all her efforts to preserve an appearance of calmness.

It seemed to her that a known calamity, however terrible and irremediable in its nature, would have been much more easy to be borne than this state of suspense. Alas! she was too soon to be undeceived on this point.

The third day brought a hasty letter from Ainslie to Mr. Matthews, simply stating the sudden demise of Colonel Franklin without any mention of the attending circumstances. This was a relief, a melancholy one indeed; but still, Lucy felt it as a relief, because it seemed to set some bounds to her apprehensions. It seemed natural too, that Ainslie should be employed to write at such a moment. The sudden affliction might have rendered Franklin incapable of the effort. Lucy now awaited the result with comparative tranquillity.

But the second letter of Edward, written after the disclosure made by his friend, which spoke of "painful and peculiarly unfortunate circumstances which he would explain on his arrival," threw her into a new state of suspense. Here was more mystery. The first letter which summoned Franklin away had appeared to be unnecessarily dark and doubtful. The last renewed all the wretched Lucy's doubts and fears.

On the second day after the receipt of this letter, Lucy was sitting alone by the parlour fire. It was late in the afternoon, Mr. Matthews and Aura were absent administering to the wants of the poor, and distributing clothing to the destitute in anticipation of the approaching inclement season. Mrs. Matthews and her sister were busied about their household affairs. Lucy was musing on the memory of past joys and painfully endeavouring to conjecture the reason of Franklin's mysterious silence, when the door opened and Edward Ainslie stood before her, haggard and weary with his journey, and evidently suffering under mental perplexity and distress. At that moment he would have given the world for the relief of Mr. Matthews' presence. He felt as though possessed of some guilty secret, and his eye was instantly averted when he met her searching glance. He had hoped to encounter some other member of the family first and instantly felt his mistake in not having sent for Mr. Matthews to meet him elsewhere. But retreat was now impossible. He felt that he must stand and answer.

Lucy had advanced and presented her hand as usual, but with such a look of distressful inquiry as went to his inmost soul. With an old and tried friend like Ainslie, ceremony was out of the question.

"Where is *Franklin?* Is he well? Is he safe?"

"He is well. Be composed, Lucy. Do not look so distressed." Ainslie knew not what to say.

"Is he well! Then why—Oh why are you alone, Edward?"

"There are certain painful circumstances, which have prevented his accompanying me. You shall know them—*but*—"

"Oh tell, I intreat you, tell me all. I have borne this terrible suspense long enough. Any thing will be preferable to what I now suffer. I have firmness to bear the worst certainty, but I have not patience to endure these doubts. If he is lost to me, say so, I charge you."

There was a vehemence, a solemnity in her manner, an eagerness in her look, a deep pathos in her voice, which Edward could no longer withstand. He trusted to the strength of her character and determined to disclose the worst. With averted eyes and a low, and hardly audible voice he replied,

"Alas! he is indeed lost to you!"

She did not shriek nor faint, nor fall into convulsions, but placing her hand upon her brow, reclined against the mantel piece a moment, and then left the apartment.

Ainslie lost no time in finding Mrs. Matthews, and apprizing her of what had passed and that lady instantly followed her young friend to her apartment. She had over-estimated her own strength. The sufferings of this last week had reduced her almost to exhaustion and this stroke completed the prostration of her system. A violent fever was the consequence, and for several days, her life was despaired of. The distress of Ainslie during this period may be imagined.

CHAPTER XIV

Active Benevolence, The Best Remedy for Affliction

◊   ◊

On Ainslie's communicating to Mr. Matthews the circumstances which he had learnt from Franklin, and bitterly lamenting his precipitate disclosure of them to Lucy, that good man appeared anxious to alleviate his unavailing regret and to bring forward every palliation for what, at the worst, was no more than an error in judgment. He could not permit his young friend to consider himself responsible for the consequences, since the stroke could not have been averted and could scarcely have been made to descend more gently upon the heart of the devoted girl.

A further disclosure was yet to take place, and never in the whole course of his ministration among the wounded spirits that had required his care and kindness, had this worthy pastor been more severely tried than on this occasion. He meditated, communed with his friends, sought for Divine assistance in prayer, and when at last the returning health of his tender charge rendered it not only advisable but necessary that she should know the whole, he came to the trial with fear and trembling.

What was his joy to find that she received the disclosure which he had so much dreaded to make, not with resignation merely, but with satisfaction. It brought a balm to her wounded spirit, to know that she had not been voluntarily abandoned—that the man on whom she had placed her affections had yielded to a stern necessity, a terrible fate, in quitting her without even a last farewell. She approved his conduct. She regarded him as devoted to his country, herself as set apart for the holy cause of humanity; and in accordance with this sentiment, she resolved to pass the remainder of her life in ministering to the distressed, and promoting the happiness of her friends.

Nor did she delay the commencement of this pious undertaking. Aided by her revered friend the Pastor, she entered upon her schemes of active benevolence with an alacrity which, while it surprised those who were not intimately acquainted with her character, and justified the exalted esteem of her friends, served effectually to divert her mind from harrowing recollections and useless regrets.

Among the earliest of her plans for ameliorating the condition of the poor was the founding of a little seminary for the education of female children. She chose a pleasant spot near the Rectory, a quiet little nook, bosomed among the wooded hills and commanding a view of the village and a wide expanse of soft meadow scenery; and there she caused to be erected a neat little building, a specimen, one might almost say, a model of Ionic architecture. Its chaste white pillars and modest walls peeping through the surrounding elms, were just visible from her own window, and many were the tranquil and comparatively happy moments which she spent, sitting by that window and planning in her own mind the internal arrangement and economy of the little establishment.

She had it divided into several apartments and placed an intelligent and deserving young woman in each, to superintend the different parts of education which were to be taught. In one, the most useful kinds of needlework, in another, the common branches of instruction in schools, and in another the principles of morality, and the plainest truths and precepts of religion; while, over all these, there was a sort of High School, to which a few only were promoted who gave evidence of that degree of talent and probity which would fit them for extended usefulness. These, under the instruction of the preceptress of the whole establishment, were to receive a more finished education than the rest.

Into every part of the arrangement of these matters Lucy entered with an interest which surprised herself. She delighted in learning the natural bent and disposition of the young pupils, and would spend whole hours in conversing with them, listening with a kind interest to their artless answers and opinions, and often discovering, or supposing that she discovered in them the elements of taste and fancy or the germ of acute reasoning or strongly inventive power.

But it was in developing their affections and moral capabilities that she chiefly delighted. There was a field of exertion in which the example of the patroness was of infinite value to the instructers. Her own education, her knowledge of human character and of nature, her cultivated and refined moral taste, and, above all, the healing and religious light, which her admirable submission to the trying hand of Providence had shed over the world and all its concerns as they appeared to her view,—all these things served to fit her for this species of ministry to the minds and hearts of these young persons.

In these pursuits it is hardly necessary to say that she found a tranquillity and satisfaction which the splendid awards of fortune and fame can never impart.

CHAPTER XV

Church and State

◇   ◇

Edward Ainslie had finished his studies at the University, where he had so distinguished himself as to afford the most favourable anticipations of his future success. He was in some doubt as to the profession which he should embrace. Inclination prompted him to devote himself to the church. His father was anxious that he should become a political character; probably being somewhat influenced by an offer, which he had had from one of the ministry, of a diplomatic appointment for his son.

This interesting subject was under consideration at the very time when the events, which we have just been recording, transpired. Edward had returned to London after witnessing the perfect recovery of Lucy, and the discussions concerning his future career were renewed with considerable interest.

On the evening after his return, he was sitting in the parlour of his father's splendid mansion. All the family except his father and himself had retired. They lingered a few moments to confer on the old subject.

"Well, Edward," said his father, "I hope you are ready now to oblige our friends in a certain quarter, and strengthen the hands of government."

"Indeed, sir, my late visit to the country, has served rather to increase my predilection for the life of a country parson."

"My Lord Courtly says it is a thousand pities your talents should be so thrown away; and though I should not regard the thing in that light, yet I think that your country has some claims upon you. Let the livings of the church be given to the thousands who are unfit for, or unable to attain the promotion that is offered to you. If you accept a living, it is ten to one you disappoint some equally worthy expectant."

"Perhaps I shall do the same if I accept this diplomatic appointment."

"Little danger of that, I fancy, when the appointment is so freely offered you—when in fact you are solicited to accept it. Let me tell you, Edward, you know not how splendid a career you may be refusing to enter upon."

"I fear, my dear father, that you have not duly considered the cares and anxieties, of political life. It is a constant turmoil and struggle for distinction. All the sterner feelings of our nature are brought into action. All the generous emotions and amiable weaknesses of humanity are regarded as fatal to one's success. A blunder in state affairs is considered worse than a crime."

"I think there is no profession," said the Baronet, "in which a crime is not more fatal to success, in the long run, than a blunder. However, we are wandering from the subject. In one word, Edward, I think that you may carry all your strict moral principles and your high and generous sense of honour into public life, without in the least endangering your success."

"What you say may be strictly true, sir, but I have feelings and partialities which cannot fail to prove a hindrance. I shall sigh for seclusion and domestic enjoyment amidst the splendour of foreign courts, and never pen a dispatch to be sent to old England without longing to see its fair prospects of green fields and smiling cottages. I love to converse with nature in her still retreats and if I must mingle with my fellow men, let it not be in the vain strife for power and distinction; but rather in the delightful intercourse of social life, or in the more interesting relation of one who cares for their eternal welfare. If I were rich, the character I should most wish to figure in, would be that of a useful, benevolent and religious country gentleman, as the advice and instruction which I could thus impart would not arise simply from official duty and might be rendered doubly efficient by acts of benevolence. Since that may not be, I am content with the humbler office of a country parson."

At this period of the conversation a servent entered with a letter directed to the Baronet, saying that it had been brought by an express. He opened it and hastily running it over, exclaimed,

"Well, my boy, you can have your wish now. See there!" handing him the open letter.

It was from the executor of a distant relation who had taken a fancy to Edward in his childhood, and had now bequeathed him the whole of his large estate, situated in the North of England.

Astonishment and gratitude to the Divine Disposer of events were visible in the countenance of the youth as he silently lifted up his eyes in thanksgiving.

After a few minutes pause, his father said, "Well, you will visit your property immediately, of course?"

"Yes sir; but I wish to visit Hampshire for a few days before I set off for the North." And so saying, he bade his father good night and retired.

CHAPTER XVI

An Engagement

◊　◊

Before leaving London, Ainslie called at the late residence of Mrs. Franklin, and was surprised to find the house in other hands. On making further inquiries of his father, he learnt that she had embarked for New York with the whole of her family. On reflection he was satisfied that this was the most natural and proper course for her. America was the land of her nativity, and the scene of all the happiness she had enjoyed in early life, England, the country where she had known nothing but misfortune and trial. Her young sons, too, would be able to figure with great advantage in the new country, and its existing friendly relations with that to which her oldest son owed allegiance, prevented her feeling any uneasiness on the score of his present employment in the India service. Edward's father also informed him that Mrs. Franklin's affairs in England were intrusted to the most responsible agents.

Being satisfied that there was nothing further which friendship required of him in that quarter he set out for Hampshire with rather different feelings from those which oppressed him on his last visit there.

We will not attempt to analyze his feelings at this time; but rather follow him to the Rectory, whither he hastened after a half hour spent at his father's seat. On entering the parlour, he found Mrs. Matthews and Mrs. Cavendish, and learnt from them that the young ladies were gone to visit Lucy's favourite school.

He determined to take a short cut to this place; and accordingly strolled along a shaded pathway which led from the garden towards the spot. The sun was just approaching the horizon and shed a rich splendour over a pile of massy clouds which reposed in the west. As he passed rapidly along a turn in the path revealed to him the solitary figure of Aura Melville, in strong relief against the western sky as she stood on the edge of a bank and gazed upon the last footsteps of the retiring sun. He approached unobserved, and just as he was on the point of speaking, heard her say in a low voice, as though thinking aloud,

"How beautiful! How much more beautiful it would be, if a certain friend were with me to pronounce it so!"

Laying his hand gently upon her arm, he murmured in the same soliloquizing tone, "How happy should I be if I might flatter myself that I were that friend!"

She turned and the "orient blush of quick surprise," gave an animation to her features which made her lover own to himself that he had never seen her half so lovely.

We have already hinted at Aura's partiality for Edward and when we apprise the reader that he had long loved her with a respectful and devoted attachment, which he had only been prevented from declaring by his dependent situation and uncertainty with regard to his pursuits in life, it will readily be supposed that they were not many minutes after this in coming to a perfect understanding.

With lingering steps and many a pause, they turned towards the Rectory long after the shadows of twilight had begun to fall. The rapture of those moments, the ardent expressions of the youth, the half uttered confessions, the timid glances and averted looks of the maiden, and the intervals of silence—silence full of that happiness which is never known but once—all these must be imagined by the reader.

On their arrival at the Rectory they found that Lucy, who had been left at the school by Aura, had returned by the more frequented road, and the family were waiting their coming, while the smoking tea urn sent forth its bubbling invitation to the most cheerful, if not the most sumptuous of all entertainments.

CHAPTER XVII

The Table Conversation

◇ ◇

"Well, Edward," said the good Rector, as he slowly sipped his favourite beverage, "this is an unexpected pleasure. I had supposed that the wishes of your father and the rhetoric of the minister had prevailed over your philosophical resolutions and that you were already half way to Saint Petersburg. Perhaps you are only come to pay us a farewell visit, and are soon to set off for the North."

"Indeed, sir," replied Ainslie, "I am soon to set off for the North, but shall hardly reach the court of the Czars this winter."

"To Berlin, perhaps."

"Too far, sir."

"Peradventure to Copenhagen."

"Hardly so far, sir, as the 'Land o' cakes an brither Scots.' I am to sojourn for the next few weeks among the lakes and hills of Cumberland."

"Cumberland!" exclaimed three or four voices at once.

"For what purpose can you be going to Cumberland?" said Lucy Blakeney; "I never heard of any court in that quarter except that of queen Mab."

"I am going to look after a little property there."

"I never heard your father say that he owned any estates in Cumberland," said the Rector.

"But my great uncle Barsteck did. You remember the old gentleman who used to visit my father and take me with him in all his strolls about the pleasant hills and meadows here. He has long been declining in health and the letter which brought us the melancholy intelligence of his decease brought also the information that he has remembered his old favourite. I could have wished to be enriched by almost any other event than the loss of so good a friend."

The remembrance of his relative's early kindness came over him with such force at this moment that he rose and turned away to the window and it was some minutes before he was sufficiently composed to resume the conversation, in which he informed his friends that he had given up all thoughts of public life and was resolved to devote himself to more congenial pursuits amidst the romantic scenery of the lake country.

It may readily be supposed that this determination was highly approved by the worthy pastor and that in the private interview which he had with Edward the next day, it had no small influence in procuring his approbation of the suit which he then preferred for the hand of his fair ward.

After a few delightful days spent in the society of his friends at the Rectory, Edward set forward on his journey to the North.

CHAPTER XVIII

An Adventure

◊   ◊

Edward's estate was in the neighbourhood of the romantic vale of Keswick. The mansion house lately inhabited by his uncle, was an old fashioned but comfortable house situated on the southern declivity of the mountain Skiddaw, with a beautiful garden and extensive but uneven grounds, laid out in a style entirely suited to the surrounding scenery. The view from the balcony, in front of the house, was one of singular beauty and sublimity. A long valley stretched away to the south disclosing in the distance the still glassy surface of Derwent-water and terminated by the bold and fantastic mountains of Borrowdale. On the east the lofty steeps of Wallow-crag and Lodore seemed to pierce the very heavens, whilst the towering heights of Newland bounded the view on the West, displaying the picturesque varieties of mountain foliage and rocks.

The cottages and farm houses of his tenants were scattered about in such points of view as to afford a pleasing sort of embellishment to the landscape. Many of them were constructed of rough unhewn stone, and roofed with thick slates, and both the coverings and sides of the houses were not unfrequently overgrown with lichens and mosses as well as surrounded with larches and sycamores. Edward made it his first business, on his arrival, to visit his tenantry and he found no little pleasure in studying the characters of these humble minded people, whose residence amongst these sequestered mountain regions had preserved their primitive manners from the tide of refinement and corruption which had swept over less fortunate portions of the country.

As he was taking his customary ride on horseback one afternoon, he arrived at a part of his estate remote from the mansion house, and where he had not before been, when he was struck with the picturesque appearance of one of the stone cottages which we have mentioned above.

It was of a very irregular shape and seemed to have received additions and improvements from several generations of its occupants.

The orchard too had its trees of all ages, and one craggy looking apple tree, which stood before the door, seemed by its accumulation of moss, and its frequently protruded dry branches, to be coeval with the house itself. There was a little garden with its shed full of bee hives, and its narrow beds of herbs and borders of flowers, and a small but noisy rill, that came dashing down from the rocks in the rear of the cottage, and sent a smile of verdure and a fairy shout of melody over the whole scene.

Edward alighted and entered the cottage, where he was received with a hearty welcome. The farmer himself was away among the hills; but the good dame was "main glad to see his honour, and hoped his honour was coming to live among them, as his worship's honour that was dead and gone had always done."

He assured her that such was his intention.

"I am glad your honour has come here this afternoon," she proceeded, "for more reasons than one. Your honour must know there is a poor distressed young creature in the other room, who wandered here yesterday after a weary long journey. She is come of gentle blood, and talks of her relations, who seem to be all lords and ladies. But sure enough the poor thing is quite beside herself, and a woful sight she was, when she came to our door yesterday, with nothing in the world but an open work straw bonnet on her head, and a thin shawl over her shoulders, poor soul, in such a biting cold day. Would not your honour please to be so good as just to speak a kind word to her? I'm thinking she's come from the South, and would be cheered at the sight of one from her own part of the country, and of her own degree too."

It will be readily supposed that Edward expressed a desire to see her, and he was accordingly conducted from the neat sitting room, into which he had first been invited, into a small back room, where to his no small astonishment he saw, seated in an easy chair by the fire, and attended by a little girl, the unfortunate Lady Mary, the wife of Sir Stephen Haynes.

Her attire consisted of a soiled travelling dress, which had once been rich and showy—her countenance, though thin and wasted, was flushed and feverish, and there was a wildness in her eyes which told the saddest tale of all, that not only was the wretched lady forsaken by friends and fortune, but at least partially deprived of the blessed light of reason.

She started at the sight of Edward, and exclaimed, "Ha! so you have come at last. Well, there, I have been crying here all this livelong morning! My husband the Duke is to be beheaded on Tower Hill to-morrow morning for high treason! But," said she, grasping Edward's arm, and whispering vehemently in his ear, "I came within an ace of being queen, for all that."

"Then too," she continued, weeping bitterly, "they have imprisoned me here, and the constable of the castle has taken away my jewels, and sent away my waiting maid, and left me nobody but this simple maiden here to attend upon me. I could have forgiven them all this but they have taken away my child, my pretty boy, with his bright eyes and his golden locks. Oh, why do they let me live any longer!" And she wrung her hands as one not to be comforted.

"Poor creature!" whispered the good woman of the house, "she has not been so raving before."

"I am acquainted with the unfortunate lady," replied Edward, in a low voice, "but she does not seem to know me."

"Know you!" shrieked Lady Mary, catching his last words, "Yes

I do know you, Edward Ainslie, and I know, too, what you are come here for. You have come to preach to me on the folly of ambition—to upbraid me for deserting my friends and protectors. But you may spare yourself the trouble. I shall answer for all to-morrow. I will die with my husband."

She said this with great energy, and then, after pausing a moment and looking thoughtfully on the floor, she burst into tears again, exclaiming, "But my poor boy! what will become of him. I pray Heaven they may not destroy him. Surely he has done no injury to the state. If the king could look upon his innocent little face, surely he would spare him."

Edward, perceiving that his presence could be of no service to her, left the apartment and directed that every attention should be paid to her, and promised ample remuneration to the family for their trouble. Then hastily mounting his horse, he rode to the nearest medical attendant, whom he despatched to the cottage before he returned home.

The Consequences of Imprudence

◇　◇

For several days after the occurrence which we have described in the last chapter, Lady Mary continued in a high fever, and the physician gave little hopes of her recovery. Edward visited the cottage every day to inquire after her, and was at length happy to learn, that by the unremitted kindness and care of the worthy family, she was safely past the crisis of her disorder; that her reason was restored, but her weakness was such, that she had not been permitted to attempt giving any account of the manner in which she came into the miserable state in which she was found.

She was assured that she was under the care of a friend who had known her in early life, and would visit her as soon as her strength would permit. Satisfied with this assurance, she recovered rapidly, and, in a month from the time of Edward's first visit to the cottage, was able to sit up a great part of the day, and to receive a visit from him.

The interview, as may readily be supposed, was an affecting one to both parties. Poor Lady Mary seemed to be thoroughly humbled by misfortune, and was desirous of nothing so much as to see her early friends, and receive their pardon for her unworthy conduct in deserting them. Edward assured her that their affection for her was the same as ever; that they had regarded her as misled by designing and artful persons; and that nothing would afford them such heartfelt pleasure, as to welcome her once more to their hospitable home.

Thus soothed and encouraged, she informed him of the events which we have already narrated concerning her elopement, and the subsequent desertion of her husband. She proceeded to say that she had lost her child, a beautiful boy, born at the Gothic cottage of which we have so frequently spoken; that after the marriage of Craftly and Theresa, which out of regard to that young lady's taste was celebrated with considerable parade, she had continued to reside with them in the cottage, in a state of indescribable wretchedness from the neglect of her husband.

She said, that one day when the rest of the family were out on an afternoon visit, she went into one of the chambers to look for a book; which, Theresa had told her as she went out, might be found in a drawer there. She pulled out one drawer of the bureau after another in vain, till she came to the lower one, which came out with considerable difficulty. When, at last she succeeded in drawing it out, what was her astonishment, to find a great part of the letters which she had written to her husband and friends, tumbled into it, after being broken open. There were a great many more letters, and some among them directed to Craftly, in her husband's hand writing.

Convinced that she was suffering by some vile conspiracy, she felt herself justified in taking the whole to her room, after first closing the drawer to avoid a speedy discovery.

Besides her own and Sir Stephen's letters, there were several of Theresa's to her mother. Before the family returned, Lady Mary had read through the greater part of them, and notwithstanding the bewildering and oppressive emotions which impeded her progress and distracted her mind, she was able to make out pretty clearly what her situation was.

Her husband was living in Paris, immersed in dissipation. Craftly had been instructed by him, and was repeatedly charged in the letters, to suffer no communication between her and her friends, and, what shocked the unfortunate lady most of all and deprived her of recollection for some moments, was a determination expressed in one of the letters never to see her again, accompanied with the declaration, that although she supposed herself so, she was not really his wife.

After recovering from her fainting fit, she hurried through the remainder of the letters, with many tears and many prayers to Heaven for support.

"Never in my life," said she, "did I pass an afternoon of such complete and thorough wretchedness. I thought myself lost beyond all hope. Surrounded with enemies, and without a single protector or friend! Before the family returned, I restored a greater part of the letters to the drawer, and when desired to join them at tea, I sent an excuse, and was glad to be left neglected and undisturbed in my room until the next morning.

"During this time I had considered all the circumstances of my situation. It was apparent from the suppression of Theresa's letters, that she had not from the first been a full participator in the plot against me. Yet it was not possible for me to give her my confidence, now that she had become the wife of Craftly, who was the chief instrument of the conspiracy. The mother and sister of this hypocrite were so fully persuaded of his honour, that they would have considered me a maniac or a calumniator, if I had disclosed the truth to them. I had found out by the letters that Craftly was paid for my support by my husband, who relinquished the interest of a mortgage on Craftly's estate as payment. This I regarded as a tacit acknowledgment that I was his wife. But the evidence of Theresa, which I supposed could be drawn from her at some future time by my friends, I considered of still greater value.

"I had no reason to fear that I should be left in absolute want, or that I should be treated with open unkindness by any of the family. But it was dreadful to me to know, that I was living under the roof of a man who had conspired to deprive me of every thing that is valuable in life. I could not look upon him without a secret shudder running through my frame. After revolving the circumstances of my situation for several days, during which I with difficulty preserved an outward appearance of composure, I at length came to the resolution to seek shelter with Mr. Matthews, and endeavour to recover the favour of my relations.

"But how to effect my escape, with any prospect of ever reaching my friends, was a difficult question. I had no money nor jewels of any considerable value; but there were a few valuable laces which I might dispose of for enough to defray my travelling expenses. I accordingly packed them up with great care, and learning that there was to be a fair in the neighbourhood, I determined to dispose of them there. On the morning of the fair, I informed the family that I intended to take a walk, and spend the day in visiting the cottages in our neighbourhood; I hope the deception will be forgiven me. I put on my travelling dress, concealed my treasure, and set forward, with mingled emotions of gladness and apprehension. I sold the laces without difficulty, though for considerably less than their value, and I have reason to believe that I was mistaken for one of those persons who gain a subsistence by smuggling articles of this kind from the continent. This however was a trifling consideration, I could have consented to pass for a gypsy or a fortune teller in order to escape from my persecutors.

"My next object was to secure a passage in the mail coach, which went South. Here was a greater trial of my courage, since this exposure was a continued one, while my other was but momentary. I played my part however as confidently as I could, and although my unprotected state exposed me to suspicions which the innkeeper, his wife and even the servants were at no great pains to conceal, yet I was enabled to bear up against it all, without a tear, and arrived at the end of the first stage without any accident.

"The fatigues of the last two days, however, were so great, that I was nearly overcome when we arrived at the inn which was at the termination of this stage, and I retired to a room apart, as soon as we arrived. I observed a newspaper lying in the window seat, and after refreshing myself with a cup of tea, I took it up, half hoping to see the name of some friend in its columns. Judge of my horror on reading the fatal record of my husband's death. He had fallen in a duel in Paris. I had loved him, oh too well!"

Here Lady Mary became too much affected to proceed with her narrative. Indeed she had little more to relate; for the shock had proved too great for her reason, and from that moment she recollected little more than that she had wandered from village to village, pitied and relieved by some and derided by others, until she found herself in her present asylum, restored to perfect recollection by the care of the good people around her.

Edward had listened to her narrative with the deepest interest and compassion, and assured her of the protection and support of her *friends,* whatever might be the determination of her relations. He gave directions for her further accommodation at the cottage during her convalescence, and it was arranged that as soon as her strength would permit, she should take up her residence at his own house.

Having been delayed only by his desire to learn all that related to her, and to provide for her comfort, Edward set off for the South as soon as these arrangements had been completed, leaving Lady Mary under the care of the worthy family at the cottage.

CHAPTER XX

An Old Fashioned Wedding

◇   ◇

The time would fail us to enumerate the multiplied works of charity in which Lucy Blakeney engaged herself. She was not content with occasionally visiting the poor and administering to their more urgent wants; but she made the true economy of benevolence her study. Her knowledge, her taste, her wealth, were all rendered subservient to the great cause. Without officiously intermeddling with the charities of others, she became a bright example to them. Her well timed assistance was a stimulus and an encouragement to the industrious poor, and her silent and steady perseverance was a strong appeal to the better feelings of the rich. She received the blessing of him that was ready to perish, and the unheard praise and unsolicited imitation of those who had abundance of wealth and influence.

As the nuptials of her friend Aura Melville approached, her attention was directed to the proper mode of honouring that event, and at the same time rendering it memorable among those who had long regarded both these young persons as the joint guardians of their happiness. Mr. and Mrs. Matthews and Mrs. Cavendish too, were all for having the marriage celebrated after the fashion of the good old times when the poor not only looked up to the gentry for protection and friendship, but took a lively interest in their domestic affairs, were depressed at their misfortunes, and proud and happy in the fame and happiness of their patrons.

Nor was Edward Ainslie backward in promoting this design. Accordingly the preparations for the marriage were made with a view to interest and gratify rather than to dazzle the guests. The bridal array was rather plain than sumptuous; the carriages and horses of Edward and his family, were decked with ribbons, and the church ornamented with flowers and evergreens, prepared by the pupils of Lucy's establishment, who also walked in procession and had their dance upon the green, to the music of the pipe and tabor. The villagers crowded the church to witness the ceremony, and repaired to the Rectory to partake of the bride cake, while the poor who had been invited to celebrate Lucy's birth day, found an entertainment not less substantial and exhilarating than the former one, prepared for them at her friend's wedding.

A long summer's day was spent in the festivities of this happy occasion, and when late in the evening the full moon was seen rising behind the church tower and shedding his quiet lustre over hill and valley, streamlet and grove, the music was still sounding, and the merry laugh of the light hearted guests was heard in parlour and hall.

None seemed to enjoy the day more deeply and feelingly than Lucy. She had learned the great secret of woman's happiness, to enjoy the happiness of others. Selfish gratification was no concern of hers. She had entered into the previous arrangements with all her heart, and as her object had been not to lay her friends under heavy obligations and astonish the guests by show and parade, but to promote the real and heartfelt pleasure of all concerned, she succeeded; and none derived more satisfaction from partaking of this festival of true joy than she did from its preparation.

When, on the following morning, Edward and his bride set off for the North, she with the rest of the family bade them a tender adieu, and returned to her usual benevolent occupations with that tranquil and calm spirit, that firm reliance on the Righteous Disposer of all things, which, in every situation of life, is indeed the pearl of inestimable value.

Conclusion

◊　◊

Several years rolled away after the event recorded in the last chapter, without affording any thing worthy the attention of the reader. The persons to whom our narrative relates, were enjoying that calm happiness, which as has frequently been remarked, affords so little matter for history. We must accordingly conclude the story with the incidents of a somewhat later period.

It was the season of the Christmas holidays. Edward and his blooming wife with their two lovely children, were on a visit to his father, and had come to pass an evening at the Rectory. Lady Mary too was there. She had recovered from the wreck of her husband's property enough to support her genteelly, and had found an asylum with her old preceptor and guide, in the only place where she had ever enjoyed any thing like solid happiness.

The Rector, now rapidly declining into the vale of years, afforded a picture of all that is venerable in goodness; his lady retained her placid and amiable virtues, although her activity was gone; and the worthy Mrs. Cavendish, still stately in her carriage, and shrewd and decisive in her remarks, presented no bad counterpart to her milder sister.

Last but not the least interesting of the cheerful group which was now assembled around the fireside of the Rector, was Lucy Blakeney. Her beauty, unimpaired by her early sorrows and preserved by the active and healthful discharge of the duties of benevolence, had now become matured into the fairest model of lovely womanhood. It was not that beauty which may be produced by the exquisite blending of pure tints on the cheek and brow, by fair waving tresses and perfect symmetry of outline—it was the beauty of character and intellect, the beauty that speaks in the eye, informs every gesture and look, and carries to the heart at once the conviction, that in such an one, we behold a lovely work of the Creator, blessed by his own hand and pronounced good.

The Rector was delighted to find the three orphans once more met under his own roof, and apparently enjoying the blessings of this world in such a spirit as gave him no painful apprehensions concerning the future.

"I cannot express to you," he said, "how happy I am to see you all here again once more before my departure. It has long been the desire of my heart. It is accomplished, and I can now leave my blessing with you and depart in peace."

"You cannot enjoy the meeting more highly than we do, I am sure," said Aura, "the return to this spot brings back a thousand tender and delightful associations to my mind, and I regard among the most pleasing circumstances which attend our meeting, the degree of health and enjoyment in which we find all our old friends at the Rectory. But how do all our aquaintances among the cottagers? Is the old sergeant living?"

"He is in excellent health," replied the Rector, "and tells all his old stories with as much animation as ever."

"And your protegés, Lady Mary, the distressed family which you found out?" rejoined Aura.

"They are well, and quite a happy industrious family," answered Lady Mary, with a slight blush.

"How goes on the school, Lucy," said Edward, "I regard that as the most effective instrument of benevolent exertion."

"I hope it has effected some good," answered Lucy. "There has been a considerable number from the school who have proved useful and respectable so far; several of the pupils are now married, and others are giving instruction in different parts of the country. A circumstance which has afforded us considerable gratification is, that a pupil, whose merit has raised her to a high station in life, has visited us lately, and presented a handsome donation towards rendering the establishment permanent."

After a short pause in the conversation, Mr. Matthews expressed a wish that they might have some intelligence from their absent friends.

"I have this day received a letter from America," said Edward, taking it from his pocket and looking inquiringly at Lucy.

"I think you may venture to read it to us," said she.

It was from Mrs. Franklin, and informed him that she had purchased a beautiful seat on the banks of the Delaware, and was living there in the enjoyment of all the happiness, which was to be derived from the society of her family and the delightful serenity of nature. One circumstance only had happened since her departure from England to mar this enjoyment, the account of which must be given in her own words.

"My oldest son, your friend—no doubt you have often heard from him. He soon grew tired of the India service, and was at his own desire exchanged into a regiment which had been ordered to join the army in Spain. There, his career was marked with the heroism and generosity which had ever distinguished his character. A young officer is now visiting me, who accompanied him in his last campaign. He informs me, that my noble son never lost an opportunity either of signalizing himself in action or relieving the distresses of those who suffered the calamities of war.

"In one of the severest battles fought upon the peninsula, it was the fortune of my son to receive a severe wound, while gallantly leading his men to a breach in the walls of a fortified town. The English were repulsed, and a French officer, passing over the field, a few hours after, with a detachment, had the barbarity to order one of his men to fix his bayonet in him. His friend, who was also wounded and lay near him, saw it, but was too helpless himself to raise an arm in his defence.

"The same night, the town was taken by storm. When the English force advanced, the unfortunate officers were both conveyed to safe quarters, and my poor son lived thirty-six hours after the capture of the place. During this time, the story of his inhuman treatment reached the ears of the commander in chief. Fired with indignation, he hastened to the quarters of the wounded officers.

" 'Poor Franklin,' says his friend, 'was lying in the arms of his faithful servant and breathing heavily, when the illustrious Wellington entered the room. It was apparent to all that he had but a few moments to live.

" 'Tell me,' said the General, 'exert but strength enough to describe to me the villain who inflicted that unmanly outrage upon you, and I swear by the honour of a soldier that in one hour his life shall answer it.'

" 'Never did I see the noble countenance of Franklin assume such an expression of calm magnanimity as when he replied,

" 'I am not able to designate him, and if I could do it with certainty, be assured, Sir, that I never would.' "

"These were his last words, and in a few minutes more his spirit fled to a brighter region."

If there are sorrows which refuse the balm of sympathy, there are also consolations which those around us "can neither give nor take away." Through the remaining years of her life, the orphan daughter of the unfortunate Charlotte Temple evinced the power and efficiency of those exalted principles, which can support the mind under every trial, and the happiness of those pure emotions and lofty aspirations whose objects are raised far above the variable contingencies of time and sense.

In the circle of her friends she seldom alluded to past events; and though no one presumed to invade the sanctuary of her private griefs and recollections, yet all admired the serene composure with which she bore them. Various and comprehensive schemes of benevolence formed the work of her life, and religion shed its holy and healing light over all her paths.

When the summons came, which released her pure spirit from its earthly tenement, and the history of her family was closed with the life of its last representative; those who had witnessed, in her mother's fate, the ruin resulting from once yielding to the seductive influence of passion, acknowledged, in the events of the daughter's life, that benignant power which can bring, out of the most bitter and blighting disappointments, the richest fruits of virtue and happiness.

FOR THE BEST IN PAPERBACKS, LOOK FOR THE

In every corner of the world, on every subject under the sun, Penguin represents quality and variety—the very best in publishing today.

For complete information about books available from Penguin—including Pelicans, Puffins, Peregrines, and Penguin Classics—and how to order them, write to us at the appropriate address below. Please note that for copyright reasons the selection of books varies from country to country.

In the United Kingdom: For a complete list of books available from Penguin in the U.K., please write to *Dept E.P., Penguin Books Ltd, Harmondsworth, Middlesex, UB7 0DA*.

In the United States: For a complete list of books available from Penguin in the U.S., please write to *Dept BA, Penguin*, Box 120, Bergenfield, New Jersey 07621-0120.

In Canada: For a complete list of books available from Penguin in Canada, please write to *Penguin Books Ltd, 2801 John Street, Markham, Ontario L3R 1B4*.

In Australia: For a complete list of books available from Penguin in Australia, please write to the *Marketing Department, Penguin Books Ltd, P.O. Box 257, Ringwood, Victoria 3134*.

In New Zealand: For a complete list of books available from Penguin in New Zealand, please write to the *Marketing Department, Penguin Books (NZ) Ltd, Private Bag, Takapuna, Auckland 9*.

In India: For a complete list of books available from Penguin, please write to *Penguin Overseas Ltd, 706 Eros Apartments, 56 Nehru Place, New Delhi, 110019*.

In Holland: For a complete list of books available from Penguin in Holland, please write to *Penguin Books Nederland B.V., Postbus 195, NL-1380AD Weesp, Netherlands*.

In Germany: For a complete list of books available from Penguin, please write to *Penguin Books Ltd, Friedrichstrasse 10-12, D-6000 Frankfurt Main I, Federal Republic of Germany*.

In Spain: For a complete list of books available from Penguin in Spain, please write to *Longman, Penguin España, Calle San Nicolas 15, E-28013 Madrid, Spain*.

In Japan: For a complete list of books available from Penguin in Japan, please write to *Longman Penguin Japan Co Ltd, Yamaguchi Building, 2-12-9 Kanda Jimbocho, Chiyoda-Ku, Tokyo 101, Japan*.

FOR THE BEST IN CLASSICS, LOOK FOR THE

□ **HARD TIMES**

Charles Dickens

A powerful portrait of a Lancashire mill town in the 1840s, *Hard Times* stigmatized the prevalent philosophy of Utilitarianism which allowed human beings to be enslaved to machines and reduced to numbers.

328 pages   ISBN: 0-14-043042-3   **$2.25**

□ **GREAT EXPECTATIONS**

Charles Dickens

In the story of the orphan Pip and the mysterious fortune which falls into his lap, Dickens developed a theme that would preoccupy him towards the end of his life — How do men know who they are?

512 pages   ISBN: 0-14-043003-2   **$2.95**

□ **WALDEN & CIVIL DISOBEDIENCE**

Henry David Thoreau

"If a man does not keep pace with his companions, perhaps it is because he hears a different drummer." Conveying Thoreau's wonder at the commonplace and his yearning for spiritual truth and self-reliance, *Walden* is both a naturalist's and a Transcendentalist's account of the beauty of solitude.

432 pages   ISBN: 0-14-039044-8   **$2.95**

□ **JANE EYRE**

Charlotte Brontë

One of the most widely read of all English novels, *Jane Eyre* depicts the refusal of a spirited and intelligent woman to accept her appointed place in society with unusual frankness and with a passionate sense of the dignity and needs of women.

490 pages   ISBN: 0-14-043011-3   **$2.25**

You can find all these books at your local bookstore, or use this handy coupon for ordering:

Penguin Books By Mail
Dept. BA Box 999
Bergenfield, NJ 07621-0999

Please send me the above title(s). I am enclosing _____ (please add sales tax if appropriate and $1.50 to cover postage and handling). Send check or money order—no CODs. Please allow four weeks for shipping. We cannot ship to post office boxes or addresses outside the USA. *Prices subject to change without notice.*

Ms./Mrs./Mr. _____

Address _____

City/State _____ Zip _____

Sales tax: CA: 6.5%   NY: 8.25%   NJ: 6%   PA: 6%   TN: 5.5%

FOR THE BEST IN CLASSICS, LOOK FOR THE

☐ **WUTHERING HEIGHTS**

Emily Brontë

An intensely original work, this story of the passionate love between Cathy and Heathcliff is recorded with such truth, imagination, and emotional intensity that it acquires the depth and simplicity of ancient tragedy.

372 pages   *ISBN: 0-14-043001-6*   **$2.95**

☐ **UTOPIA**

Thomas More

Utopia revolutionized Plato's classical blueprint of the perfect republic, and can be seen as the source of Anabaptism, Mormonism, and even Communism. Witty, immediate, vital, prescient, it is the work of a man who drank deep of the finest spirit of his age.

154 pages   *ISBN: 0-14-044165-4*   **$2.95**

☐ **THE SCARLET LETTER**

Nathaniel Hawthorne

Publicly disgraced and ostracized by the harsh Puritan community of seventeenth-century Boston, Hester Prynne draws on her inner strength to emerge as the first true heroine of American fiction.

284 pages   *ISBN: 0-14-039019-7*   **$2.25**

☐ **WINESBURG, OHIO**

Sherwood Anderson

Introduced as "The Tales and the Persons," this timeless cycle of short stories lays bare the lives of the friendly but solitary people of small town America at the turn of the century.

248 pages   *ISBN: 0-14-039059-6*   **$4.95**

☐ **CANDIDE**

Voltaire

One of the glories of eighteenth-century satire, *Candide* was the most brilliant challenge to the prevailing thought that held "all is for the best in the best of all possible worlds."

144 pages   *ISBN: 0-14-044004-6*   **$2.25**

☐ **PRIDE AND PREJUDICE**

Jane Austen

While Napoleon transformed Europe, Jane Austen wrote a novel in which a man changes his manners and a young lady her mind. In Austen's world of delicious social comedy, the truly civilized being maintains a proper balance between reason and energy.

400 pages   *ISBN: 0-14-043072-5*   **$2.25**

FOR THE BEST IN CLASSICS, LOOK FOR THE

☐ **THE ODYSSEY**

Homer

E. V. Rieu's best-selling prose translation captures both the delicacy and drama of the hero Odysseus's journey and allows the freshness and excitement of Homer's well-knit plot to delight us as much as it did the ancient Greeks.

368 pages   ISBN: 0-14-044001-1   **$2.95**

☐ **THE PRINCE**

Niccolo Machiavelli

This treatise on statecraft — in which the author uncompromisingly proposes what most governments do but none profess to do — holds such power to shock that at one time Machiavelli was identified with Satan himself.

154 pages   ISBN: 0-14-044107-7   **$2.25**

☐ **HEART OF DARKNESS**

Joseph Conrad

Written in the last year of the nineteenth century, *Heart of Darkness* represents in many ways the first twentieth-century novel. Conrad's story of Marlow's search for Mr. Kurtz provides an extraordinary exploration of human savagery and despair.

122 pages   ISBN: 0-14-043168-3   **$1.95**

☐ **THE CANTERBURY TALES**

Geoffrey Chaucer

Told by a motley crowd of pilgrims journeying from Southwark to Canterbury, these tales — bawdy, pious, erudite, tragic, comic — reveal a picture of four-teenth-century England which is as robust as it is representative.

526 pages   ISBN: 0-14-044022-4   **$2.95**

You can find all these books at your local bookstore, or use this handy coupon for ordering:

Penguin Books By Mail
Dept. BA Box 999
Bergenfield, NJ 07621-0999

Please send me the above title(s). I am enclosing _____ (please add sales tax if appropriate and $1.50 to cover postage and handling). Send check or money order—no CODs. Please allow four weeks for shipping. We cannot ship to post office boxes or addresses outside the USA. *Prices subject to change without notice.*

Ms./Mrs./Mr. _____

Address _____

City/State _____ Zip _____

Sales tax: CA: 6.5%   NY: 8.25%   NJ: 6%   PA: 6%   TN: 5.5%

FOR THE BEST IN CLASSICS, LOOK FOR THE

☐ **THE RED BADGE OF COURAGE**

Stephen Crane

Certainly one of the greatest novels written about the heat of battle, Crane's story ultimately concerns the battle waged in young Henry Fleming's mind as he reacts to "reality," confronts duty and fear, and comes to terms with himself and the world.

222 pages ISBN: 0-14-039021-9 **$2.95**

☐ **McTEAGUE**

Frank Norris

This searing portrait of the downfall of a slow-witted dentist and his avaricious wife is a novel of compelling narrative force and a powerful and shocking example of early American realism.

442 pages ISBN: 0-14-039017-0 **$5.95**

☐ **SELECTED ESSAYS**

Ralph Waldo Emerson

With these essays calling for harmony with nature and reliance on individual integrity, Emerson unburdened his young country of Europe's traditional sense of history and showed Americans how to be creators of their own circumstances.

416 pages ISBN: 0-14-039013-8 **$4.50**

☐ **SISTER CARRIE**

Theodore Dreiser

This unsparing story of a country girl's rise to riches as the mistress of a wealthy man is a pioneering work of naturalism, especially so in this unexpurgated edition which follows Dreiser's original manuscript.

500 pages ISBN: 0-14-039002-2 **$4.95**

☐ **UNCLE TOM'S CABIN**

Harriet Beecher Stowe

A powerful indictment of slavery that brought the abolitionists' message to the White House and beyond, *Uncle Tom's Cabin* was hailed by Tolstoy as "one of the greatest productions of the human mind."

630 pages ISBN: 0-14-039003-0 **$3.95**

☐ **THE ADVENTURES OF HUCKLEBERRY FINN**

Mark Twain

"All modern American literature comes from one book by Mark Twain called *Huckleberry Finn*," wrote Ernest Hemingway. An incomparable adventure story and a classic of American humor, no book has a better claim to the title of The Great American Novel.

336 pages ISBN: 0-14-039046-4 **$1.95**